City
for
Conquest

City
for
Conquest

Aben Kandel

With a new introduction by Leonard Quart

LOST URBAN CLASSICS

Transaction Publishers
New Brunswick (U.S.A.) and London (U.K.)

First paperback printing 2015 by Transaction Publishers, New Brunswick, New Jersey.

Originally published in 1936 by Duell, Sloan & Pearce. Copyright © 1936 by Aben Kandel.

All rights reserved under International and Pan-American Copyright Conventions. No part of this book may be reproduced or transmitted in any form or by any means, electronic or mechanical, including photocopy, recording, or any information storage and retrieval system, without prior permission in writing from the publisher. All inquiries should be addressed to Transaction Publishers, 10 Corporate Place South, Suite 102, Piscataway, New Jersey 08854. www.transactionpub.com

This book is printed on acid-free paper that meets the American National Standard for Permanence of Paper for Printed Library Materials.

Library of Congress Catalog Number: 2015005977
ISBN: 978-1-4128-5606-5
Printed in the United States of America

Library of Congress Cataloging-in-Publication Data

Kandel, Aben, 1896-1993.
  City for conquest / by Aben Kandel.
     pages; cm. -- (Lost Urban Classics)
  ISBN 978-1-4128-5606-5 (softcover : acid-free paper)
  1. New York (N.Y.)--Fiction. 2. Urban fiction. I. Title.
    PS3521.A42C58 2015
    813'.52--dc23

                                        2015005977

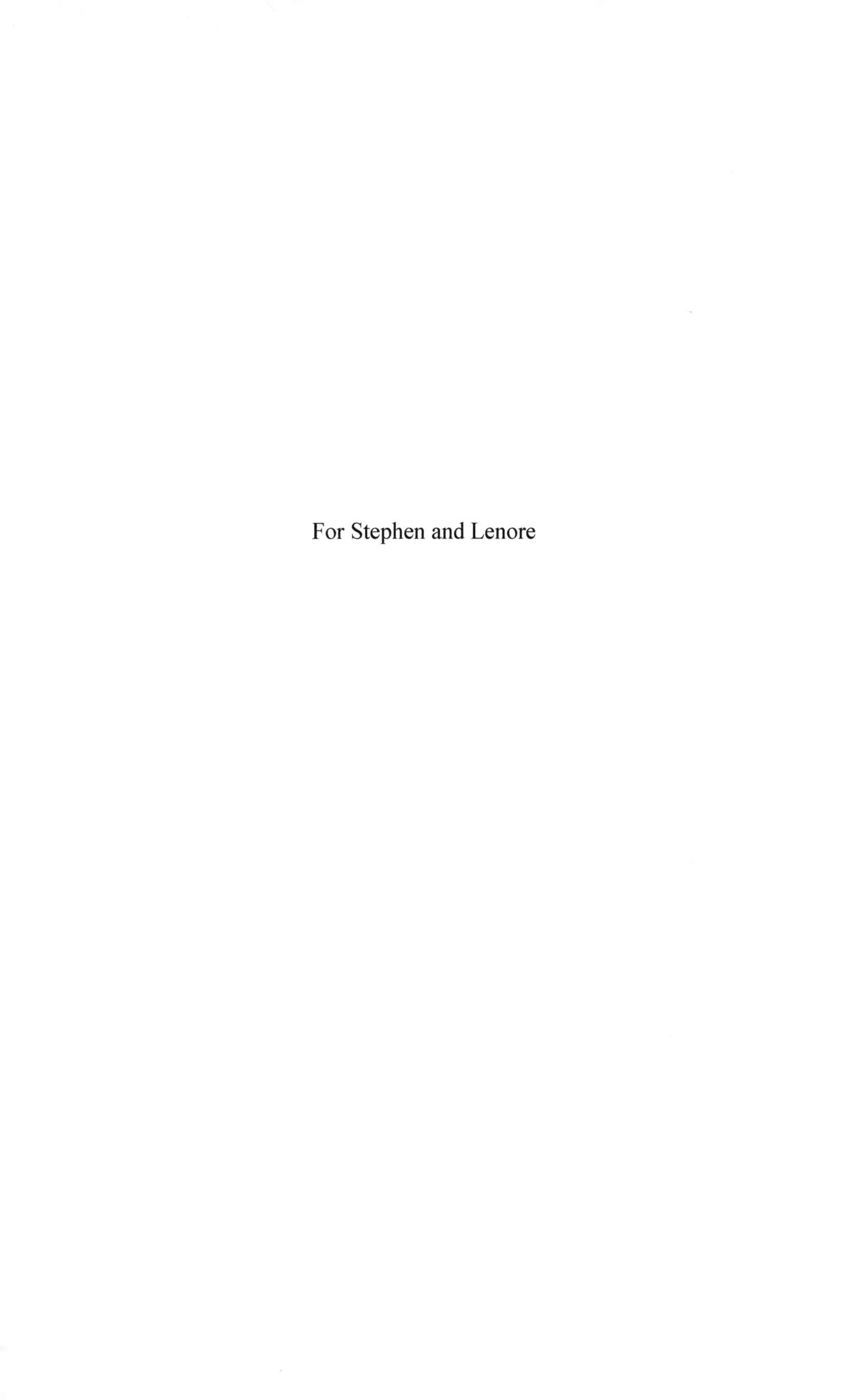

For Stephen and Lenore

CONTENTS

INTRODUCTION TO THE TRANSACTION EDITION

BY LEONARD QUART

Aben Kandel was one of the last screenwriters who wrote for the American "B-movies" of the 50s—*I Was a Teen Age Werewolf* (1957)—but his career began much earlier as a novelist. He produced a number of novels in the 20s and 30s—*Vaudeville* (1927), *Black Sun* (1929), *Rabbi Burns* (1931), and *City for Conquest* (1936)—his most distinctive work that was turned into a successful, if very sentimental, conventional film with Jimmy Cagney for Warner Bros. in 1940. The novel was a panoramic New York work, like Dos Passos' better known and more formally imaginative *Manhattan Transfer* (1925), which is a flashier and more stylistically experimental and expressionistic opus (fragmented narratives, scraps of newspaper stories and song lyrics inserted into the text, and bits of stream of consciousness) than *City For Conquest*. Kandel's novel uses a much more stylistically traditional and accessible style in depicting, through a set of clipped episodes, a set of characters from different social classes and ethnicities, who often fortuitously interact, to evoke the complex and contradictory patterns of city life. The book is vivid, overwrought, and blatantly melodramatic, and conveys a city defined by powerful dreams and a nightmarish underside from the turn of the century into the twenties.

City for Conquest's New York is a volatile, dynamic city inhabited by the very rich, the criminal, the idealistic, the bohemian, and the driven, the entrapped, and impoverished, it's Kandel's symphony to a city where almost every one of his characters is feverishly pursuing "how to make a dent in this town." The city devours some of them, but others remain greedily "at the trough, sucking away, grunting, gorging at the meat and blood of New York."

The book sets out to capture a number of strains of New York life during those years: the impoverished, immigrant Lower East Side where a number of the book's central characters begin their life on its teeming, roiling blocks; the world of corrupt contractors, developers, and politicians who work in concert to plunder the city; organized crime (bootlegging), boxing, and show biz; and Wall Street's calculating, high flying financial manipulators.

For Kandel, the city was a monster—a world of immense inequality (just like current day New York) where "six blocks from Wall Street, people haven't got a dime, six blocks from duplex apartments, people live in hovels." But he doesn't really explore the social and political dynamics of inequality. He also tries to convey the essence of the city by cataloguing the city's places and smells. He describes taking a trip on the El going below 14th St., and cutting across Cooper Square, passing Bowery flop houses, where "from cubicles upstairs, one can smell old underwear peeled off dejected, unwashed bodies" and on to Chinatown, "where the lights are low, chop suey, chow mein, pickled duck . . . dried blood of tong wars, opium, Park Row, and City Hall." And he depicts the warfare between the evil vapors given off from "the mountains of refuse, garbage, burnt coal, excreta, and the appetizing cooking smells, water and soap, green vegetables and fruits, melting tar, and flowers." The itemizing provides Kandel with the opportunity to write heightened, somewhat florid descriptive prose, and also conveys his pleasure in observing the infinite variety of positive and negative sensations the city emanates. But Kandle projects a vision of the city that is more than his flamboyant lists.

Kandel sees the city as one divided by dark and light forces without much that rests in between. But it is his dark vision of New York that dominates the novel. The one character—the delicate, sensitive, lonely Perry (a rich man's son)—who has dreams of creating a better, more livable city, is ineffectual. He may make a bit of headway in turning the Lower East Side into a more habitable place, but the book sees the forces of avarice and exploitation arrayed against him as too powerful for any real change to be achieved. They even see his slum clearance project as a way of picking up more money in contracting work.

Perry is the only character in the novel with even a glimmer of a social commitment—one that offers a vision of how life in the city could be altered that is more idealistic aspiration than truly possible. The other characters mostly obsess of moving up the class ladder and achieving the

American Dream of money and success ("making it" is their mantra)—without any criticism of the values they pursue; some of the characters make it, others stumble along the way.

Kandel rarely rewards his virtuous characters. Joey, the innocent, honest, big-hearted Lower East Side boxer loses the girl he loves, Bella, to her futile dream of becoming a star dancer/performer. There is pathos in the inarticulate Joey's simple, repeated affirmation of love for Bella ("you're my goil"). Predictably, she breaks his heart.

But controlled, driven, tormented Peter, who grew up with Joey on the Lower East Side, and whose impoverished father worked in a garment factory and on the side peddled cheap jewelry to the Irish in bars, flees his past and class without looking back. He marries a cool, moneyed woman who is in the Social Registrar, and becomes a wealthy financier. Since early on Peter's aspirations have been to make money and ascend the class ladder, he ultimately achieves his goals. His existence may be cold and soulless, but Peter claims to be satisfied (if not happy) with the comfortable, untroubled life he has chosen. He has found ide of perfection.

Googie is another of the Lower East Side boys, but his life veers in another direction. His role models are the crime bosses he sees in the movies. His rise from small time hood and killer to becoming a top crime boss himself is inexorable. At the novel's conclusion he lives lavishly in a penthouse, but his "eyes still glowed with a murderous gleam." Googie was one more of Kandel's dark versions of the American success story.

There are other characters—a farmer's son, and a vagrant, who both come from nothing and nowhere to become enormously successful as a real estate developer and stock and bond salesman respectively. Kandel observes their mad pursuit of wealth without making overt moral judgments, but there is no question that the novel offers an implicit critique of a society so besotted with money and that most of its characters' humanity is lost in the process of acquiring it. As one character says: "The slogan of this town—is every man for himself." And another character, an intrusive homeless philosopher (a hoary Kandel conceit), states that "the city hates all the little people" that inhabit it. But Kandle never offers a political alternative to a city dominated by the moneyed.

There is one figure in the novel who stands strikingly outside this Darwinian struggle—Eda the successful journalist. She is the only distinctive female character in the book, who asserts: "I am sick with love of this town. I am big with NY." This demonic, erotic bohemian does not believe in the city changing, "except from its own ferment." Her image of herself is as a "lithe, clawing creature loosed only for an orgy of self-destruction" in the "fearful jungle of the city."

Eda is a woman of extremes, and her utterances are always extravagant. Through her feverish voice Kandle often conveys his own love affair for the city: "Crush of New York, stone, handclasp of five boroughs, when I am still my bones shall ache with nostalgia, when my eyes have been picked from their sockets, tunneling winds will spray my tears over the town."

Kandel, however, is not Eda. She feels betrayed by her lover and by the city—for her they are one of the same, and the intensity of her love may elevate her, but at the same time it is also a dirge. By the novel's conclusion, Eda jumps off the Staten Island Ferry into the ice cold waters of New York Bay.

Kandel concludes the novel in a similar apocalyptic vein. He sees a flood engulfing the city (prefiguring Hurricane Sandy) and "the town will drown in its own arteries . . . and a terrible silence will descend upon the city." It ends without hope, though *City for Conquest,* is too filled with energy and anger at inequity to be an utterly nihilistic or pessimistic work.

City novels like James Farrell's *Studs Lonigan* trilogy (1932–35) or Henry Roth's great *Call It Sleep* (1934) make the city one of the prime characters in their books. Its social dynamics and forces shape the lives of its characters. *City for Conquest* may not be in the same league in literary terms, but Kandel's churning, ever-changing New York imposes itself as well on the consciousness and reactions of its many characters. None of their lives are hermetically private or particularly introspective. For Perry, Peter, Googie, and the other characters that populate the book, the public world is an integral part of their lives—it permeates their very being. Kandel offers descriptions of how the world they inhabit functions. For example, the book incisively depicts the machinations of real estate developers and the building of a skyscraper, the workings of the stock market, and the atmosphere and social structure of a local dance hall. Kandel can be very pointed about how the city evolves: "In New York, there is no such thing as a fresh start. One begins by destroying what you hope to supplant." (Think of Lincoln Center and the World Trade Center, and the areas of the city and lives they were built over.) The city is omnipresent in almost every chapter of the book.

City for Conquest is not an elegantly written novel—its prose is frequently overwrought and exhibitionistic, but one can feel Kandel's passion for the city's dynamism and life force coursing through the book. If one wants to remember what the city felt like in a time rife with contradiction—a boom where fortunes were made, and other people lived in impoverished slums (a close parallel to contemporary New York)— *City for Conquest* is the consummate urban artifact. It has been out of print too long.

BOOK ONE

BOUQUET OF THE BOROUGHS

1

Across Manhattan a lean wind blows, a late August wind, eastward out of the Hudson. It's a wiry, muscular island, Manhattan is, from the South Ferry tip where the Ellis Island boats disgorge the greenhorns, to the gash cut by the Harlem River where the fat Bronx begins. It juts out like an unruly thumb in the clenched fist that is New York. It's a gun pointed at the Atlantic. Span the middle from Thirteenth Avenue to Sutton Place and it's an old man's walk, only fourteen avenue blocks. But try to work your way across from a tenement fire-trap flat on Death Avenue to a terrace apartment overlooking Welfare Island, and it will age you. There's a stop signal on every corner.

The town is sore. Sore from growing pains, griped from over-eating, raw-knuckled from pummelling, sore from being bled, angry as a cinnamon bear in spring. Rome was a pompous city and Athens an heroic place, but New York is an angry town. Out west, you drive under an arch of fragrant trees and a wide banner beams across the road, "You are now entering Flowerdale, the celery center of San Jacinto Valley. Welcome."

But there are no welcome signs in New York. You get off at Grand Central or at the Penn Station, and the fall training squad of redcaps swarms all over you. Before you've cried the cinders out of your eyes, you've been hustled into a gyp cab and you've shelled out two bits. For what? For carrying a tangled mess of dirty laundry, a deck of cards and a few samples. Or an imitation leather valise, betrayed at the corners, but clamped tight upon the great unpublished manuscript and a pair of sporty flannel trousers in case you're invited to a Long Island week-end by an elderly patroness of the arts. Come in on the Jersey side and your ears are stuffed with coal dust and you shiver and yawn on the slowest ferry ride you ever took. Enter from Europe, steerage, and the immigration officials delouse you, examine you for rabies, leprosy, pink eye, syph and poverty, and mutter, "Greenhorn, this is nothing; wait till you're in." Come back as a third generation Americano, and they tap your spine for Swiss watches, rip into your trunk for false bottoms, tear up a set of harmless dirty postcards and shove you through. Home again. But look back over your shoulder and the Statue of Liberty has the flaming torch planted right on her nose.

There are no welcome signs in this town. Get off a freight car with your wrists stiff and blue and the vomit in your throat, and the railroad bulls slap you around for exercise and steal the two bucks you sewed into your coat lining against the day when the richest city in the world would economize by calling off its breadlines. Hike in on your caked socks and blistering feet and you keep hiking. The cobblestones sing back the song of the bluecoats, "Keep moving, brother." It's only when you take the Twenty-third Street ferry to Greenpoint, that the jolly alderman greets you on the rotting dock and blowing smoke in your face, shillabers, "Greenpernt—the garden spot of the woild." You can have it.

There's no welcome in New York—no farewell. From Tottenville to Canarsie, from Van Cortlandt to Columbia Heights, it's a twenty-four hour town that can spare anyone from the mayor down. Every day, winter, summer, spring and fall, they come in like locusts, tens of thousands, on foot, rail, steamer and automobile, endless thousands come in, shaking their fists at the big town, and every day tens of thousands slink out, shaking their fists at the big town. Shake, brothers, shake.

Across Manhattan, fanning over to Brooklyn and Queens, down to Richmond and up to the Bronx, a lean wind blows, eastward out of the Hudson. Under the streets, sewage flows, subways roar. Up from the pavements, the skyscrapers stand erect. The city is deep and high and angry. Come in and you're swallowed. Leave and you're not missed. What a town. New York.

Sunning himself between two garbage cans, the Swami stands, the centerpiece of a Forsyth Street frieze. Every morning he clumps down the stairs and enters the picture like one of the living statues in a vaudeville act. The letter carrier, lopsided under his burden of foreign mail, blows his whistle and the Swami swings his beard. The voice of the mailman rings through the hall, long, foreign names, and hearts beat wildly on the third and fourth floors. Slattern wives, with hair-wisps across their cheeks, hobble down the steps and haggle in the grocery store; boarders, husbands and grown sisters go off to work; the kids, like puffs of factory steam, fly off to play. But the Swami stands. The Negro garbage man, colored light by refuse, yells, "whoa" to his nag, and in a graceful arc of ascent swings two garbage cans into the dump wagon. One gives off a sudden, penetrating stink; the other, a delicate shower of powdery ashes. Kris Kringle, the first snowfall of summer by special arrangement with the Department of Sanitation. The butter-yellow sun drips down, street voices rise to the roof-tops, but the old Swami stands still.

"Why should I move? Everything I want in life is here."

Summer Saturday in the life of Forsyth Street, twelfth assembly and eighth congressional district, New York City, year of the nineteen-seven panic, guaranteed by the goatees and vandykes of that period to be the last, absolutely the last panic in the United States.

They were laying the new road-bed for the Second Avenue electric car lines on Forsyth Street. Way for the shining trolleys, and a cheer for the stalwart nickel snatchers. A four-foot strip had been ripped from the center of the gutter. All summer long, the Eyetalians had worked. One man held the sharp spike, while the other swung the iron hammer, driving it into the hardened tar. The wops are a musical folk and the beat of the hammer on the spike rang out like a church bell, tsong, tsong, tsong. Hallowed chimes—but when the swinger missed his mark he crushed his fellow-worker's wrist into a bloody pulp and the poor dago lost a hand or an arm. Yet the road-bed was being laid . . . "in accordance with specifications, the rails to be laid upon a continuous bearing of wood blocks, the said blocks to be held in place by guard rails secured to metal ties." . . . From Grand to Houston Streets on Forsyth, then up Second Avenue to the car barns where Manhattan narrowed into Harlem. A hand, an arm, a foot, a leg, thrown into the big cauldron to the music of the chimes.

In the deep rent, gravel was strewn, blue-gray chips, the size of chicken eggs. The kids on the block loved them because, in street fights, they were easy to throw and every hit meant a dented shin-bone, a gash on the cheek, or gory glory, a hole in the head. Mutt, the undisputed dope, had his eye gouged out by one of the earliest stones, and he became the snooty-snoot of the neighborhood, first with the sinister black patch over his vacant socket, and then with a fancy glass eye, donated by the Tammany district leader, whose heart was broken. The kid walked with his head in the air, for a glass eye (not to be confused with being plain cockeyed) elevated him to a higher social plane.

Ah Forsyth, with its royal neighbors, Rivington and Stanton Streets—good old English names, moats, castles, armor, fox-hunts, ale and partridges, droits de seigneur, and the old Swami sunning himself between two garbage cans, while the brown dago gnomes ring tsong, tsong, tsong on the smooth spike-heads. In the shadow of a castle stood a bower of saplings, the young shoots of the street, heads clustered together over a crap game, the stakes of which were the campaign buttons of the politicians who were running for office at the following November elections.

"Shoot three buttons," cries Joey. The buttons are tossed out. One is McClellan with a fly speck on his aristocratic nose, the other, a jovial alderman with silken mustachios, two chins, and that merry "I-kiss-babies" twinkle in his eye. He wants to serve the people once more. Just one more term, he pleads, and he can retire. He's willing to pinch the cheeks of mama and kiss the baby for papa's vote. The third button bears the picture of a strong, dismembered arm clutching a torch. "Faded," cries Danny, flinging a penny down and picking up two buttons, for the market quotation on politicians that day is five for a cent. And now, if Joey can throw a natural, he'll pick up a penny and a button. Pennies are important, for with five of them two kids can go to a moving-picture show, those new caves of fantasy and laughter that have sprung up in abandoned stores on the Bowery. Pennies are rare on Forsyth Street, for with panic in the land, even the parents treasure them.

Peter Mendes, the Sephardic Jew, clutches his penny in a moist palm. When banks close and factories shut their doors, and the workers are forced out of poverty into starvation, an investigation is launched. One melodramatic financier blows his brains out and Peter Mendes' spending allowance is cut down to one cent every month. But when times are good, Peter gets one cent every week.

Joey gathers up the dice. He is past twelve and a tough sheeney. Even the micks on the block admit that. Cradled in the gutter, he loves it, and is at home only in the street. Breathing space, elbow room, my worthies, in the narrow gulch between two rows of tenements, in and out of trucks that rattle up the street. The two-room flat (toilet in the hall, two families to a privy; the better dwellings don't have them in the yard any more), his crowded home, is merely a place for sleep after the day's adventures, and to bounce out of early in the morning. Joey even finishes dressing in the street, fastening the last few buttons of his shirt on the stairs outside the flat. He forages for food in the street, stalking fruit peddlers, hot-dog vendors, old women with pickle stands and herring barrels, Turks with halvah, old Jews with wash tubs filled with steaming corn on the cob, trundling baked sweet potatoes or hot chick peas in rolling ovens. Sometimes, he hunts with the pack, often alone. He plays, learns, fights, eats, loves and grows in the gutter.

At twelve he is as tall and promises soon to be heavier and stronger than his father. He is five feet three and weighs one hundred and eighteen pounds. His hair stands up in a brush of hard bristles, his forehead is narrow, split sullen by a frown, dark, smouldering eyes deeply imbedded and banked by high cheekbones, a nose like the butt-end of a gun and a mouth like a clamp. He is slow to speak and slow to understand. But he is quick to sock. And because no one rises after being socked by Joey, he is looked up to by all the boys on the block. He is regarded as a particularly strong asset on the school basketball team for when it wins a game in a hostile neighborhood, in the fight that invariably results, Joey marches the team home over prostrate bodies, scoring a second triumph for good old P.S. 20. Already his shoulders force the cloth, his chest bulges, his calves rise in a beautiful arc, and there is a firm, lean right-angle from ear-tip to chin-cleft.

The settlement worker, pencil aloft, stands up to inquire what Joey's diet has been. I'll tell you, little bonnet. For breakfast, a mug of coffee and a roll, buttered when there's butter, dry when there's none. We skip the golden orange juice, the cereal in its pool of heavy cream, the eggs and the crisp bacon (bacon! God forbid!) and the pint of bone-building milk. For lunch, a purplish hot-dog dipped in yellow mustard, swathed in sauerkraut, laid to rest in a soft roll and washed down with a glass of lemonless lemonade. This was in affluence. Otherwise, the heel of a bread gnawed with an apple, a sweet potato, or anything that could be taken by force or cunning.

But every Friday night, famine or plenty, there was a beautiful ceremonial dinner at home, with a pint of beer which the father and mother shared.

In this diet, there was no proper balancing of vegetables and meat, certainly more roughage than proteins. But who has ever computed the vitamins in a kashe knish, stolen red hot from a lamenting Jew and eaten in a cellar with the relish of escape?

Joey rattles the dice in the cupped palm of his right hand. Near him crouches his brother Bert. Although three years younger, Bert is in the same grade as Joey, and promises to become the youngest graduate of the school since the hunch-back child phenomenon of the class of '99. Bert, in contrast to his older brother, is fair, with a faint blue vein delicately traced on his right temple, lost under his smooth skin and re-appearing on the lower part of his cheek near the pointed chin. His hair is curled, straw-colored and already his forehead suggests a brow. His nose is long and bony, the skin drawn taut across his pale face. He is a fast runner, but after a fifty-yard dash he collapses, his heart beating as though it would crack through his ribs. He does his brother's homework, prompts him in the classroom, shields his secrets at home, and worships him because Joey is everything that is worth while on Forsyth Street.

Joey rolls the dice. The other boys fold around him like the petals of a flower at sundown. The life of the street goes on. Gnomes pound on steel, neighbors talk across windows, horse-drawn trucks rattle by, the "giddiyap" of throaty truck drivers rending the air. But while the natives play, the Indians are coming.

A band of dark Italians from Mott and Elizabeth Streets across the Bowery suddenly appears. Deployed into two units, shock troops from the south and a surprise onslaught from the north, they rush around the corners towards the center. They swirl onward in a burst of color and clamor. Clad in gay stockings like bicycle riders, in their father's cast-off vests, in weird coats worn inside out, the sleeves flapping like the arms of animated scarecrows, the invading wops come howling down the street like demons, hurling gravel and hard corn-cobs, the leader a shrieking devil with a knife drawn for hand-to-hand combat. The Forsyth Streeters are caught unawares.

Bert took one look at the approaching fiends and shrieked in terror. His fair skin tinged greenish with fear and a nausea seized him. He fled for cover into a doorway, crying, "Joey—the guinees are here—look out!" Then, quivering against the wall, hating himself for his fear, he furtively watched the combat.

Joey's clamp of a mouth ground tighter. He commanded the boys to seize stones, cans, baseball bats, and any other missiles and weapons that were handy. He yelled quick instructions to Danny, the Irish kid, Peter Mendes, the strange Sephardic Jew, Chick, Mutt, even to Googi, the Italian Shabbas goy of the block who was in a dilemma, torn between his blood tie to the Sicilian invaders and loyalty to the sons of his best customers.

Stones flew, and the air filled with wild cries. The workmen ran into hallways for safety, merchants closed the doors of their shops and prayed for their plate glass store fronts, and mothers screamed from windows. The air grew thick with flying missiles, for the ammunition was endless, lying in the deep gravel pockets in the gutter. The Forsyth Streeters, outnumbered, out-yelled, were losing ground.

Joey suddenly decided upon a strategic move. He abandoned the gravel, and, shielding himself with his arm, ran for the invading leader. He could always depend upon his chunky fists—hard, rough, unerring fists which pounded like stone hammers. The leader, shrieking a foreign curse, lunged at him with knife drawn. Joey swung to the left of him, and, with a quick jerk of his foot, tripped him. The dago fell on his face, the knife clattering from his hands. Peter, from a vantage point, felled an aide with a tomato can. Joey quickly lifted the leader from the ground, held him in position with his left hand, and socked hard with his right fist. A scream shot through the air as the swarthy skin split in two and a line of blood spurted. Exultantly Joey socked again as a stone struck his head.

By this time the cries of the hoodlums and the crashing of glass windows had interfered with the siesta of Walrus the cop, who drowsed in the back room of Sullivan's saloon, awakening only to sip his beer and blot the suds from his luxuriant moustache. He panted out, his enormous paunch fluttering, pounding his club on the pavement, rattling oaths in his throat against the damned foreigners. As his blue uniform, gray helmet and swinging club came into view, the invading devils, carrying their stricken leader, whooped out of view. The gay colors of their stockings vanished like a rainbow sucked back into the sky, and the normal sounds returned to the street. It's after the battle, mother. Workers resumed with pick and hammer, stores opened again, women ceased to scream from windows, and the regular gutter flow began once more.

Joey, more concerned with the fat guardian of the law than a hole in his head, had allowed himself to be helped into a hallway by Peter Mendes. His brother Bert, who was blue with fright and deathly sick at the spreading, dark blood that stained Joey's hair, sheepishly asked, "You hurt much, Joey?"

Joey scowled at him. It was the major cross of his life that his own flesh and blood, his own brother, was a coward and could not stand up side by side with him and trade wallops with the enemy. Yet he did not hold it against him, hoping he would outgrow it. Joey put his hand to the back of his head, examined the smear of blood on his fingers with the unconcern of a scientist and scowled, "It's nuttin'! But you shouldn't tell mudder." Then they all went over to the corner drugstore, while Walrus returned to his comfortable chair in the saloon.

The pharmacist, a Russian student with cascades of black hair worn like Robert Louis Stevenson and heavy-lensed glasses, gruffly ordered Joey into the rear room. "Loafers, bummers, always fighting," he muttered, pushing him towards the sink. He cut away some of the matted hair with a finger-nail scissors, washed the wound, applied some iodine and sadistically watched Joey screw up with the burning pain (that will teach him a lesson), and finished by putting some adhesive tape across it. As the battle-scarred Joey, now a bandaged hero, walked out of the store, the man cried after him, "You shall tell your mother this costs ten cents." Just to keep his record clear, Mutt lifted a box of chocolate laxatives from the counter.

The pharmacist watched the boys disappear and sighed. Short of major surgical operations, he performed most of the medical work of the neighborhood. The housewives could not afford doctors (fifty cents a visit in the office, one dollar at home) and so they brought him all of their ills. His remedies were direct and simple. He divided the human body into two equal parts. Castor oil for all pains below the navel, aspirin and a cold compress for all aches above it. But when mothers of four and five asked to speak to him privately in the rear of the store, he sold them ergot for you-know-what. A philosopher and a humanitarian, he was also ambitious. With the help of his sister, a shirtwaist operator, who was proud to support him through medical school, he would soon become a doctor. Then he planned to open an office in the same vicinity. And when the families would prosper, the grateful wives would remember the pills cast upon the waters.

In Yorkville, three doors away from Eighty-eighth Street, where the Second Avenue tracks would presently be laid, or exactly four and one-half miles due north from Forsyth Street, in a third floor rear flat of a tenement, a six-pound daughter was born to Maria and Jan Pajalski; Maria, (née Schleisig) of peasant and domestic stock, and Jan, of the roaring Pajalskis from a village near Crakow, peasants, sots and wife-beaters for generations. Jan was a fiddler by occupation, playing at Polish and Bohemian weddings for a livelihood. He was all the generations of his glorious stock, a lecher, boozer, saufer, swine and Polish patriot. He had russet-colored hair, blue-watery eyes, a Norman nose and mustachios like a brigand. After each dance it was his gallant custom to drink the health of the bride. And generally, before the ceremony was performed, he found himself involved in a fight with the bridegroom over his ardent attentions to the bride. Thus, while Jan was tuning up his fiddle on the draughty platform of the Yorkville Casino and casting a rooster's eye upon the assemblage of women, his wife was delivered by a Jewish interne, assisted by two neighbors. The baby was called Gina.

Tsong, tsong, tsong, ring the iron hammers on the shining, spike-heads. Firm wrists like the ones that clutch the Socialist torch on posters, and the unerring aim of the swarthy, sweating gnomes whose powerful jaw muscles bulge out as if a marble was concealed in each cheek. Music above the clamor of the street. A city torn up and rebuilt, a city growing to music. Tsong, tsong, tsong, like the chimes in some far-off peaceful churchyard.

Let us saunter through the peaceful churchyard. On the east corner, Sullivan's saloon with a twenty-five foot bar, a mirror that ran the length of the wall, and two deft bartenders skilled in blowing suds into a ten cent growler. And in the rear, a little room with three tables and comfortable chairs, where ladies, sports and roundsmen could cool their throats with mellow beer. On Sundays, when the main entrance was closed, the customers could enter through a side door, and taper off the Saturday night drunk. Next to the saloon was a four-story tenement, and then Moscowitz's Roumanian Cafe. Within, men in shirt sleeves, with fine dark moustaches and dark, gleaming eyes, played cards and sipped small cups of Turkish coffee. The sediment in each cup was thick and heavy, but the men drank into the dregs, flavoring the bitter granules, and endlessly smoking cigarets which they rolled on machines at home. No one ever ate at this cafe; even the proprietor sent out for his meals. The one aromatic spot was Rosenzweig's barber shop, with its beautiful peppermint stick constantly revolving in patriotic colors, and the florid script on the window, "Tonsorial Parlor," and its cool smell of bay rum and hair tonic and the short, dapper barbers with their soft, clean hands. An old brick house separated it from the grocery store, filled with open barrels, trays of rolls and bread and fly-paper murals. All the housewives mocked at the fumbling grocer who couldn't add and was helpless without his shrewish wife. Every time she bore a child, the business went to ruin because her husband gave away more money in change than he took in. Then she would rebuild the trade and just when the store showed a profit, passion would fell both her and the business once again.

In the center of the block there stood that marble counter-part of Roman elegance and decadence—Lepke's "mikvah." The hot springs of Forsyth Street. A vivid three-tone hand-painted sign, a beautiful example of primitive east side art, announced its hidden wonders, eight tub baths and two plunges. A melancholy bather sat in the tub on the right hand side. He had one big, round eye, a sad eye in the center of his profile, a shaggy brown moustache, and a brown pelt upon his head; and he was nude up to where the slightly irregular line of the tub cut across his abdomen. The artist, a slave to realism, had boldly indicated that the man had one breast.

But not the lady who sat in the companion tub on the other side. This Madonna of the tub had a crown of hair piled so high and heavy upon her head that she resembled an Italian mother balancing three bread loaves. There was an aristocratic tilt to her nose, and a wistful look in her eye, but alas, she had no breast. She was washed clean and flat in a censorial swish of pink paint from her cheek to where her virginal body sank into the water. The tubs cost twenty-five cents and the plunges fifteen. There were no showers in Lepke's mikvah, thus guarding against the possibility of emerging clean.

Tsong, tsong, tsong, the chimes grow sadder. The old Swami stands still, and gently the wind blows through his beard. In the house next to him is a plumbing-store with a large display window, in which, framed like a still-life, is a glistening white toilet seat atop a marble bowl, arched like a fish-jaw. A thing of beauty and remote as a star to the good residents of Forsyth Street, although it was rumored that in the new houses going up on Second Avenue each apartment came equipped with such an ornament in addition to a white ice-box and a marble bath-tub. On to the ladies' hair-dressing parlor, one floor level above the street, where the only regular customers were the sporting women, for good housewives had no time and no call to beautify themselves, except on special occasions such as births and weddings. Behind the two wax busts with their delicately curved and tinted lips and their rosebud nostrils, there was a dark bedroom which could be rented for assignations. The landlord listened with dramatic indignation to many complaints about this den of sin, but alas, he had once compromised himself with a Galician hussy in that very dark room and so was estopped from evicting the tenant. On the corner was a tombstone shop, a cool, dusty place, in which rose simple marble and granite headstones without ornamentation, for no Jew likes to have angels dance on his grave when his bones are returning to dust. On summer nights, the boys sat on these sample tombstones and harmonized in doleful melody.

> *"You made me love you;*
> *I didn't wanna do it—*
> *I didn't wanna do it. . . ."*

On the opposite corner was a soda fountain and candy-store. A sloppy, slippery place, where rose tonic, a sweet and fragrant drink, cost two cents a glass and American Beauty Cigarets were four for one cent. But a spendthrift, preening before his girl, would buy a single Turkish Trophy cork-tip for one cent and wear it behind his ear until he was ready to smoke it. In the adjoining basement was a job-printing shop which specialized in posters for organizations that ran dances, outings and picnics. Thus, "Annual Dance of the Forton Social and Athletic Club at Stuyvesant Casino, Gents, fifty cents, Ladies, free." Or "The Buckowiener and Galatz Masque and Civic Ball—Come in Costume"—although the only disguises were pressed pants and stiff collars.

And the Irish with their clam-bakes—"the East Side Democratic Club," or just a plain racket run by a hoodlum for his own benefit—"The Tony Bastano Association," for which two tickets would be forced upon every shopkeeper in the neighborhood on threat of having his bones and windows broken. And now the poolroom, ten cents a cue, where to get in you had to wear long trousers, and where everyone smoked and swore. Great secret plots were hatched here among the taunts and oaths of men, as each young blood clutched a cue like a spear in His Majesty's Lancers. Here you received your first real recognition as a man among men when the gang leader whom you worshipped and for whom you were proud to run errands addressed you as an equal. You thrilled to his friendship, even though it led in a few brief years from your first pair of long pants to a jail sentence.

In the basement on the other side of the stoop was a bird and dog store, a fetid interior with the odor of bird and animal droppings, and a mute owner who seemed to have been silenced by the noises of his pets. Then a row of two-story brick houses, now in decay, relics of the period when the "gemutlich" Germans dwelt there, when each house boasted a tree in front and a garden patch in the rear—long before the Irish invasion had forced them into better neighborhoods. Now the Irish had been ousted by the Jews, who in turn felt the hot breath of the Italians down their necks.

The block ended with Rosoff's drug store, with a maroon glass jar in the window, the sign of the apothecary.

Tsong, tsong, tsong. The belly of the gutter had been ripped open in a deep four-foot gash. Gnomes sweated in the pit and around them a complete city flourished. On Forsyth Street you could be born, live and die—even order a tombstone—without going off the block. And beyond that were other, similar blocks. From river to river, Battery to Harlem, across bridges to Bronx, Queens and Brooklyn, by ferry to Richmond, a city made up of infinite lesser cities, each a complete entity, sufficient unto itself. New York.

The old Swami smiles. The cool breezes of the late afternoon blow gently through his patriarchal beard. Softly, wisely, he speaks:

"Why should I move? Everything I want in life is here."

The chimes ceased and summer darkness came over the city. In all the boroughs, in all the districts, saloons were getting ready for the Saturday night crowds. In the poorer sections, where the laboring people lived, the bartenders slipped on new aprons and took stock of their beer supply. Uptown and in the theatrical section, they slicked their hair in equal parts, dressed in starched, white coats like surgeons and made the face elastic with a genial smile. Once released from fears, envies and inhibitions, grandiose talk would rise like steam from the drinkers, rise higher than the topmost tier of glittering glasses, loud, expansive, "have-another" talk, fanned until the closing hours by the suave, smiling servitors. In Brooklyn, along the Navy Yard, on the Bowery and Fourteenth Street, the bartenders, many of them ex-prizefighters, girded themselves for the sale of hard whiskey and the sudden bum's rush they would have to give the tough huskies that came off the ships, loaded down with wages, thirst and lust. The young chippies primped and the tarts swung their wide bags in the "welcome-home" parade of flesh. The husbands of a city marched in tired brigades and freshly dressed young wives leaned eagerly from windows, for the kettle was on the fire and this was the night for love. Sunday, the man of the house could sleep late. Saturday night, and the city prepared itself to relax, to love and to rest.

At dark, Isidore Glass, the father of Joey and Bert, came home from work. He was short, of slender build, with a gentle, barely awakened face. Like a great many immigrants, to whom uprooting was a form of death, he was completely bewildered and frightened by America. Even after ten years in New York, only the memories of the life he had left behind seemed real, and the new life was a nightmare. But it must be lived. Every day, including Saturday, he worked from seven in the morning to seven at night in a gas mantle factory located on Wooster Street, a mean and squalid path in a dismal factory section. For a seventy-two-hour-week, he received nine dollars in wages and the promise of a raise to ten dollars after Christmas. But he was glad to have this job, for the panic had thrown thousands of the poor out of work.

At this period, electricity for the many was still a remote marvel and luxury; most families, dependent upon gas for illumination, used an acid-treated cotton mantle which increased the light and mitigated the horror and meanness of the bleak blue-yellow gas flame. Isidore worked as a "shaper," shaping the mantles from the strips of acid-treated cloth, sewed crudely in the form of a sock. The shaping would be done over a strong flame which withered the cloth, releasing fumes of acid which nearly burned his eyes out. All the workers in the shop suffered from eye ailments, and a few had been blinded, but they also suffered from extreme poverty, and so those who could see kept on working, grateful to have a job.

The boss was a grubby and insolent German Jew who found it a good business. Labor was cheap and the demand for mantles was great because they were sheer and crumbled easily even when carefully handled. He despised the Roumanian and Russian immigrant Jews whom he was exploiting and planned little ways in which to make their harassed lives even more miserable. He smoked long cigars brazenly on the Sabbath and then taunted his orthodox workers who were obliged to labor on the day of rest. He flaunted himself as a "free-thinker" and would express his contempt by saying, "Ich bin ein deutsche Yihoodah," as though that elevated him from every other form of Jewish life. He hated them for that dark resignation with which they accepted all of his taunts, and yet went on working for him. In all of their minds, behind their saintly patience, behind the hardships and humiliations they endured, secret deposits of strength were forming. Each one was planning, hoping, dreaming.

So with Isidore. Despite the burdens of his struggles, fears and maladjustments, ambition had touched him. There must be a way out, a path to a better life, if not for himself, certainly for his children. He had already taken his first step towards the escape. Two weeks before, he had invested most of his savings in a peddler's box, which he had stocked with cheap jewelry, collar buttons, tie-pins, fancy sleeve garters, key rings, pearl-handled button-hooks and other trinkets similar to those which the Dutch had used in the purchase of Manhattan Island from the Indians. And following the advice of a friend, he had peddled those wares among the Irish on the west side. The man had assured him that the Irish were a race of drinkers and spendthrifts and readily fascinated by glittering trinkets. Part of this legend he had discovered to be true, for on his first timid excursion among the Irish, he had brought back nearly two dollars in profit for only one evening's work. To-night he planned to try the same route again.

His tired wife set a plate of steaming soup before him. He soaked a crust of "Chalah" in it, left over from the Friday night feast, and asked:

"Where are the children?"

"Where should they be? Playing in the street," his wife answered.

Isidore sighed. He longed to see his children. On week-days he only caught a glimpse of them, and always they were asleep. In the chill dark of early morning, when he left for the shop, they were curled up in the big bed beside the kitchen stove, fast asleep. And often at night when he returned, especially after working overtime, they were also asleep. Same bed, same position, the same silence. Sometimes in the still of night he would be seized with a terrible nightmare that his children were dead, that they had been dead for years and were lying in the kitchen bed in an endless sleep from which he would never see them aroused. Then he would creep off his own bed, tip-toe softly across the cold floor, listen to their breathing, touch their cheeks with his bruised, tired hand, sigh, and return to bed. Yes, some day he would see them, fill his eyes with the view of his own children—alive.

Quickly, he finished his soup and carefully arranged his box of wares. He tried to instil in himself new animation, a fresh spirit that could put to rout his fears and fatigue, for he was off to earn money. Ambition touched him, but he was small and gentle and tired. Carrying his peddler's box closed, like a valise, he trudged down the stairs, illumined by a small blue gas flame, just a finger-tip of light. In winter, gusts of wind often blew it out and the gas would hiss through the jet, endangering the lives of the tenants. Automatically, Isidore clothed the dismal flame with a mantle as he walked out of the long, bleak hall.

At Stanton Street he boarded a horse-car, which rolled and dipped like a ship on the high seas. There were two narrow rows of seats against the walls with an open space in the middle for a stove in the winter time. Despite the frantic efforts and curses of the richly bemoustached driver, the horses rarely pulled the car on an even keel and the more delicate passengers frequently became seasick. Isidore transferred at Sixth Avenue for an uptown car, got off at Twenty-Third Street and walked over to Seventh Avenue. This was his territory. Here the saloons were bright and the merry and lavish Irish foregathered.

Near the swinging doors of a saloon in the middle of the block Isidore adjusted the straps of his peddler's box, cast a final look at his wares and girded himself to enter. Here was an entrance that required courage. Under the imitation cameos and the green garters, his heart beat wildly. He could hear the revelry, the hoarse, important voices that poured over the doors, blending with the cigar smoke and the smell of beer suds. It was clamor, lit up. He pushed through the doors, and paused for a moment within. A blare compounded of light, sound and fumes, enveloped him. His eyes, burned from the long day's exposure to acids, smarted and sudden tears rolled down his cheeks. Through them he gazed blurredly at his prospective customers. Some two dozen huskies were standing at the bar drinking beer and whiskey. They were longshoremen, stevedores, truck drivers, motormen, all broad-shouldered manual workers, with faces like slabs of raw meat, brick red necks and large rough fists. A couple of Beau Brummells wore campaign buttons on the side of their hats and a rosette behind the ear. Little Isidore sighed, took a deep breath and advanced, for there was a dollar to be made.

He smiled plaintively, ingratiatingly at the bartender and ordered a beer. The man scowled and filled a glass. Isidore put down a nickel and pushed the schooner back towards the bartender. "For you," he said, and, trying to smile, he indicated his box. One nickel bribe, a goodwill offer—nearly thirty minutes' work before the open flame shaping gas mantles, carfare to Coney Island on the Bergen Street Line, twenty cigarets, a meal in an Allen Street basement restaurant—one nickel.

He advanced with his open box and timidly touched the coat of the first husky. "A nice pair of sleeve garters, mister?" The boyos took notice of him. What's this floating down the Green River? A little Haybroo to have a bit of fun with. Politics and prize-fights could wait. "Faith and 'tis Ikey, himself," said a dock worker to a man who knew half the Talmud by heart. "Come here, Ikey," and he whisked his chin with thick, clumsy fingers, the life-of-the-party imitation of an animated beard, appended to the Jewish chin—the comical, universal Jewish whiskers. "Oy bet those garr-ters are made of pae-per," and he felt them, yielding a little to their flamboyant green. "They'll be fallin' off me arrms," and he bought them.

Others laughed, others bought. A pin here for that blinding necktie, a cameo brooch to take home to Bridget, a pearl-handle button-hook to hook those bright yellow buttons on those size eleven bulldog shoes and a set of collar buttons for the celluloid collar when you go to early mass. And there you were. Sixty cents gross business. The world was full of good people, and even the goyim could be kind on a Saturday night.

But as he turned to leave, a playful boyo with a rosette behind his ear, stuck his foot out. The little Haybroo tripped, just catching himself at the bar. A howl of laughter went up. For it was Saturday night in the old saloon and the boys were whooping it up. Along the line, the drinkers got their big feet ready. The peddler looked down helplessly, frightened. He could never run this gauntlet and survive. He looked appealingly at the bartender, who scowled, but remembered the beer which the little Ikey had bought for him. He came from behind his bar and roughly escorted Isidore through the line. But the last man goosed him and he leaped through the doors in a blaze of light and laughter from behind. On the sidewalk he adjusted his box and took stock. A bit of rough-house—but thirty cents profit. Thank God for that.

Indifferent sales in the second and third saloons, and then he came to one a few blocks up. It had a mean, hostile smell about it. It bristled with low hatreds. The men had reached a stage in their drinking when all their surface geniality had been cooked out. Instead of arguing, they were snarling.

When Isidore bought a glass of beer and pushed it towards the bartender, the man flung it back and growled, "No sheeny buys me a drink."

Isidore wanted to retreat, but a group had already taken notice of him. A teamster picked up a scarf pin, but in doing so, closed his other fingers around a signet ring. But you can't accuse a two-hundred pound mammoth of stealing, so you say to yourself, "All right 'bullvan,' you like the ring, keep it—just pay me for the pin."

Another picked up a key-ring and went on talking, pounding the bar with emphasis, "And if they put any more gasoline trucks on the route, we'll be looking for a job. I can drive a team of horses, but I'll have nothing to do with those motor-cars."

A thin, quavering voice intrudes, "That comes to fifteen cents, gentleman."

"And what are you after?"

"The key-ring you took, please."

"Who, me? So 'tis stealin' you're accusin' me of?"

The other boys cluck their tongues. What's the world coming to, if you can't drink your beer peaceful of a Saturday night without being accused of stealing by a little vaudeville Ikey that walks in without so much as a by-your-leave?

A terrible silence falls upon the saloon. Into the void, like spitting pits out, he repeats, "So—'tis stealin' you're accusin' me of."

And his anger mounting as he puts the key-ring in his pocket, he rotates the beer in his half-filled glass, and suddenly tosses it full in the face of the Jew peddler. A roar of laughter steams up.

The beer smarts the eyes of Isidore, drools down his face and clothes, into his merchandise, soaking through to his heart. The suds cling to his moustache like icicles. He stands there frozen with terror and shame. Sadly, he wipes the burning beer out of his eyes, and silently turns to go. But his resignation torments his attacker. "And don't be callin' me any of them cursin' Haybroo names."

The Jew walks on, still silent. His pursuer follows and pushes him roughly towards the door. Isidore sprawls to the floor, striking his cheek against the bar-rail, while the wares spill out of his box. He gathers the trinkets quickly, picks himself up, rubs a smear of blood away from his face, and backs out. His tormentor readies a fist.

From a rear room Michael Donovan, the owner of the saloon, looks out. He takes in the picture of the retreating Jew peddler, cowering before the upraised fist of a customer and listens as the bartender snarls, "And don't ever come back here." It's only a brawl, so Donovan makes no comment. He knows from experience that a Jew is not a heavy beer drinker, and Michael is too ambitious a business man to repress his customers. "The boys are having a bit of fun," he muses and returns.

Outside, Isidore wipes the blood from his face, brushes the sawdust from his clothes, and moves northward to a friendlier saloon.

In the rear room, Michael Donovan resumed his discussion with Pat Ahearn, the district Tammany leader. The saloon owner was a portly Irishman about thirty-five, with dark hair parted in the middle and curled a little over his brow. He had a respectable paunch, a lively tongue and a gleaming sportsman's eye. In eighteen years, he had risen from cleaning spittoons and sprinkling sawdust in a west side bar to ownership of his own saloon. He was proud of himself. He had always been eager for the acquisition of money, power and prestige, and now that his interests were vested and he had taken solid root, he was expanding to politics and managing prizefighters. He owned a half-interest in a front rank lightweight, and with him as a nucleus sought to build up a stable of fighters, all of championship timbre, who would scatter themselves over the arenas of the country and bring back heavy purses to him. He foresaw the day when all the large cities would support permanent arenas and fighters could travel from city to city like theatrical stars and perform to big gate receipts.

Ahearn screwed up his terrier eyes and spoke in his confidential voice out of the side of his mouth.

"We've got to dig at least 3,000 votes out of this district for the next election. What do you think, Mike?"

Donovan listened and nodded. The Germans might be pig-headed but the Irish could be depended upon and the Italians with the promise of pick-and-shovel jobs could be induced to vote a straight Democratic ticket. Luckily, the pay-off place for the votes would be his saloon, which meant that most of the money would be spent there. Yes, he would ally himself with Ahearn; it was good business. The men rose and walked to the bar.

"I'm sure we can do it," said Donovan with lively confidence.

In a private dining-room (bedroom adjoining) of a Herald Square hotel, Eugene Murdock sat at a table, surveying the remnants of a double portion of lobster à la Newburg, and the faintly blurred vision of Polly Malone. All through dinner he had been drinking champagne, but the sole effect had been to make him see things within himself more clearly, and the objects outside himself, less sharply. The blinds were drawn, but the mid-town breeze washed in wavelets of Saturday night hilarity, which made Polly restless and eager to get on to the peak of this rendezvous. She was a buxom female in her late twenties, still pretty, but surrendering rapidly to her self-indulgent love of good living. Puzzled by the remote, engrossed look in his eye, she pouted:

"You're paying no attention to me at all. I might just as well be in Chick-ago."

"Oh yes I am, dear."

Murdock, a tall, handsome man, about thirty-eight, soothed her with a smile, poured two glasses of champagne, and resumed his inner thread. He was thinking of his son, wondering whether this boy who puzzled him so would be able to exploit the advantages which his father had wrested for him. Figures mounted like music notes in his mind. That new deal, the contract to lay the road-bed for the Second Avenue trolley, would net him as his share of the profits close to sixty thousand dollars. And this was only the first of the big, juicy plums. True, it had taken months of hard, patient work, and every cent he could muster.

And at that, if it hadn't been for the cunning of his partner in the contracting business. Dominick Ferraro, the deal would have fallen through. A strong man, that Italian, a wise man, sure of himself, a man risen from his people by his own pick and shovel. Ferraro had handled the city bosses, arranged the political split of the loot, the actual management of the labor, while Murdock solved the engineering problems and took care of the financing of the project. Well, that hadn't been easy, either.

Murdock sipped from his glass and frowned. The one feature which had impressed him most in the entire deal was the negotiations with the private banker, Seymour Henderson. How suave and unctuous the old gargoyle had been with his Union Club manners and deacon's whiskers and how sure his large cut of the pie. And for what? For lending surplus money which other people had entrusted to him, against the collateral of bills drawn on a quasi-public corporation with the security of the city behind it. The old pirate with a look as sharp as a cutlass, and a refrain like a banshee.

"Money is scarce in the panic—only the private bankers have capital. Money is scarce."

Polly rose from her chair. After all, she mustn't forget that she was an arch-temptress, one of the original Floradora Sextette—so she said. For years thousands of chorus girls, soubrettes, ingenues and burlesque hoydens would claim that same spot—the seventh girl in the Floradora Sextette. Plumply she sat on his knee, spilling a few drops from his glass as she circled her soft arm around his neck. The warm flesh-smell under the perfume wooed him back into an awareness of her. Against his cheek, she baby-talked:

"Don't oo wike oor ittle dirl any more?"

She nicked his ear and he shuddered slightly.

"Sure I do—you bet." He set his glass down and, crushing her to him, he kissed her, a thick, champagny, blood-heat kiss. He seemed to remind himself that he was celebrating to-night. Polly rose as after a conquest and, half-brazenly, half-coyly, she continued, "Don't oo want oor baby to det ready for her big mans?" He waved her into the adjoining room.

As with the turn of a spigot, his thoughts flowed back to Perry. What strange alchemy had made the son so unlike the father? The very phrase itself, "father and son" held a warm, human, almost romantic glow for Murdock. Father and son, tree and limb, one sturdy, protecting, the other nourishing upon its strength, but both alike. Yet every day Perry grew further away from him. And, moving on in his thoughts, Murdock tempered his sense of frustration with a note of gratitude. The boy was unlike him, and yet, not altogether like his mother. And that was something for which he could be grateful. He softened the criticism of his own wife. She was a good woman, one who brought dignity to his home. But she was cold. Years before, he had mistaken her frigidity for qualities of reticence and maidenly reserve. But with time, and even with the birth of a son, neither warmth nor worldliness had come to her. She was still determinedly chaste, still naively sure of the difference between right and wrong. And in recent years, as Murdock had plunged more aggressively into a world she only dimly understood, she had retreated, packing herself more and more securely into her own shell. She clung to her belief that it was a virtue not to change.

Murdock tugged at his meaty cheek meditatively.

Through the drapes that served as a door to the other room, he could hear Polly singing in nasal professional tones a frisky parody of a song of the day.

> *"His fish and worm*
> *Will make me twist and squirm,*
> *We start in to dip"*

At this moment, his wife was sitting in the cavernous living room of their brownstone home in Columbia Heights, Brooklyn. Fingers clasped in her lap, shoulders slumped forward, she sat almost inert, gazing out upon the harbor. She liked to follow the shore-lights on the rim of the city, and the slowly disappearing lights on the passenger boats that belly-crawled up the East River, some north to her beloved Boston. She sat and waited, brooding with that tight-lipped, religious expression that sealed her face against the bitter truths of a world whose rapid changes she refused to acknowledge.

Perry came down softly for his good-night kiss. At the approach of his tread, she turned her head. In his long night-gown, he resembled a girl, and for a moment Prudence sighed in regret. She had always wanted a girl, someone to knit closely to her, but a divinity whose wisdom she dared not question, had seen fit to present her with a son. Well, Perry was not rough and unruly like other boys. And certainly, he was not like his father, which was something to be grateful for. She forced back an onrush of tormenting doubts and bitter disappointments about Eugene. He too was part of the world against which she had closed herself. Prudence placed a thin hand on Perry's head and drew him towards her. Without fervor, she kissed his cheek.

"Good night, dear."

Softly, Perry retreated from the room, looking back once to see his mother outlined against the brilliant, mysterious flow of river life.

"Good night, mother."

In the hotel room, sharply cutting in on Eugene's meditations, the nasal voice confidently took new hurdles in the song.

> *"Ta-ra- ra-ta-ta-ta-ta*
> *Do a corkscrew turn. . . ."*

Eugene Murdock made up his mind. It was the banking game for his son. There was something gracefully larcenous about it. Healthy for the pocket and easy on the conscience. As soon as he got his degree at Yale, or perhaps Princeton, he would apprentice him to this very Henderson.

Polly parted the drapes and flared into the final bars of the song, undulating seductively.

> *"I love that Oceana*
> *I love that Oceana*
> *Ro-o-ll."*

Murdock scraped his chair back and walked thickly towards the drapes. Underneath her negligee, her ample breasts were like targets and the protruding nipples like bulls' eyes.

The whistle of a tugboat in the harbor, the sharp hoot of a freight train on Death Avenue, the clanging of a surface car as it crosses an intersection, the melodic ring of a bell on the handle-bar of a bicycle, the nervous laughter of a girl on the stoop with her lover, the wail of a woman in child-birth, the monastic soliloquy of a bum on the Bowery and the hot wind in an alley. The peddler shakes his fist at the town and slowly plods his way home.

When Isidore entered the door of his flat, his wife, observing his battered peddler's box, and his bruised face, ran to him with a moan. Joey, the pain of his cut throbbing in his head, cocked an eye from the kitchen bed and nudged his brother. With little rancor the father told how he had been thrown out of a west side saloon.

Then, noticing the crucifix of adhesive tape on Joey's head, he asked, "What happened to our son?"

The weary mother answered, "Another hole in the head. Is that something new? He was playing in the street."

Joey closed his eyes on dreams of vengeance. The Irish beat his father. Well, some day he would show them, with his hard, chunky fists. But Bert, who read books, was more philosophically sad. He knew all about the hardships of George Washington at Valley Forge, of the privations and courage of Daniel Boone, of all that the American heroes and pioneers had withstood. No, his little father was not a pioneer and must not wander from the safe and the familiar. No, he was not of the stuff of heroes. Not in a city where fists beat the rhythm of the hour.

Fists beat the rhythm of the hour. Fists on the walls of hall bedrooms and stinking flop-houses, on mahogany tables in swanky hotels, on mysterious doors in Chinatown, on Tenderloin gambling houses, on the iron bars in the Tombs, on the rods of freight trains coming in and pulling out; fists punch holes through the high air on roof tops and beat tattoos on the prostrate bodies of children in the cellars. Fists beat the rhythm of the hour.

Isidore Glass, Talmudist and shaper in a gas mantle factory, free lance peddler and sincere father, future citizen and voter of America, peels off his socks and stretches his toes. Already the blow in the saloon is a memory. Joey and Bert are curved up in deep sleep.

The tired mother closes the tap in the sink so that it won't drip all night, bolts the door, and turns out the light. From husband to children, she takes count of her brood and sighs, "Two wounded—but none dead."

2

"Yet I will look upon thy face again,
My own romantic Bronx, and it will be
A face more pleasant than the face of men."
—Joseph Rodman Drake
(Bronx minnesinger)

On East 164th Street near Sherman Avenue in the Bronx, Abel Hicks sat on his back porch and looked out upon his half-acre of waving corn, his two urban cows, as bland and bovine within earshot of the city's roar as they would have been on some secluded pasture. This was Sunday, Abel's day of rest, and he felt at peace with the world and with himself. He owned a valuable tract of land, had money in the bank, and what was more remarkable, a young wife who six months before had borne him a daughter. Hilda, his second wife, was forty years his junior, but he had succeeded in making her happy. She had consented to marry him, a rich old widower, only on condition that he take her to New York to live. Technically, shrewd trader that he was, Abel had fulfilled that condition. And yet here in New York he still did the only work he knew and loved; he farmed, just as he had done all his life in Stony Creek, one hundred miles upstate.

On the porch with Farmer Hicks sat Elmer, his grown son by his first wife, grimly observing him. Between father and son there was a strong rural hatred, the kind that festers in lonely homesteads, on far-off farms cut off from the world, where two people within four walls make a living, growing thing of their hatred, until it becomes necessary to their very being.

Years before, Elmer had thrown off the yoke of his father, and had run away from the farm. Abel still remembered coming upon the note propped up against a sugar bowl at daybreak one morning. The note was stark and brutal. "I'm leaving you and the farm. There's no opportunity for me here."

Like scores of barefoot boys, whose triumphs in the big city had transformed them into legendary characters, Elmer had run away to New York to make his fortune. He had not complained about the hard work on the land, the monotony of life, the loneliness, particularly since the death of his mother. It was the lack of opportunity that had driven him away. And for that he had deserted his father, leaving him alone in midharvest season.

But New York had rebuffed Elmer. He had endured hunger and want, had worked endless hours, had skimped and hoarded, knuckled under, racked his brains for opportunities, and so far all he had achieved was a job as an insurance salesman. That, on the surface, was all he could point to. But actually, he knew that at last he had come upon a positive formula for making a tremendous fortune. Real estate in the Bronx. Here was the reason and the justification for his escape from the farm for all his years of privation. He believed in Bronx real estate with an evangelical faith. But he had no money to buy even the smallest lot.

It was this hunger for land in the Bronx that brought him back to his father when he learned of the old man's second marriage and his move to New York. He had hoped that Abel would forgive him, would relent, would quicken to his dream of wealth.

But Abel could not forget that his son had mocked his authority, had deserted him when he needed him most.

The first question he had asked him after their awkward and begrudging reconciliation was:

"Well, son, have you made your fortune in New York?" And the constrained, shamefaced answer to this question had been the old man's revenge.

Now he gloated in the son's failure, enjoyed to the full his harassed, frustrated, cringing attitude. This failure was a divine visitation, a punishment for having deserted the parent. And whenever Elmer timidly broached his need of help, Abel answered, "Go ahead and make your fortune—but make it without me."

In the meantime, in exchange for a bed to sleep in and food, he exacted from him an obedience greater and more deferential than he had enjoyed on the farm.

"Come, son, let's go out and pick some corn for supper."

Dutifully, Elmer followed his father off the porch, down four steps, into the half-acre of growing corn. Corn, he thought with a bitterness that burned through him; corn for the belly. That's all the old man thought of. Corn brazenly growing on this precious land. The old man walked with leisurely but alert stride. He caressed each ear before he tore if off the stalk. He loved his corn as something to grow and eat, as produce to sell, as his gesture of contempt and defiance to the city that was herding itself about him.

"Father," Elmer began timidly, "there's something I must take up with you." The old man gave little indication of attention, walking ahead between the rows of corn, his son behind him pleading across his shoulder. "I'm thinking of starting a company—a little real estate company." He spoke in gusts.

"I'm right glad to hear that, son."

"But I need your help. You can be president of the corporation. I must have some land to begin with. If I could only start with a corner lot——"

The old man laughed. The laughter struck Elmer as it rolled over his father's shoulder.

"If you're countin' on me, forget it. I'm just an up-state farmer who don't know the ways of the city."

Laughing, he turned up another row, Elmer at his heels. They re-entered the house. The old man tossed the freshly plucked corn into the kitchen and resumed his seat on the porch.

There he sat and rocked upon a straw-bottom, hand-repaired chair, a stubborn, stingy old farmer of sixty-three who might easily live to eighty.

In seventeen years all the golden opportunities for making fortunes out of Bronx developments would be gone. But try however desperately, Elmer couldn't communicate this sense of panic to his father.

The old man simply sat with a smug, shrewd look on his face and a mocking glint in his eyes as though he could read the other's thoughts. His bald head shone with pride and his long beak, red and venous, was flung as a challenge. His cunning little eyes looked out upon his corn and livestock, a farm within the very limits of a tremendous city. He rocked contentedly on his porch as though he were a thousand miles from Times

Square, and his big-knuckled hands clutched the arms of his chair like the outstretched grip of a fighting cock. He was the monarch of what he surveyed, and a man besides. He had proved himself young at sixty-two; had married a young woman, caused her to moan in ecstasy and sired a healthy child. Who could do better?

As Elmer watched the grin spread over his father's leathery face, flow like water into the wind-bitten grooves of his cheeks, he felt a maddening rage sweep over him. He hated the old cock, hated the moronic wench who was his wife, a lop-eared slattern from an up-state sty, hated the yowling brat they had begotten. Instead of it all coming to him, upon his father's death, the valuable acre would have to be divided three ways. Nimbly, he subdivided the tract, as if the land were all his. He would keep the corner lots, mortgage the middle part to put up a large apartment house, and then watch the values leap. For all this would soon be five cents' fare from anywhere in town.

The old man watched for the dream-glow on his son's face, and startled him with speech.

"No use, son—I'm keepin' this farm to the day of my death. I like this place and nobody's goin' to push me off."

"But, father, this land's too valuable for farming. They'll be raising taxes on you every year. And all around you buildings are going up." He pleaded again, "If you'd only let me take charge——"

"No thanks. Guess I can take care of what's mine till the day of my death."

He alluded to the day of his death with the confidence of one who has made a secret pact with God to live forever.

Elmer bit his lip. Stubborn old mule. And that maddening indefinite postponement of the elite sign, "Elmer Hicks, Inc., Real Estate." Again he visualized the heavy stream of immigrants pushing the Jews and the Irish and the Italians out of the east side, across the bridges to Brooklyn, beyond the Harlem River, into the Bronx, the fat, sprawling Bronx, like a huge sponge with infinite cells, which kept sucking in wave after wave of newcomers.

"Roll me a cigaret, son."

Although Elmer hated the smell of tobacco, this was one of his filial functions. To roll cigarets for Farmer Hicks, who couldn't manoeuvre the tobacco into place on the thin paper with his own hulking stumps of fingers. He also derived a sadistic pleasure from making Elmer perform a distasteful task. And his sloppy habit of leaving cigaret butts around to stink up the house. Abel lit the cigaret and drew in sharply. A young woman appeared on the porch.

"Be careful, Farmer, with your old cigarets. You know how careless you get," she said in a shrill, proprietary voice. The old man grinned and looked at her with pride. His young wife.

"Come on over, Hilda, and set by me." He pinched the end of the cigaret with his spatulate thumb and forefinger and put the butt in his pocket. Hilda walked over and sat on the arm of his rocker. He ran his grime-lined hand down her waist and thigh. He squeezed her with increasing force and she squirmed kittenishly, "Don't, daddy."

Elmer tried to stuff his ears with his own dreams.

The farmer pursued his wooing. He pinched her young white forearm and looked out upon his half-acre of waving corn. Like a prophet he spoke.

"It's a cool Sunday and the air is nice smellin'. It's cool enough to sleep." He rose from the chair and walked towards the door. "Come on, Hilda."

She looked at Elmer, out at the field, and turned her head. Dutifully, she went.

Elmer stood alone on the porch. He stared into the space about him. Two blocks away, lay the inert jaws of a steam shovel. Excavations for a new apartment house. All around him land prices were going up, fortunes were being made and he could do nothing. A shrill giggle from the room above cut across his thoughts like a lash. Between his teeth, he spat:

"Stubborn, lecherous bastard."

There were no Sunday chimes on Forsyth Street. The tsong, tsong, tsong of the iron hammers on the ringing spike-heads, was stilled. The Eyetalian workers were at home, resting and feasting in the vermin-ridden catacombs of Elizabeth, Mott, and Mulberry Streets, west of the Bowery, in the crumbling, mice-warmed boxes where they dwelt. Big families, in number at least, just what President Theodore Roosevelt had asked for. Lusty father, high-bosomed mother, gnarled grandfather, lone-toothed grandmama, and the lucky seven squawling bambinos, the three youngest bow-legged from rickets, the next two pink-eyed, one in a white coffin, and the two survivors already at work, the boy shining shoes and the daughter in a garment sweatshop.

But this was Sunday, and the lusty sire was at home. A large tub of spaghetti was steaming on the stove, and a bottle of dago-red belly-wash, bought from a neighbor who had a wine-press in his cellar, stood on the shelf. Padre would eat until those powerful jaw muscles, which stood out like marbles, were tired, and then drink his red wine until the warmth of sunny Italy was in his blood. Then he would drive all the bambinos out into the swarming street, herd the ginning, gnarled old pair near the kitchen stove, lead the madonna into the only bedroom of the flat, and plough her like soil in the spring. For Sunday was the day of rest and recreation—and, as a by-product, procreation. During the week, when the little padre came home after swinging an iron hammer all day in the open, he was very tired. He had just enough strength left to eat his supper, smoke half of a warty, rust-colored, furiously stinking stogie, and then sink on the family bed like a felled tree. Later, the mother and three of the kids would crawl softly into the same bed. He neither heard nor felt them.

But this was Sunday. And in the cool of the summer evening, refreshed and relaxed, he would lead the family out of their dismal cells and they would sit on campstools in the courtyard. Other neighbors would creep out of their boxes and join them. An East River breeze with its dying strength would touch their relaxed faces. Someone would play a guitar or an accordion; a rich tenor voice, suddenly set free, would rise above the vapors from the yard, higher than the clothes-lines. Others would join. The air would fill with "Oh Marie, Oh Marie. . . ."

They would dream of the serene peasant life they had left behind in Sicily, of the olive groves and the fragrance of orange blossoms. They would sing and dream until the sudden need of rising early on the morrow struck them like a hammer-blow. Then, slowly, they would return to the vermy, roach-lined catacombs of Elizabeth, Mott and Mulberry Streets, west of the Bowery.

Early on Sunday Joey rounded up his gang. There was important work to be done. The November elections were not far off, and it was time to forage for wood to burn for the great election fires, huge bonfires on all the east-side streets. Here was something to plan for. Sometimes the flames mounted as high as the roofs of the tenements, cracking windows with their powerful heat, driving terrified families out of their homes, setting buildings aflame, causing harassed fire engines to scurry around from block to block in a futile battle against too many flames. For weeks there were deep charred pits in the middle of the gutters where the election fires had burned their way down. But little could be done to prevent this, for the police were busy at the polls safeguarding the re-election of the Democrats, and the repair jobs on the streets made juicy little plums for the district leaders.

Today ambition stirred through the gang. They wanted the most wood so that they could have the tallest fire in the neighborhood. An agreement had already been made with a stable-man to store the stolen wood in his hayloft, in exchange for a promise not to frighten the horses he rented out to sports who went buggy-riding on Sundays. Years later, similar bargains for "protection" would be made between the gang and the merchants.

Joey took count of his men. One-eyed Mutt, son of the janitor and a natural sneak-thief, Danny, the Irish kid, Louis, the Metzger twins, Chick, Sleepy, Itzky, and Schultz. All of the inner circle were present except Peter Mendes and his brother Bert. Pale-faced Bert, who caved in after a fifty-yard dash and who became nauseous in a fight, had made himself comfortable on the fire-escape of their flat. Here he was engrossed in an enormous book entitled "Less Miserables," by a French writer, Victor Hugo. He had already devoured all of "Doomoz" and had noted many other books which he planned to read after this. He could read for hours on end, forgetting food, surroundings, everything. He was a reading fool, thought Joey, but secretly he was proud of his kid brother who had fallen under the secret enchantment of books. Well, let him read. He was no good anyway on these foraging expeditions, where surprise attacks from neighboring gangs must be expected and where the bringing home of loot was fraught with many dangers. This was work for men, chunky-fisted men, not for dreamers who read all the time. But Joey did want Peter Mendes.

"Let's get Pete," he commanded, and the squad moved forward.

Peter Mendes, Sephardic Jew (his forebears had been exiled from Spain, through Holland to Constantinople), lived with his father and grandfather (his mother had died on the voyage to America) in a two-room flat (toilet in the hall) located in a rear building on Rivington Street, just around the corner from the drugstore.

There was a front four-story tenement with an entrance from the street, a long, dark hallway which led into a courtyard, and then a rear three-story building.

The Mendes differed from their Russian and Roumanian Semitic neighbors in many respects, but chiefly in that they were lean. There was an ascetic dimension to the family. Peter, past twelve, already preparing for his Bar Mitzvah, was tall, slender and dark.

But there was a lively, dark, luminous quality in his face. His eyes gleamed, and his hair, bluely black, combed straight back from his forehead, held a sombre, wintry light on its surface. All the other boys on the block, forever quarrelling with their unruly mops, envied his hair its obedient quality. But above everything else, there was an exotic smell about Peter, a mysterious, Sephardic smell, emanating from his hands and body, rising faintly from his clothes, a spice and coffee and sea smell. He was fastidiously clean, even well-dressed, his clothes enduring far beyond their allotted time. There was the ride of the dandy in his appearance and he was the first kid in the neighborhood to wear a breast-pocket handkerchief, The suggestion of aristocracy and superiority which came from him would have made his life miserable on the block if Joey had not adopted him.

Joey liked Peter, not because he was a fighter, but because he had ideas and knew how to plan. Thus, when they saw peddler seated near his cart upon a choice fruit box which they coveted, it was Peter who planned that Itzky the gamin engage the old man in conversation, tell him that the staff which supported the cart was slipping, get him off the box and around to the far end, while Joey made off with the wooden case and Mutt with a cluster of grapes.

When Walrus the cop tried to ferret out from the boys who broke the barber-shop window with a pussy cat, it was Peter who spoke up and asserted they had been playing basketball at that very moment in the gymnasium of the University Settlement. Peter planned, devised ways and means, spoke coolly, always contrived to have some money, and even though he was not much with his fist and loathed getting dirty, he was high up in the councils of war. He could maintain a long silence and he never betrayed a confidence. Joey liked him and let it be known that anyone who attacked Peter, offended Joey. And that was something to remember before taunting Peter, for when Joey sailed in with his chunky fists, his powerful, arched calves and his sullen clamp of a mouth, you were in for a beating.

Two boys were despatched to summon Peter. In a few moments he joined them, and the march began.

On Delancey Street a crowd had assembled to witness a fascinating and colorful street spectacle. A troupe of strolling acrobats was performing a tumbling act in the gutter which, in skill and daring, was the equal of any opening act on a vaudeville bill. The acrobats were clad in bright silk blouses, tucked into tight-fitting knee breeches with large bows, similar to those worn by sycophantic Americans presented at the Court of St. James.

One of the troupe carried a bass drum strapped to his shoulders and a padded stick attached to one leg, so suspended by belting that he could pound the drum by merely jerking his leg and still have his hands free to clash a pair of cymbals. He was a sad little man and when the blare of sound bolted from his jerky, bird-like movements, he looked frightened and apologetic. A carpet had been unrolled in the street and the acrobats performed handsprings, somersaults and backflips, all with a serious air. It was no fun for them, even if the crowd did enjoy their antics. This was their way of earning a livelihood. The boys, attracted by the cymbals and drum, ran forward eagerly. But Peter lagged behind.

Among the group he recognized his father. The elder Mendes, who had injured his spine in a street tumbling act, now performed another duty in connection with the troupe. He was dressed in a costume more garish than the others and wore a Turkish fez on his head. To his back was strapped a large copper samovar with a long spout instead of a spigot, from which he poured lemonade by merely leaning forward. His plaintive, sing-song voice filled the air. "Toor-kish-a-lemonade—two cents a glass." The populace was being royally entertained and in between stunts bought lemonade.

Sometimes, after a particularly difficult feat, a few men would fling coins on the rug, and it was Mendes' duty to pick those up. Peter blushed for his father, his lean, swarthy father with the aching spine, the Sephard who was more aristocratic than even the German Jew, who was esteemed as a man of wisdom and refinement in his clan, but who couldn't work in' a sweat-shop, and had to resort to this for a livelihood.

There he stood, dressed as a clown, peddling lemonade to street idlers for two cents a glass out of the same unwashed glass, picking up coins like a beggar. The shame of it seared Peter. Fiercely he resolved to do something to end this—for all of them. He had a way with the boys on his block, and he knew that some day he would have a way with men. He would stand apart from the dirt and danger of the struggle and direct others.

Peter caught his father's eye—and Yussef Mendes turned away. "Toor-kish-a-lemonade"—it was a wail now. He should have warned Peter. Usually, the troupe performed uptown, where the pickings were heavier. But with the panic on, and the advent of German bands, clusters of red sausages that blew into wind instruments until people were forced to give them money so that they would go away—business for his acrobats had fallen off. Now they were obliged to comb the neighborhoods nearest their own homes.

Joey and his friends watched the performers with keen interest. For weeks to come the kids on the block would be attempting those same stunts, risking their necks in somersaults and handsprings. Peter slunk into the background, his shame a cutting pain every time his father's wail rose above the crash of the cymbals. "Toor-kish-a-lemonade—two cents a glass."

"Hey, Pete—your fadder," called Mutt, jerking his thumb.

"Come on if you're going," snarled Pete. "Don't forget—the Broome Streeters are after wood too."

Reluctantly the boys began to move. The clash of cymbals, the beat of the drum, the grunts of the weary acrobats as they hurled themselves in the air while truck drivers cheered them from high, moving platforms, fascinated the boys.

In the inner rank of the spectators Joey discovered Isabella, a young girl from his block, whose mother was a widow who worked in a shop, leaving the child in the care of a grand-mother. At eleven the girl was already famed as a street dancer and would follow an organ grinder for blocks beyond her neighborhood. Color, music, crowds, drew Isabella like a wand. Her pallid face would light up and her dark eyes would become greedy with excitement. At the beat of music her thin body and legs grew alive. She seemed to abandon herself to movement.

Even at this tender age, Isabella was a cause of worry to her neurotic mother, not only because of her insatiable craving for dancing, but also because she was beginning to take notice of boys. Joey, without daring to admit it to himself, had in turn been taking notice of Isabella.

Coming upon her suddenly, jealous of her interest and pleasure in this spectacle, he seized her long braid and gave it a quick, vigorous tug.

"If I was your brudder—I'd wallop you. Git home."

Isabella began to cry and Joey, feeling strangely guilty and uncomfortable, gruffly added, "A goil should stick on her own block," and then he summoned his boys.

On the sidewalk, against a brick wall, Itzky was already attempting to stand on his head. Joey slapped him down roughly and, flanked by Peter and Mutt, walked on. Only he and Peter were sensitive to the retreating sounds. In Joey's ears was the sharp cry of Isabella. In Peter's, the clash of cymbals and the plaintive wail of his father, "Toor-kish-a-lemonade—two cents a glass."

Time out for a dash of statistics. After all, there are readers with orderly minds, their feet solidly planted on the ground, with an appetite for facts. They want to know things. They leap at you with darts in the dark. What was the population of New York in 1907? How many lunatics walked the street of Manhattan in 1910? Or, the mother of an attractive daughter, confronted with an embarrassing question. Is there any morality in the Bronx? For these, a brief parade of facts and figures.

In 1908, the total population of all five boroughs comprising New York City was 4,152,860. By 1927, these had grown to six and one-half millions. No negligible village, this, *mes amis*. It bloats like a gigantic sponge, except that it has no soft cells. It breeds another million in the time that it takes a farmer to wear out a pair of overalls. In 1908, fateful year, 771 men committed suicide on the island of Manhattan and only 223 women. More women had more faith. In 1909, 95 died from alcoholism in Brooklyn, much to the embarrassment of the Prospect Park section. In 1907, there were 12,547 fires in New York City, but its water consumption by gallons was in excess of half a billion. Its building construction figures in any year would stagger you and its budget is terrifying. In 1911, 92 persons were indicted for homicide in Manhattan and 42 were convicted, a comforting record for judicial leniency.

And through it all the birth rate mounts, the air grows thicker, and the cries for life madder and more desperate.

As for its morality, it has always been the most moral city in the world—for the unmoral. On those rare occasions when a rainbow spans the island from the East River Morgue to the paneless windows on Thirteenth Avenue, the city is illumined with its quaint inscription, "Blessed are they—that goes after what they wants." Its morality is relentless in that it applies only to those who fail. Each man climbs over the backs of others, swinging the spiked club left and right. Stand on top of your own little heap of arched spines. Kill, steal, lech, guzzle and gorge—there are more confessionals than brothels in New York, there is more absolution than sin. This is no town where the village whisperers destroy a reputation. In the sweat-band of each Tammany derby is perforated this whimsical slogan, "Who the hell cares?"

So much for statistics and morality. A reader rises who has taken correspondence courses in the development of chest, biceps and genitals and wants to know, "Is there fresh air in New York?" Frankly, there isn't. Alas, there is no fresh air in New York, and I would be the last to libel my city.

But there are rare, marvellous smells here. Smells that not only defy description, but dare you to ignore them. Ah, ah, I catch the aroused eye of the sensualist. You with your secret vices, you who shudder delicately while sugar melts at the bottom of a teacup, or crunch autumn leaves under your feet in ecstasy, or linger near bootblacks to inhale shoe-polish, or sink your fingers in fox-fur and scratch for thrills, or ride back and forth on the ferry to inhale the special ripe watermelony smell of New York waterfronts: to you I recommend the tantalizing distillations of New York, the special smells of ambition and of defeat.

For instance, stand on the highest peak of Manhattan, on the very flagpole topping the tallest building and breathe deeply. Surely, in these upper regions, the air should be pure, virginal. But, through the ozone, you sense the thin trickle of garlic and ground steer emanating from Warshaufsky's Wurst Geshäft on East Houston Street, and across it like the plaits of a braid, the bouquet of Bellodgia from the bathroom of a fifteenth-story suite in the Ritz Towers, where a lovely blonde is touching with a glass rod the pink nipples of her flawless breasts that soon will be worshipped by the cupped palms of a middle-aged broker. Together, they constitute the aggressive perfume of ambition. Monsieur Warshaufsky wants to make the best wurst in the world and the blonde desires a Peggy Joyce career. And as the sharp sensories inside your nostrils endeavor to dissect this smell, there burns across it the sudden, final stink of carbolic acid, wafted by Manhattan winds from a Bowery lodging house where some bum has just converted himself into a suicide statistic. These rare smells of ambition and defeat are the special emanations of Manhattan. They rise above the battle of smells that goes on constantly in New York—the warfare between the evil vapors given off from the mountains of refuse, garbage, burnt coal, excreta, and the appetizing cooking smells, water and soap, green vegetables and fruits, melting tar and flowers. Ah, the fragrant flowers of New York. Yes, inside each florist shop there are soothing smells.

Or suppose you invade Brooklyn. Cross the Williamsburg, Manhattan or the old Brooklyn Bridge, enter from Queens across the fetid Newtown Creek, steal into this vast borough through any of its apertures—and pause to smell. Chill settles on the nape of your neck, your flesh creeps. You stand rooted, nailed by terror. A heavy vapor rises from the ground. Brooklyn—yielding up the odors of its dying and its dead.

There are other ingredients—a stained glass ecclesiastical smell, the widespread dankness of melancholia, the stench of Flatbush smugness, the bleak staleness of Bushwick, a righteous Catholic aroma, an outer rim of sea-food, the Sunday outing smell of the millions who go to Coney Island, the drooping, withered smell of their return, the conglomerate smells of the alrightnicks, the first families, the Polacks, the Greenpoint scavengers. Statistical insert: The highest elevation in Brooklyn, 210 feet, is in Greenwood Cemetery. The dead rise higher than the living. But to remember its aroma until the day you return to rot in its embrace, stand still—inhale—Brooklyn—yielding up the odors of its dying and its dead.

Complete the tour through the Bronx, the sour milk from the Mott Haven dairies, the sweet milk from the million mothers bending over perambulators, the jungle odors from the zoo. The constant smell of brick, lime, mortar—for buildings are always going up. And the filled-in swamp smell of Queens, and the far-away freshness of Richmond. But above it all, where the high winds rise to battle, from east, west, north and south, they blow upon the city an unforgettable bouquet—the special smells of ambition and defeat.

3

$\mathbf{G}$uglielmo Zucco, or Googi, the Shabbas goy, who was sought by Joey on their wood-stealing expedition, lived in a three-room tenement flat on the Bowery between Stanton and Houston Streets. It was an old, sooty-colored crumbling structure that hung limp between the Grand Hotel, a Bowery flop house (25 cents a room, 15 cents a bed, showers free) and a loft building occupied by a wholesale crockery house and two paper-box manufacturers. Zucco père was a brigand of a Sicilian who, years before, had been separated from his savings by a pair of obliging countrymen who had sold him a money-making machine. They assured him that if he left fifteen ten-dollar bills in the machine (which they sold him for only fifty dollars as a special concession) he would find ten times that amount at the end of a week. Then they sat down and figured out with him that ten times $150 is $1,500 and with that tidy sum he could return to his native village and live out his years in affluence. And while he re-laxed, the machine would re-vitalize inself for a second miracle. Zucco wanted to believe and bought the contrivance. To guarantee results they volunteered to insert the money properly for him. Didn't he give them his savings with his own hands and didn't he watch them insert the bills with his own eyes? Every night for six days he came home from work and prayed before the mysterious box with its magical arrangement of spools and wires.

On the seventh day he came home, set down his tools and locked himself in the bedroom. He tried to control himself before this shrine of money, but it was impossible. He plunged for the box and, with trembling fingers and a heart that banged against his ribs, he opened the money-making machine. He discovered a bundle of Sapolio coupons and some newspaper clippings trimmed to the size of currency. He howled in agony, kicked through the door in rage and collapsed. For weeks he went about in rage and grief, looking for the benevolent countrymen who were now operating among the bohunks in Pennsylvania mining towns.

When the ache and fury subsided, Zucco decided never to work again in order to compensate for his misguided years of industry and saving, and cast the entire burden of supporting the household upon his wife, his two daughters, and eight-year-old Googi. From a jovial Sicilian he became a hard overseer. He beat them all unmercifully and devoted himself to making sure that they worked. He collected all of their earnings, spent his days in a pizzeria on Mulberry Street and found life full of compensations for a disillusioned landowner.

As a bootblack Googi was charged by his father with making at least ten shines a day (five cents on a chair, but only two cents on the wing). Twenty cents he must bring home every night. When he fell short his father accused him of squandering his earnings or loafing, and beat him with a razor strop.

Poor Googi, spindly-shanked, rib-revealing, yellow-pallid wop, survivor of rickets, bandy legs, diphtheria and scarlet fever, tortured by sties in the eyes because no one had known enough to wash them with an antiseptic, and nearly blinded when a neighbor applied hot urine as a sure remedy, never-kissed starveling and gutter rat, body bitten by bugs and razor strop, slinking up the street with the shoe-shine box strapped over one shoulder like a knapsack—soldier in what war?

On winter mornings, he was thrust out of the house shivering with cold, his eyelids unwashed, pasted together, clumping along in shoes too big for him, with the soles loosened and slapping against the pavement, slappety-slap-flappety-flap—a soldier who made his own rhythms.

After he had shined his first pair of shoes, he could stop at the corner stand and buy a hot dog, ground up from meat not government inspected, and wash it down with a glass of sour lemonade. This was breakfast for the little man. Hey, you orange-juicers, you cereal eaters, you bacon and egg toasters, you drinkers of rich milk and fine cocoa and hot coffee, you wearers of shoes with sound heels and soles and stockings that cover instead of exposing the legs through their holes, hey, you who sport woolen overcoats that button snug and tight and a good-bye kiss still warm on your cheek—do you see what Googi ate and wore?

When the truant officer kept after his father, Googi went to school. But he was too hungry to learn, too tired to concentrate, and too tense to forget that he would have to work all the harder after hours. School was no place for a dago that had to come home every night with a twenty-cent admission fee or be socked by a razor strop with bevelled edges that swung and curled all around him, stinging and burning like lashes of hot steel. The teacher, a high-bosomed Germanic spinster, a flaccid dope with granules of good meat in her cavities, considered him an incurably bad boy and often left her pudgy finger-prints on his dusk-yellow face.

On Saturdays he would eke out his earnings by lighting the gas burners in the Orthodox Jewish homes. The first time he performed this rite, he was terrified. A Jewish kid had summoned him:

"Hey walyo—wanna make a cent?"

The boy had led him upstairs to a cleanly swept flat. "Light the gas," the kid said. An old bearded Jew stood in the corner, with his back upon this desecration of the Sabbath.

"Dat's all you want?" Googi asked. The awakening cunning and suspicion of his gutter mind were at work. Why should anyone pay a hard-earned cent for lighting the gas? It was too simple. There must be a catch in it. He struck a match and the old bearded Jew winced. Googi's fingers trembled. Maybe a curse was being laid upon him. Or a fierce arm would suddenly encircle his neck and break it off. He lit the gas. He turned it high, he turned it low, he turned it right. The old man indicated with this beard one penny on the mantelpiece. Googi swept it off and fled. At the door he heard them ask him to return next Saturday. There was nothing to it. Jews were crazy, that's all. And in time, he became the official Shabbas goy to Forsyth Street.

Sometimes on hot summer nights Googi came home, turned over his small earnings, received his beating, and, sobbing, crawled out on the fire-escape. The heat in those rooms, the stinking fumes from those walls, trussed and vised against brick layers on both sides, with the hot rails of the Third Avenue "L" like radiators outside their window, the heat roar from the rumbling trains and the rising steam from the bums and nags below were unbearable. The heat of the torn mattress, plagued by bugs and disintegration, and of three writhing, unbathed bodies seeking rest in one bed, made of heat a living thing, a powerful demon, a great bear with a smothering embrace.

Googi would crawl out upon the fire-escape and look at the life around him. Four flights below were the hot, putrid side-walks of the Bowery, and the cobble-stones like hard sores on the gutter, so that a wagon rattled across it like a load of bones fleeing from the devil.

And like the trill of an early bird, the shrill, off-key, in human singing of "Mary Sugarbum"—saint of the dark corridor, patroness of the black alley, strutting Manhattan wreck.

Hey there, fragrant Daughters of the American Revolution, plant the lorgnette on the aristocratic beak, and roll your peepers on "Mary Sugarbum" as she struts down the Bowery in all her beery, razzle-dazzle glory. Prize exhibit in American womanhood, giant backyard dahlia, flourishing only in the soil and bird-drop of the Bowery. There's a flopping lid on her wobbly head—a wide-brimmed straw, spattered with mud, a plume like the tail of a drowned cat—and a corsage of flowers, lately a funeral wreath nailed to a door, now plucked from an ash-can. Under the hat, wisps of stringy, rusty-gray hair hang down to be blown askew by gusts of alcoholic breath. Her face is grimed and lined like a toiler's palm—O Lord Jesus, how does a human face degenerate into that? Hag and sot, come forward grinning, with one eye blue from a blow, with sagging cheeks grit-lined, nightmarish gums barren of front teeth, low-hanging teats, distended stomach, gin and show those old decayed fangs and carol to the Bowery night in your croaking voice. The soiled, twisted dress, the swinging bag, the torn stockings, the high-laced shoes, lopsided at the heels, and ah—that love of life. Strut, stagger and sing down the Bowery. Just a gay old bird. From doorstep to Welfare Island to Potter's Field.

Little Googi sits on the fire-escape and looks across at the broad expanse of the Bowery, across the north- and southbound tracks, into the windows of the trains that rumble by with men stretched out upon the seats in troubled sleep (sleep the night through for only a nickel fare on the Third Avenue "L"), into the windows of the flop-houses where, under the dim lights, the bums pick lice from their shirts and scratch themselves like weary monkeys, into the hot, panting sky that offers no hope. Summer idyl in New York. The Salvation Army's at the rescue; God's in His Heaven and the Mayor's at the trough.

This Sunday, something stirred in Googi's spare and bruised body. He awoke early and looked out of the window. The butter-yellow sun dripping through the railroad ties made plaid checks on the cobble-stones below. Googi dressed quickly, silently, swung the sweaty strap of his shoe-shine box across one shoulder and walked out. Except for the searching cats, the street was at rest.

Something stirred in Googi. For breakfast, he bought a scoop of pulverized ice, doused with an artificial orange flavor. He walked along lapping his tongue in and out of the mound of sweet ice. Near Rivington Street on the Bowery he passed a store front which advertised the new moving-picture, "The Great Train Robbery." He paused before the vivid lithographs and a great yearning filled him. He stared open-mouthed at the figure of the terrified hero tied with heavy cords to the railroad tracks, the monster train approaching and the wide-eyed, mutton-sleeved heroine, yellow tresses in the wind, racing madly to reach her lover first. Five cents to get in, to find out whether she saved him. Five shoes to a high lustre, polish on tip, polish on sides, polish on heel, brush, brush, spit on tip, flam, flam with flannel rag and one cent earned. He must see the picture.

He walked on. In an undertaker's window, alongside of a beautiful baby coffin, there was a potted palm. Googi stopped to look at the soft, satiny white interior of the coffin, and the green of the leaves above it. It roused a hunger for beauty in him, a yearning for nature. Another ambition welled up in Googi. He longed to go to Central Park. For years, ever since a boy had held him spellbound with a recital of its blossoming wonders, Googi had wanted to visit it. To-day, somehow, it moved within the realm of fulfillment. For it was Sunday in New York, and there was a holiday spirit in the air.

Tunnelling into the orange ice, Googi passed the Mills Hotel. This was the architectural adornment of the neighborhood, a place where poor, self-respecting men could sleep, but not too late, for it's reveille early in the morning and everyone out to work. One of the residents, just a big hotel man, called him over and, leaning against the stone wall, ordered a special Sunday shine. Googi on his knees, as in prayer, polish, brush, spit, flim-flam, the other foot and the man tossed him a nickel and said, "Keep the change, walyo."

This was the day for Googi, as he licked the paper clean of the melted ice. Central Park by day, and the "Great Train Robbery" at night. He was lucky enough to get four customers in a row, for Sunday is the shoe-shine day, and with thirteen cents in his pocket, Googi set out to conquer the Central Park menagerie and explore its green pastures. He was afraid to ask a policeman for directions, because all cops were anathema to him. They chased him when he found a good spot in front of a school or library, often forcing him to let a customer go with one shoe shined, and they were always breaking up harmless crap games with a swing of the club on the buttock which would leave its blue imprint for a week. He got his information from a cigar-store man, a keen fellow of great wisdom and gold teeth and long black cigars, who instructed him to take the subway at Spring Street and get off at Columbus Circle. He leaned over and puffed smoke into his eyes. "You know—Christopher Columbus—a wop justa lika you."

Googi followed directions and discovered the park. There were benches where serene families sat at rest, green meadows, tall trees, impressive statues, and a lake where boys his age, clad in smart sailor-suits, were floating toy boats on the quiet waters. Googi marvelled at so much peace and innocence in the world. Big boys with nothing to do but float toy boats! What tender angel arranged their lives? In wonderment he spoke to one of the boys, "Cheez, kid—how you maka dat ship stay on top of da water?" The well-bred scion looked at him tight-lipped and alarmed and a superior nurse promptly led him away.

Googi made no further efforts to break into the social life of the park but confined himself to shining shoes. This he did furtively, for the police were even fiercer here than in his own neighborhood, detecting as they did that he was out of bounds. For lunch he ate a box of popcorn and drank it down with some water from a public fountain.

Then he inspected the wild animals, more savage than his father, and studied the shameless way in which monkeys exposed their genitals. With awe, he gazed at the llama, the elephant, the zebra. In the late afternoon he fell off to sleep on a park bench from sheer exhaustion, clutching his shoe-shine box to his bony bosom.

It was dark when he awoke. An entire day had been spent in rapture. But he was still hungry for beauty and he was determined to see the "Great Train Robbery." He would get a beating anyway, and he might as well store up all the beauty and excitement he could against the wrath of his father and the hot night of pain and crying.

He made his way out of the park and had the street sense to get back to his own territory. He walked down the Bowery to Delancey Street, paused for one moment before the vivid lithograph and with his last nickel bought his admission. He entered and sat down upon a hard bench. Next to him a fat man wheezed. Flickering figures moved on the bright screen and suddenly they vanished into a hole of light as the celluloid snapped in the operator's shack. There was a howl of disappointment from the audience, stamping of feet and shrill, derisive whistling. A pugnacious bouncer rolled down the aisle and swished his whip against the shins of the noisy kids. The film was patched and the picture went on, and open-mouthed silence returned.

Googi, bootblack and patron of the cinematic arts, saw the "Great Train Robbery." In the excitement of the approaching train which threatened to mangle the hero his smarting eyes nearly popped out. Googi knew the terror the hero felt. He was an old railroad man himself. Often, from his perch on the fire-escape, he had seen the "L" trains approach with a fierce thunder, and had had wild nightmares in which he was cast to the knifey tracks by his villainous father. But in this picture the heroine, with her yellow hair, arrived in time to flag the engineer and save the hero. As they embraced, Googi wept. There was hope in life. He wept at this discovery. There was hope.

He came out of the nickelodeon clutching his shoe-shine box and stood before the billboard, bewildered. It was difficult to shake off the illusion which the picture had cast upon him.

Standing there, alone, uncertain, dreaming of hope and far-off beauty, a gang of older toughs from Broome Street set upon him and quickly brought him back to the realities of the Bowery. They searched his pockets and were enraged to find nothing. Again, he was penalized for being poor. They socked him, took his shoe-shine box away, kicked him around the sidewalk and ran off. Googi picked himself up, completely sobered. This was far from a casual crying situation. This was a crisis. It was one thing to report to his father that he had lost all of his earnings and then take a beating, but to come home without the business, without the tool of production—that was very grave indeed. He couldn't explain that to the ogre. He thought of staying out all night, a practice which boys on the block followed when they had done something very wrong, but no one went on the "bum" alone. Besides, he was too tired, too disillusioned. Slowly, resignedly, he walked home. A new crime—a new punishment. H;s father would undoubtedly go from razor strop to razor.

Googi entered the hallway of the tenement. A feeble gas light sputtered, throwing weird shadows upon the walls from which paint had been scaled off, leaving big, scabrous patches. He walked slowly, softly. At the foot of the stairway he clutched the rickety banister. He stopped. Behind the stairway he heard voices. Not words, just thick sounds.

Softly he retraced his steps and went around to investigate. Aside from his father, there was little that he feared. The dim light had almost died, but Googi could see. Before him was spread lesson one in what a young boy should discover only from Shelley, Keats and Swinburne, Inc. "Beneath the stars, my love. . . ." Or even Elinor Glyn, Ltd. "Lady Cheswick, shall we sit this dance out? May I lead you on the piazza? Your shawl, Lady Cheswick. Ah, the moon, the stars, the lake, the ripples, the night, the dancing moon. Your gleaming eyes, your ruby lips, your pale hands. My strong arms, my hot kisses. Ah Lady Cheswick, ah, ah, lady."

Googi crept closer. On the floor behind the stairway "Mary Sugarbum," the Bowery pushover, was clutching to her flabby bosom the drunken stoker of a freighter that had come in that day. It's a cinch. You buy the tramp a few drinks and then you drag her into a dark hallway. Behind the stairs, under the dim gaslight, on the mousy floor, love will find a way. It's a cinch. Years later, in some far-eastern port, you die of the black dog.

Googi looked on. The determined lovers were panting. Their heaving subsided. The man rolled over in a drunken stupor. The lady lay inert.

Googi waited. They were stretched like the dead. On the stairs leading down to the cellar he could hear the scuttle of a rat. Stealthily Googi crept over. Ever so gently, he put his fingers into the man's pocket and withdrew two bills. Under the feeble light, he identified them as a single and a five. More money than he had ever owned. His heart beat with triumph. *There was hope.* The heroine with the yellow hair had flagged the train in time.

On tiptoe, he climbed up the stairs. At the first landing, he removed his right shoe and stocking. He would give the dollar bill to his father and explain that he had found an El Dorado where one shined shoes all day and at night left in safe-keeping the heavy box. But the five, Googi would keep. He secreted the bill against his foot and drew his torn stocking on. How cool and strong and comforting it felt. He would sleep with his stockings on and in the morning he would step into a new world. No more shining shoes at a cent a shoe. He had advanced himself. He had discovered a new game. All day he would play and eat and drink, and at night he would prowl. The Bowery was full of hallways and the hallways were full of drunkards rolling over each other in the dark. And he would roll them. Rolling the lush—a new game. A game? A career!

Googi walked upstairs. Ambition beat high in his narrow chest. He would climb out on his fire-escape and shake his fist at the Bowery—at all New York. Hey, Big Town, I've got a formula for beating you. No more razor strops, no more hunger, no more pennies. Googi came into the door. The grumpy brigand with bristles on his chin and his long underwear crinkled like an elephant's hide stood ready to flog him. But Googi extended the dollar bill. The explanation didn't matter. "Maronna mia—gooda boy." A train rumbled by. The house trembled. Googi looked out at the flop-house across the street and felt sorry for the bums without hope. He crawled into bed. The cells of his brain were dark hallways peopled by drunks, and a song surged through him, "New York-I'ye found a way to beat you."

In Sheridan Square, Greenwich Village, the Latin Quarter of New York, in Gypsy Marie's little restaurant, conversation poured thick as smoke from tireless throats and smoke blew freely as words from the lips of the emancipated, and both blended to fill the low-ceilinged room with a vapor so dense that faces were discernible only by their glow. It was an intoxicating atmosphere filled with the abandon of those flavoring for the first time a new freedom. They were free to live their own lives. The word Art was passionately inscribed in smoke, in beautiful, flourishing chirography, Art with a capital "A." And a national joke, as virile and long-lived as the Ford joke, was being born. The joke about long-haired men and short-haired women. In all the vaudeville houses of America the mere mention of these symbols of deranged lives was sufficient to provoke laughter. But the union of these comic symbols bred a national scandal. Free love.

Yes, in a small territory, west of Washington Square, north to Fourteenth Street, a plot upon which you couldn't grow enough alfalfa to nourish a small herd of cattle, was born the shocking idea of fornication without courtship. Escaped middle-westerners and exiled New Englanders cast off the shackles of the love conventions of the hinterland and made a cult of free love and creative freedom. This was the social contribution of Greenwich Village to America. What it contributed in art, in the theatre, in prose and poetry, in sculpture and dancing, in the technique of having a good time and in shrewd methods for amassing real estate fortunes is a matter of record.

And so, at a small table in Gypsy Marie's, encircled by tall words forcefully spoken and by lovely dreams pronounced as if they were nightmares, two young women faced each other at a table. Neither had known the other until they had been seated at the only unoccupied table in the Bohemian restaurant by the picaresque husband of the picturesque Marie. The girls lit cigarets, then the first movement in the symphony of feminine emancipations, played with open defiance to man-made conventions, and regarded each other sympathetically. The older girl spoke first.

"I'm Agatha Crabtree." She was about twenty-four, rather squarely built, with a sober, dark face, faintly masculine features, very bright eyes and a definite voice. The other giggled pleasantly, a shy, mounting, musical giggle. "My name's Sally—Sally Rollins." She paused with a sharp intake of breath and giggled again. "Kansas City—it's written all over me, isn't it?"

The other smiled indulgently. "I guess we all come from somewhere else. I've yet to meet a native New Yorker. I'm from Vermont—Rockport." Mentally she added, "Historic American stock. Mother goes back to the Mayflower, and father is still a Pilgrim."

Sally's rosy complexion, with the most delicate blond fuzz on her cheeks, made one think of a ripe peach. She had soft blond hair, bobbed—but not too radically—blue eyes, a small, narrow nose, lips that were never dry, rounded arms and legs, and a trick of ripening at will under the warm stimulus of masculine attention. Coming to New York alone (she had defied her storekeeper father) was the great adventure of her life. She wanted to be gay and with gay people.

"Isn't it too wonderful how neighborly everyone is?"

"Yes, especially in the Village," agreed Agatha. Thinking back upon her home, she added, "You could be born in Rock port, but, if your parents came from somewhere else, you were still regarded as a foreigner."

Agatha, too, had dreamed of New York, but not as a gay lark. She had come full of purpose to make a career as an illustrator and to escape the atmopshere of Rockport, in which she felt herself surely strangling. She was interested in no man. On the contrary, and quite unlike the girls she knew, she did not even enjoy talking about men. That was another thing she wanted to get away from—the endless twaddle and cackle about men—what Robert said at the church social and what William did at the strawberry festival. At home, the time was drawing close when, if she didn't link her life with some man, she would be regarded as an old maid. She had never given serious thought to this indifference, almost a repugnance to men, except to attribute it to her great ambition to succeed as an illustrator. All her energies, all her life must be poured into this mould.

There were no parental blessings to speed her on her way. But fortunately, through her maternal grandmother, a thrifty crone, a small income came to her and she needed no financial reliance upon her father.

"I suppose you want to go on the stage," said Agatha. Naturally no young and pretty girl came to New York to become a stenographer, a waitress, a chambermaid, a Bronx housewife, or a Tenderloin call girl.

"No, I want to be a model. But only for special artists—not for a group." Sally had drawn her ideals from "Trilby" and from the glamorous adventures of Evelyn Nesbit.

"How interesting. I'm studying art. Perhaps you could pose for me."

At a neighboring table, a young man with a strangely matured beard, spoke savagely. "The French have denounced all their classical poetry. I tell you, Da-da-ism is the thing."

Konrad, the picaresque husband, also the cook, dishwasher and waiter, shuffled towards their table and set down two steaming dishes before them. "Roumanian stuffed peppers, fit for a queen," he said sadly, looking from one girl to the other. His face became more melancholy as he brooded. "The Village fills with beautiful virgins. They come from the north, the west, the south—beautiful virgins, tender as stuffed peppers—but I can do nothing."

The girls pronged the food, not without a sense of adventure, for the meat was hidden within a soft green coating, covered with gravy.

"Do you live nearby?"

"On West Fourth," said Sally, wrinkling her nose. Agatha felt herself attracted by the pretty face, by the cute gesture of wrinkling her nose. "A bitsy room—they're certainly stingy with space. But I can't afford any more." She looked up just a little helplessly.

"I have a rather nice apartment—on Macdougal. It's next to a stable, but it's quite roomy." Agatha hesitated for a moment. The fact that such an impulse could even come to her was proof that she had forever shaken off the inhibitions of Rockport. And she was drawn by the peachy face and the white rounded arms. "Perhaps—to cut down expenses—you could move in with me." The boldness of the idea constricted her throat so that the food nearly choked her.

"I'd love to," said Sally quickly, "and you could help me find work as a model." She was quick to lean on anyone sympathetic—in a pinch, on anyone. "And living together—will be loads of fun. You get so lonesome by yourself."

Miss Crabtree spoke with animation and her face took on a glow. "Yes—one is lonely—although I mean to work very hard." Under the sobriety of her resolution she felt a strange elation at this new relationship she had formed. It was part of the new freedom, the great adventure of living the art life in New York.

The savage young man with the beard turned from his dinner companion, a male who ate with mincing movements, and looked boldly over at Sally. She warmed under his glance, but Agatha, quickly wounded, touched her hand.

Konrad shuffled over and set before them a pastry dripping with honey, cut octagonally, its flaky crust glistening.

"What do you call this?" asked Sally, like the little curious child she had just been to the man with the beard.

Konrad regarded her deeply, sadly. He continued to brood. "Such a sweet face, so well tinted and rounded, and such a tender bosom." A deep sigh rent him. "The Village fills with virgins—and I can do nothing."

"Well—what?" insisted Agatha.

"Kibabbe," he nearly sobbed and he shuffled away.

The room reeked of unrealized ambitions. Smoke blew, words tumbled, faces glowed, hands cut the air in determined gestures. The major escapes from life, art, theatre, poetry, fornication, were being avidly discussed. Agatha felt herself a definite figure in this pattern of boldness.

"Do you suppose—you could move in—tonight?"

"Why not?" Sally giggled musically. "Of course—I must insist on paying my share." With vigor, "I do hate my room." The girls gathered their things and walked out, Sally clinging to Agatha's arm.

In an hour, they were installed. It was all so Bohemian, so unconventional. The apartment was next to a stable and consisted of one large room, one small room and a tiny kitchen. The bathroom was shared with a lone lodger on the other side of it and when you went in, you had to remember to fasten both doors from the inside.

The excitement of meeting, of moving, of new friendship, kept both girls awake until midnight. Then Sally, nearly exhausted, moved languorously towards the smaller room. There was no door between the rooms and Agatha watched the younger girl undress, observed all her feminine movements, the stepping out of the dress, the kick-off of the slippers, the unrolling of the stockings, watched all hungrily with an absorption that excited her. Then the light was extinguished and a yawny "good-night" was tossed in her direction.

Sally closed her eyes and stretched luxuriously. So many new and satisfying sensations that she almost felt replete. A new friendship, a new strength to lean against. She was about to sink into sleep when thunder rolled over the house. The stamping of the restless horses in the adjoining stable, the cloppety-cloppety nags that were being led out of stalls down a corduroy runway for night shifts on delivery trucks, loosed itself with a sudden fury. The thunder of their hooves penetrated the thin wall, rocked the house and terrified Sally, who felt the stampede of wild horses was leading right to her bed. She shrieked and cowered under the cover. But the stampede drew nearer and nearer. Wild-eyed, she ran from the bed.

"Agatha—Agatha—what's happening? I'm scared."

The older girl spoke with a strange calm. "Don't worry, my pet—you'll get used to it. It's just the horses leaving for the night. In the beginning I used to be afraid, too. But now I've got so that I listen for it—every night."

"I'm terribly frightened," Sally whimpered.

Agatha took her hand gently and drew her towards the bed. "Lie down with me—for a while."

Sally crept in. Another stampede descended upon her and she flung herself against the older girl. Agatha began to comfort her, smoothing her hair, caressing her cheeks, her shoulders. How smooth her skin, how fragrant. How fresh and virginal, how like a beautiful child as she lay against her, her eyes closed in terror. The delivery horses were led out. The beating of the strong hooves subsided. Silence fell upon the house and Sally fell asleep in Agatha's warm, protecting embrace. But Agatha could not sleep. The thunder of the hooves was in her blood. She was curiously, ecstatically happy, as though an old and bewildering longing had at last been gratified.

When Sally awoke in the morning, breakfast was already upon the table. Agatha bade her a cheery good morning and brushed a hand across her tousled hair. Sally seemed vaguely to remember the touch of the hand but like the terror of the horses it was all part of the night, the night which had receded.

Agatha fed her morsels and watched her eat with pride. And Sally enjoyed all the little attentions.

As the older girl prepared to leave for her art class, Sally giggled musically and said, "Do you mind, Agatha, if I don't pay my share of the rent now? I need some new clothes. And after all, I must look smart if I'm to get a job."

Agatha placed her hand against the younger girl's cheek. "Don't worry about it, pet." There was a quiet, possessive tenderness in her voice. "And be sure to wait for me for dinner. We'll eat—together."

Let us return to Elmer Hicks, a twenty-seven-year-old bachelor, an insurance agent without bad habits, who was suffering from an advanced case of vision. In the evolutionary ascents of Manhattan idols, Paul the Peddler, Phil the Fiddler, George the Garbage-man, vision must be analyzed not as a dream glow, a poetic strain that lights up the life of the man destined to succeed, but as a definite pain in the side like the attack of an enraged appendix. Elmer, the young farmer who had run away from land in the country, now suffered from land hunger in the city.

That was his vision and his malady. And he found it a painful one, for when he closed his eyes he saw the vision he wanted to embrace as a faith, but when he opened them, there was the mocking reality which he hated. The Bronx was growing and it seemed to expand within the confines of his narrow chest. It seemed to puff itself out within his own brain, producing a constant ache, a gnawing, a straining from which he must soon burst.

Again, with a masterful patience and cunning, he was explaining his dream, his vision, to his indifferent father.

"Now look, father. Two German and one Eyetalian steamers came into port yesterday, crowded with three thousand immigrants. You can read that right in the papers. And except for a few Swedes and Polacks—nearly all of them stay in New York. But where are they going to live?"

Farmer Hicks frankly was not concerned. For all he cared, they could cling to the sides of the boats like barnacles.

Elmer resumed with greater fervor. He must persuade his father to open those mean, cunning eyes that stubbornly refused to see this vision.

"They can't all go to the east side—because that's overcrowded already. And even if they do—they've got to push others out. And where are those others going to live? All right, some go to Brooklyn, some to Long Island, a handful to Staten Island—but most of them come to the Bronx. Yes sir, right here. People don't like to cross a body of water to get to work and back to home. There's a fog and there's frost and there's danger—and besides, it costs more. But it's natural for them to move to the Bronx. Only five cents' fare from anywhere—and lots of room."

Elmer closed his eyes. Behind his glasses, they were screwed up in a painful grimace as he flavored the bitter tang of his vision. Hordes of east-siders, partially Americanized, swarming into the Bronx. Better jobs, better standards of living. Big apartment houses going up to shelter them, houses with modern plumbing and bathrooms, and courtyards for sunshine instead of narrow air-shafts. Newlyweds in their first romantic glow leaving the squalor of their youth to start life fresh and beautiful in the Bronx. And all this meant higher rentals. Land would become precious.

If only he could control the land of his father and enhance it with the two adjoining acres he could buy from Devitt. He started! Could buy? Why—he was already pledged to buy it. That very afternoon, in a panic lest someone get there before him, he had withdrawn all of his savings, $500—carefully put together in half-dollars, in quarters, yes, in dimes and nickels, from petty insurance commissions, and he had bought a thirty-day option on the Devitt acreage. He could see the buildings rise on the land, financed by banks, for could there be better security than realty? The corner lots held for stores—and the land growing more and more valuable—every grain of earth a gain of gold. How could his father be so blind?

He resisted a maddening impulse to shake him, to seize him by his scrawny neck and throttle him into this vision. Instead, he licked his dry lips and drove on.

"Yes, father—all those foreigners coming in all the time—Eytalians, Russians, Germans, Irish, Roumanians—all the time—pushing the others into the Bronx." He leaned forward tensely. "Now, father, if you'll lend me the money to buy the Devitt land—I'll give you back a purchase-money mortgage and put up an apartment house. That'll make your lot more valuable. You'll be my partner—and we can start a real estate company—and in a few years—why—before you know it———"

Abel Hicks yawned. His thin upper lip curled to meet his venous beak and his sawed-off whiskers lowered. He bared his hard teeth, stained by tobacco, but all still sound. Then he spoke, reminiscently, maddeningly. "I saw a Rooshian once in Quaker Village—but I've yet to see a Roomanyin."

Slowly, he extended his tobacco pouch and the straw papers for Elmer to roll him a cigarette. He moistened the tip with his purplish tongue, lit it, inhaled and then shook his head like a prophet.

"No, son—I spent fifty years of my life on a farm and the towns around me didn't change much. A workingman likes to make his home near the place he makes his living. There are no factories around here. And it'll be a long time before all those buildings you speak of will be put up in the Bronx."

A note of irritation crept into his voice. "And anyway—I don't want them foreigners around me. I'm getting old—" he paused to allow his son to contradict him— "and what I own I'm keeping. When I die you'll get your share of the land, same as Hilda and the baby. If you want land so bad, work for it. Save your, money—and in a few years——"

"But father, in a few years there won't be any low-priced land around here. It'll all be bought up." There was an hysterical note in his voice. "Prices will be sky high and I won't be able to touch it."

"Well," Abel yawned, "I'm not chasing trouble at my age. What I have, I keep. I'm satisfied."

"Then do it for me." Hope, self-abasement, desperation were blended in this cry.

Abel rubbed his chin meditatively. For a second it seemed that he was weighing the impulse to relent, to be generous.

"Please do it for me. After all, I'm your own flesh and blood."

Abel's hatred sprang into the open.

"Why should I?" he cried. "When I needed you—you threw over the farm, sneaked away like a thief, leaving me alone. You were going to make your fortune in the big city. Well, go ahead and make it."

Elmer fought back the impulse to leap at his father's throat. The old man cowed him with a look, flavored for a moment his triumph and then dismissed the issue between them.

He looked around smugly at the warm, cosy interior, at his young wife setting the table. Then a light flashed into his jujube eyes. Playfully, he motioned Elmer not to move, not to speak. The old clown tiptoed behind his wife and suddenly ran his thick finger down her spine. She shuddered and screamed while Farmer Hicks squealed in laughter, his face growing red, and the tears rolling down his furrowed cheeks. Then she slapped his hand and in a high-pitched possessive voice reproved him while he gathered her, struggling, into his arms.

Elmer stared upon this scene of domestic frivolity and erotic friskiness, and his gorge rose. He hated his stubborn, cruel, senile father who amused himself by tickling this young slattern while his own brain was bursting with the vision of a Hicks empire in the Bronx. Toothing back his rage and frustration, he stamped out of the room. If he didn't acquire land soon, his vision would shatter him. He could no longer imprison it within him.

On his twelfth birthday Perry Murdock was relieved of his Little Lord Fauntleroy suit by stern command of his father and fitted into a dark blue serge suit with the balloon of the knickers falling well below the knee and a double-breasted jacket of a mannish cut. His high-button shoes were replaced by oxfords. But the most drastic change of all was visited upon his hair, which he had worn long and in ringlets, and which was now cruelly trimmed to a boy's length.

Perry was tall and of slight build, with brooding circles under his eyes and a patient, gentle manner of speaking. He rarely raised his voice, not even in play. His skin and hair were smooth and fair, and his hands had that wax-like quality of those not fully alive. He lacked vitality, impulse, but especially he lacked emphasis. He did have a capacity for suffering and for reacting to the suffering of others, but that only added to his general air of unhappiness.

When his proud and determined father, after a grunt of approval, sent him in to be inspected by his mother, she brushed her eyes with a lace kerchief and wept genteelly, "You've become a man so soon, my little Perry."

Prudence Murdock, née Saxton, came of old and genteel Boston stock and had ideals in life to which she stubbornly clung and which she tried to implant in her son. Lately this had grown difficult because Eugene Murdock, the two-fisted aggressive New York contractor, was different from the young road engineer who had courted and won her in Boston. Sometimes she doubted that he was now the same man. In that gently romantic period they had read Dickens together, attended the better plays and concerts and had even been present at a lecture by Oscar Wilde. But since they had moved to New York, where there were bigger opportunities for him, he had sunk himself more and more in his work and had become almost vulgarly rugged and far too democratic. Lately, he had been associating with all sorts of low foreigners, such as Jews and Italians, and even Irish.

This was shocking. In Boston no Irishman had been permitted to cross the Saxton threshold. When she gently remonstrated with Eugene, he explained to her that he had to make these associations on account of business, that in New York your best partners were the pushing, cunning, aggressive foreigners rather than the scions of old families who were your social equals. And thinking of Henderson, who was of very old American stock, he was tempted to add that these foreigners were also more honest.

But Prudence would never be convinced. Her own father had once been a prosperous and respected physician, but had lost his entire practice to a pushing Irishman with a jovial bedside manner and a nervous Jew who was becoming the wonder surgeon of Massachusetts. She consoled herself, however, with the thought that she had done her best to foster her ideals of gentility, of social superiority, of a repugnance to all foreigners in her son. She was brushing Perry's soft hair back from his pale forehead when Eugene came into the room, smoking a cigar. Faintly ill, and with the echo of a whine in her voice, she said:

"Don't you think those clothes make him look too old, Gene?"

"Nonsense, Prudence—the lad's growing up. The sooner he becomes a man, the better I'll like it."

Eugene looked at Perry's gentle blue eyes, at his air of not being personally involved in any mortal transactions, and wondered by what alchemy he could implant in those innocent eyes the suave, coolly larcenous gleam of the private banker, Seymour Henderson; wondered by what magic he could transform that gentle chin into an aggressive, battling jaw held up firmly to the world.

Perry felt sad and alone on his birthday. He hadn't been given a party because most of the boys and girls who attended the Harrington Private School with him were off in the country. Not that he really missed them, but it would have been jolly to laugh and play games with his school chums. But unfortunately, he had come down with the grippe at the beginning of vacation and the doctor had advised his parents to keep him away from the country because he was so sensitive to pollen. And besides, he was easily frightened by thunder and lightning.

They might have taken a house at a fashionable Long Island beach but Prudence had refused because Mr. Murdock had to be in town and she didn't want to leave her husband entirely alone.

She was beginning to worry about what he did on all those endless evenings away from home. She knew that he was drinking too much for a respectable householder and sometimes she sniffed the clinging vapors of a hostile perfume on his clothes. Yes, and long, blond hairs on his coat. Some day, when she felt stronger, she would confront him with that. It was trying, because there hadn't been a scandal in any branch of the Saxton family since a nephew had run off to join a minstrel show. She wondered, too, how he could possibly spend so much time with those Italians and Jews and Irish in those negotiations about a contract to lay a road-bed. Of course it was a big job—he had mentioned some fantastically large sum he would get as his share—but Prudence preferred not to concern herself too deeply with money transactions. She would be glad to help in her own way, and even permit him to invite the proper kind of business associates to his home for dinner. But there her interest stopped.

And so the family remained in Brooklyn, on the promise that when the contract was finished they would all take a jaunt to Europe. The summer had passed pleasantly enough. The house had been fairly cool for the harbor breezes blew in through the windows and there had been trips in their automobile.

But it had been a sad summer for Perry. It came to him on his birthday, in a sudden shock of realization, that he wasn't having any fun. He knew that most of the boys and girls he saw in the street laughed a great deal and enjoyed themselves. But he never did. You can't ride a two-wheeler all day on the sidewalk, or just watch the boats, or listen to the clamor of life on the other side of the harbor.

Occasionally strange kids from distant neighborhoods, rough-mannered, wild-speaking, badly dressed, would invade the Columbia Heights section. They howled and fought and laughed with the abandon of pirates. They seemed to be having great fun and even though they were poor and dirty, he couldn't help envying them. But he never got to talk to them, for, heeding his mother's caution, his nurse took him right upstairs. The idea was to shelter him, protect him from any contact with the lowly, the vulgar, the raw.

Eugene went forward and seized his son's arm. "Some day, we're going to have big, hard muscles." He pressed the biceps, squashing the yielding flesh.

Perry winced and looked up at him, bewildered. "Yes, father," he promised, in an enfeebled voice. The father wanted to surprise his son with a gift, not only the gold watch he had bought him, something personal, something which would brighten up the kid. He slapped his thigh smartly. He was trying to engender an atmosphere of male heartiness.

"I've got it, Perry. Suppose you come with dad and see the road-bed I'm building down on the east side."

The boy's eyes brightened and he looked to his mother. The father spoke up for him. "I'll take Perry along, Prudence. I've got an appointment with Tony." She raised her eyebrows. "We'll go in the motor-car."

The car, a single-cylinder Cadillac runabout, with acetylene head-lamps and ten horsepower, was kept two blocks away in a blacksmith's shop, the owner of which was already planning to lease more space to house the rapidly increasing automobiles in the vicinity. Eugene put on a linen duster and goggles, helped Perry into the seat beside him, and started. Across the Brooklyn Bridge, Murdock teased the big syringe of a rubber horn every time they passed horse-driven trucks. But with the occupants of other cars he would exchange glances of dignity and understanding, for car owners in 1908 were definitely members of the upper crust.

They drove down Park Row and turned into the Bowery. But when they honked up Delancey Street, the street gamins began to run after the car, flinging their caps before the wheels and yelling derisively, "Get a horse—get a horse." Perry was frightened by the recklessness and ferocity of those kids. Some of them even threw missiles at the car, and Murdock, swearing at the grinning devils, grumbled, "Those damned kykes and wops—it's a wonder they don't all get killed in the streets."

The car turned left on Forsyth Street and came to a halt in front of Sullivan's saloon, where Murdock had the appointment with Ferarro, his partner. Murdock removed his goggles and pondered upon his next move. He didn't dare take Perry into a common saloon, for the report of it would infuriate his wife. And then it was too early to set an example in drinking before his son. So he left him in the seat, monarch of the motor-car.

"I won't be long, Perry. If anyone bothers you, just honk the horn."

Perry; alone, sat back and looked around him. The street gave him a definite, electric shock. It was vibrant with the rhythmic movements of the Italian workers, who had paused only to salute the "bigga boss," with the song of the rolling peddlers, with the fierce activity of the kids playing in the torn gutter.

Near the corner was an iron trough, the size of a large bathtub, filled with dirty water. Years before it had been donated by a lover of animals so that horses driving through the sultry streets in the hot summer might pause and refresh themselves. The water was rarely changed and collected on its surface dirt, refuse and scum. Occasionally, a delivery truck would stop near by, the sweating driver would loosen the reins and the heaving nag would lower its long, ungraceful neck, lap up the dirty water, shake the foam from its heavy lips and wearily trot off.

As Perry looked on, awed by the clamor and intensity of the life around him, he saw Mutt gallop up, harnessed like a horse and driven by Joey, who paddled him with a long stick. Mutt clumped up to the edge of the trough, looked around to see that all eyes were upon him, neighed like a horse, dipped his moronic face into the filthy water and drank some of it while the kids howled. Nausea gripped Perry, but he couldn't tear his gaze away.

Peter, standing apart, coolly appraised the lone occupant of the motor-car. He seemed to appreciate the gulf that lay between the delicate youth with the greenish tinge in his cheeks and himself. But Perry saw nothing except the imbecile with his face in the dirty, foamy water. Joey drove his charge away. Just then Murdock swung out of the saloon. Perry, agony in his throat, turned to his father. There were beer suds clinging to his moustache, suds like the foam from the trough. As his father reached for a handkerchief, Perry slumped over in his seat and vomited.

Above everything else Isabella loved to dance. She would follow an organ-grinder for blocks, pausing when he did, to dance without embarrassment before new clusters of admirers on each street. And the Italians who rolled music into those streets knew her and loved her because whenever she danced, crowds gathered and that meant pennies for the organ-grinder. Isabella danced naturally, tirelessly, a dancer with light breathing, tossing her reddish hair, flashing her dark eyes, moving her delicately-muscled legs and her stem-like body to the admiration of onlookers. Dancing alone before groups fascinated her, luring her on and on, until suddenly she would realize that she was blocks away from home, and that if her mother returned from work before she did from play, there would be a scene. Then suddenly, even before a dance was ended, she would break into a run and vanish like Cinderella before the stroke of twelve.

On Forsyth Street she was a familiar dancing figure and although the boys on the block jeered at her exhibitionism, which was the properly masculine thing to do, Joey in his gruff way saw to it that no harm befell her. What alarmed Joey was that of late, whenever he was near her, he had a strong urge to touch her. He felt ashamed of this urge as though it were something unnatural. He wouldn't dream of giving in to it and touch her with tenderness, so that when he discovered her dancing, astray from home, he would wait until she had finished, observing her graceful movements with pride and admiration, and then he would cuff her and curtly order her home.

One day Isabella danced alone in the yard of the house in which they all lived. Joey and Bert were sitting out on the fire-escape, Bert engrossed in a huge book entitled "The Wandering Jew." Joey was wondering if, by using the clothes line as a cable, he could cross into the next yard. Suddenly, he espied Isabella in the yard below. How gracefully she moved, her body swaying like the stem of a flower, the movements of her hands, the way she tossed her hair, the arc she described with her toes! Cat-footedly Joey lowered himself down the ladder of the fire-escape, quietly down three flights, jumping the last one and landing on the balls of his feet like a visitation from above before the startled Isabella. But she recovered quickly and smiled at him.

"You're always jumping," she greeted him.

"So I'm always jumpin'."

"And all the time you're fighting."

"And you're always dancin'," he said gruffly.

"I like it," she answered, and began to cut circles with her left leg. She was thoroughly at ease and took pleasure in his discomfiture.

"Don't you ever do nuttin' else?"

Teasingly, she smiled, danced close to him and put her arm about his shoulder. "Come, Joey, I'll show you how to waltz. You know what my teacher said? Among the rich kids even the boys learn how to dance. Come on now."

She clasped his hand. The touch of her warm fingers shocked Joey, caught him completely off guard. He stood still. Then, cautiously, he looked around. High up, above the tracery of the fire-escapes and the iron ladders, his brother sat reading, far too absorbed to see what was going on below. None of his friends were there to mock him. Joey yielded and put his arm about Isabella's waist. He felt the touch of her arm around him, her small hand in his, the warmth of her tiny breasts brushing his chest, and he stood there paralyzed.

"Don't be so stiff, Joey," she instructed.

Then she began to hum a waltz tune and her low humming tingled in his ear. He tried to move but he was rooted. He stared into her dark eyes and suddenly brought her close to him with a fierce pressure. Both stood hushed and yielding and seemed to grow up in that moment. "Joey," she said softly, "Joey," clinging to him. He felt an ecstasy which was terrifying in its beauty. For the first time in his life, he knew fear.

Suddenly he pushed her from him and ran out of the yard, ran to drive this new, strange and frightening impulse from his blood. For days he avoided Isabella.

4

In Bryant Park an old man sat. The noon heat cooked the town. There was a fire under the streets and a roaring furnace in the sky. The air smelled of heat, scorching the nostrils. The old man stirred, scratching himself. He wore woolen underwear, three pairs of pants, four vests, two jackets and over everything a long overcoat, securely buttoned. His broad face was sunk in hair, a single derby upon his head. A matted beard tingled from his shin and grapevined all over the exposed parts of his body. Only his glistening cheekbones and his marmoset eyes faced the world. The old man munched slowly from a grease-spotted bag. He chewed and scratched himself.

A young tramp, tall and cadaverous, sank down beside him. "You couldn't spare part of the grub, could you, mister?" he whined.

The old man moved his forested neck, and paused in his munching. "I never give anything except advice."

The young tramp licked his parched lips and whined, "All right—I can use that, too." He leaned his hot face forward, exhausted, starved, and asked eagerly, "Tell me, mister—how do you make a dent in this town? I rode in on the rods, I've walked the streets with blisters on my feet, I've slept in parks, I've washed dishes, I've panhandled, I've been pinched—but I'm always sliding down. I can't get my teeth in this town. Tell me—old man—how do you make a dent in this town?"

The old man munched and, from a dark gullet, spoke. "Young feller—I'll give you the secret of this town—and I know it—because I got clothes on my back."

He closed the paper bag and put it carefully in his pocket.

"New York is a snake. Strike the head in Queens and the tail swings in Staten Island. Yes—and remember this—when a milk-can rattles in the Bronx—a corpse turns over in Brooklyn."

The old man scratched himself. The young tramp rose and walked away.

Perry Murdock was down with fever again. He couldn't erase from his mind the vision of the east side kid drinking dirty water from the iron trough. It had begun as a persistent nausea and had penetrated, sinking deeper and deeper into his consciousness, until now, every time he closed his eyes, he saw reined figures dancing towards the trough. There was dirt-foam on the imbecilic lips of Mutt, but when he looked again this picture changed into beer-foam on the moustache of his father. He hoped his father would never touch him again. It was something he could not dispel, and yet something he could not, dared not, talk about. He could only lie back on his bed, hot and tormented.

"He always was a delicate child," his mother explained to the doctor, with a note of pride, as though a delicate condition of health were a special mark of gentility and good breeding.

"Nonsense," the father growled. Prudence was ashamed of the smell of brandy on his breath and tried to check him, but he went on, quite irritated. "The lad was feeling fine yesterday, when he went out with me. I can't make it out. He comes of strong stock and has had every care and attention in the world, and yet he's always ailing." The doctor nodded his head wisely, while Murdock grew more savage. "Now take those sheeny and dago kids." Mrs. Murdock shuddered delicately at such language. "I see them playing all the time in the gutter and in the road-bed. They eat out of garbage cans, get their heads broken every day and never take a bath. Yet they look strong as horses." He bit his lips. "But my Perry———"

"Environmental adaptation," said the doctor sagely, and looked over for approval to Mrs. Murdock. It was becoming fashionable to use long, psychological terms. "But Perry will be all right." He wrote out a prescription. "Here, Mrs. Murdock, this will settle the little man's stomach and quiet his nerves. Have it made up right away. And when he gets over this, it might be a good idea to send him to the seashore—just to sharpen his appetite. There's nothing to worry about. I'll have a look at him in the morning." He smiled brightly and left.

Perry tossed on his damp bed. Dimly he was aware that a nurse was coming towards him with a glass. What he saw more clearly was the iron trough. It grew bigger and dirtier. There were reins around his shoulders and he was being driven towards it—being forced to put his head in it—forced to touch his lips to the dirty, foamy water. The nurse was pressing his head down, forcing him to drink the full glass with the foamy bubbles, just what the doctor had ordered to quiet him. But Perry retched and fainted.

Ambition bedeviled Elmer Hicks.

All through dinner he tried to eat, but the food choked him. Through his glasses he watched his old father eat with noisy relish, mopping up the gravy with spongy chunks of bread, lifting his head back so that his whiskers were almost horizontal and thrusting the food into his mouth like a stoker feeding a furnace. The old man loved food, loved life.

"Something wrong with a young feller that can't eat," the farmer said, winking to his youthful wife. This was the vaudeville opening of which he never tired. He implied that Elmer was in love, and in harmony with the classical tradition, the young swain craved no food.

"Where you hidin' the gal, Elmer?" and he roared with laughter.

Elmer hated his stubborn denseness. Did the old man really think that anything as trivial as a girl could convert him into this single-tracked maniac? Love? There was no love in him. Just a lust for land. "Sheershay la femmie," the farmer wagged and roared again, his wife joining in the laughter. Elmer hated the bond between them, the implied boast of the old man that he was younger, stronger, more masculine than his son.

"No, father—I got something on my mind, and it's far from being a girl." He must try to be civil.

"Whatever it is, I wouldn't let it get in the way of my stomach if I was you." The unctuous, self-satisfied way in which he mouthed "stomach."

"There was a builder over from Brooklyn this morning," said Elmer, "to look at the Devitt piece of land. Offered him $11,000 for the full acre."

"That's mighty good money—but 'tain't worth it."

"It is to the builder. And when he puts up an apartment house the land will be worth three times that much."

"Will he pay cash for it?" the farmer asked shrewdly.

"Nobody pays all cash, father, but the security————"

"That's it," he broke in triumphantly. "Just wildcattin' speculatin' with honest people's land and money. Well, I don't like it." He pounded his table.

"But you have to do things, like that now. It's dealing in futures. Now if I could only get that Devitt land before———"

"Don't count on me, son." That was spoken with such finality that he resumed eating. "When I go, like I said before, you'll get your share of the ground. But—" and a chuckle began to spread across his furrowed face—"if you don't eat more you're like to go before me." He cackled out loud and his young wife dutifully cackled back.

Elmer could not laugh. He knew there was truth in the old man's jest. There was a good chance that he would devour himself alive, and pass on before the old man—not through lack of food, but because of this fiercely thwarted ambition. If a stranger bought that Devitt land and built on it, it would kill him. It wasn't only the five hundred option money—although God knows he had pasted that pile together with enough bitter sweat—it was his life he was in danger of losing. The baby, squawling in the crib upstairs, roused him. Elmer pushed his chair back. "I've got to see a prospect tonight. I'll come back late."

"Come in quiet," the old man said with galling authority. "We'll be asleep—because we're going to bed early."

Elmer started for the door, but his father called him back. "Before you go, son, roll me a cigaret." He indicated the pouch of tobacco and the book of papers on the mantelpiece. It was another form of humiliating him, for Elmer could not smoke the cigarets his deft fingers rolled for the farmer, who had a thumb like a stump. Elmer rolled a cigaret, handed it to his father, replaced the tobacco and papers on the mantel-piece and walked out of the door.

On his long walk over to the Third Avenue "L," Elmer went over the old man's routine. It was maddening how clearly each step was engraved upon his mind. The farmer would light the cigaret, sit down in his rickety rocker and read the paper. He read the Bronx Home News because he got it for nothing, and always turned first to the obituary column. It gave him a grim satisfaction to read of the deaths of other people. Once or twice in the course of the evening, while Hilda was washing the dishes, he would rise, stealthily tiptoe into the kitchen and run his thick thumb down her spine. She would shriek in pretended fright, slap his hand, and then they would both howl like children. When her chores were completed they would go upstairs, arm in arm.

On evenings when he stayed at home, Elmer, from his nervous seat below, could hear them upstairs, laughing and playing like two moronic children. Their uncouth carryings-on, their crude and brazen love-making, infuriated him. He resented it bitterly. He didn't need love in his own life. All he wanted was land, a parcel of ground in the Bronx, wanted it more than life itself.

As he rode downtown on the "L," the resolution to go through with the plan which had kept him awake for many nights became fixed in his mind. He had to do it. Again, he told himself, it wasn't only the five hundred—it was life itself.

He shrank inside himself, small and secretive, and went through movements as one who dwelt within, protected by an outer casing. Mechanically he got off at the Eighty-sixth Street station, walked north for two blocks, turned east, and entered the dimly-lit hall of a four-story tenement. With a lightness he hadn't felt in months he began to climb the stairs. Nimbly in the morning, wearily at night, how many, many stairs in how many stinking tenements he had climbed to get that five hundred. He knew the door, because he had a natural memory for every detail of houses, although curiously enough the name escaped him. It was some long, foreign-sounding name—Pij—Poj—ah, Pajalski. A week before, the mother had taken out a $200 policy on the life of her new-born daughter, Gina. A quarter a week. But even that little quarter had been missing when he called to collect and she had asked him to return in the evening. No more quarters, no more climbing of smelly stairs, no more visiting with greasy foreigners—for soon that elite sign would be hung out, "Elmer Hicks: Real Estate."

He knocked on the door. Voices rose inside as though set free by his knock. The door was opened, first cautiously, then wide enough to let him enter. In a corner sat the man of the house, Jan Pajalski—a brigand with a long moustache, watching him suspiciously. The foreign husbands were always like that, full of hostility and suspicion towards all strangers who brought progress into their lives, but the mothers somehow were friendlier, managed to put something by for their offspring. In a basket set upon two chairs in the center of the room rested the baby. Elmer pretended to smile at the baby—you always had to—it was good business—and the man of the house grunted through his heavy moustaches. The woman silenced him in a deep, throaty voice, a voice whose passion and intensity penetrated for one brief flash the outer casing of Elmer. Then, untying a knot in a kerchief, she loosened a quarter which she handed him. Elmer receipted her card, pinched the cheek of the baby and left. No one would call it smart business to spend ten cents carfare to collect one quarter.

And yet it might prove a life-saver. For instance, if a finger were to be thrust under his nose and a crisp voice were to ask, "Where were you on the night of the 27th?" he could answer truthfully, "I was calling on an insurance client—the Pajalskis of Eighty-eighth Street, Yorkville. One hour to get there, one hour trying to sell them a bigger policy, and one hour to get home."

It was after ten when Elmer returned. The entire neighborhood was silent, dark. The house itself stood serene and dark. Quietly he walked up the narrow footpath which led to the rear of the frame dwelling.

A few blocks away, across vacant lots, he could see the outlines of a steam shovel. It stood inert and huge like a Balinese God with a monstrous jaw. All day long it had scooped up great mouthfuls of dirt for an apartment house foundation, and now it rested. And like a god it gazed upon its handiwork and was content. Reverently Elmer bowed before it. It was his god.

He stood still before the kitchen window. A cool early autumn wind fanned his face. It blew the waving corn—corn rising grotesquely from ground where every inch should support its share of an apartment house. Beyond the peaceful field he could see a few lights from the clusters of two-family houses that were springing up, and far beyond them, the faint glow from the teeming city below. The glow seemed to light up the sky. The city was reaching out; first it flung its spears of light, then it groped with its luminous hand, beckoning with its muted call, and then it would bear down with its bricks and mortar and glass, deafen with its roar until it all became one city, brilliant, clamorous, crowded, alive and terrible. This was the city he wanted to speed into this peaceful acre where the corn now waved in the wind, and where there was silence and darkness.

Jerkily, with the movements of a man suddenly roused from a reverie, Elmer looked around. He saw no one. He deftly pried open the kitchen window. Not the usual way to enter the Hicks domicile, but then Elmer, if anyone asked you, had lost his keys, and the thoughtful son was reluctant to disturb his revered father and his revered father's lovely young bride.

He let himself in across the window sill, moved knowingly through the kitchen and into the parlor.

On tiptoes, he advanced towards the mantelpiece. Like a nervous pianist, he tapped along the stone. Ah, here was the tobacco pouch and the little book of papers. He rolled a cigaret, lit it quietly, cupping the light in his hat, and puffed at it. The taste of tobacco nauseated him and it was only with violent effort that he prevented himself from coughing. He drew fiercely on the cigaret. The fire around the tip was like an army of red ants devouring the cigaret. When it was half gone, he moistened the end again and pasted it to the stone mantelpiece. In a few seconds the glow died, the paper drying to the stone and adhering to it. No matter what happened, they would find a thin fragment of cigaret paper dried to the stone. Tch, tch, tch, careless old farmer, leaving lighted cigaret butts around the house, so that an early autumn breeze could blow some sparks from it to a newspaper left lying on the rocker. And to leave the rickety old rocker with its seat of dried straw right near the kindling wood stairway that led to the bedrooms above.

Kneeling, Elmer lit a match, fed it to the newspaper on the rocker, watched the flames curl around the paper and ignite the straw in the seat, waited until the leaping tongues licked at the dry, cracked wood of the bannister. He had a wild impulse to walk up with the flames, as though he were personally conducting the fire. Again, he roused himself, retreated through the kitchen window, lowered it securely.

Slowly, he walked from it. There was a faintly sardonic wrinkle in his brain which told him there was no hurry. The old man would sleep as one drugged. He always did after an amorous encounter with his up-state slattern.

At the end of the path he looked around. Not a soul had seen him. He turned once for a farewell glance at the home.

As he looked, the windows of the parlor suddenly leaped into orange, a vivid, violent orange glow, as though a last sinking sun had spilled its death light into the room and set the very glass aflame. Elmer closed his eyes and fled.

Two hours later, exhausted after walking steadily, Elmer returned. The bonfire had been seen for miles around and a large crowd had gathered. From a long hose firemen were still playing water on the ruins of the house. A few charred, upward-pointing poles remained and the lonely bricks of the fireplace. It was miraculous how thoroughly, how quickly a fire devoured. Flexing his arms, crushing his heart quiet, he forced his way through.

A fire marshal stopped him. "Where do you think you're going?"

"But this is my house." He flavored the word "my." "I'm Elmer Hicks—something terrible's happened!"

"Oh, you're Mr. Hicks." Bad news, grim news. "The bodies were removed to St. Mary's Hospital. Yes, all three of them. But it's no use. Dead on arrival, I should say—dead before arrival—the baby burned beyond recognition."

"Tch, tch, tch."

"Just an old tinder-box—a death-trap—fire spread so quickly—they were all caught. Must have been fast asleep."

"Tch, tch, tch—but what caused it?"

"That's what we're trying to find out."

Elmer whistled out his breath and tried to quiet his heart. The big city was full of such fires. Every day the Metropolitan papers carried a story which began, "Fire, of *unknown origin,* took its toll of three lives yesterday and burned to ruins the home of Abel 'Farmer' Hicks, at East 164th Street near Sherman Avenue in the Bronx. The dead are. . . . And would you believe it—the old man had his arms around his wife."

"Tch, tch, tch. . . ."

"What do you think might have caused it?"

"Well," he faltered as if gasping for breath. Then, as if suddenly remembering, "father was a little careless with his cigaret butts. Used to leave them lit around the house."

"That might be it. Sparks with a brisk wind."

"Tch, tch, tch—and tonight of all nights I had to be away. Yes. I was calling on a prospect—I'm in the insurance game" (inside cackling, it's real estate now) "yes, calling on a party down in Yorkville—foreigner, you know, Pajalski's the name—devil of a long time explaining a little clause in the policy—a policy on a baby. Tonight of all nights, tch, tch, tch."

Elmer went to a hotel downtown to spend the night. He bolted the door of his room and sat down on the bed to think. The land was all his, free and clear. Moreover, with the insurance money and tidy sum the old man had in the bank, he could easily acquire the Devitt tract. Yes, he would call Devitt in the morning, receive his condolences and tell him to have the deed ready. He would take title after the funeral. Four acres of land. He would raise a mortgage on the entire tract and put up an apartment house. Something with a nice lobby, a fancy entrance and a lot of rooms: Call it Hicks Court in memory of the old man. Ah, but he would hold on to the corners; no matter how many buildings he put up, he would hold on to the corners.

He had sat there so long revelling in this vision that his joints were stiff. He eased himself off the bed. He drew the shades all the way down and put out the lights. He wanted to be utterly, completely alone with his vision. He removed his clothes and lay down on the bed.

Raising his eyes casually to the window shades, he was suddenly petrified by terror. Terror held him in a vise at the neck. The shades were a livid orange. He looked up at the ceiling. The ceiling smote him with its livid orange color. He flung himself around and dug his head into the pillow. But inside his eyes, deep inside and within the tightly shut lids, was a sheet of livid orange like a last, sinking sun spilling its death light into his eyes.

Along with the land and the insurance money, this was part of his inheritance. But unlike the others, he could never dispose of this. He would have to live his days, yes, and his nights too, with this livid, orange flame.

All along the waterfront, the boats come in and disgorge the immigrants. They're seasick green and the women wear red bandana handkerchiefs decorated with a picture of the vessel that brought them. A souvenir of the ocean voyage from the steamship company. They're eager to spring at the town, taut as coils in a clock—but what patience has been packed into those bodies. The repressed hopes that have been kept alive, the dreams tended like fires in the rain. The years of waiting and toiling to save up the passage money, or the sacrifices of those in America who sent it. The first terror of uprooting, the agony of parting, the long and bitter journey. The smuggling across borders, the herding in third class trains, officials with badge and sabre, cattle-steerage on boats, bad food, mal de mer, examinations, probings while their hearts stopped beating, officials with a badge and pencil, Uncle Sam's guests at Ellis Island and the ultimate bewildering clamor of the Battery. Too many heroes—too little confetti. But the town just blots up the greenhorns.

And every day the trains push off the huskies from the farms. The men compounded of honest ham, honest bacon, honest eggs, honest manure. Shy, big-wristed huskies who know the Abe Lincoln legend and the John D. Rockefeller fairy tale, fighters from the backwoods who have come in to lick the town. They must begin at lesson one—how to breathe in the big city. It takes months to learn how to breathe in New York. There's no air in the town—only the bouquet of the boroughs. It takes months to pick out the particular smell upon which you can nourish and to get the knack of breathing through one nostril. And the apple-cheeked wenches from upstate, ample-bottomed maids for house-work (a pinch for the master thrown in) for hotels and factories and crib-houses, adventure-loving lassies who've heard about city slickers and want to know more. Greenhorns and natives, across the ocean, across the bridge, they pour into New York, chinking material.

Every day the town grows denser. The orders come flying through the smoke. Hey there—we need five thousand Eyetalians to build a new subway. The big scoop digs into the steerage hold of a vessel, into the vermy catacombs behind the Bowery and brings them up, squirming on a steel platter. Swarthy little gnomes, miracle workers who live underground. All you give them is a back-breaking job, a hole in the wall, and a street fiesta every year. Saint Parasite's Day.

Hey there—send up an order of Russian Jews for the garment sweat-shops. Presto, they're on the streets. Hollow-chested soldiers on a long, long trail. From the garbage-ridden ghettoes, from the slimy, slinking streets, Mangin, Cannon, Scammel, Ridge and Pike, across the Williams-burg Bridge to Seigel, Moore and Varet Streets, into Brownsville and East New York they come; the long, long, file—fathers, mothers, brothers and sisters, on to the machines.

And the Irish for bullet stoppers and brick-handling, and the Poles for janitors and mills, and the Negroes for porters and filth-cleaning, and the Chinese for laundries—every color, creed and nationality right on tap. Anyone for anything, and for every job a dozen takers. Densing the town, thickening the mulligan, the black belt grows, the yellow belt grows, Little Italy breaks out in several rashes, the Jews "Mogen David" a neighborhood overnight, Armenians stake out a couple of blocks. The Scandinavians hedge in a piece of Brooklyn. The Irish battle for the waterfronts and the gas-house district. The Germans solidify Yorkville, each belt grows and the town fills to bursting. New York becomes niggardly of space. An inspector with a lamp walks along a street and spies a blade of grass. He is shocked. A blade of grass—a pore in the earth through which fresh air may pass—tch, tch, tch—we'll have to report that.

So many feet trample on the town, it blisters. So many nationalities go into its gullet, it heaves, it suffers. What a diet. Who can digest all those peoples? The town bloats, the town heaves, the town retches. Buildings are wrecked so that others can be built in their place, so that they can be torn down to make room for bigger structures. New streets are cut and worn smooth in a day. Lime, cement and human bones, buttons, thread and coughed-up blood, rails, gravel and mashed wrists, cavities, tunnels, highways, bridges, singing wreckage, rising higher than the needle-point of the tallest skyscraper, and above it all an upraised arm shaking its clenched fist at the sky. What a town!

At the end of January, graduation exercises were held in P. S. 20. It was a festive day not only for the school and pupils, but for the entire neighborhood. For weeks the parents had been economizing on food so that their children might wear new shoes and new clothes (true, these were carefully put away for the Easter and Passover holidays) to the last day in school. The candy and stationery stores did a thriving business in confections and in albums for autographs, even the poorest graduates allowing themselves the sentimental luxury of leather bindings and fancy cover designs.

It was a great day for all except the teachers, who would soon have to drone the same subjects all over again to another eager class which in turn would pass from their lives leaving them to their endless monotonous posture of marking time.

Within the school there was the excited chatter of an awakened forest. And then a gong clanged, its authoritative vibrations falling like a blanket over the noises it sought to still, its music ending with the silence it had induced. The pupils were hushed. The doors which divided the large assembly hall into class rooms were rolled back and the eight squares melted into one spacious auditorium. The parents had already been herded into one section.

Picked students from the lower grades, who were to participate in the singing and dramatic exercises, marched to the heavy roll of "Die Wacht

Am Rhine." And then, in a well rehearsed entrance, the graduates swung in. For them was played on a thunderous organ, Shubert's "Marche Militaire." Here was the marching youth of New York, glistening graduates with their shoes shined, their faces scrubbed, their hair slicked, their white blouses and blue coats. The exercises began with a reading from the Bible by the principal.

Fathers and mothers, looming big and broad as comedians from their schoolboys' seats, eyes beaming in bewildered yet entranced faces, sat inert, silenced and awed by a language they did not understand, revering the teachers, the principal, the great picture of George Washington framed in the American flag, but above all choking with pride for their offspring, cognizant that a definite goal had been reached in a bitter, foreign land. In the language of their children, first base had been touched.

Mr. and Mrs. Glass were there, early arrivals. They sat in the front row. Small, gentle Isidore was at once exhilarated and saddened by this spectacle. He was sad because only one of his sons was being graduated. When he had requested permission to take half a day off (to be deducted from his wages) the boss had gruffly asked for the reason and Isidore explained that his son was getting a diploma from public school.

"He must be a big feller," the boss commented, puffing importantly at his cigar.

The father hung his head. "It ain't the big one—he don't graduate. You know how some boys are—he don't like school." Then his face brightened. "It's my younger son, Bert—only eleven and a half—and already he graduates. He makes a speech, too."

Although Isidore and his wife would have loved nothing better than to have both sons graduate (we'll work our fingers to the bone and send you through college) the bitter truth was that Joey would never receive a diploma from P. S. 20. In fact, he was not even permitted to enter the school to witness from afar the glory that would never be his. In the eyes of his teachers he had disgraced himself—although for all time he would remain a legend among the pupils at the expense of a diploma.

It had happened one tantalizing week before the end of the term. Otto Goebbels, his teacher, who believed and practiced corporal punishment as the only means of securing respectful attention in class, used to discipline unruly boys by commanding them to come to the front of the class and to extend their hands, palms up. He would then take a firm, yard-long ruler from his desk, a wand weightened by a steel band through its center, roll his owlish eyes, sigh hypocritically, and strike. From long practice and shrewdness, he knew that the boys withdrew their hands as the ruler descended. Hence, he struck at a target in the region of the wrist, and always landed on the palm. He enjoyed this little exhibition of sadistic marksmanship. It bolstered him up, compensated him for having to knuckle under to the principal, and so he created frequent opportunities to practice it, when he might readily have overlooked minor infractions.

On this occasion, he had summoned Joey to the front for making objectionable noises with his lips. Joey, familiar with the ritual, extended his palm; but, feeling grown up with graduation so near (he had been pumped across the passing marks by Bert) and to show his contempt for this child's punishment (he who had taken so many rocks on the head and fists in the face), he did not withdraw his hand when the ruler fell. Thus it landed on the part of his forearm covered by his coat sleeve, causing no pain, bringing forth a derisive laugh from the class, and also the blush of deep embarrassment to the meaty cheek of Herr Goebbels. In the frothing rage that followed, Goebbels struck again, this time with the knife-like edge of the ruler.

It hit its mark, but it shot beyond the limit of Joey's tolerance. He clenched that same right hand into a fist like a hammer-head and socked. It was a beautiful swing which caught the amazed teacher flush on the chin, rocking him off one fat leg and flinging him against his desk for support. And because Joey had been faithfully practicing the one-two punch, he crossed with a quick left which demoralized the Teutonic beagle of the schoolmaster. There was a gasp of astonishment from the pupils, a fainting shriek from the teacher, and Joey fled. He realized he had struck an institution.

And thus Joey completed his academic education. He knew how to read, write and the lesser complexities of simple arithmetic, and was also dimly familiar with certain inaccuracies concerning the history of his country and the length of rivers in Brazil. But he could run a mile in five minutes, shoot a goal from three-quarters of the field in a basketball game, and lead a fight against any odds. He had neither cunning nor wit, neither gifts of grace nor language, no special skill with fingers, no craftsmanship, not even a simple pattern for his life. But he had learned one fundamental truth: that the only way to discourage the strong from devouring the weak is to bite first. But he had learned that lesson in the gutter, and not in school.

Bert, however, more than atoned for Joey's scholastic backwardness and disgrace. He was the youngest graduate in his class and also its valedictorian. For more than a week now, with the help of an English teacher, Bert had been composing his farewell address, at the same time devouring chapters of Balzac's "Cousin Bette." And now he sat, his heart pounding, awaiting the call when he would have to deliver the long speech, punctuating with the graceful gestures the elocution teacher had contributed.

Children with young, fresh voices sang "Santa Lucia," and the seniors enacted the funeral scene from "Julius Caesar," and when Mark Antony wept—

> *"Bear with me.*
> *My heart is in the coffin there with Caesar*
> *And I must pause till it come back to me."*

—hearts were broken.

At last Bert was called upon to deliver the valedictory address. A small, thin, pallid figure, in a young, quavering voice began, "Honorable principal and teachers, beloved parents and fellow graduates." He paused for a moment and looked deep into the array of faces before him.

In the street, around the corner, Joey was sullenly practicing to span the gutter in three leaps. Bert soared to oratical heights, paid homage to learning, to his alma mater, to his parents, and saluted the future with grave confidence. Some of the fathers and mothers prematurely aged, sat huddled and listened stony-faced.

But Isidore Glass wept. The tears beaded his eyes, and through a blurred and smarting vision he watched his son, his own flesh and blood, gesturing with the grace of a trained orator, rolling off sonorous phrases with marvellous ease. That boy would become somebody. He gripped the furrowed hand of his wife. She too was weeping. One thought joined them. Bert must have the chance the parents had been denied. Anyone who could speak so fluently, with such magnetism, would be a great lawyer, possibly a judge. Well, mother and father were prepared. (We'll work our fingers to the bone and put you through college.) Then Bert was rewarded with a medal, diplomas were distributed, parents dried their eyes and the ceremonials were concluded with the singing of the "Star Spangled Banner."

Mrs. Glass went back to the kitchen, and Mr. Glass returned to the gas mantle factory, but with a lighter step. He had conquered a little.

Bert exchanged autographs with his fellow graduates and several of his teachers signed their names in his book over fragments of homely advice which they themselves had studiously avoided. And so, loaded with wisdom and sentiment, Bert bade farewell to his public school.

In front of the house he met Joey, still sullenly trying to span the gutter in three leaps. Bert had a quick impulse to hide his diploma as though merely to carry it were to flaunt it.

One, two—the powerful legs spread far, the taut body sprang as a coil, and a—three. "You did it in three, Joey," cried Bert.

Joey crossed, ginning sheepishly. He touched the ribbon around the diploma and his face sobered. "You know the boys are still talking about the way you socked Goebby."

Joey loosened the ribbon and opened the sheepskin, examining the florid script and the gold seal as if it were a foreign document. "What the hell," he grumbled. "You always was the smart one. I'll git my workin' papers—and git a job. And twict a month later on I can fight at the Forton Athaletic Club."

The brothers regarded each other a little awkwardly. There were many unspoken thoughts between them—but there was also affection and a respect for each other's talents. Awkwardly Bert put his arm around Joey's shoulder. He wanted to press him warmly to assure him, to share his triumph with him—but he was afraid it would be silly. Together they went upstairs.

A winter sadness fell on Forsyth Street, fell on the town. Howling winds gathered along the Hudson, along the East River and raced madly for the Battery. And coursing downward they flung chill forebodings of the cold days and the cold nights to come in all the boroughs. The rich of the city fled to the French and Italian Rivieras and to Florida.

In the poor, crowded sections the great winter hibernations began. Humans crawled into cells like insects and a spot near the kitchen stove was a place in the sun. Street cleaners, peddlers, janitors, newsdealers, the all-day workers in the wind, were hooded and swathed in their odd winter raiment, old sweaters, foreign shawls, ear muffs, and the purplish blue of the New York north settled on their faces. There came a lull in the life of Forsyth Street.

Bert, now a student in the De Witt Clinton High School, became one of the vast army of subway riders. Every morning he trudged, hugging books and lunch bag, up Rivington Street across the Bowery he still dreaded, to the Spring Street station. Ten stops north and he was at Columbus Circle, from which Googi had once gone off to view life among the upper world, and then westward on 59th Street, through blocks inhabited densely by Negroes, to the impoverished Death Avenue Irish and the school edifice itself, a vast educational mill which ground learning into four thousand pupils, youths that poured into it every morning and streamed out again in the afternoon. And in all the city high schools, the same thick flow was repeated. White, black and yellow, all creeds, races and religions, all stations in life, some so poor that they walked miles to save the nickel subway fare, others delivered by chauffeurs in cars, all rubbing together in the monstrous educational treadmill, and in each the special spark of Cosmopolis—ambition.

Joey found a job in a printing plant on Lafayette Street as a delivery boy. Hours, seven-thirty to six; wages, five dollars a week and a chance for a sturdy pair of legs to save a bit on carfares. Almost overnight he had become a man, wearing long pants, doing a man's work, earning weekly wages.

And though his clamp of a mouth bit back any complaints, his work was very hard. The bundles he delivered were made up of closely packed paper or lead type. When there were a great many to take out, he would pile them on a delivery cart, take it down with the freight elevator and trundle the car through the city traffic. There were always arguments and bickerings with elevator men and receiving clerks, but Joey worked faithfully. And no matter what time he returned from his route, he had to sweep out the shop, a huge loft.

In the beginning he used to come home so exhausted that he could barely go through his meal. His heavy lids would droop, his shoulders sag, and his face become ashen from the poison of fatigue. When his mother uttered a word of tenderness or sympathy, he snarled. He wanted no pity, no commiseration. His fingers were cut and bruised and his hands so blistered that he could hardly hold a knife and fork. His little father looked at him and felt sad. He, too, was familiar with hard work and it was this life he had sought to avoid for his son. But his own child had chosen it.

Yet, after a few week's, Joey's powerful body and his great spirit hurdled the work. He learned to glory in it because it helped make him stronger, because it sent him home hungry and pleasantly tired. His back, shoulders and arms were bolstered by new muscles. In the evening, when he returned from work, he would wash the grime carefully from his hands and face, change into better clothes, and demand great portions of soup and meat and bread. He was a good boy now, no longer a problem, a comfort to his father and mother. Regularly he turned his wages over to them, receiving a small allowance for himself. And from this and what he saved in carfares on errands, he was able to give Bert an occasional quarter.

A change came over Joey, He was no longer sullen. He was an adult, sharing the responsibilities of the family with his parents, and also their pride in the younger son Bert, who was beginning to make scholarship records at high school. The atmosphere at home became more serene. Panic left it. It was a pleasant phase in their family life, a change in gear from second to high, the group rolling along, each member in his appointed path. Bert, an honor student, on his way to fame as a lawyer; Joey on his way to a big business career, and the parents breathing relief as though the crest of the hill towards which they were pulling the burden were already in view.

There were changes on the street, too. The tsong, tsong, tsong of the musical hammers had been replaced by the nervous clangor of the new electric cars. The swarthy gnomes had been scooped off the streets and lowered into subterranean pits where they labored at new subway excavations. The belly of the gutter had been sewed back with molten tar and asphalt. The gang which had reached the peak of its achievement in the memorable election fire was broken up. The Metzger twins had been taken to McKeesport ("Pennsylvania State," they quoted), where their father was going to work in his brother's general store, a dry goods emporium which catered to miners and tin-mill workers. Danny, the Irish kid, moved to Harlem, and Mutt, who had defied the teachers of 6B for three terms to teach him anything, was given his working papers and had now become a messenger boy for the A.D.T., earning the descriptive name of "all day tramp." He was as proud of his uniform as he had been of his glass eye.

And silently, in shadowy movements, on a blue winter morning, Peter Mendes and his family moved out of the neighborhood. The season for the street acrobats had long ceased and with it had vanished his father's meagre income from the sale of Turkish lemonade. It was too cold even in the sun for crowds to gather around a troupe of tumblers and no one wanted to drink icy lemonade when his lips were already blue from the winter chill.

During one winter, his father had attempted to coax a living by the sale of "halvah," "rahat," and cakes made of caraway seeds, but this required endless tramping in the cold, with a peddler's tray, and because of his weak back he could not endure the exposure and strain. And even when he did remain out all day, the profits on the penny sales were so small that with all of their thrift and self-denial they could not accumulate the rent, let alone money for food.

The only thing to do was to move and Peter made the decision for the family. He, too, had leaped suddenly to manhood. Although he had received his diploma along with Bert, he had taken no part in the exercises. They were too childlike for one who felt himself older than his teachers. He saw clearly, without pity and only with self-appraisal, the task before him. He would have to become the provider. He would transfer himself to a preparatory high school at night and find a job at once.

In the meantime, with the help of a distant relative, he had found an apartment in a neighborhood that was even cheaper and poorer than the one they occupied. It was located far downtown, on the dismal side of New Bowery.

The name of the street was Roosevelt, so called in honor of the most famous American family, but certainly no credit to it.

Some Spanish Jews still lived there, in a cold, steel-blue poverty which was their own concern. For neighbors they had the most impoverished layer of Italians, Greeks, some Irish and a sprinkling of Chinese who had ventured out of Chinatown. The rent was seven dollars a month for two rooms, a zinc sink in the kitchen, loose, creaking floors weakened by mouse holes, and toilet in the yard.

The few family possessions had been piled upon a junk cart hitched to an old nag that seemed depressed by the prospect of a journey into deeper and bleaker slums. Father and the parchment-like grandfather were helped into the cart. As Peter tossed the last bundle and was about to climb up beside the driver, Joey passed on his way to work. He stopped in surprise.

"Hey Pete, you movin'?"

"Yes—to Roosevelt Street."

"Cheez—Roosevelt Street. I never hoid of it." It seemed far away, remote as in another city, and it was sad because it would carry Peter out of his life. Next to Bert, he liked him best of any boy on the block and many's the sock he had delivered in his behalf. Peter also felt the wrench, but he pretended to be absorbed in tightening the bundles.

"Well, I hope I see you sometimes."

"Sure—I'll come down to the Settlement House."

Joey walked on. Then abruptly, he retraced his steps. Timidly, he held out his rough, bruised hand. "Just for luck, Pete." The boys regarded each other and their glances turned aside, both embarrassed by this show of emotion. Peter shook his hand silently. Then he climbed up beside the driver.

There was a flick of the rein, the driver spat in the gutter and the nag moved. Upon the chill blue air there fell the tinkle of bells as the junk cart moved.

5

Standing on the roof of the Stock Exchange on Broad near Wall
Street, Mike Donlin, baseball idol of America, could have batted a baseball
in a straight line from the richest point in the world, the absolute center
of wealth, to the poorest and most hideous plague spot in the world,
Roosevelt and Cherry Streets.

Here, in the back garden of Wall Street—just a few blocks southwest
of the Exchange where brokers, bankers, speculators, plunderers all,
grovelled gracefully for millions—there bloomed a scabrous, pus-running
poverty. Time, between the scarlet sore and the apple of the eye there lay
a thick eyebrow of indifference.

Here was a city vineyard famous for its cultivation of the tubercle
bacillus, famous as sections of France are known the world over for their
special wines and cheeses, and already known to connoisseurs of slums
and plague spots as the "lungers' blocks." Here dwelt Greek bootblacks,
Jewish sweat-shop workers, Spanish house-to-house peddlers, and Italian
diggers in a poverty at once so hideous and fantastic that it became one
of the sights to show out-of-towners on the rubber-neck tours.

Here was a vicinity whose anthem was the consumptive's cough, and
whose colors were the same red, white and blue that waved above the
U. S. Treasury Building—white for spittle, red for flecks of bloody lung
tissue, and blue for the convulsed face that ejected it.

And here, in a two-room flat, Peter entered upon the second segment of
the formative period of his youth. Three men, three generations of slender,
aristocratic Sephardic Jews, hanging up a God Bless Our Home sign over
a rent in the wall, in two bleak caves. Peter, eager and determined to wrest
success from the world; his father, with a spine stiffening in paralysis; and
a gaunt, parchment-like grandfather who dwelt silently as if in a trance,

80

secure in his pact with the God of his people. The grandfather moved his lips in prayer and placed his wafer-like hand on the head of Peter.

"Remember, my child, there is no truth, save in His book—and no way of living save in His light."

Peter stood still and inwardly crushed the dream of the two old believers. He would never devote his life to God. New York was no place for a rabbi—a pastor to a small, select Sephardic flock. He would have a way with men—but he would exercise it not for their own souls, but for his own betterment. The streets had drummed that lesson into his very fibre and this new descent into poverty, this fresh degradation, did not increase his belief in the wisdom and mercy of God.

It did not take long to scatter their belongings around the two-room flat. Then Peter, man of the house, left to look for a job.

He began by exploring the neighborhood, which in itself was an adventure. He followed Roosevelt Street down to where it dirt-trickled into the waterfront as South Street swept across it like a broad, strong current, washing from it the feeble burden of the last few eyesore hovels, paneless and crumbling, targets for the gales from the East River. As he came into the opening, an avalanche of violent smells assailed him. This medley of stinks rose from a mountain of garbage plied on a scow, moored to the refuse dump of the Department of Sanitation.

Quite naturally, in the eyes of the city fathers, the foot of Roosevelt Street was a better place to dump garbage than, say, the site of the Yacht Club at 96th Street and Riverside Drive. Since there were no bathtubs in the houses, nor bathing facilities in the neighborhood, since in some of the two- and three-room flats as many as eight and ten people lived together in unwashed and diseased embraces, since the toilets were in the yard and the garbage cans stood on the sidewalks in long rows like sentinels, the addition of a little more refuse and malodor could not seriously change the character of the neighborhood. Through the heavy vapors from the dumps spiralled the persistent, unconquerable smell of fish, for the Fulton Fish Markets were near by.

In the years to come these odors were to be the constant companions of Peter. In wintertime they would wait for him out in the street, and as soon as he emerged they would seize him by a nostril on either side and escort him against his will until he climbed the more fragrant heights of the city when, with a violent effort, he shook them off. In the summertime they would forcibly enter through the open window of his home, through the door and keyhole, and become the unseen but certainly not the absent visitors at his side.

Peter walked along the teeming, amazing south waterfront of New York, passed the freighters of the United Fruit Lines that went south to Cuba, the old Bay State boats that went north to Boston and other New England ports, saw the saloons with the two-story hotels for seamen in with many months' pay, passed the husky, noisy dealers in wholesale foodstuffs, and then came to a pier about which were gathered a group of well-dressed people.

Their attire was as different from the garb of the habitués of the neighborhood as the huge passenger liner at which they looked was different from the freighters Peter had seen. On deck, many of the passengers bound for Europe were waving and calling out to those below.

A great hunger seized Peter. These were the fabulous people who sailed across the seas, not in stokeholds or in steerage but on the top decks.

He glanced up and saw a face he recognized. Once he had seen that face in an automobile and a gulf of wealth and society lay between them. Now, he saw it above him and that same gulf divided them. On the top deck, bundled in a warm hat and heavy overcoat and flanked by his mother and nurse, stood Perry. But the face, Peter thought, was exactly the same. Whether in the automobile or on the top deck, in summer or in winter, it was peaked, unearthly and tinged with a greenish nausea. Peter stared at it fascinated. The band was playing, but his face was green.

Eugene Murdock, one of the first down the gangplank, brushed rudely past Peter. He hated sentimentality and it embarrassed him to prolong the farewell until the last warning signal routed all of the cloying friends and relatives of the passengers. He swung once around and waved to his little son, saw the hand flutter towards him, turned his back on it and continued down South Street.

As he neared the Battery, the icy waterfront wind whipped his coat about his legs, stung his cheeks, froze the breath on his moustache and made him walk as if the devil were pursuing him. Well, there was one comforting thought; his family was off. The doctor, that genteel, long-worded practitioner of the bedside manner, had diagnosed the persistent nausea of Perry as an "inner war with his incompatible environment" and had prescribed a winter in the south of France. Eugene had kissed his

wife—how frigid and dutiful her caress had been—and in an overpowering impulse had crushed Perry to his breast as if to instil in him a final
charge of masculinity.

"Perry," he said thickly, "I want you to get strong—and become a
real man."

And then observing the greenish pallor of his cheeks, the fright in his
eyes, and a little ashamed of his own show of emotion, Eugene stepped
back and added more gruffly, "And for Christ's sake don't get seasick."

The mother quickly snatched the boy to her side and looked reprov-
ingly at her husband. Such language—and at such a time. This parting,
however, was no occasion for a scene.

So Eugene took his leave, tormented by his love for Perry and the
fierce hope that the boy would return the man he wanted him to be. Just
a final pat on the frail back—and Eugene turned away to blow his nose.
Walking along now, he still felt the wrench. What irony—with his career
flowering beyond his wildest dreams, with every chance for him to become
a millionaire—to have a milk-sop for a son. Well, perhaps the European
influence would strengthen the lad. There was a tradition about money
in Europe and a great respect for it.

In the meantime he was free to concentrate upon his new deal, an
impending contract to build an extension of the west-side subway. This
was getting into the real money. True, as his operations expanded there
were more politicians to bribe, more silent partners to cut in; but it
meant no diminution in his profits, since the city and its people bore the
ultimate cost.

At South Ferry he took the local to Astor Place and walked west to the
Hotel Brevoort on Fifth Avenue. He had an appointment with his partner,
Ferraro, and two representatives of the interests they would have to cut in.

When Murdock arrived the three men were already sitting around a
table. He made his apologies for being late and Dominick made the intro-
ductions. Meet Mr. Donovan, Michael Donovan, the west side alderman
and saloon-keeper (step in for a drink when you're over my way) and
Mr. Finkel, Max Finkel, the labor man. Donovan held the portfolio for
Tammany and Finkel was the dummy for a Commissioner of Accounts
who swayed considerable power in the awarding of contracts. Murdock
shook hands with the portly, theatrically dressed alderman with the dark

hair parted in the middle and curled a little over one side. Then he clasped the soft hand of Finkel, a short, bald, bland-faced Jew with a pronounced Russian accent which he made no effort to overcome. It was remarkable, thought Murdock, knowing who Finkel's boss was, how the Irish in power were getting to trust Jews, and how the Jews, when they attained power, delegated their confidential work to the Irish. The Irish seemed to be able to arouse greater loyalty from the Jews than from their own kind. And both, whatever their religious differences were, found harmony in this mutual embrace of the city's plunder.

Murdock, ordering a double Scotch, invited them all to have a drink. Only Donovan accepted, Dominick taking a cigar, and Finkel a glass of tea. When Murdock urged him to take something stronger, Finkel shook his round head, laughed with a Puck-like billowing of his cheeks, and said:

"Vone drink and I'm rollink on the floor like a shikker."

Then the smile quickly vanished from his face and he said, "Vell, gentlemen,"—and from the look he exchanged with Donovan, Eugene could see that those two had already agreed on what they wanted and Finkel was the spokesman. "Vell, to come to the point, ve are quite sure about getting the contract for you—it's only a qvestion of how to share up the profits." He licked his pursed Cupid's bow of a mouth. "Shall ve say—four equal parts? Organize a holding company to control this contract—and each of us holds twenty-five per cent stock."

Murdock, a little shocked at the brazen thievery of their demands, looked over at Dominick who with a glance warned him not to object. "If we do-a dat," rolled Dominick, "then we forced to raise him up da bid."

"That's right," Murdock added quickly, grateful for Dominick's inspiration, "we couldn't split four equal ways on the old figures and make any profits for ourselves."

Donovan consulted Finkel with a glance. "Sure—raise the bid—but keep it within reason."

Murdock smiled relief.

"There's only one more condition," added Donovan. He extracted a card from his actor's vest. "You'll have to buy your materials from this concern."

Murdock took the card from his pudgy hand, with the large square-cut diamond on the middle finger. "Acme Supplies." He knew all about that.

A company that dealt in building materials and was owned by the brother of a Tammany Sachem. Well, that too would have to go into the bid.

"Okay," said Murdock. "I guess we can arrange that." Now all the men leaned back in their chairs and glowed.

"Well, gentlemen," said Murdock expansively, "I would say this calls for a little celebration."

And quite suddenly, with the new contract so easily arranged, he felt lonely, twinged again by the parting from his son (this moment he was speeding away from him). He scanned the faces of these men eagerly for a friendly emanation, a human touch. He was willing to dispel his loneliness with these strangers, even if they meant nothing more to him than fellow marauders. "How about dinner at Mouquin's—then take in this new Follies show—they tell me this young Zieg-feld picks them like a genius—and finish up with supper at Reisenweber's."

Again Finkel shook his bland, bald head. "Every Friday night ve go to East New York and eat by my mother. Such knoedlech and chulint—" he rubbed his expansive girth—"a vonderful belly-ache—but I have to eat it."

Murdock turned to his partner. "How about you, Dominick?" The Italian laughed heartily. "No—all my bambini, they fighta like hell if I'm no home. And tonight my woman is make chicken cacciatora—Madonna mia—and Chianti that I make, and my Rosa sing—" he slapped Murdock heartily on the back—"you coma with me."

Murdock tried to smile and shook his head.

Donovan muttered a quick, "Count me out, too. I got to be on hand tonight to do favors for my voters."

Loneliness again seized Murdock. It was emphasized by the family claims of these men, their social obligations. He had never looked forward with great joy to going home. One side of his mouth lifted in a sardonic smile, as he contemplated what dining at home would mean. Well, here he was a successful contractor, lonely as hell, without his son and without a single crony in the town. But of course there still was Polly.

The men regarded one another in a final appraisal before taking leave. An Italian, an Irishman, a Russian-Jewish immigrant and a New Englander—three foreigners and one Yankee—New Yorkers all.

They scraped their chairs back and shook hands. On his way out, Murdock stepped into a telephone booth.

The boat moved away to music, and when the fabulous passengers were no longer visible, and the music was faint, Peter, heavy-hearted, turned away. He had been standing so long he was nearly frozen. He began to run northward, fell into a maze of streets which angled into each other like carpenters' joints and suddenly came upon a scene which astounded him with its clamor and activity.

On Broad Street, in the wide gutter near the Stock Exchange, more than one hundred bedevilled men, clad in woolen stockinged hats, sheepskin coats and galoshes, were fingering madly, gesticulating with digits and yells, to as many confrères who leaned dangerously out of open windows in office buildings above the street, and who in turn shouted and twisted their fingers to them. He had never witnessed such frenzy in his life. Was there an earthquake imminent? Were these men warning each other about a great fire, a calamity which would wipe out thousands of lives?

What priceless thing was at stake to call forth this apoplectic display? Why, here was a man who leaped in the air as if bitten by a bloodthirsty hound, he plucked his hat off and waved it like a mad flag, he shouted hoarsely until the cords nearly burst on his neck. For what? Another sprang like a Jack-in-the-box and whooped like an Indian on the war-path. And the general clamor grew more and more deafening. Peter stood there, thrilled and awed by this spectacle.

He had witnessed street fights where heads were broken in enraged combat and blood gushed, he had heard the blood-chilling shriek of fire-engines on their way to election fires, he had heard the screams of mothers rescuing their babies as they clawed their way out of burning tenements. But he had never seen or heard anything as violent, as melodramatic as this.

When Peter dared to turn his head, he noticed several other spectators, all of them grown up. Timidly, he edged up to a rotund, kindly-faced man, and in a hushed voice asked:

"What's the matter, mister?"

The man laughed, a curiously clear and melodic laugh in that medley of harsh cries. "Why, nothing's the matter, son."

Peter gestured beseechingly with one upturned hand. "But—what are they doing?" He waited breathlessly for his answer.

"They're making money." And the little, round man laughed again.

Peter was crushed. They were making sport of him. He knew how money was made. You tumbled in the streets until you broke your spine. Or you sold Turkish lemonade for two cents a glass. Or you owned a grocery store, or drug store, and you sold articles for more than what they cost you and you made a little profit. To be sure there were fabulous millionaires, but nobody knew how they got their money.

He turned again to his informant and with tears in his eyes pleaded, "On the level, mister—what are they doing?"

The rotund out-of-towner had patience. "On the level, son—these men are buying and selling money."

Peter moved away. He looked around at the tall grim buildings, felt again the swift, nervous current of people, heard anew the clamor of the street, and some ancestral memory awakened in him and suddenly he grasped the essential feature of the bourse. These men were dealing *directly* with and in money. Not for them the grosser forms of merchandise. He felt in himself a lyric response to this awakening and he forgave these leaping and shrieking fiends their frenzy and insanity. The force of money was strong enough to make these men lose their reason, endure any cold and hardship. And he understood, too, that it was because of money that the slender boy with pale, pinched face was on the steamer that moved beyond the horizon to music, while Peter, penniless, stood below and watched it hungrily as he froze.

He shook off the dream-quality of this spectacle and walked to the corner. The sign-post gave the name of the two streets. Wall and Broad. And High, too, he thought. But scale it he must. He would come early to-morrow, freshly scrubbed and as neatly dressed as possible, and look for some thin crack in this wall and try to get in.

6

The main thing in New York is to get a start, to make a dent in the town, to jump off. Once you've battled your way into the breast of the stream, the current will sweep you on-ward, upward. The New York current ever climbs. Each year the buildings encroach more and more upon the sky. The towers stretch for the moon. The highest peak rules the city, but only for a little while. One morning when the darkness lifts a higher peak looms above it. The newest, tallest sky-scraper in the world has just been completed.

There's no standing still in the current of the town. A man decorates a hole in the wall with the fringes of a palm tree and sells pineapple juice— "Hawaii's National Drink." Thirsty New Yorker tastes it and smacks his lips. Mmmmm—and it's great for your bowels, too. Overnight the town takes on a tropical air, palm trees sway from all corners and the juice of the pineapple floods New York. Pineapple is king—until Orange Juice displaces him. And his régime is immediately threatened by Apple Juice. New York won't stand for just one hole in the wall; it must have itself thoroughly perforated. And while the war of the fruit juices rages, buttermilk, sour milk, zoolak, and the other lacteal havens for the benevolent intestinal microbes are gathering strength for their assault on the town.

It's an ever-climbing current. A man opens a little store to sell dresses that he bought cheaply at a bankruptcy sale. Thrifty citizeness buys one. She goes home to beam. In an hour, an army of women descends upon the little store. Overnight, Union Square is roped off for the sale of cheap dresses and I. Klein becomes an international name.

No one builds a home. From the soil of subdivisions there sprout solid phalanxes of two-family houses—hundreds of them. Between sunrise and sunset they fill with humans as if by magic. Streets line the swamps and lights swallow the darkness and a new suburb gleams. In all the boroughs those who claw their way to the breast of the current fatten, grow big, travel swift. Dreamer today, millionaire tomorrow.

But the main thing in New York is to get a start, to make a dent in the town, to jump off.

The years go around. Once again, summer cooks the town.

> *"In the good old summertime, in the good old summertime,*
> *Strolling through the shady lanes, with your baby-mine."*

There's a Roumanian folk dance called the "Horra" which has found great favor with all classes. A couple glides out on the floor, one hand upon the partner's shoulder. They face the guests in a horizontal line and sway to the music. Soon others join, one, two, three, sway and kick, one, two, three, sway and kick. The line grows and becomes a circle, all dancing around and around, swaying to the bleating shepherd's music, every-one in this, hands on shoulders, fifty legs raised in unison, a rhythmic sense of everyone being linked. One, two, three, sway and kick.

The summer heat was a folk-dance that linked the town. Day after day heat blew up out of the manholes like the blare of trumpets in some hot band playing in the lower intestines of the town. Heat blew up and linked itself with the heat that poured out of the apartments, that steamed up from the narrow gutters, linked itself with the heat that fell from the sky, forming a wall of dancing heat waves around the city. The town was hooped with heat and it gasped.

But the work of New York had to go on. Up in the Bronx The Hicks Arms Apartments, a five-story citadel for sixty-four families, was nearly finished. Certainly it would be ready for September occupancy. From dawn to midnight, from the ecstatic moment when the first steam shovel had dug its jaws into its first mouthful of his earth, Elmer Hicks had watched the work go on. Before the foundation was up, he could visualize every window, every door, almost every brick. And even on Sundays he sat on a box near the watchman and discussed the building boom with him.

As the structure rose, it attracted attention from the people in the neighborhood. Some, already planning to desert their older houses, made inquiries about rentals. Others came up on holidays from the lower east side; entire families, equipped with lunch boxes, would sit around on the grass that hadn't been torn up yet and picnic on his lot while they looked yearningly at the new building. A family outing on the threshold of their new abode, for many were thus moved to lease an apartment.

It was all as Elmer had visualized and the accuracy of his prophecy gave him deep pleasure. From a couple of four-family houses he had gone to this. Yes, even before the roof was up, the east side had stormed his house and taken possession of it. Every apartment rented at his own figure. And the same was going on in the Flatbush and Bensonhurst sections of Brooklyn. He regretted he was not two men, to be able to perform the same miracle in both boroughs. He did hope, however, that when his next building was up, his fever would abate a little so that he could have some respite.

The big trouble was that he could not sleep. When he lay down at night, his muscles twanging piteously, his head aching with the roar of construction, his eyelids suddenly became aflame with a hideous orange light. He would shut them tight, try to strangle the flame that burned within his sight; but instead the orange linked itself with other torment- ing colors, blazing, bright colors—maroon, vermilion, green, and finally, a return to a sheet of orange. Then the colors which had rolled before him like discs now squeezed themselves into weird, monstrous shapes, nightmarish patterns, menacing gargoyles, and he would bury his face deep in the pillow and carry on an agonized battle against the flaming colors until, before dawn, wrung limp, he would sink off into a tortured sleep, only to be aroused by light again in the morning.

But the apartment house was nearly completed. And already he was scheming to get more land, to build more houses.

In the good old summertime, Eugene Murdock sat in the library of his Columbia Heights home poring over blue prints, plans, columns of figures, a cigar between his lips, a decanter of Scotch whiskey by his side, and, within, that same persistent loneliness and concern over his son. The letters he had been receiving from his wife were schoolgirl descriptions of historic places, written in a round, innocent hand.

Occasionally a note was included in the small script of Perry. After a long rest, the boy had been placed in an élite school at Zurich, where he would consort with European gentlemen and be exposed to classi- cal education. He was studying foreign languages, French, Italian and German, under the tutelage of native teachers.

In the good old summertime, Eugene Murdock was studying how to make profits with the help of foreign gentlemen, one thousand Italian diggers, a handful of German timekeepers and some French draughtsmen, precise little guys who worked like hell. A good place to read Dante's "Inferno" in the original Italian would have been in the subway pit of the west side extension, and the ultimate Latin classical touch was to watch a swarthy gnome lay aside his tools and remove from his bag a "wop sandwich"—half a bread cut through, with a layer of pork sausage between and devour it with a pair of jaws that snapped with the force of a crocodile's.

Well, perhaps Murdock would take a trip in the fall and visit his son and discuss foreign cultures and influences with him and see for himself how rapidly he was becoming a man.

From the harbor he could hear the moan of a tug. Ship lights, shore lights, building lights snapped on, snapped off—a city lighting, re-lighting itself, routing darkness in a million corners. He pushed the blueprints away, thought shudderingly that he couldn't live long enough to build all the subways this city would need, peered horrifiedly into an endless dark pit, the grave of the city, and poured himself three fingers of Scotch whiskey. Standing near the window, he downed it, knew it was too hot to drink so much, mumbled the hell with Polly and walked unsteadily towards his bed.

In the good old summertime, Maria Pajalski lifted her soft, round, beautiful baby out of a tin bathtub full of water, wrapped her tenderly in a fleecy towel and, shielding her with a broad peasant back, spoke over her shoulder to Jan, the sot who sat muttering in a chair.

She said, "I'm a patient woman and I have stood for much, but if you so much as try to touch Gina while you're drunk, I'll crack your head with a stovehandle."

He lifted his blue-bleary eyes to her and gurnbled, "Now that she's got her baby, she won't let me touch her. Well, the world is full of wenches. All I have to do is fiddle and they dance to me."

And Maria shushed him as she hummed a German lullaby to her little three-year-old Gina, beautiful Gina, sleeping in a wicker basket made soft with half the feathers from the mother's own pillow.

In the good old summertime, sand itched the sleepers on the Coney Island beaches, the bums stank against the damp grass of Jackson Street Park, and sleepers were cramped on east side fire-escapes, although despite the heat youth bundled on the roofs. But on Riverside Drive the breeze from the Hudson answered the prayers of the pious rich who dwelt behind the cool, open windows.

And in the good old summertime, Joey awoke at six. The butter-yellow sun dripped bars of light across one wall of the kitchen. In the dark corner, his back towards humans and his face towards God, his little father stood, phylacteries wound around his left arm, the holy word encased in a leather box upon his forehead, praying quietly. He resembled a gentle unicorn.

On the fire-escape Bert was already seated, reading a book. He went to sleep with a book under his cheek and awoke with one in his hands. In the early morning light the blue vein could be traced upon his cheek and around his temple. He was pale and tired and every few moments he opened his mouth as if gasping for breath. Whew, it was hot, and yet he seemed utterly lost in his book. The mother's day had begun and she was already downstairs buying the groceries for breakfast, a quarter pound of sweet butter, a jug of loose milk, four "beigel" and some fruit for the younger boy who was a finicky eater.

Joey felt a sadness for his little father with the hot leather bands around him, for his frail brother breathing through his pale mouth, for his mother all wilted and tired even before the day had really begun. He couldn't suppress a feeling of triumph that he was different from all of them. The gutter had made him strong and tough. He laughed at heat and cold and fatigue. He went through the days like a well-oiled machine and at night he rested. Yes, and he could fight, and they could not.

He clenched his rough hands into big fists and bounded off the bed. There was a feeling of elation within him that laughed at the aches of the town. Heat or no heat, he had a schedule to follow that day. This was real man's work, not at the shop, for he was enjoying his week's vacation. He was fifteen now—nearly five foot six and weighed one hundred and thirty pounds stripped. Joey was in training for his first professional prize-fight. And he must begin.

Joey trod cat-footedly to the window. He peered for a moment over Bert's shoulder and suddenly he seized the book from his hand. Bert's long fingers followed the book instinctively like hands lifted in prayer. Startled, he swung around. Joey tried to read the title, "Brothers—Kar-a-ma-zoof—by—Dos-to-off-ski." Grinning, he returned the book. "Cheez, Bert—you sure readin' fat books." Even though he laughed, it was not in mockery but with pride. He loved his brother, was awed by the books the kid could read—real face-crackers. He put a hand on his shoulder (mustn't touch tenderly when you really like some-one) and then pressed hard. Bert ouched and jerked the hand off.

"Come on, kid," Joey urged, "train wid me to-day. Foist ting—a little road woik—we run acrost the bridge."

Bert sighed. It was much easier and pleasanter to read, but on Forsyth Street there was real glory in tralning with a prize-fighter. And he was proud of his brother, happy to be seen with him, particularly in the capacity of an equal.

"That bridge is too long for me, Joey—I can't run a mile and a half. And back, too."

"Who's askin' you to run? Tell you what I'll do: I'll rent you a wheel. You'll ride while I trot. Come on, Bert, I got to get in me road woik."

Joey put on a sweat shirt, long flannel trousers and sneakers. In the oval mirror that hung in the front room, he stole a glance at himself. He enjoyed all the garb and paraphernalia of the prize-fighter. Bert swung out upon the window-sill as his mother entered, her arms full of bags.

"And where are you children going so early in the morning? There isn't a dog on the streets yet."

"Gotta train, ma," explained Joey. "Just a little run acrost the bridge."

The little father paused in his prayers, looked over his shoulder at his son, and spat as one does at an insane person. It was sheer madness to run on such a hot day, but he dared not interrupt his prayers to speak.

Joey munched a "beigel," drank a glass of milk, while Bert bit into an apricot. He was never hungry and couldn't even think of eating until midday. Then, they left the house.

The early morning workers, in wilted regiments, were on their way to the shops. They began the day hot, tired, limp. The men carried their coats folded across their arms, shirt sleeves rolled up, straw hats in hand. The girls wore shirtwaists, or middy blouses, long dresses (the more daring permitting a short slit up one side), cotton stockings and high-top shoes. They marched, an endless parade of workers, pouring out of the tenements, joining the fattening ranks, marching to work as if the city itself had blown a whistle.

Around the corner on Rivington Street an Italian organ grinder, one arm cut off at the elbow, the other turning the crank of the tambouriney music-box, ground out a march. The music had spirit and, as the workers passed its rhythm, they seemed to respond to it, to straighten and lift their legs a bit higher; but as soon as other city sounds drowned out the march, they lagged again. But the organ grinder played on, every morning for three hours, a fine-looking Italian with a large moustache and a florid face. Some of the workers dropped pennies into a cup he had on top of the organ. When school children replaced the workers on the sidewalks, the organ grinder ceased making music and with his one good hand trundled his box across the Bowery and disappeared in some courtyard.

Joey and Bert walked down Forsyth Street and turned east on Delancey Street towards the Williamsburg Bridge. Here the flow of workers downstream was so thick in the direction of the gloomy factory streets across the Bowery, towards Crosby, Mercer, Greene, Wooster, and all the streets from Lispenard to Chambers, that it was difficult to walk against it. For convenience they chose the gutter, dodging delivery trucks drawn by deflated nags, Joey moving in springy steps, Bert hurrying to keep pace.

In a bicycle shop on Norfolk Street, two blocks from the entrance to the bridge, Joey rented a two-wheeler for Bert. The charge was ten cents an hour and a one dollar deposit against overtime, damage to the bicycle, or possibly theft.

Bert felt like a man when he snapped the metal garters around the cuffs of his overalls. He was not a very skillful rider but he mounted the seat with spirit and under the watchful eye of Joey he maneuvered a zig-zag course to the entrance. The policeman on guard would not permit Bert to ride on the smooth upper roadway reserved for pedestrians, so they had to take the lower, rough and dirty path across which all the bridge traffic passed. Bert began to pedal uphill. He knew at once that it would be hard work. Joey took a deep breath, clamped his mouth, placed his elbows against his sides and began an effort-less trot.

Through the heat a breeze blew from the East River, a thin breeze that squeezed itself between the bridge railing and the wall of tenements that followed it down to the riverfront. Here was a glittering lump of city filth. Here were rat and cockroach-infested houses that wilted under the sun, cowered under the rain and snow and yet, year after year, stood up. Here were the first hovels to be condemned as unfit for human habitation in the powdery reform waves that periodically dusted over the city, and yet humans were born, lived and died in them unmindful of the tender hearts that had bled a little for them.

And under the bridge, in the cool, dark and dank bowels of the bridge, flourished the markets, the peddlers in wares for those whom even Bert and Joey considered the poor. Here was a special lower life, a mysterious jungle life that went on in thickets of poverty, in clumps of unbelievable squalor, dark, impenetrable, a challenge to social explorers. And here it could flourish safely, because it was under cover, away from the eyes of man and law.

Joey trotted uphill easily, drawing in long breaths compounded of rotting vegetables, stale fish, tenement stench, horse manure, axle grease, and through it the fresh breeze from the river and the aroma of coffee beans it bore on its crest from the opposite shore. He filled his lungs with the air and moved his strong legs like pistons. But Bert suffered. This was more than he could endure. His wrists were almost riveted to the handle bars, and his legs ached so that every revolution of the wheel was a carousel of pain. Sweat poured down his pale face and the overalls clung to his body. But he pressed his lips into a determined line and tried to avoid being run over by the trucks that rattled by. Whenever he dared to lift his eyes from the path, he stole a glance at his brother, running at an even pace, admired the strength and stride of him; and once, when their eyes met, they both smiled as if here indeed was youth at play.

Presently they reached the highest level of the bridge, the span across the narrow waters of the East River. Boats moved serenely—squat tugs bearing flats with railroad trains on them, coal barges, lighters, freighters, river boats, passenger steamers bound for New England ports, moving coolly, serenely. But around the edges of the water the city grew so dense and feverish that Bert had the feeling that some giant pair of hands, pushing from behind, could gather up the whole waterfront and shove it in the East River.

They passed the crest and the down hill path to Williamsburg began. While there was no more pedalling to do, the strain of applying the brakes so that the bicycle would not fly away with him was almost as painful. Finally Bert rolled off the bridge and with his last strength wheeled himself against the curb, stopped, slowly, agonizingly, pried himself off the seat and sank exhausted on the curb-stone. Joey came to a stop alongside of him.

"What's the matter, Bert? You ain't quittin'?" Bert wiped the perspiration from his face and opened his mouth to breathe. In Williamsburg the air hung just as low and heavy as on the other side. The city was growing hotter.

"I can't go back," confessed Bert. "Can't lift a leg." He tried to straighten his hand and pain shot through his whole arm. "And my wrists feel like they were sprained. Gee—I never thought it was so hard."

Joey grinned understandingly. As Bert sat there, crushed and exhausted, he was so definitely his kid brother, the scholar, the reader of fat books on the fire-escape, but certainly not the strong arm guy.

"Come on, Bert—" he helped him to his feet—"I'll ride you back on the handle-bar. That's as good road woik as running acrost."

He lifted him upon the handle-bar and with Bert's legs dangling, Joey pedalled the wheel up to the north side of the bridge, returning to Manhattan. Bert, his arms and legs comparatively free from torture, had a good opportunity to study his city from on high.

The thin river breeze cooled his face and he enjoyed travelling in an upper box. That was the way he liked to see life. The tenements hugged each other, the wash hung from the roof lines, and the people seemed stuck to the sidewalks like flies on paper. Below, it seemed hard to breathe, hard to lift a foot. But on high, life was cool and graceful and pleasant. That was the way to live—to be wheeled on high. His reverie was broken by the swift and hazardous descent, for Joey was not as cautious as Bert had been. Curving in and out of trucks, winding under the very nose of a horse, Joey bounded off the bridge and back to the bicycle store, where he reclaimed his deposit.

And now for a shower. Joey led the way to the public baths on Allen Street under the Second Avenue "L." For a penny one bought the use of a towel and a sliver of rubbery, yellow soap. In the good old summertime a long line always waited to get in, for the dozen shower stalls were quickly occupied and the bathers were constantly hounded by attendants who urged them to hurry. But Joey knew the guard, a cousin of the district leader (how else could he get a city job), who fancied himself a tough guy because he bossed the immigrant poor who waited for baths. And in his rôle of a tough, he made special concessions to the young men who trained for prize-fights. He always admitted them at once. Perhaps there was a measure of self-preservation in this custom. Thus Joey and Bert (he's my trainer) were admitted at once. They went into stalls, turned the wonderful water on, first warm, then cold, Joey slapping the muscles of his arms and legs, kneading them, after the manner of a masseur in a champ's training camp.

Then, cleansed and refreshed, they walked home. Joey ate two eggs and drank another glass of milk. Bert surprised himself by eating one egg and sipping a small cup of milk. Then, he sank exhausted on a mattress left to air on the fire-escape. In his book he tried to find ease from his pain, and soon he melted the ache of his legs and wrists in the higher anguish that tormented Karamazov.

But Joey went downstairs to arrange the remainder of his day's training, which was to consist chiefly of practice bouts with any of the boys who were willing to put the gloves on with him. A gabby newcomer to the block, Livingston Cohen (one of the first of the Livingstons, Monroes and Fenimores to be prefixed to Jewish names) had done considerable unsolicited bragging on behalf of Joey, as if he were his press agent, so that four "shtarkers" from neighboring blocks put in an appearance. They were curious to test his strength and speed, for Joey lately had frowned on street brawls. It was not in the code of the professional. Besides, he might break a bone or kill an opponent. And there was his future to consider.

The boys were corralled and led into Joey's back yard, where they discovered Isabella and some of her friends dancing. The girls were roughly shooed away like so many buzzing flies, but when Isabella looked coquettishly at Joey, he gruffly granted her permission to watch him from the fire-escape of her flat, two flights up.

The afternoon heat hung like a ceiling over the yard. Within their small rooms, mothers and babies panted for breath. But so great was Joey's excitement that he warmed up by skipping the rope, first with both feet, later, alternating left and right. Then he slipped the gloves on, glanced up once like a knight in armor to his lady fair, who was seated in her fire-escape loge, and called for his first opponent.

Joey felt good with the sixteen-ounce gloves on his hands. He was exalted by a frequent though never voiced prayer.

"Thank God—I'm not like Bert or my father. I've got strong hands and a heart and I can sock."

He called encouragement to the first kid. "Hit me hard—I won't hoit you." And he had no intention of hurting any of them. He merely wished to block blows and he egged the lad on to throw his punches fast and furious. Only once, to keep faith with his lady love in the balcony above, did Joey uncork a blow which promptly ended the first exhibition bout.

The third boy, however, a lout of sixteen, heavy, clumsy, surly, and already adept with the brass knuckles, had secretly planned to upset Joey's party. He waddled towards him, attempting to wrestle by encircling him with a bear's grip, but Joey wriggled out. They clinched again and as Joey broke out of the clinch and before he could put his guard up, the lout pelted him and snickered. This was the first serious test of Joey's new resolution to control his temper while fighting. Instead of rushing him, he jabbed at his nose from long range, tossing color on it with skill that sang. Then he tried a one-two on him, poked with his left and crossed with his right, lowered the attack to the stomach, all the time listening to the music of the pounding of the gloves.

As he flayed the lout, his muscles sang to him that he could punch his way beyond all the thick walls of the tenements, from backyard to green fields, from poverty to riches, from obscurity to fame, yes, even to the little lady who sat with her dancer's legs crossed on the fire-escape and gazed on with admiration.

In the late afternoon the day's training was tapered off with a plunge in Lepke's "mikvah," the, "ole swimmin' 'ole" of the entire neighborhood. Here was a stagnant, underground pool, wooed more ardently than the babbling brook that courses through English poetry. Here came the hoodlums and young prize-fighters to be cleansed and cooled and conditioned. Here also came, a little furtively, the tough wops from across the Bowery to be washed of sins and to be kept from paying penalties, for Lepke's "mikvah" was a good hide-out for young thieves in a jam. And in among these professionals there splashed a little timidly the innocent kids of the block who were merely cooling off or learning how to swim.

Once every summer the water was changed, and that was at the beginning. And after its winter slumbers, the water did not gurgle, but actually fell through the drain pipe. An examination of one of its drops under a microscope would have split the glass. The water was alive not only with its original molecules, but with all the gifts that can flow from human pores and other apertures or be washed from human skin. But it was the only body of water in which to cool off after a boiling day, and the only place to dive even at the risk of a cracked skull or an infected ear; and so it was heavily patronized.

On Fridays a smaller pool was filled with boiling water and in it orthodox Jews, cleansing for the Sabbath, used to lower themselves with such piteous moans, gasps and sighs that even God must have heard these subterranean cries. The young boys would watch these bearded grannies in stark amazement, for it was impossible to dip even a hand into the water. But the old Jews had developed a technique of their own. First, one bumpy and skinny shank, but stealthily, as if to deceive the water itself, and then the other, and no disturbing of its surface, for the others already immersed would have killed you. And then the thighs; a "Sh'mai Yisroel" yelp as the belly, like an awning let down, submerged; and finally the whiskers like a tangle of kelp. An initiate would remain hunched and motionless for many minutes, and then, as the breath returned to him, would he dare to speak. An orthodox Jew would remain in this cauldron until he was boiled and when he emerged he resembled, ironically, enough, nothing so much as a ham ready for carving.

But even on rainy days, or when it was cool, you could always find a few Italians hiding out from irate fathers or the police—meagre walyoes wedged into narrow dressing booths, their swarthy bodies corrugated with goose pimples, their lips purple from cold.

It was in Lepke's "mikvah" that Joey came down for a plunge, stroked about for half an hour, cleansed himself under a faucet, dried himself and went home for supper.

Darkness drew over the town. Heat steamed back from the pavements and the tired dwellers sought sleep. As Joey stretched out on his bed in the kitchen, every muscle in him sang and he felt the glow that only the perfect in health ever achieve. He had put in a day's training.

> *"You'll be my tootsie-wootsie,*
> *In the good old summertime."*

7

Googi was learning about life from lithographs. The vivid, hysterical figures in the three-sheets had become his patron saints. Still vivid in his mind was the first motion picture he had seen, although nearly three years had passed. In his own mind the rescue of the flaxen-haired Susie, in the "Great Train Robbery," was inextricably linked with his own rescue from poverty and death. That picture had taught him to have hope and his faith had borne the luscious fruits of soft living. For the years following his discovery of his new game, "rolling the lush," had been the fattest and most interesting of his life. He was out of the amateur class and enjoyed the life of an expert.

He had a fixed routine. He would begin at Canal Street and work north. Like a wily ferret he prowled among the hallways of the Bowery, sniffing for mushy drunks. Sometimes he encountered them on the streets, and in order to manoeuvre them into hallways he had developed a special approach. Every drunk was usually followed by a gang of kids who would hurl corn "shots," trip him up, and in other annoying ways express their disapproval of drinking.

But Googi would break into such a scene like a hero on a cue. He drove the hooting kids away, picked up the sloppy lid and placed it tenderly on the drunkard's conk, and then, taking him by one arm like a brother, he would say in a special, wheedling voice, "That's all right, Johnny—I'm taking you home."

And so, for a block or two, he would walk the lush, guiding him like a frisky nag, agreeing with him, singing with him, yes, almost weeping with him, until he came to the hallways he knew were safe and with a quick jerk he would lead Johnny in.

"Sure I'm takin' you home." Or, sniggishly, "There's a great piece of hide waitin' fer you."

And when he had him inside, behind the stairway where it was dark and lonely, he would trip him up suddenly and let the big hulk land on his bean. It was too bad about the skull cracking but you had to work fast in this game. Down on your knees and with quick, practiced fingers into all the pockets, around the waist for a money belt, in the lining of the fly where money was frequently concealed, and then you straightened up and nonchalantly whistled your way out.

Since you didn't read the papers anyway, how could you ever find out about an unidentified man suffering from a skull fracture as the result of a fall while intoxicated? After all, it was all in the new game, "rolling the lush."

And with the money thus garnered Googi bought immunity from beatings from his father, and for the first time in his life, bought food and clothing. For himself he did the things his parents had been unable to do.

Not that the ways of normal living came easily to Googi. It took him months to learn how to eat the food that all civilized people eat. Not mincing table manners, or the point-counter-point of salad fork and soup spoon, but the actual process of eating. For so long had he been nourished on an erratic diet—a mound of artificially flavored ice, a hot dog winter-coated with mustard, black licorice sticks, a dish of leftover spaghetti, rancid butter and stale foods—that in the beginning he felt a repugnance to honest, normal foods.

But again, the lithographs came to his rescue. Outdoor billboard and wall advertising was just beginning to grip and befoul the country and Googi was one of the first patrons of this vivid and lopsided art. And the men, women and children in these pictures were his idols, just as the food at which they yum-yummed, the tobacco they smoked and the clothes they wore became his goals.

And so, with the aid of a rose-tinted lad with cheeks like a hussy's buttocks, Googi learned how to eat bacon and eggs. But his big triumph was his first cup of cocoa. Somehow, cocoa smacked of the upper stratum, of the elegant life that went on behind the tall casements where, on thickly carpeted floors, a pert maid proffered a tray upon which reposed a cup of cocoa so proud of itself that the vapors it gave off were like clouds in heaven. It was sweet and rich to the taste, and caressing, in time, to his own starved palate; for in him there was a deeply buried hunger for the sweet and rich in life.

In his progress towards normal living the only picture that baffled him was that of a mother bending over to kiss a baby. That kiss bewildered him, because he had no memory of ever having been kissed by his mother. Or for that matter, by any other woman. It dawned on him, not without amazement, that there were homes in which mothers kissed their babies.

He acquired his first pair of shoes bought in a reputable store with the premeditated intention of fitting his particular feet. The few pairs of shoes he had worn in his life—and they were few, for like the agrarian heroes Googi went barefoot in summer and into the fall—came either from cellar stores in the Bowery or pushcarts on Orchard Street, where they were acquired only after endless haggling. At best they were factory misfits, second-hand, stolen, or just pulled off the feet of the dead. Before his feet found hospitality in them a long battle went on between the creases and arcs of the shoes and the demands of his own toes. And by the time the shoes began to fit comfortably, they were so worn that only the ties of poverty bound them to his feet. Thus a new pair of shoes to fit his feet, to be worn instantly without agony, was a memorable triumph in his life. Equally memorable was his first pair of trousers that came fresh and pressed from a clothes-rack, instead of wriggling off his father's sweaty hips.

Of course the business of shining shoes was utterly out of his life and he sold his "Shabbas goy" concession to a younger Italian for fifty cents, warning him that he had discovered the only weak spot of Jews. His days he spent in the streets, foraging, petty thieving, but especially in sizing up people from the angle of prey, slyly wondering how this one could be mulcted and how much that one would yield when frisked.

Evenings he spent at Joe's poolroom and billiard parlor, ten steps below the level of the street. Here a cellar life went on, secretive and predatory, tunnelling into the life of the people who trod the pavements overhead. His long trousers were his card of admission but it required a siege of many months before he was admitted beyond the threshold. And so these were his days and his evenings; his nights, of course, were given over to prowling the Bowery and, on lean nights, even the waterfront in his quest for game. He lived by day like a mongrel dog and by night like a sleek, tenement rat, And upon this life he throve. He no longer feared his father, although with that ingrained Italian sense of filial obedience, he occasionally allowed him to beat him. But as the razor strop curled around him, not paining half as much as in the days when there was no flesh on his ribs, Googi would snarl, "Some day, you sonofa bitch, I'll slit your belly open."

While the figures in the billboards and lithographs taught him the refinements of living, his mentors in the actual business of getting on in New York were the older habitués in Joe's poolroom. Here were the wise gazaboes of New York—and it was his ambition to grow into a full-fledged all-around wise gazabo. A wise gazabo apparently never worked, and yet lived like a lord. He wore the best of clothes, slept late, ate the finest of foods, played pool all day and with a flourish, always carried a thick wad of money with a rubber band around it, was idolized by a group of disciples who fought for the privilege of running errands for him, knew and lived off women, and took no guff from anybody.

Here were the gay caballeros living a serene sub-stratum life, moving in a small circle of slothful, undramatic activities; and yet, on rare occasions when one of their tempers broke loose it was terrible to behold. A maiming, a cutting, even a killing was the result. And now and then one of them would disappear, and the explanation for his absence was that he was "away for his health."

Googi, couldn't help contrasting the cushioned life of the wise gazaboes with that of the honest boobs around him. When he saw his mother stagger in from the sweatshop with a bundle of raw coats in which she had to sew linings at home, he laughed, a special wise-guy snarl, half lifting the side of his mouth and snorting through his nostrils. His black eyes gleamed and he laughed in derision, no pity moving him. One dollar for stitching all night. And he laughed, too, when he saw those battalions of Sicilian laborers returning from work, compact swarthy automatons, gnomes with ragged coats slung over their shoulders, sucking on a stinking pipe or a stogie butt. Two dollars a day for this back-breaking work. Well, that was all right for the old wops; but for him, a New Yorker, he would become a wise gazabo.

And so in Joe's poolroom, after months of fawning around the cuffs and running endless errands, Little Rocco, a wily leader, finally took official notice of Googi. One afternoon he touched him on the head with a billiard cue, in the manner of knighting him, and said, "Hey walyo, what's your name?"

Googi blushed and trembled with joy. To have Little Rocco display such interest in him.

"Googi," he faltered.

Rocco laughed. "Who wished a handle like that on you? I wouldn't use it on a dog."

"You know—from Guglielmo," Googi nearly wept. Inwardly he cursed his father for having handicapped him with a name like that.

"Commere, Googi," the smile suddenly vanished from Rocco's face. He set the cue down, planted a toothpick in his mouth and pulled Googi around to face him so that the diamonds in his horseshoe tie-pin blistered in the boy's eyes. Without disturbing the position of the toothpick, he slid a few words at Googi.

"Listen, kid, I been watchin' you. Yeah, Little Rocco don't let nothin' get by. Now take the wax out of your ears and listen. You wanna do right by yourself? You don't wanna be a punk all your life. You wanna be a wise gazabo?"

"Sure, sure," said Googi, feverishly.

"Then how's about a little wagon-bouncin' for me? It's a pipe."

Googi licked his lips. He was being initiated into the inner circle. "Anything you say—anything."

A course in wagon-bouncing for the apprentice "wise gazaboes," it must be explained, was to major stuff in crime what Lawrenceville is to Princeton. You learned the ropes, inhaled the right atmosphere and met the sort of people who would be your friends for life. It was a popular practice on the west side, but was spreading through all New York with the speed of the gospel. Its technique was simple and it was more like a game than a vocation. A team of two played it. The boys would saunter through a middle-class neighborhood and wait for a delivery wagon from one of the department stores to drive up. "Whoa." The sleek horses come to a halt. The boys wait in a doorway while the driver hitches the reins and jumps off his seat. He opens the back of the wagon and removes a parcel for Mrs. Davenport.

As soon as he's gone one of the boys leaps on the wagon while the other watches for a cop, removes a fair-sized parcel and tosses it to his confederate, who promptly skidoos with it. The gleaner then jumps off the wagon and vamooses in the opposite direction. To make the game safer and more colorful, the boys come equipped with special caps which resemble the headgear of department store drivers. Thus a suspicious officer is lulled.

Rocco with the tip of his tongue deftly swung the toothpick to the other side of his mouth. But his velvety purring was not interrupted.

"I'll team you up with a mick from the west side and I fence all the stuff youse guys bring in. And we split fifty-fifty. Now how's about it—you gonna be a punk—or a wise gazabo?"

And so Googi's social life expanded to include a new friend, a kid from Hudson Street, the freckle-faced accidental offspring of an Irish teamster, a snarling lad for whom the world was an oyster with ground glass in it. And Red Finnigan had a few wrinkles of his own. So that when a garlic-laden breeze blew out of the Battery and he sniffed the arrival of a great steamer, Red would rent a horse and wagon and, with Googi beside him, drive down to South Ferry and pick up a lonely immigrant who had neither friend nor relative. They would show him the town; reading the card pinned to his lapel, they would agree to deliver him safely, together with all his baggage and his secret store of money.

And they had a merry time of it. Googi led the way to his special Bowery hallways which he knew so well, where the gullible immigrant, fresh from his embrace with the Statue of Liberty, would receive his first lesson about life in the great metropolis.

Yes, it was a gay life and Googi was making progress. His body, which seemed to have cowered for years through fright, suddenly shot up, seized flesh for its bones, whipped some red corpuscles into his cheeks, routed the pains and ills which had always menaced him. And as he grew physically, he grew in cunning. He developed a special street sense which permitted him to scent danger as an animal does in its own woody preserves. He knew his way around, he had warm food in his belly and good clothes on his back.

Yes, the main thing in New York is to get a start, to make a dent in the town.

Friday night, at the Forton Athletic Club, on Grand and Orchard Streets, Joey fought his first professional fight. His nom de guerre was Young Samson, for of all the Hebrew learning which had been drummed into his ears by a weary *melamed,* all he remembered was the legend of Samson's strength. On his purple trunks he wore a "Mogen David"—the six-pointed star of David. In a four-round preliminary bout he was matched to meet Mickey Callahan, the west-side flash, a fledgling under the protective wing of Michael Donovan, who, now that his political career was moving along, was beginning to build up his stable of fighters.

Sitting around tables in the rear rooms of saloons, or at the Democratic clubhouses, or even at brothels of a Saturday night while waiting for a favorite floozie to wiggle downstairs, the sporting men who discussed prizefighters agreed that the Jewish lads had speed, cleverness and ring generalship, but lacked the killer's heart. And without that you were not a fighter, only a dancing master. Witness Abe Atell, the cleverest boxer that ever donned a pair of gloves, the featherweight champ; he lacked a killer's heart, and had to take nearly all of his victories by decisions. And of this whole crop of Jewish fighters, not even excepting Leach Cross, all were able to make a monkey out of an opponent but hardly any had the flint sledge-hammer punch that fells a man to the canvas, rigid and dead to the mournful tolling of ten. And they all agreed, Donovan among them, that the great pugilistic find would be a clever boxer, a long-range marksman with phantom legs, who also packed a K.O. wallop.

At the ringside were Donovan and Murdock and his partner Dominick, for Donovan always made a little pin money by selling tickets for prizefights and outings to his business associates. And besides, it was an occasion for a social evening in the course of which some new details regarding the subway contract could be discussed.

And behind in the dollar seats were Googi and his partner, Red, both younger sportsmen and patrons of the fistic arts.

Alone, several rows removed, hunched over with fear and tension, biting his knuckles, sat Bert. A stir down the aisles, a puff of commotion as the boys clambered through the ropes. There was something Hellenic, classical, in the beauty of the young gladiators as they entered the ring. Shorn of their ill-fitting clothes and their defensive grimaces, they displayed only their youthful, glistening bodies and the air of incipient ring idols.

The announcer, a plump clown with a voice that vibrated in the last cobweb of the hall, introduced the combatants. "In this corner we have Young Samson, the Forsyth Street shtarker, one hundred and twenty-two pounds." Googi led a small contingent in wild cheers, but Joey only frowned, for he believed he was being mocked at. "And in this corner, Micky Callahan, the west side flash, one hundred and twenty-four pounds." A shrill cheer came up from the micks, in which Red joined to the great annoyance of Googi.

Out of his deep-set eyes Joey looked at the contemptuous Irish features in the opposite corner, at the belligerent freckles and the confident grin that illuminated them when a west side admirer yelled, "Kill the sheeney." Joey glowered, the sullen split in his forehead like an ominous cleft, his shoulders slightly hunched over, his long arms by his side. But the perfect symmetry of his body was beautiful to behold, the flow of deep chest into thin waist, the fistfuls of muscles at his shoulder blades, the arch of his calves, the sheen of his skin. From what Judean gladiator was this a heritage?

The ferocious second from the club blew whiskey fumes into his ear and whispered hoarsely, "Kid—come out fighting. That's all you gotta do—come out fighting."

And at the same time, Callahan's second was assuring him, "The little mock can't hoit you."

The referee summoned the lads to the center of the ring, told them to break at his command, not to hit in clinches, and to go to a neutral corner after a knockdown. Then he whisked them to their corners. The boys barely had time to limber up on the ropes when the gong sounded.

Callahan tore out of his corner like the west-side fury he was. He had been reared in the tradition of Terry McGovern, nourished on tales of the terrible mick. Swarm all over your man like a centipede and destroy him in the first minute. He threw punches from all angles, wildly, furiously, viciously. Joey, a little bewildered by the ferocity of this attack, thought of the many times he had been obliged to dodge bats, bricks, bottles, cans and stones. This kind of attack was fast, but it was not new to him.

In his rear seat Bert, his face blanched and yielding around the edges to the greenish tinge of nausea, sat hunched over and shivering. Every blow that glanced off or struck Joey resounded in his heart. And when a smear of blood appeared on the tip of Joey's nose, Bert grew horrified. He wanted to shriek when that same bloodthirsty and badly controlled voice yelled, "Kill the sheeney!"

Joey weathered the storm. Some of the blows he blocked, some glanced off his elbows and shoulders and a few found his face and body. But after two minutes the fury of the whirl-wind attack subsided and Joey, feeling the decreasing power of the blows, suddenly lunged forward and socked. It was a beautiful right swing, well uncorked, with growing venom and bottled up strength behind it. Sock—and it resounded on the chin of the west side flash. Callahan spun around on one leg like a top and collapsed against the ropes. The referee who saw and heard the blow caught the astonished look in Mickey's eyes, that flash that blinks once in the eyes of a steer as the hammer falls.

He waved Joey to his corner, and as he began his count, he mentally appraised Young Samson. A featherweight with the wallop of a two-hundred pounder. Add cleverness, maturity, ring generalship, and put a shrewd manager behind that punch—and you could have a champ. At that very moment Donovan was making those same calculations. "Five, six, seven," and the bell saved Callahan. While his handlers kneaded his muscles, dangled a whiff of ammonia under his nostrils and sponged his face, the same second kept saying, "Kid—the mock can't hoit you." And Joey's second, fever in his throat, shouted, "What did I tell you? Come out fighting."

Donovan watched keenly. He had no special sympathy with his fledgling. He was out to build a stable of fighters. And this round would tell whether the little yid had a killer's heart. Googi's voice was falsetto from yelling. The knuckles on Bert's hands were as white as his face.

The gong sounded and Joey tore out of his corner. He suddenly remembered what had happened to his little father in a west side saloon. This was no longer a contest—it became a crusade. No fly-swatting attack now, no delicate exchange of jabs. He tore in the way he did in a street fight. The very useful and deadly one-two. A left to the bread basket and a right cross to the chin and the west-side flash was dimmed. He lay on his freckles for a long count.

Bert, who had been watching pop-eyed, faint with fear, echoing to each blow, subsided with relief and suddenly wet himself. He felt sick with shame.

Donovan left his seat to talk to the matchmaker. He wanted an inside track on Young Samson. Now that it was over Joey liked the applause, the cheers from the boys on his block; but as he walked up the aisle he wondered why Bert looked so crushed and avoided his glance.

Then he reviewed some figures in his mind. He had sold thirty tickets at a dollar apiece, out of which he retained fifteen. And for his winner's end of the purse the matchmaker had promised him fifteen dollars. That gave him a bankroll of thirty bucks. Twenty he would give to his father, the little father, nearly two weeks' wages, and tell him he had won it in five minutes of prize-fighting. And two he would give to Bert, just for spending money, and warn him not to read so much because it was affecting his eyesight. And the remaining eight he would blow in on a spree with Isabella. Yes, with Isabella, his girl.

In the dressing-room, Donovan sought him out. Joey couldn't help being impressed by this portly gentleman, smoking a fat cigar, who walked arm-in-arm with the matchmaker of the club. The square-cut diamond on his finger and his flamboyant vest awed Joey. He placed a kindly and appraising hand on Joey's shoulder in the manner of appraising a race horse.

"Tell me, kid, how long have you been boxing?"

"Dis is me foist fight."

"And you sure flattened him. I bet you like it, too?"

"It's easier than woik."

"So you've got a job? And what at?"

"In a printin' shop."

"I'd like to do something for you, sonny. I'll fix you up with a soft city job so's you can train. I'm thinking we can make something out of you. And by the way—where do you train?"

Joey grinned. "In me back yard."

"Well, let's take a look at you Monday night in a real workout. Here"— he gave him a card—"this will get you in at Stillman's gym. Don't forget, Monday night. I'll be there!" The matchmaker whispered a word of congratulation in his ear and left.

Joey stood alone in his glow of triumph. Money in his pocket and victory in his chunky fists.

The main thing in New York is to get a start, to make a dent in the town.

On a bench in Stuyvesant Park Mamie the prostitute sat. Wistful and shocked writers from New England and the middle west could have written volumes about this poor girl of the streets, this victim of circumstance or of a vicious economic system. But Mamie, the hustler built like a buffalo, simply sat, completely innocent of the latent springs of literary inspiration locked up within her. She sat with her lumpy thighs well apart, each leg resting on the little box of a heel, her piggish eyes sleepily eyeing the men who passed by.

At the other end of the bench sat an old man. He was covered with hair and puffed with clothes, a black derby on his head and woolen mittens on his hands. He rustled through a paper bag, withdrew a piece of cake, stuffed it through the matted adit of his beard and let the sugar flakes gently shower him.

A clock chimed in Stuyvesant Church. The hour rang four and the little hand of the clock obediently pointed to the numeral. The old man paused in his munching and spoke to the prostitute.

"Sister—all the clocks in this town are wrong, and I ought to know because I got clothes on my back." She regarded the three coats he wore and the two pairs of pants. "Sister, this is a twenty-four-hour town and when it's eight o'clock for you it's twelve o'clock for someone else. Yes, when it's time for you to get up, somebody in Brooklyn is going to sleep. It's night-time for you when you go to a show but it's morning for the actor who's just beginning to work. It's the last hour for a man who's dying in Staten Island, but it's the first minute for a baby that's just born in the Bronx. It's always the wrong time for somebody in this town. That's why all the clocks are, wrong."

The old man resumed his munching. Mamie stood up, her little feet squealing at the quivering weight imposed on them.

"Right or wrong," she said, "it's time for me to hustle. I got a pimp to support and a son in private school."

She walked off slowly, a wide beaded bag swinging from her wrist.

Opening of the Hicks Court, ta-ra!

The morning the imitation Persian rug was nailed down in the lobby, indicating the completion of the building and a subtle mistrust of the world, should have been ushered in with the rolling of thunder, salutes from the fleet and floral tributes from leading citizens, so momentous had that moment loomed in the anticipations of Elmer Hicks. But the Bronx was racing along too rapidly to pause. What's one little building in a borough that sprouts them like weeds? Alas, it was dramatic only in Elmer's mind, and even for him the feeling of triumph was quickly desecrated. He had hoped for a regimental march of grateful tenants bearing banners from the east side and being led to their apartments by their great saviour and leader, Captain Elmer Hicks.

But instead, a few thrifty families had moved in even before the decorations were complete, thus appropriating a few weeks' free rental. And such is the intensity of life in the Bronx that one baby squawling can make an entire barracks echo with its lamentations. One morning, as he approached his beautiful *arc de triomphe*, he saw a begrimed ice-man with a cake of ice on a burlap bag across his shoulder enter the citadel and drip up the floor. So great was his shock that he forgot to order him around to the tradesman's entrance.

There lay the root of his sadness, the lack of a definite cleavage between dream and reality. It all blended together, like taffy on the rack of a pulling machine.

But there was no time to grieve. Elmer was already immersed in his plans to acquire more land and to begin another, a larger apartment house. The boom was on in the Bronx. Jewish, Italian and Irish builders materialized out of nowhere and descended like an army of beavers intent upon building. They bought and connived options on land, mortgaged the land to secure money for construction, then mortgaged the buildings to get money for more land. It was an enthralling, exciting cycle, each man battling for the opportunity to owe so much that merely on the strength of his debts he would be rated a rich man. Branches of the large downtown banks were opened to finance and control these projects, and as usual the bankers reaped the real fortunes. Somehow all the little blueprints that grew into houses were held by steel threads in the hands of the bankers. They tugged the threads that bound the dreamers and schemers to their projects with the skill of marionettists. But it was a long and flexible leash, let out and drawn in many times because there was a little fee to be raked off at every step in the construction of a building.

But despite the frenzied competition, Elmer regarded himself as lucky. Other men had to go home to wives and children, seek solace and rest on Sunday, or hunt for forgetfulness in pleasure, or be restrained by scruples. But not Elmer. There was no woman he loved, no children he had begot, no religion to comfort him, no conscience to halt him, and no possibility for rest. When he was alone in a room, he would fling himself on a bed to relax, to let the furies die down in him. But just as their black wings ceased whirring within his brain, the windows of the room would suddenly become aflame with the orange blaze that was his own personal hell. And he would be driven to deeper work as an escape.

Elmer was also lucky in that he was alone in his operations. Other builders had been obliged to form partnerships, so limited was their capital. And if they grew, so did their debts grow, which was safe so long as they moved with the upward current of a land and building boom. But the first waves of recession would engulf them all and wash them up on the shore as debris, the flag of the bankers safely nailed to the roofs of the buildings the schemers and toilers had sweated to put up.

But Elmer kept reserves of liquid capital which would be augmented now that revenue was flowing in from his building in the form of rents. He also regarded himself as lucky because his personal needs were so few. He had set aside a one-room apartment on the ground floor which served as an office and home to him. He cared little for food, was indifferent to clothes, needed no amusements and was suspicious of his fellow man.

His sole diversion consisted in tramping through the Bronx. On foot he explored all the undeveloped sections, and in his mind covered them with houses, for he knew that some day booms would spring up in all these districts where land could now be bought cheaply and held for a future rise. The West Farms region, the part lying northwest of Bronx Park, and even in more populous districts there would be small acreages which one could pick up on the settling of an estate or on fore-closure sales. His plan was to buy cautiously, only when other people had to sell or were being sold out, so that he could buy on his own terms. While the active side of him was engaged in putting up apartment houses on the land he had taken from his father, the dreamer side of him speculated upon the site of the next boom. Who knew where it would strike?

One winter a section lay stony and wooded, almost impenetrable, in a little known region of the Bronx. Then a builder discovered it and miraculously, by summer, a development was complete, housing a population greater than that of Cheyenne, Wyoming, or Baton Rouge, Louisiana, its residents already clamoring for a subway station. One day an unfinished apartment house stared blindly through its dark windows at the street below and the next, as if by magic, lights glowed in each window, curtains flew in the breeze, children howled and sang, food steamed, brides moaned in bedrooms, and a bumper crop of babies wet the sidewalks of the Bronx. Naive names, the builders' coats of arms were inscribed in florid script on the marquees, "The Shirley Court," "The Irvidore Arms" or elegantly, "La Parisienne," or simply, "The Ginsberg Annex."

As Elmer had envisioned, the tide of newcomers from the east side was ever-flowing. One Orchard Street tenement. humanely emptied and redistributed so that every human being could scratch himself in comfort, could fill a Bronx block. And a Bronx block moved intact to a western city would have gladdened the population statistics of any Chamber of Commerce.

And Elmer, looking around, coveted a parcel of ground along Jerome Avenue near 168th Street. Upon it was a hog farm operated by a man who himself was greater kin to swine than to humans. The hogs, for the sake of economy, were fed garbage which the owner collected in a big truck daily from the hospitals, restaurants and public institutions of the Bronx. He would bring the garbage back, piled high, a volcano of stink, dump it upon a heap in an avalanche of refuse and turn his pigs loose. They grunted and swilled at this malodorous banquet while he looked on, unmindful of the fumes or the swarm of flies, thinking only of the hams, bacon and pork sausage these hogs would soon become. In summer the stink was unbearable, covering the man, the hut he lived in, the sties and the ground like lava—a crusty stink, layers deep and promising to harden into a permanent covering. Although there were few buildings directly around the farm, a strong breeze could easily permeate the entire neighborhood with the aroma of this porcine haven.

But Elmer coveted this land, first because it was in a direct line of development and would some day be very valuable, and secondly because he knew no competitor would want it, let alone invade it to make an offer. Late one afternoon, while the pigs were reducing a hill of garbage, Elmer came upon the land to talk to the hog raiser. A powerful stink embraced him like a welcome, but the owner was hostile. He was a blubbery clod, dressed in slimy dungarees.

"What do you want?"

"Nothing—just a neighborly call." Elmer extended a cigar, and although he never smoked, he hoped this hulk of a man would, so that the smoke might screen the putrescence.

"Ain't got no neighbors," the man said, lighting the cigar. He looked a mouldering green. "Just a lot of kikes and Eyetalians moving up around here." Elmer was familiar with this kind of cantankerous talk.

"Well,' said Elmer sharply, "I'm a man of few words." He had to be, then. "I may open a restaurant nearby and don't want people kept away by bad smells. Would you be interested in selling this land just to clean it up?"

"I sure would," the man answered gleefully, "but it ain't mine."

Puffing leisurely, he told Elmer that an erratic spinster in Boston owned the land and let him raise pigs on it just to show her contempt for New Yorkers and because she liked the smoked bacon he sent her as her share of the products.

"She'd take a price for it, wouldn't she?" Elmer was hopeful. The hog raiser suddenly stooped, picked up a large stone and hurled it at a porker who had mistaken his mate for a side of garbage.

"No, she's got all the money in the world."

The man tried to discourage Elmer. The land was no good anyway. It was infested with insects and rodents and the stink would remain there for years. But Elmer was persistent and succeeded in getting the names of her New York attorneys before he left.

He had formed a little plan in his mind for securing this land, and all it required was some political assistance.

And for that he knew where to go. Many had told him that the person to see about a favor downtown was Michael Donovan, a west side saloon keeper who was very close to the Tammany chief and could get anything done for a consideration in any part of New York.

A block away, looking back on the parcel of land, he could already shed the memory of its stink. It was on an elevation, and his heart warmed at the thought that after he had acquired it other speculators would marvel at his cunning.

8

Sun rose out of the East River and spread over Battery Park. The light rays tapped on the eyelids of Clarence Dale and he stirred, tearing the damp sheets of newspaper he had spread under him the night before. He rubbed his eyes, yawned, scratched his head and sat up. Always towards the end of summer, with election drawing near, the cops were instructed to let the bums sleep in the waterfront parks unmolested. This was in exchange for the only thing some of them still owned—a vote. As Clarence looked around the bay, the sun lit up the buildings grown together like teeth in the mouth curve of the waterfront. He was stirred by this sight and yet he couldn't help asking himself whether this superb view would yield one doughnut and a cup of coffee.

Quickly he overcame his cynicism, for on this day he was determined to end his period of starvation in New York. The dewy grass felt fresh to his touch, the streets looked less hostile, and an atmosphere of friendship hovered over the park. Even if only the warm emanations from the Gulf Stream were the cause, they lulled him. For the first time in that nightmarish period in which he had bummed, starved, lick-spittled and blistered in New York, he felt the town friendly. Some days are like that. We shed a skin of despair and emerge as trustful as a pampered baby. Yes, as Clarence expanded with this fresh hope in him, he had the feeling that New York regretted a little the pummelling it had given him and was now prepared to make amends. The town was going to show him its better side.

Around him some of the sleepers still snored. As they lay there in cramped and agonized postures, whistling and wheezing at the city through their ugly apertures, this seemed to be their *raison d'etre*—to toss up little sounds into the great discord of the city. The bum nearest him moaned in his sleep through a begrimed mouth and had rolled up one dirty trouser, revealing a vermin-bitten leg with long, infected scratches where the

115

dirty fingernails had sought relief. That leg by itself was the epitome of ugliness and failure. Here was a human being already in the first stages of decomposition, even before death. He had no name, no age, no home, no ties to the protoplasm that spun around him, a sleeper on sod long before he was to be lowered into it—just a diseased leg. Clarence looked at the man and turned his face away, revolted. God, this must not be his destiny.

He stood up, pinched his flesh alive, and moved. There was an exhilaration in his walk. This was his day and he felt transformed. He who had begged from the city, had held his lips up for its drippings, thanked it for its cast-off food, even humbled himself for its free advice—he still remembered vividly what the wizard in clothes had told him in Bryant Park—he was going to master the city.

Clarence walked to the rim of the city. An excursion boat with pennants flying in. the morning breeze crunched water softly. How inviting the water looked. It made him think of the lake outside of Youngstown, the long swims he had enjoyed there, and the girl he had disgraced. That's what had broken his mother's heart, shattered suddenly the entire pattern of the life which had been cut out for him, and had sent him running away. He had a way with girls, but he must be careful. Even when they gave in, they won. And another episode like the first would destroy him forever. Quickly he banished all those uncomfortable creeping-vine thoughts— mustn't think any longer about broken-hearted mother, disillusioned sweetheart and the home he had befouled. He straightened himself for the start of the new day.

He approached a sailor, a husky just off a boat, walking with a jaunty roll. He tried not to look like a beggar, as he stood in his way.

"Listen, sailor, would you lend a guy a dollar? I'm out to get a job to-day. I need that buck bad."

The sailor's lucid blue eyes smiled at him. "Nothin' cheap about you, brother."

"But I'll pay it back—honest I will." He rummaged in his torn pockets and produced the stub of a pencil. "Here, I'll write your name and address down, and I'll send it back to you. It won't be long." All the sincerity he could muster was packed into his plea.

The sailor looked up, intrigued. "Gee, you know how to write and—" he broke into a laugh— "you're a bum just the same." When he had threatened to run away to sea, his father had warned him that unless he acquired an education he'd wind up in the poorhouse. Yet here he was, with four months' pay in his jeans, playing Lord Bountiful to a man who could write and read. Probably a prize scholar. Well, that was one on the old man. This feeling of triumph was worth a dollar.

"As long as you're payin' it back," he grinned, "take this." He handed him a dollar bill. With dark claws, Clarence crumpled the bill in his palm. Its feel against his hand made his heart beat like mad. This was his day. Feverishly he wrote on a piece of paper. "Jerry Moore, care of Seaman's Home, South Street." Fighting back the tears in his eyes, he added, "I'll never forget this."

The jaunty sailor tossed back over his shoulder, "Yeah—and don't forget to take a bath. You stink." And, roaring with laughter, he walked on.

Clarence tramped down Broadway, nearly deserted at such an early morning hour, for the white collar workers, along with their illusion of superiority, were granted an extra hour of sleep. But when he passed the entrance to the Brooklyn Bridge and turned into Park Row, he walked into the first contingents of workers for the vast printing plants and the leather tanneries that gave the little labyrinth behind the Bridge its special smells.

He continued down Park Row to Chatham Square and here stepped into a crummy beanery. In flourishing script, its menu was written on the window in white soap. A complete meal could be eaten here for fifteen cents, in as many minutes. But its effects would last for a month. Only those who for regular fare picked food from the restaurant garbage cans could dine here with relish. The others held their noses and shovelled. Clarence remembered a hamburger steak he had once consumed at such a place. For two days it held his stomach in a wrestler's grip. Well, no use taking any chances now. He bought himself a mug of coffee for two cents and a doughnut for one cent. The change he received from a dollar bill was a fortune in coins. During this time the "L," street car and subway had been disgorging workers, so that now he marched against a stream of toilers which made him all the more eager to join their ranks.

He turned up Division Street looking for a ragpicker's shop where he might pick up a pair of pants to replace the ones he wore, which were ludicrous. He observed a Macy delivery wagon stop in front of a store. The trim uniform of the driver, who jumped off his seat and withdrew a parcel from the rear, filled Clarence with envy. How wonderful it was, how safe, to belong to something solid and respectable merely by virtue of the clothes you wore. All he needed was a suit and a clean shirt and he would be reinstated in the class from which his own folly had exiled him. As he stood there for a moment, he saw a swarthy, ferrety youth walk briskly to the rear of the wagon, extract a large parcel and calmly but awarely move off with it. The professional despatch with which he performed this act branded him as a thief. Clarence knew this game although he had never mustered the nerve to try it. Well, this is my lucky day, he thought as he followed the sneak thief.

Googi walked rapidly for a block with the package under his arm and turned to the right on Catharine Street. What a cinch, he thought, what an easy life.

Clarence, directly behind him, and both out of the danger zone, yelled suddenly, "Drop that bundle, you crook." Googi, startled, caught completely off guard, dropped the package and ran.

Clarence quickly picked it up and ducked into the first tenement. Up four flights of stairs he bounded and on to the roof. Here, behind the chimney, he deftly opened the package and discovered a suit, a beautiful gray flannel suit. But when he tried on the coat, his heart fell, for it was several sizes too small for him. But this was his day for alert thinking. He discarded the tell-tale box, wrapped the suit in a newspaper and came downstairs with it. His pulse beat with fear, but no one was there to arrest him. He made his way back to the Bowery, and walked confidently into a second-hand clothing shop. Necessity made him glib, persuasive. A joke-book Hebrew approached him with a gleam. "Looking for a bargain, gentleman?"

"No, I've got one for you. Look, a wonderful suit, mister. My uncle sent it to me for a present, but he forgot my size." He was talking the lingo of the clothing salesman. "Feel the goods—and it's brand new."

"I don't think if we can use it—but how much do you want for it?"

"Not a nickel—in cash." The dealer's eyes lit up. "I'm making a trade. Look, you keep this beautiful suit—and you give me a second-hand blue suit to fit me, and throw in a pair of shoes and a hat."

Fortunately the dealer, who knew merchandise even better than he knew human nature, coveted this sporty flannel outfit. And Clarence, pounding at this weakness, improved the deal to include a shirt and a necktie.

With his new outfit carefully wrapped in a bundle tight under his arms, he continued down the Bowery. Near Delancey Street a crowd of derelicts stood outside a slave market, reading the want ads written in chalk on a blackboard. "Men wanted."

Men for the Maine woods, for lumber camps, for railroad building—men wanted. Clarence knew all about that gag. "We pay the fare." Any time they pay your fare, it's your turn to be wary. These vast employers would scoop up carloads of these down-and-outers, take them away to isolated regions, work them for twelve-hour-days, feed them impossible food, house them in vermin-infested hovels and, when they had used them sufficiently, would make conditions so intolerable that most of the men fled. In fleeing they forfeited their rights to return fare, so that what little money they had left was spent in getting back to New York. And like figures in an endless nightmare, they would find themselves again, broke and homeless, standing in front of the same blackboard. "Men Wanted."

Clarence passed that up quickly. No manual labor for him. He was going to use his wits and his tongue and his personality in this town. With a jaunty step he walked into the Moler's Barber College on the Bowery, near Rivington Street. Here one could get a shave and haircut free, if one was willing to entrust face and neck to a freshman. These ambitious but murderous Sicilians who sought an escape from the pick and shovel in the aromatic delights of barbering would hack away at a derelict's stubble, nip up little islands of skin, cleave away patches of neck, and send their victims out scarred for life.

But Clarence was wary. For a charge of fifteen cents he avoided the young guitar players and got an upper classman with a beautiful pompadour to shave him and trim his hair. This barber, almost ready for a diploma, leaned lightly on his razor and blew his garlic gently into his patient's face. And then, remembering the parting shot of the sailor, he engaged a tub of water in the rear of the barber shop and there cleansed and soaped himself until his skin sang.

When he emerged, shoes whole, suit pressed, shirt clean, face smooth, hair combed, he lifted his hat and saluted New York through the elevated rails on the Bowery. He had sold himself to the town that day. And now he was out to sell the town.

The main thing in New York is to get a start, to make a dent in the town, to jump off.

They leave the town, too. A thrifty German has saved up four thousand dollars in twenty years. He sells his little cigar store to a syndicate which is buying up corner locations, bids farewell to the wooden Indian out front, and returns to Leipzig with mama. He will buy a small hotel on the Sturmplatz and call it "Der New Yorker." And each year, during the fair, his place will be crowded with the merchants and their families who come from all over the world to see what's new in commerce and pick up bargains. Without stress, he will earn enough to support himself in comfort among his own people in a land which he never really abandoned. After his sojourn in America, his cronies will ask him for stories, he will be regarded as a traveller, an observer, a speaker of foreign languages (ach das Americanisher shprache, you should, August, zome-times zpoken hear it), a citizen with dash and daring and, in short, he will be quite a guy. That's an old age to look forward to. His sons can remain in New York. Let them become Americanized, but he has had enough of tummel and sweating and saving.

A Sicilian slinks back steerage. He came by way of New York and returns through Boston. Who can trace his crime now? He, too, will become a wise man among his people. True, he has not saved much money, but in the little village where he came from a few dollars will go a long way. His faithful wife awaits him and the children are all grown. He will tell tall tales about New York. Would you believe it, there are buildings forty stories high, and there are Americans who bathe every day, and he crosses himself. Perhaps he can wheedle a job from a steamship company to induce Italians to become immigrants. For a consideration he will repeat the fable that the streets of New York are paved with gold. The steamships need passengers and New York needs replacements in the pick and shovel brigade for there are new subways waiting to be built.

And the Poles and the Swedes and the Ukrainians go back. They return to the farms, to the villages, to the towns they came from and they sing a grand chorus, better a peaceful life here than a chance for plenty in that volcano, New York. But they lie. They have come back to die, and even as they lie inert, the clamorous, greedy, terrible city is real in their memories and the peaceful hills among which they live become a mirage. You come to conquer and you leave defeated. You come to conquer and you remain . . . defeated. Yes, they leave the town, too.

But more pour in.

9

Sitting in his library, a whiskey and soda by his side, Eugene Murdock regarded the letter from his son. The foreign stamps, the small, thin script, thrilled him. He tore the flap and spread the letter.

19 May

Dear Father;

Mother was disappointed because you had to change your plans at the last moment about coming over to see us. (But not you, thought Murdock petulantly.) We've been getting along very nicely and Mother is now accustomed to the European milk. I enjoy my school very much and am now able to read books in French and German. I have grown quite tall and have become very friendly with a German boy whose name is Ludwig Baum. (A radical, I suppose, thought Murdock.) He reads all the time and knows a great deal about literature and economics and political history. and is interested in world affairs. How many things I have found out, Father, that I never dreamed existed. He certainly is different from the boys and girls I knew at the Harrington school in New York. We discuss a great many problems and I like to be with him. He has invited me to visit him in Berlin during vacation and Mother may give me permission to do so as she wants to travel through Germany next summer. I hope you'll be able to come over. (But not too soon, muttered Murdock.) Thanks for your presents, but I must ask you not to send me so much spending money, as there really is nothing I want to buy.

Your loving son,
Perry

121

Murdock slapped the letter aside, and again pondered the irony of a son like Perry. He had wanted a roistering, daredevil son, a lad who would sow a few wild oats, get into complications from which he would be extricated by his father. He would have given anything for a cablegram from some American consul urging him to take the first boat to free his son from an entanglement with the foreign police. But instead, Perry gave himself over to discussions. And think of a son who complained because he was receiving too much money from his father! He had hoped the boy would develop a money sense, an awareness of its importance, an ambition to accumulate it some day in mountainous heaps. Instead. he wanted less and less of it. He was still immune to the disease of money.

Murdock left his chair and walked to the large window from which he could look across at the downtown skyline of New York. He stood there, and shook his head. Then he gulped his drink.

Agatha's course had taken definite shape in New York. Clarity to see her life and courage to live it, had come to her, dispersing the mists of doubts, bewilderment and distrust which had enveloped her in her home in Rockport, Vermont. Little wonder her bones had ached for the freedom of the big city; now, breathing deeply, thrusting her arms out forcibly, she marvelled at the puny threads of fear which had so long tied her to a life that had been alien to her. What beauty, what contentment there lay in living the life which God—in her case, a slightly impish God—had designed for her. Fear and restraint faded into the past.

Her drawings were beginning to receive favorable attention from the magazines, and occasionally commercial assignments fell her way. She was economically independent. And her companionship with Sally was both beautiful and satisfying. But she realized that its serenity depended upon how well she nurtured Sally, and how completely she dominated her. With greater clarity than Sally herself, she realized that the vague ambitions which had sent this pretty but mentally insecure girl from Kansas City to New York would have to be dispelled. Luckily, Sally's own laziness, the very vagueness of the methods by which she had planned to rise, were Agatha's strongest allies. Like a great many pretty girls in New York, she was inert, and depended upon a force stronger than herself to move her from place to place. Well, Agatha would see to it that no men moved her Sally.

Studying her own condition in books that could never have been obtained in Rockport, Agatha was fortified with strong arguments. She made Sally frightened of men by depicting all males as beasts, vulgar, hairy animals who would despoil the fruit-like lushness and beauty of Sally, whereas Agatha sought only to preserve and worship it. By making her dependent for food, shelter, clothing and companionship upon the older girl, by surrounding her with tenderness, with firm guidance when her frail mind wavered, Agatha was drawing Sally closer and closer to her, moulding a yielding psyche.

She spoke to Sally as a male lover would, sought to impress her with the far reaches of her ambition. "Some day I'll be a great woman in New York. I'll design stage settings for the theatre. You'll be proud to know me, Sally, proud to be loved by me."

And Agatha was in earnest about a career in the theatre, for she had joined a little art theatre group which had taken over a former stable and converted it into a stage. Here was a centre of excitement and glamour into which she promised to draw Sally, but only on condition that Sally would not become entangled with any of the lecherous, penniless actors, writers and directors who buzzed about the theatre.

And in time Agatha became an important member of the group. She had the strong mind of a male, the directing and executive talent of a long line of maternal ancestors who had ruled their men under the trick of yielding to them, had hoarded, husbanded and built up fortunes and reputations by controlling the work of their men.

So when Sally came to meetings of the group and to its first rehearsals, the importance of Agatha, her Agatha, filled her with awe and pride and her radiance blinded her to the furtive preludes of some of the Bohemians who were far more interested in sex than in art.

Agatha continued to triumph. Yes, in New York she could breathe deeply, relax, thrust her arms out forcibly. She could not only become somebody. She could be herself.

Summer Sunday, mercifully cool. Bert sat upon his fire-escape, easing the hardness of the rusted iron strips by a pillow under his back and another at his head. He leaned back, as in some secluded garden, and held a book up to his eyes.

"As the sun went down over the ridge, beyond the savannah, the whole western sky changed to a delicate rose-colour that had the appearance of rose-coloured smoke blown there by some far-off wind, and left suspended—a thin brilliant veil showing through it the distant sky beyond, blue and ethereal. Flocks of birds, a kind of troupial, were flying past me overhead, flock succeeding flock, on their way to their roosting-place, uttering as they flew a clear, bell-like chirp; and there was something ethereal too in those drops of melodious sound, which fell into my heart like raindrops falling into a pool to mix their fresh heavenly water with the water of earth."

Bert looked up from the book. Around him webbed the rusty tracery of the fire-escapes, the wash-lines strung to poles like webs spun by giant spiders, and below the cracked wooden fence, like withered brushwood that separated the yard of his tenement from the Eldridge Street tenement that backed it. Right and left, the view was unending. Fire-escapes, wash-lines, bleak poles and the undressed back walls of houses.

The approach of a tenement from the street has some lure, some color, as though to brighten the heart before it is swallowed up by the dark corridor. The brass rail on the front steps is polished to a lustre, a few ripening girls cluster in short dresses, laughing and singing, a store-front beckons to customers, a lacy curtain flies at a window like a flag of hope. But the rear of a tenement is just a wall with windows, unvarnished, unpainted, unadorned. The best it can offer to relieve the eye is baby-stained bedding left out to dry, and the remnants of food on the window ledges. I'm showing you my rear end, says the tenement. Like it or lump it.

But Bert, as if he were in some secluded garden where life was gentle and beautiful, read on.

"Far above me, the tender gloom of one such chamber is traversed by a golden shaft of light falling through some break in the upper foliage, giving a strange glory to everything it touches. And in the most open part of that most open space, the shaft reveals a tangle of shining silver threads. . . ."

A strange glow warmed him. The eye on the word, the word on the brain, the glow in the heart. The terrible strength of the printed word, its power to evoke beauty, its crushing weight in sadness, the far distances it traversed, the torment and ecstasy it brought. The word turned the wheel, the riches of the mind, the cruelty of man, the benediction in a phrase, the ultimate sin, the first word, the last word.

Bert read on.

"And then slowly, imperceptibly—for I did not notice the actual movement, so gradual and smooth it was, like the motion of a cloud of mist which changes its form and place, yet to the eye seems not to have moved—she rose to her knees, to her feet, retired, and with face still towards me, and eyes fixed on mine, finally disappeared, going as if she had melted away into the verdure."

Tears came to his eyes and the words danced from the page, but even in their wiggly outlines, he felt for them. Humble and prayerful and devotional. For years, he had been walking through a long, dark corridor, lit up only by words, tapping hopefully on stone walls. And suddenly a door had opened. He had found his love, his life. Not bread was the staff of life, but the word. Willingly, joyously, he surrendered himself, his flesh and his bones and his heart, to be bound in a book, condensed to a page, compressed into one unforgettable phrase, distilled into a single, ecstatic word.

From the kitchen came the pungent odors of meat stewing in the generous juices of onions. Emanations from other open windows, below and above, tangy bubbles from the steaming pots, joined the vapors and ordors that blew along from the far ends of the city, frolicsome smells which blended waterfront spice with cellar stink and brushed the nostrils of the town. Shadows lengthened on a tenement wall, darkening a decaying bunch of radishes on a window-sill, and from the smell of the cooling wind and the color of the patch of sky that hung above his fire-escape, Bert knew that it was sunset over Forsyth Street.

But the halo of the glowing word was drawn around Bert's head. And not the pungent mal-odor of the city smells nor the rusty corrosion of the city poverty could defile him in his securely locked-up richness, his seclusion, his utterly private nobility.

At the end of the dark corridor he had opened the door. Over and over, with fervent lips, he fashioned the word.

Love also came to Joey. Early in the morning, he had taken Isabella to Coney Island, not by the cheap way through Williamsburg, but with an extra fare to Brooklyn Bridge and then on the Smith Street line. Yes, we travel like sports, Bella, and there's nothing too good for Joey's girl. An hour and a half in an open trolley car, jammed to the gunwhales with poppa and mamma and the squealing, slippery kids (try to seat five of them in one row), and sweethearts self-consciously holding hands and the old folks out for a Sundzy airing, all laden with picnic baskets, bundles containing extra diapers, black-nippled milk bottles, sweaters and bathing suits. Joey and Isabella sat quietly at the end of a bench, their bathing suits rolled neatly and tightly strapped in a leather belt and carried at their feet like quiescent dogs on a leash.

The jammed car plowed and clanged its way across the Brooklyn Bridge, leaving behind the Sunday death that falls on lower Broadway, a funereal pall upon City Hall and its neighboring court buildings that moves down, spreading its hush over the legal and financial districts and ends only at the holiday life of Battery Park. Upon the East River a slow tug was bearing two railroad flats, one on each side, like idle wings outspread. Sharp glimpses of crooked streets like old streams that pour into the waterfront and the glowering, furtive Sands Street section under the bridge. They cut across Fulton Street with a view of Borough Hall and the Brooklyn cluster of court buildings (in all the boroughs, the wretched administration of justice went on with costly pomp and intricate ritual), and from the somnolent life of lower class Brooklyn they came to the gaudy parade of cemeteries. The endless cemeteries of Brooklyn, where so many of the city dead lie buried. Catholic cemeteries with ornate tombstones, flamboyantly carved crucifixes, modern improvements on the cross that Jesus bore to Calvary, angels dancing in family plots like performers in a verdant arena. And the Jewish cemeteries, husband and wife huddled close together under caressing stones (sh'mai Yisroel), the wind blowing through the bright nourished grass, the wails of the last prayers, the final wrenching laments as the inert are lowered into the last cave. And the odors of the dead filtering through the foliage of the cemeteries.

But beyond Prospect Park Brooklyn spreads itself, offers space and fragrance to its residents, long stretches without a single house (why, it's like living in the country), and then abruptly the car swings around and deposits you in the jangling clamor of a carousel. Red horses snorting fire run around you as you stretch your cramped feet and murmur "Coney Island."

The sun beats down on a city seeking air and fun and escape. Some have travelled nearly twenty miles in street cars to escape New York.

Timidly Joey took Isabella's arm. The soft touch of her skin shocked him. He had always felt with his knuckles and his clenched fists and rarely with the inside of his hand, his palm, his finger tips. His fingers nuzzled against her arm as walking lightly, he led her across the broad expanse of Surf Avenue. They paused before the newly constructed Municipal bath houses (we do things for the unwashed poor of our city—only ten cents a locker). There were two lines, one for men and the other for women. Joey closed a quarter in her small hand—it was marvellous to give her things—and said, "Your line is shorter, so you'll be foist. Wait for me on de steps." He wanted to use soft, tender words, but he knew none. Wait for me on the steps seemed to sum up everything he had to say. Even to speak to a girl was still a challenge to his masculinity. But it was different speaking to Isabella. And abruptly he looked around with his sullen frown and his clamp of a mouth, looked around at the men waiting in line as if to say, "and I'll sock the foist guy that gets fresh wid my goil."

It was still early and officious attendants disposed of the line readily. A minute to undress and place his clothes in a steel locker, and soon Joey was on the steps leading to the beach. She ran lightly towards him. The shock of Isabella in a bathing suit, supple, young and fresh, the dancer's grace of her tread, choked him. And Isabella, more awakened than Joey, became aware of his perfectly formed body, the sweep of his chest and strength-line of his muscles, the beautiful arc of his calves, the waist just wide enough to support his torso, his effortless movements. They were happy as they clasped hands. Venus and Adonis. And why not, you cynics? Strength bred in the gutter and shop, suppleness acquired in leaping in and out of trucks and eluding gangs and cops, courage trampled in by the mountainous feet of poverty and necessity, the sturdy flower of New York civilization. As for the flower-like beauty and swan-like grace of Isabella, you can only explain it by saying that she had never seen a field of daffodils bending in the wind, or a swan on a shimmering pond.

Joey rushed towards the water, Isabella screaming as he tugged at her hand. She had not enjoyed the privileges of Lepke's "mikvah," and so swimming to her was new experience and water something to be dreaded when it rolled like a sea monster on its back. Joey placed her near the ropes, and, with her eyes upon him, plunged through a wave, ducked and swam out with great release and enjoyment. He wanted to cool himself, steady himself in the water. But he could not remain long away from Isabella. He swam back and, luring her into a depth above her waist, he suggested, "I'll loin you how to swim. Don't be afraid—I'll hold you up."

She paused for a moment and looked at him. Overhead there hung a perfect summer sky. The air was filled with the Sunday cries of released workers. Joey extended his hands. A bathing cap neatly framed her head and upon her face there glistened a few beads from the Atlantic Ocean. Without fear she moved towards him, and Joey, his heart thumping, flexed one arm under her waist. She splashed femininely; a vital wave rolled in; in lifting her up, his wrist brushed against the conical up rising of her firm young breast. A wave thundered through him, and with its force, rising from the dark and terrible grottoes of the ocean, he crushed her to him and kissed her moist, salt lips. He 'held her tight against him, his back to the horizon, standing off the entire Atlantic, while she, a little frightened, nevertheless yielding to his force, until a roaring benediction of water washed over them. Isabella screamed, gasped and sputtered, but Joey, unable to move a muscle of his face, his voice lost, only his heart beating, tenderly floated her in.

They sat on the hot sands, legs touching, staring out into the bobbing ocean, at the impenetrable blue of encircling waters. Joey was silent, but Isabella found words, spun them softly, marvelling that she could arouse such silence in him, frightened by it. Yes, at Coney Island, love came to Joey, a tight band around his heart and tape across his lips.

Refreshed and health-tinted, they left the beach early because Joey wanted to protect Isabella from sunburn. For the after-noon, he bought combination tickets for Luna Park so that they experienced all the thrills and laughs this gaudy labyrinth offered. They had hot dogs at Feltman's and then they returned on the boat. Joey placed two campstools on the upper deck, and they sailed home with their eyes on the moon and the shimmering waters. The songs of returning revellers, the shouts and quarrels of drunkards came to Joey as from a vast distance. Nothing touched him except the tired little girl who sat close to him and soon fell asleep, her head resting against his shoulder. All the way home Joey was silent, the deep serene silence of a man to whom has been revealed one truth, and who feels that truth with great intensity. He was at peace with himself, no complexities, no doubts to plague his mind. He wanted Isabella and the lightweight title and he felt that no power on earth could keep him from attaining both.

At her door he held her face up for a moment. In the bright sunlight or in the dim gaslit hallway it was still beautiful. Her face was a little puffed from sleep, and her drowsy eyes smiled happily.

"Bella—you're my goil." His clipped words were at variance with the deep tenderness he felt. She parted het lips and said, "Yes," softly. "And soon," he continued, "I'll be takin' you to rackets at Stuyvesant Casino." She awakened a little. She longed to dance in a real hall, to a real band. "I'll take you every-wheres wid me." Then, as though to reaffirm it, he repeated, "Bella—you're my goil."

She brushed his cheek lightly with her lips, "Sure, Joey, I'm your girl."

It was his own intensity that got Peter a job in the offices of Seymour Henderson, capitalist and private banker. He had been turned down by twenty-six securities firms in that same building, but something Henderson had glimpsed in the fiery, purposeful eyes of the boy after the accident of his being in the reception room had secured an interview, awakened a spark in the old usurer. That, fortified by a letter of high recommendation from the principal of his public school and the fact that Peter working at six dollars a week would replace a ten dollar a week office boy, got him the job.

From the very beginning Henderson liked Peter, although not enough to move him to generosity. He liked the despatch with which the boy ran errands, his faultless memory for names, places, faces, his quickness with figures, his precise and legible handwriting, and his personal neatness. The lad was clean, sharp, smooth; his movements direct, ordained; his mind and habits organized. He had all the virtues that Henderson could wholeheartedly commend, including the one of working for little money. And he was scrupulously honest. Henderson had tested him with stamps, a sly ordeal through which all of his new employes had to pass. In an office where a great deal of mail goes out daily the temptation to filch a few stamps and sell them at a rebate is one that leads many an under-paid office boy into his first petty larcenies. And such was the special organization of Henderson's business that the larger issues took care of themselves, affording him ample time to count up stamps, compute the time errands took, note who arrived late and all other trivial, unimportant details. Henderson owned a seat on the Stock Exchange but traded only in certain substantial securities. The commissions he earned just paid the interest on his investment in the seat. But it brought him prestige and gave him rights which were very valuable. His big money came from private loans, trebly secured, and his underwriting of ventures in which there was no element of speculation and through which he acquired stock in going concerns.

It took weeks before Peter even dimly grasped the extent of these holdings, but step by step it became clear to him that the man who every Saturday noon gave him an envelope containing six dollars was a fabulous capitalist and many times a millionaire.

And on these six dollars three men lived in their Roosevelt Street flat. Peter, his father, and his grandfather. As time passed, the pain in his father's back become more and more acute and he lay in bed for days at a time, which made any work impossible for him. Upon his parchment-like grand-father fell the cares of the house, the shopping and cooking and cleaning, and also the praying, for the ascetic old believer saw his son slipping into an alien grave, and his grandson moving further and further away from the word of God into the money-changers' market.

At night Peter attended a preparatory school designed to hasten him through enough knowledge to convince a Regents Board that he was eligible to study law. To all of its students this preparatory school was a continuation at night of what the factory was by day—although, paradoxically, it held out the only hope of escape from the shop. Here in a few terms the equivalent of a high school education was ground into the memories of weary students so that they knew just enough to answer the recurring questions on the regents' examinations, provided they didn't fall asleep at their tests from sheer exhaustion. And when enough regents' counts were earned, the student was eligible to enter an institution of higher learning.

Most of Peter's classmates were ambitious immigrants, educated in their European homes, driven to America either by pogroms, starvation, or to elude military service, now temporarily enslaved in factories and seeking the shortest road to the life of a human being. They were preparing for pharmacy, dentistry, medicine and law, the professions which offered the quickest returns and immediate openings.

In spring, with the windows open, the night noises of the throbbing street would rush in. The teacher, himself a slave seeking escape, would plod through his lesson in a low, monotonous drone. In Seward Park across the way blades of grass were beginning to push through the hard, trampled ground. Children playing, girls laughing, trucks rumbling, peddlers shouting, the thin notes of a young fiddler practicing the "Humoresque," and the regular clamorous beat of hearts, lights arid voices on East Broadway filled the classroom. A pallid student with curly hair, just beginning to cough up blood, puzzling over the hypotenuse in a problem in plane geometry (five counts) sat back for a moment, listening to the music of the voices, the gentle caress of the spring air, and dreamed.

"O, to be in Brownsville, now that spring is here."

O, to be in Brownsville on a spring evening to take a chair out in front of the two-family dwelling, to turn your tired face to the winds that blew across from distant Jamaica Bay. Or to wait for your sweetheart, attending an American high school by day as God had ordained, to take her arm and walk up Pitkin Avenue, look into the bright window fronts, nod to friends, pause to exchange a few words. O Lord, for once to be strong enough to keep awake at midnight when sleep pummels the workers into submission, when lovers yearn to be alert and alive. To listen, as you caress a soft hand, to the faint murmurs of a city which subsides for a few hours after its clamors all day, to talk softly with the one you love, perhaps to kiss and quickly compute how and with what means one could take up life in a better apartment, to lay plans for music, books, walks and love. O, to be in Brownsville now that spring is here. To sleep through the nights without coughing, to awake refreshed and cool, to look once into the new day through eyes that are not burning, to hold a cheek to the morning breeze that is not feverish. O, but to live.

A bell clanged and the pallid student moved on to French, a romance language.

The quantity and the intensity of the ambition generated in one evening at this preparatory school was sufficient to equip all the idle sons of all the millionaires of America. And the knowledge that Peter absorbed in several semesters came filtered through this atmosphere of the fierce ambitions of men who were risking tuberculosis, anemia, heart trouble, insanity, men who worked ten and eleven hours by day, studied evenings, and tried to memorize facts far into the night, knowing no rest, no recreation, no surcease throughout all the years of their young manhood, knowing no youth in order that they might live as grown men. Here truly was a lost generation, sacrificed to ambition in a war against the town. And the knowledge that Peter absorbed in this atmosphere had a bitter tang.

But his road lay clear before him. First law, and than finance. Even Henderson stood in awe of the shrewd lawyers who could contrive new financial set-ups, who knew the corporation structures which protected the capitalist from the legislator and the investor.

Yes, Peter knew his road. First law, and then finance.

10

In due time Googi wormed his way into the confidence of Little Rocco. On evenings after a particularly good harvest of petty thefts the leader would even condescend to shoot a game of pool with Googi, and in this gracious mood win back Googi's share of the loot. Or sometimes he would put an arm around his shoulder in the presence of the mob, which stamped the former bootblack as a coming favorite. And now and then Rocco would slyly hint that he had big ideas for Googi's future. And Chick and Monk and Lou the Goneff would gravely nod their heads and agree. One evening when Googi entered the poolroom Little Rocco swung him over with a swift upward jerk of his head, directed him into a corner with his black eyes and there he whispered curt directions to him. Secret instructions. Googi's heart beat wildly. The words that sent him on his first job came to him as in a benediction. "You're through being a punk. From now on—you're one wise gazabo."

Early next morning, Googi stood on line in front of a loft building on Lispenard Street. There were six men ahead of him and four behind, all waiting to apply for the job of elevator operator in this building. Googi was dressed in working clothes which consisted of yellow hightop button shoes with bulldog tips, heavy trousers tightened at the waist with a wide leather belt, a dark blue flannel fireman's shirt, the collar raised high, bound tight around the neck, the points clasped together by a gold-plated safety pin, no necktie, a swagger checked cap-band, a toothpick carelessly pending from his lips.

Now that he had learned how to eat and had put on weight, he looked like a willing worker. And even though his face was sallow, his dark eyes had a lustre born of his new ambition. There was a gay, glamorous life ahead for the tenement rat and even if he had to work occasionally, it was all part of the greater pattern.

The superintendent of the building who was interviewing the applicants was also ambitious. He was trying to run the building for as little money as possible and so all he offered was nine dollars a week for a twelve-hour day, work every other Sunday, with the added chore of sweeping out the halls of the building after the long shift on the elevator. The line melted quickly. No one wanted the job except Googi. Sure, he ate up hard work. Sure, he was the soul of ambition and nine dollars was a lot of dough to an ambitious dago who was careful with his money and had to support a blind mother and a father.

So Googi got the job and the elated superintendent, to prove his gratitude, made him a present of his predecessor's glove, a caked, stinking mitten to protect his hand from cuts and bruises when he unhooked the heavy iron door of the cage. There were no further ceremonies and Googi began his work at once. It was a rickety, worm-eaten eight-story loft building, resounding with the whir of machines, the thunder of presses, the roll of wheels across floors. A noisy, dusty, drafty, stinking structure. But on the fourth floor, behind the sign on the glass door— "Levine Bros.— Silks"—were stored many bolts of silk, precious rising-market silk.

Googi came down to the poolroom that evening exhausted after his first day's work. It was a long time since he had worked so hard, up and down, helping delivery boys with their heavy bundles, and then sweeping eight hallways full of choking lint and dust. But there was a gleam in his eyes as he reported the layout to Little Rocco. He thrilled as he held his attention. The leader was listening to him now. There was a necktie factory on the first floor, a bookbinder on the second, a job printer on the third, and the silk merchant on the fourth. This was where he paused and Little Rocco moistened his lips. But of all the undeserved luck, the fifth floor was vacant and used as a storeroom by a cap manufacturer who occupied the seventh and eighth floors. There was more to tell, but before spilling it, Googi broke into a chuckle, a low, cooing chuckle which had the lining of the gutter in it, the cold of winter and the heat of summer, the hard, defiant, knowing chuckle which held out the hope of escape. "And the boob tells me that I gotta work on Sundays." They both roared at this. It was perfect. "And I tells him sure I'll work on Sunday. Me, I eat up work." Perfect. Sunday was the day.

The superintendent of the building was tickled. The labor turnover on elevator operators had been very great, and usually the best he could get was some doddering failure, some old derelict who burned out in a week.

But this time he had picked a winner, a willing wop who not only sang Sicilian melodies during his twelve-hour shift, but stayed on to give a hand to plagued tenants. Why, on Wednesday he had seen him help the shipping clerk of Levine Bros. carrying bolts of silk from the new shipment. Not just with the small car, but actually help bring them into the loft, count them, assort them, and help pile them on the shelves. Say, here was a worker.

On Saturday the superintendent handed Googi nine dollars and told him, "You can take off tomorrow—but next Sunday you'll have to be on the job." Googi didn't mind. That was just the way Little Rocco had outlined it. You can't pull a trick the very first week, but after you've worked a couple of weeks everyone forgets you're a newcomer and they're calling you by your first name, they're used to your face and nobody gets suspicious.

Sunday was the day. He awoke early, girding himself for conquest. The Sunday pall had fallen on the downtown loft district. The deserted buildings blinked sleepily through their smudgy windows, bewildered at the sepulchral quiet. Here and there an orthodox Jewish firm which closed on Saturday broke the peace with the whir of machines, but in the main the district was under the grey hush of the day of rest.

Googi arrived on schedule. Only the necktie manufacturer put in an appearance. He wanted to look over his figures and determine whether or not it would be profitable for him to go into bankruptcy. On entering he handed Googi a cheap cigar and talked pleasantly to him. Googi sat on his chair out front and greeted the private policeman who patrolled that district for some of the manufacturers. "Nice little guinney," the old uniform thought. Directly after lunch the necktie man left. "Coming back?" asked Googi. "No—I've finished," and they smiled genially to each other, for the business man had decided to file a petition in bankruptcy and save himself the annoyance of paying off his creditors in full.

Googi's heart began to beat wildly. He was alone with the building. He must take his first step. At a quarter after on the hour, the private, cop waddled by and everything must be timed correctly. Well, the job itself wouldn't take fifteen minutes once the preparations were complete. Googi rode himself up to the fifth floor. He hooked the door back and held it agape with his chair. Since no tenant occupied the loft, the loft door was open. Googi entered and walked to the rear window. Opposite him was a blank wall which would shield him from view. He climbed down the fire-escape to the fourth floor. He bound his right hand with a handkerchief and, with the instrument Rocco had given him, cut a window pane. Then he stuck his hand in, opened the lock, and drew up the window. He entered. There were one hundred bolts of silk piled on the shelves. He chuckled as he used their own phone to summon Little Rocco, Chick and Monk, who were waiting with the truck in a Greenwich Avenue garage. Then he opened the door from the inside, went back upstairs through the fire-escape and came down into his elevator cage. Just as he readjusted his chair outside and swung another toothpick into his mouth, the private cop passed. He nodded and went on. "Nice little guinney," he thought, "having himself a well-deserved rest on Sunday."

Five minutes later a truck resembling an American Express car rolled around and pulled up in front of the building. Little Rocco and Monk jumped off, clad in delivery uniforms. With velvety despatch, Googi took them upstairs. Working with expert rapidity, they piled all the bolts into the cage, carried them into the truck. Bolts of silk were made for thieves. They're neither too heavy nor too bulky and they bring a big price, especially on a rising market. Two trips, and the loft was cleaned out. The truck rolled away. Googi promptly rode back to the fourth floor, locked the door from the inside, went up the fire-escape to the fifth, closed that window and let himself down to the street floor again. There was a chuckle in his throat like the song of a poet. He leaned his chair against the wall of the building and dangled his toothpick with high glee. The old uniform passed again, and automatically thought to himself, "Nice little guinney sitting out his Sunday shift."

Excitement beat high in Googi that night, but he obeyed orders. He kept away from the poolroom and went directly home. He could hardly sleep, chuckling to himself all night. So far it was a cinch. But in the morning—well, they'd have a hell of a job proving anything against him.

Early next morning Googi was on the job. The superintendent, who was a few minutes late, smiled contentedly at him. "Was there much doing yesterday?" Googi answered casually. "Nothing at all. Only Mr. Gupson, the necktie man, showed up. That's the only ride I took all day." Workers in the various lofts filled the cage and he took them up and sent them forth to their little dark places at the machines.

At eight o'clock on the tick the shipping clerk of Levine Bros. arrived. A natty young man with a pigeon-pout strut as befitted a coming merchant who soon would be doing a little commission business for himself. They were old friends now. Many's the time the elevator boy helped him empty a small truck of bolts. "How's it coming, wallyo?" "Great," chuckled Googi. He let him off at the fourth floor. The young shipping clerk withdrew a bunch of keys from his pocket and jingled them with an air, for he was a trusted employe.

Googi watched him fit the key into the door. He had a burning curiosity to see his expression after the door opened, but the buzzer registered impatiently. Somebody wanted him downstairs, wanted to go up quickly so that his pay would not be docked. Googi rode down, but he had hardly slid the door open on the landing, when the buzzer complained violently. The little numeral four was hollering "Help, help." It continued to shriek as if to burst into a thousand fragments. "Gee—somebody's in a great rush." He shot up again to the fourth floor and before he could open the door there was a frantic pounding on it with frantic open palms. The shipping clerk was white with fright. "We've been robbed—robbed! They cleaned us out. Every bolt of silk. Police! Police!" He was hysterical now.

Up and down the building the news spread quickly. The superintendent phoned police headquarters and then tried to solve the mystery before their arrival. The necktie man, the printer, the bookbinder, the cap manufacturer all put their heads together and formed a chorus of commiseration. "How did they get in?" "The door was locked—" the shipping clerk was strangling for breath— "but a window-pane was cut out." The superintendent felt it his duty to question Googi. But Googi's answers were rehearsed. "I didn't see nothing. Taking it easy outside. I took the necktie man up and down just one trip—" "Yes that's right," agreed the necktie man— "and I was chewing the rag with the private cop outside all afternoon—you can ask him." One of the Levines arrived and tore his hair when he was told of the disaster. "Max," he glared at the shipping clerk, "you had the keys." The shipping clerk paled and threatened to faint.

Presently two men from headquarters arrived, Detectives Flannagan and Scala. "Now let's begin at the beginning." They questioned everybody and looked for leftover clues and fingerprints. "An inside job," thought Flannagan shrewdly. "Are you insured against theft?" he asked Levine. "Very little—they wouldn't give me much unless I put in a burglar-alarm." He tore his hair. "And silk is going up." An inside job, determined Flannagan, eyeing the shipping clerk and his boss. They simply move the merchandise, collect the insurance and then go into business again.

But Detective Scala, as he hummed an aria from "Pagliacci," thought it might be the wop. There was a gleam of cunning in the over-zealous elevator boy and then again—he wasn't frightened enough. To be sure he told a straight story and he would check up with the private cop on the detail of his greeting him every time he made the rounds. And yet a few socks on that blue-black head with a rubber hose might open that mouth of his. Better to tail him for a couple of days. At best he was a punk fall guy for some real silk thief. Well, he would watch the ferices in town.

For a week Googi wisely went on working as though nothing had happened. Evenings taxed him most, for he was burning with eagerness to go down to Joe's poolroom to get his share of praise and loot from Little Rocco. But he restrained himself as per rigid instructions and instead visited the God's Providence House, a slum settlement on Broome Street, where he indulged in such innocent diversions as checkers and croquinole. And all the information Detective Scala gleaned about Googi pointed to his innocence. So he pocketed his face in a fold of his memory and turned his attention to a new and bigger silk robbery.

But on Saturday night the summons came. Room 609 of the Bangor Hotel on West 47th Street. It was only a second-rate tenderloin hotel catering chiefly to race-track touts, bookies, green goods swindlers and confidence men, vaudeville actors and sporty drummers, but Googi was awed by its splendor and the glitter and life of its lobby. Here were the real swells, stylishly gowned women and nattily dressed men, moving with ease and loud confidence through the uptown life. He rode up in a real elevaror, chuckled inwardly as he compared it with the rusty cage he had been operating, and knocked timidly on the door of 609. The knob was turned cautiously and Monk admitted him. Little Rocco beamed on him.

"Googi—looks like you're gonna be a wise gazabo. Shake." Googi felt the blood warm his cheeks. He hoped they wouldn't laugh at him because he blushed. Praise from Little Rocco. "Sure—he ain't no punk," agreed Monk. "He done the job like an old-timer."

"Sit down." Little Rocco smoothed him into a chair. Then he shot the bolt of the door and drew down the shades. He paused a moment, his eyes smiling. "Like I told you," said Rocco, reaching for a wallet, "there's plenty of easy dough for the wise gazabo." He withdrew a thick wad of money, bills in denominations larger than any Googi had ever seen. Twenties, and fifties and hundreds. "Now, Googi," Rocco clipped his words, "I'm splitting three ways, see. You're as good as me—and I'm as good as you." He adjusted the blazing horseshoe in his necktie. Googi was overwhelmed. "Jeeze, Rocco, you're one white guy." Rocco deftly dealt the bills like cards. "It comes to a thousand apiece, but I'm only giving you five hundred." He pushed over six fifties and ten twenties. "The other five hundred goes into a kick. In case we get into a jam—why, we got money for a mouthpiece and bail. See?" Googi's mouth opened in astonishment. Such wisdom, such foresight, such a leader. The money felt silky in his hands and his eyes smarted with tears. Suddenly the money was swept off the table into pockets and the air cleared. The men rose. Little Rocco, in an amiable voice, said, "Come on with us, Googi. We'll have a little blow-out and tomorrow put you wise on how to dress yourself. You're through being a punk."

In a large rented touring car they drove to an address on West Sixty-third Street and stopped before a brownstone house with all the blinds drawn. Rocco rang the bell, and a middle-aged woman in a kimono opened the door. All three slid into a velvety interior, dimly illumined by rose-tinted lights.

"Hello, tanty," greeted Rocco, "I'm bringing you a cherry," and he pushed Googi forward.

The woman laughed in Rocco's key and tugged playfully at Googi's hair.

"We want a real feed with plenty of wine," ordered Rocco, "and get the big blonde for the little wop." He turned with admiration to Googi. "What a pair of knockers—what a pair. I'm throwing her to you because I went you to have the best."

A wise-eyed mulatto dressed like a hospital nurse led them to a private room upstairs. The men threw off their coats, loosened their collars, Rocco carefully adjusting his diamond stick pin with a safety catch. The girl returned with an ornate ice-bucket and popped a bottle of champagne. Rocco poured three glasses and Googi felt like Alice in Wonderland. "Drink up," ordered Rocco, and Googi gulped down a swallow. "After every big job we have a blow-out." He infected Googi with a tremendous, pulsating love of life. The real uptown life behind drawn window blinds under rose-tinted lights. This is what he had dreamed of. This was the reward.

A steaming roast was brought on and directly behind its aromatic vapors, like figures summoned by a fairy's wand, came the three sirens. They, too, were rose-tinted and clad in lacy, heavily perfumed negligee. Porto Rican women starved and slaved for weeks to provide these hussies with delicate under-things which were put on only to be taken off. Googi could not eat. The blood began to flow thickly towards his throat and he tried to dilute and cool it with wine. Furtively he glanced at the big blonde and at her powerful breasts. Rocco slyly caught his look and, removing a drum-stick from his mouth, laughed, "Some pair of knockers, like I told you."

The blonde put a soft, perfumed arm about him and said wistfully, "So you're the cherry."

There was no use asserting his masculinity here, for even if he had experienced a few furtive back-yard and cellar experiences, this was his first affair with life, the glamorous uptown life under the sheltered rose-tinted lights. Gently, almost maternally, she led him out.

He was plunged into a deep and astonished silence by the sight of her perfect navel.

At two o'clock in the morning the same touring car bore them all down to the Turkish baths on Forsyth Street. Here Googi was steamed and scrubbed, massaged and cleansed. Here he marvelled at a real plunge with clean cold water, utterly different from Lepke's mikvah.

At noon, he awoke, relaxed and refreshed, and ate an ample and leisurely breakfast. The afternoon was devoted to a shopping spree. On Sunday, the stores displayed their finest wares and hummed with activity for that was the one day in the week the workers were free to make their purchases. Googi bought three suits from Witty Brothers on Eldridge Street, the coats silk lined, the trousers fashionably narrow. Then he splurged on a hat and a pair of shoes to match each suit. In the evening, he entrenched himself in a rented room on Tenth Street near Second Avenue, opposite St. Mark's Church where Peter Stuyvesant lies buried.

He sat down in his first rocking chair, looked at the bed which he was to occupy alone, and tried to think clearly. He had spent a remarkable night, had bought a beautiful wardrobe, paid two weeks' rent in advance, and now he had one single twenty dollar bill left and some silver change. He recalled how Little Rocco had urged him on to spend. "Spend big—easy come—easy go," and after all, he wanted to be and live like Little Rocco. But the money had been unreal to him and so was the fact that it was gone.

But there was more money to be had. At the poolroom later on Rocco swung him over with a glance. Gone was the laughter from his voice and he slid his words out carefully. "There's a little job in Bridgeport. The layout is a cinch." Instead of silk, this was woolens.

Googi was thrilled. Travel. What opportunities and luxuries his career brought. The rewards of success and loyalty. Travel in a big car from New York to Bridgeport, eat and drink at the best roadhouses, wear silk-lined clothes and, after each coup, a blow-out.

But even as he thought dreamily of the big blonde, he was chilled with the contact of a piece of metal that Little Rocco slipped into his hand. He looked down at it. An uncontrollable tremor passed over him as he saw for the first time his own hand clasping a gun. Tensely he sped it into his pocket. Now, surely, he was a full-fledged equal.

Rocco caressed his diamond horse-shoe and seemed to be talking with his eyes.

"Googi—you might as well carry a canister." His bright eyes held him hypnotically. "Just in case——"

Bending over the fires in the gas mantle factory, the workers fanned the rumor that a machine had been perfected which could manufacture 20,000 mantles a day. Some scoffed at it; others, like Isidore, hoped it was not true. One worker with a sense of the vivid described it as a huge, iron monster with deft steel fingers and a back that never tired, a diabolical machine which could easily take the place of six men and four girls. The scoffers mocked at it. Nonsense. How could a mechanical device with iron hands shape a fragile mantle which powdered to ashes at the merest touch, blow it into its proper form, hang it on a hook to dry. Absurd. In other countries, in other times, older workers had scoffed at the advent of the machine and had changed their derision to curses and despair. There were far too many ambitious inventors in New York, eyeing everything done by hand as a challenge to their ingenuity.

And then one Saturday morning the boss came in, his face limp, his eyes bewildered. He walked tragically into his little office, forgetting even to blow smoke in the faces of the orthodox workers. He called for the foreman and in sunken tones announced that he was closing the shop. Yes, that diabolical machine actually existed. He had just lost his biggest customer to a rival who had secretly installed it and who, as a result, was able to sell gas mantles at half the cost he could produce them for with human labor. Abruptly he would go out of business. There was no sense in investing capital in a larger machine, especially since all mantles were doomed with the increase of electricity in all new houses. He paused for a moment to comfort himself with this thought. His rival would not profit long, for newer inventions and cheaper electricity would in turn displace him. And anyway, the boss had enough to live on for the rest of his years. As for the workers—well, it was just too bad.

He called his workers together and told each as he handed out a pay envelope that the shop was closing. On Monday, he announced, he would dispose of the machinery and fixtures to a second-hand dealer. The good will was negligible, since the first rival to undersell him could take away his oldest customers. "Good-bye and good luck," he finished, leaving his employees holding their little pay envelopes and staring after him with stunned faces.

The real tragedy in a worker losing his job, is its lack of ritual and melodrama. Often curtly, even casually, he is snipped off from his job. One moment he is part of an industrial process, the next he is outside a dull brick wall. Not like losing an arm, a leg, a fortune, a mother, a child. No sudden wrench of pain, no cry of anguish, no wail of sorrow. He carries his death with him, and even as in death, there is a false, lulling hope of release. When workers, bludgeoned under the thuds of routine, welded to a job, are suddenly turned out, there stirs within them an undying hope that perhaps something better will come of their undesired freedom, a more gracious form of slavery.

But Isidore felt no hope. He was an ageing man in an alien land, familiar only with the path that lay between the shop and its return. He had transferred all his hopes and dreams of achievement to his children. To him, the loss of his job was stark tragedy, undecorated by black, unlit by shrieks, unrelieved by any ritual, made dull by the realization that he was too old to learn a new trade and that it would be very difficult for him to find a new job. He would have to resign himself to peddling, exchange the warm bench in front of the flame for the winter cold of the street, give up the security of the shop for the hazards of the saloons.

In the late afternoon Isidore went to synagogue and returned with the first evening star to tell his family that he was out of a job. His wife said, "God will help," and Joey gruffly advised his father not to worry. Donovan had kept his word with Joey and had transferred him to a soft city job as an apprentice compositor in the Board of Education job printing plant, where he now received ten dollars a week and had a great deal more time for training. And hadn't Donovan always told Joey to bring his problems to him? "You do the fighting—and I'll do the thinking for both of us, my lad."

After supper Joey summoned Bert, and together they walked over to the west side to Donovan's saloon. Donovan greeted him kindly but said, "I never like to see any of my fighters in a saloon."

Joey reminded him of his promise to help whenever he was in trouble and asked him to sign him for a fight. But Donovan shook his head. Ever since that first fight in which Joey had so impressed him he had kept him away from any encounters, merely supervising his training, waiting for him to mature a little longer, until he could carry through a definite campaign for him. "Don't worry, my lad—I'll get your father something to do. Send him around to me—and I'll see you at the gym tomorrow night." Donovan was familiar with such stories. The growth of his power and prestige was due to his ability to get jobs for his faithful voters, to get the husbands off when they committed minor infractions, and arrange bail for the sons when they broke the law.

At dawn the following morning Isidore was up from force of habit. Joey looked at his father as he wound the phylacteries about his arm. How tired and old he had suddenly become. He went over to him and, with what tenderness he could muster, said, "Don't worry, pop. Me manager will get you a soft job. Go back to sleep." Isidore fought back the tears in his eyes. His own son was regarding him as an old, worn out man. "What foolishness, my son. I should go back to sleep? A fine spectacle—me stretched out in the bed like a bridegroom. No—I'll find some work—and without the help of goyim."

11

The idea was to get your foot inside the door. That's what the crew manager had drummed into Clarence's head. And to Clarence, this technique of forcible entry was symbolic of his whole nightmarish year in New York. For a year he had tried to pry open the door of the big town and always it had been slammed in his face. But now it was different. You began by putting your foot inside a small crevice. Later on you tackled the big door.

Get your foot inside the door, give 'em that dimpled smile, and talk a mile a minute. That's the formula for success. Take a street in Bensonhurst. There's a brand new row of two-family houses, like peppermint drops in a box. Everything is fresh; the street has just been opened, sidewalks freshly raised, gas newly piped, electricity wired, and a hole in the ground punched through for the subway stations. Newlyweds and young married folks abandon Williamsburg and Bushwick and Greenpoint to take up life behind a blade of green grass. Yes, take any street in Bensonhurst.

You begin with the first house. You ring the bell. The little lady of the house comes to the door because they can't afford a maid yet. When she goes from Bensonhurst to Ocean Parkway, she'll have a maid. She opens the door and you put your foot in. "Good morning, madam."

Ah, sweet mistress. A young married woman in a mother hubbard and a dust cap over her hair. A few strands escape, bringing to the artless face the faintly beddy morning look. Her plumpish arms are bare and speckled with a healthy color. In a hand distinguished by the wedding band she clutches the broom. "Good morning, madam," and the position is perfect. Foot inside the door and the full dimpled smile. She tries to look hostile, but underneath her suspicious stare there is a gleam of interest. And why not? Clarence is young, tall and handsome. He wears a neat blue serge suit and a clean collar, his face is freshly shaved, and his accent is not

New Yorkese but smacks of the middle-west, which sounds better, even if it isn't.

"Madam, I'm sorry to interrupt you, but I know you'll end by thanking me." An introductory line which he had invented himself and which he kept a secret from the crew manager. And now, a quick plunge into the regular sales talk. "I represent the Zenith Vacuum Cleaner Company, the machine handled by the biggest department store in Brooklyn (local touch). Now, I'm not trying to sell you anything, madam (disarmed you there, my pretty mistress), I merely want to know whether you'll be kind enough to let me demonstrate our latest model vacuum cleaner in your home some day next week. You see, I'm the division demonstrator (big title, that) and I'm just making appointments."

Telling word, appointment, brushing the edge of assignation, with its faint overtones of romance. And as she stands there, clutching the broom, pursing her morning-kissed lips, he goes on. "No doubt you have very expensive rugs in your little home (a note of flattery, there, implying Persian and Chinese rugs instead of the ones woven in the Yonkers factory) and we'd like to demonstrate how you can protect them. There's absolutely no obligation involved—and you don't have to buy a thing, because (again that dimpled smile) I get paid merely for introducing the machine into these fine Brooklyn homes." (A lie but it makes him important, the big handsome introducer of a machine.)

The little appointment book is out and the smile is hypnotic while the pencil is held at attention and the housewife thinks to herself, not a bad looking young man and it costs nothing and anyway, the rugs will get a free cleaning, because those hand cleaners merely take the dirt from one place and put it in another. "Well, all right, if you want to come. Wednesday morning."

And so the appointments are recorded. Three on one side of the street and four on the other. "You're sure to average two sales," the crew manager says. That great law of averages will protect you, even when God fails.

Early Wednesday morning Clarence is driven to his base of operations by the crew manager. He consults his little appointment book and proceeds at once to his first prospect. This woman is really in the market for a cleaner without any monkey shines. She opens the door briskly, admits him with business-like despatch and he plunges into his demonstration. He attaches the plug and the machine leaps to life, the bag fills with wind and the motor whines.

Clarence enjoys his work and his audience. He is like a ventriloquist with a mechanical dummy. As he rolls the sweeper, the convincing words he had so carefully rehearsed fall from his lips. "The brush won't hurt the warp and woof of the most expensive rugs. This sucks up all the grit and sand without breaking off the threads. It adds years of life, and preserves the sanitation of the house."

Masterfully he pelts the woman with arguments, but her mind is made up. She wants one. She buys. Clarence interrupts his demonstration and tries not to look too eager as he rattles the order blank. He places the fountain pen in her hand and she signs. Then she gives him the first payment. Eight dollars. A thrill of triumph surges through him. Those eight dollars are his commission. They belong to him. He thinks of the blistering days when he had nothing to eat, when he was a ragged derelict on a park bench, when his bed was the damp grass or a bleary hallway. What strange power did he tap in himself to make money by pelting people with words, by persuading people to buy? And he had that power within himself, like a religious fervor, locked up throughout all the days and nights of his privations. But now he knew. And it opened for him all the vistas of prayer.

The second woman did not want to buy, but he was just as gracious and eloquent, confident that some day his powers of talk would melt her sales resistance, even as constant prayer ultimately produces rain. The third woman was only mildly interested and postponed a decision until her husband could see the machine demonstrated. Clarence cheerfully made a note of this in his book. Husbands were easy because you mowed down their resistance, not with logic, but with an appeal to chivalry. Are you the kind of a man who permits his wife to toil like a drudge, break her tender back in slavey's work? And the sheepish husband signs. Oh, there were endless arguments, just as there were endless prayers, one to suit every occasion.

The fourth prospect was very special. Clarence straightened his tie and recalled the young housewife with the health-speckled rounded arms and the sweet domestic swing of her hips. He rang the bell and she came to the door with that same look of determined hostility. She pretended that she had quite forgotten about the demonstration and Clarence was thrilled by the mask she had put on for his benefit. Ah there, my pretty housewife, I have come to talk of cabbages and kings and the Zenith vacuum cleaner. His foot is within the door. "But I'm really very busy, what with housework and putting up the dinner," and she tries to look cross. But Clarence is smilingly persistent. Come, come, the demonstration will only take a few minutes of your time and why wear out those fine legs and rounded arms beating rugs and furniture when we can find much better use for them. Clarence has been eating regularly for weeks and when the novelty of a full belly has worn off, other hungers take up their barbaric cry.

He closes the door behind him and removes his hat with a flourish. And he pelts her with gentle words. Cosy little parlor, Mrs. Smith, an adornment to Bensonhurst. "All you do is attach the plug, turn on the switch"—he clutches the rod of the cleaner as though it were part of his anatomy—"and it works. A child can operate it. Here, you take the handle." He bands her soft arm with his electrical fingers, and draws her to the machine. She runs it back and forth and he still clings to her arm, guiding her. There is a pleasant vibration which makes them both tingle, which surges in waves from the socket through the handle into their bodies. She bends over, the provocative curve of a housewife bending over, and asks him a question. He comes from behind her good, mature haunches and answers the question. A little unspoken wish, springing from both, tingles in the air. "Of course it cleans furniture as well as rugs." "Is that so? There is a love seat in our room, plush covered—my husband is a bookkeeper." Sits all day, thinks Clarence, with a pen behind his ears, peering through heavy-lensed glasses at figures. "I can never get the dust off that." "Why, let's go up," invites Clarence, and under his skin, we'll make the demonstration complete. There's nothing like a satisfied customer to recommend another. And so they go upstairs, she leading the way, up a short flight of carpeted stairs, he behind her—the quick view of the den, bathroom, and the bedroom, the room which is intended to come alive only at night. How demure the bed looks with its pink spread and the doll sitting upright at the head. And here is the stubborn love seat that clings to its dirt. Well, we shall see. He attaches a smaller nozzle and plugs in the cleaner. Again the whining as the motes are sucked into the bag. He draws the little housewife closer, "you see how easy it is, Mrs. Smith." Suddenly the words get stuck in his throat and as he presses her to him, she yielding, but murmuring against the tingle in the air, "well, I never, you mustn't, you mustn't," but ever so faintly.

And so Clarence, not quite on schedule, completed his demonstration. His order blank is under her bewildered fingers and his voice pelts her softly. "Mrs. Smith—because you've been so sweet to me, I'm going to do something which is against company orders. I'm going to split my commission with you. All you pay me now is only half of the first install-ment—eight dollars—please."

A major social event on Second Avenue—the annual dance of the Forton Athletic Club at the Stuyvesant Casino, with music by the New-port Serenaders, five apprentice bandsmen who had never been north of Van Cortlandt Park but who knew a classy trade name when they saw one. Directly inside the vestibule, as couples dressed in their ballroom best crowded in, the beefy, jocose special officer, with his badge like a chest protector, barked, "Check your guns at the door," while debutantes on Fifth Avenue at swankier coming-out parties checked their corsets to give their upper-caste breasts freer play.

Joey, nearly eighteen, sullen and proud, gingerly escorted Isabella, now sixteen. She shimmered with excitement, for this was her first grown-up dance in a real ball-room to the music of a professional jazz band, escorted by her "feller." In the crowded ladies' room the girls primped nervously, chattered like aroused birds, strategists of a city forest, plan-ning to crush the last drops of pleasure out of the one free night of the week, planning love and conquest and future. Then, as they linked up with their waiting beaux, they subdued their excitement and walked up the carpeted stairway in a measured tread, their eyes dancing at the first glance of the floor polished like a shimmering pond, their blood leaping at the first call of the music.

> *"I'll be down to get you in a taxi, honey,*
> *Better be ready 'bout half-past eight."*

Flowerlike, Isabella swayed in the current of her excitement. The bleat of the band, the reflection of the floor, the color and perfumes of the girls intoxicated her so that she had to clutch suddenly at Joey's arm, and only the firm clasp of his strong hand steadied her. He drew her to him and they spun out on the floor. He, too, felt an exaltation, holding her close to him with a fierce possessiveness, for he was dancing with his girl at the annual shindig of the old Forton A. C., admission—gents, one dollar, ladies, fifty cents.

Joey was a good dancer, gliding gracefully, rhythmically, but his danc-ing lacked passion. At best, it was one of the minor graces of his life, now that he had begun to fight professionally as his real career. But Isabella's aroused yearnings demanded a partner to whom dancing was life itself, as it was to her. And on the stag line at the annual dance of the Forton A. C. there were such bucks.

Hovering around the rim of the swaying and gliding couples cruised the lynx-eyed sharpshooters, the dance-hall aristocrats, the "spielers." Here was a species of young male that devoted itself exclusively to ballroom dancing. For them dancing was a drug, dancing was all of life. Nothing else existed. Winter, summer, spring and fall, every night, they followed the popular tunes on waxed floors, spinning and turning like dervishes. In recreation centres, settlement houses, summer schools, public dance halls, in the Grand Central Palace, midtown, at Hunts Point Casino, Bronx, at Midland Beach, Staten Island, in the Parisienne, Brooklyn, they danced not with pleasure but with lust, as one takes drugs. They constituted an inner, disdainful fraternity, tall, pallid lancers, clad in narrow high-waisted trousers, narrow suede-top shoes, double-breasted vests, form-fitting coats, a colored shirt with a tightly drawn collar to match, and a strangled necktie. They could not work because nights of constant dancing wore them out so that they had to rest by day. They were exiles from home, pariahs in the midst of workers, and yet they bore themselves with great disdain for their inferiors—those who were not experts in the dance. No achievement mattered alongside of skill in the "Peabody," dexterity in a fast one-step.

Following these "sharpshooters" around in this cycle of dance halls were jazz-crazed girls as madly devoted to them as the girls who follow the fleet. Young girls, sucked into the inner hub of dancing, music and rhythm-crazed girls who were happy only when they were weaving in and out in intricate steps guided by a slightly bored and disdainful "sharp-shooter." These young men and the girls who clung to them so slavishly competed in the dance contests at the various balls and many of the male partners lived by selling the silver loving cups they won.

King of the cruising spielers at the Forton A. C. dance was Murray Burns, a Harlem alumnus, who was not only famous in the dance halls of Bronx, Brooklyn and Manhattan, but who had already appeared professionally in a small Atlantic City cabaret. His dreams, like Isabella's, were also of conquest through the dance. He was tall and cadaverous-looking, with a blanched face the pallor of which was relieved only by his bright eyes and the disdainful slope of his mouth. He wore side-burns but slicked the rest of his brown hair back in a neat sweep. His trousers were a shade narrower than anyone else dared wear them and came just to the edge of his chamois-topped shoes. His shirt was purple, with a stiff purple collar that gripped his neck as if it were in the clutch of an angry cuckold. He moved superiorly, a champion with an admiring coterie, while the dance-crazed girls angled for a turn with him like American debutantes after the Prince of Wales.

Joey knew him vaguely, as one knows by haphazard legend of a local boy who has made good, broken an athletic record, married a wealthy girl, or killed a policeman. But when Isabella saw Burns dance, she felt a quick leap inside her. Here was dancing.

The beat of the music, the intoxication of her own dreams, brought her a beauty that filled Joey with dread. He glowered protectively beside her. When a friend asked her for a dance, Joey clenched his fists instinctively and then abashedly realized that there was a code of etiquette even on Second Avenue which permitted friends to dance with your girl. Fearfully he suddenly realized that men in packs like wolves would hunt Isabella, that he would not always be able to protect her, that keeping her entirely for himself through life was something far more complicated than the simple "You're my goil—I'm your feller" relationship he had hoped it would be. He began to wonder whether he had done wisely in bringing her to the dance.

In the course of the evening, Murray Burns took official cognizance of Isabella. Ordinarily he would have crooked his finger and expected her to run, but one of his retinue warned him. "Take it easy, big-timer, she's Young Samson's goil." And since he dared not risk a punch in the jaw, he went over with an emissary who paved the way with an introduction. "I wanna knock down a friend of mine—Murray Boins—and this is Isabella and Young Samson. I guess you guys hoid of each other." The go-between laughed, then, noticing Joey's expression, grew nervous. Joey glowered, but upon seeing Isabella's face light up he repressed himself. "I'm pleased to meet you."

Isabella primly raised her eyelids and lowered them. Upon the platform, the fiddler was scraping strings and the cornetist blew experimentally into a brass funnel. Isabella raised her eyes again. She could see the invitation to dance forming itself on Murray's lips, and Joey could read acceptance on hers. Joey, dreading the first definite bars of the dance music which would lure her away from his side, tried to console himself with the logic that since he did not care so much for dancing, there was no reason to interfere with Isabella's innocent pleasures. Oh, to be sure, he would see to it that the pleasures were innocent, and the first guy that made a dirty crack or a bum pass would get socked.

Preliminary scrapings and furtive scales suddenly blared into definite music. Burns, faintly mocking, eager despite his veneer of disdain, bowed and parted his arms. "How about this dance?" Isabella looked over for

Joey's approval and he sullenly nodded his head. The claw of Burns encircled her waist and they were off on the floor.

> *"When you wore a tulip, a sweet, yellow tulip,*
> *And I wore a big red rose. . . ."*

Throughout the entire labyrinth of his most intricate and flashy steps Isabella followed with plume-like grace and weight. Drug that it was to him, dancing was sheer joy and release to her, and something of her own ecstasy beat out upon him in recurrent waves so that he became dramatically aware of her. His mockery, his disdainful superiority drained from him, and at the end of the first half of the dance, he permitted himself a note of admiration. "All I've got to say, kid, is—you take the cake. You sure can spiel—and believe me I've tripped the light fantastic with the best." Isabella was flattered and murmured, "Thanks. At first I was a little nervous. You're perfect." But Burns was generous. "You followed me like a ghost and you fit like a glove."

What she liked about him in addition to his amazing grace and sure leadership was that at the first lull in the music he did not suddenly reach for a kerchief, or pant or show signs of exhaustion. Then, as if with sudden inspiration, he said, "Listen, kid—will you be my partner in the contest to-night? I'll shake the kluck who thinks she's tied to me, and you and me will do some real stepping."

The second half of the dance music hurtled across the floor, and he seized her to him in something more than a dancer's embrace. His bony fingers tapped impatiently upon her spine and she became aware of another force in him. "Please—don't," she whispered, pushing him away. "Joey is watching—and he gets awful jealous." Their interest joined in the dance.

Isabella had never been so happy. As she passed the sullen eyes of Joey she felt that she had suddenly grown up. On this very. evening she had walked to womanhood, up a carpeted flight of steps, upon a shimmering dance floor. Two men, each with distinction in his own field, desired her. She could feel Joey's possessive eyes pursuing her and against her smooth cheek Burns spoke. "Kid—you ought to be up on Broadway—and I'm the guy that can put you there. Why, only the other day, my agent—and he books acts for Keith's time—he said to me, 'Murray, if you had a real partner, we could fix up a first class dance-act and I'd get you the booking.' But he says to me, 'For the love of Beejesus—get yourself a girl with class.' And kid, I'm telling you—you sure got class."

Pelting her with dream talk, nourishing the ambitions that used to light up in her eyes when she followed Italian organ-grinders and danced in the streets. As Isabella drank in his talk the last of her childhood disappeared like sand before an incoming tide.

The music rode into its off-key ending like a train off a track and Isabella returned to Joey. He claimed her for the next dance, but his glowering thoughts weighted him and she found him clumsy and burdensome after the nimble Burns. When she asked for permission to enter the contest as the partner of Murray Burns, Joey clenched his teeth. "Why don't he leave you alone?" His anger stiffened him out of step, and suddenly the fear of not being able to dance in the contest brought tears to her eyes. Joey glimpsed them and crushed her to him. The saxophone mocked:

"What do you wanna make those eyes at me for?"

In a choking voice, Joey said, "Gee—Bella—I can't stand seein' you wid another guy. But alaright—stop cryin'. You kin dance wid him—only tell him you're my goil, Bella—remember—you're my goil."

Twenty-five couples entered the contest. The men had numbers pinned to their backs and grinned self-consciously at their partners. But Burns, a veteran winner of many contests, rested against a pillar, one ear cocked for the opening strains. The judges stood on the side-lines, pencil and paper poised importantly. A fox-trot was launched on angles of discord and the dancers swung out. As each couple glided by, a friendly group, their particular claque, broke into a spatter of applause. Once completely around the floor and the judges eliminated the first five, calling out the numbers of the survivors.

Never before had Isabella experienced such thrills. As a newcomer to the ranks of the upper class dancers, she excited comment. But as the chosen partner of the great Murray Burns, she aroused envy. And even the girls had to admit that she was a "natural-born" dancer. No practiced gymnastics here, but a beautiful willowy grace which anticipated the most intricate of steps and executed all with consummate artistry. Presently all but three couples were eliminated and the judges announced a regular dance for all, to be followed by the final round of the contest.

Isabella danced next with Joey, but he knew that she was not thinking of him. Her lithe form quivered in his arms, quivered with excitement for the dance that would follow and not because of any emotion he aroused in her. Her words came to him from a distance, her vision was fixed on a moon behind him, and he realized with a sinking feeling that some fierce ambition of hers had come between them; to keep her to him he would have to bind her with new cords.

A roll of drums, a sudden hush over all, and the announcement of the final round of the contest, with the spokesman holding the silver loving cup aloft. The surviving couples came out like gladiators, their friends crowding around them, narrowing the circle within which they were to perform. Even the music was muted, the angular blare of the fox-trot giving way to the gracious swing of a waltz.

> *"I lost the sunshine and roses,*
> *I lost the heavens so blue. . . ."*

After the first few turns it became evident that Murray Burns and his new partner would win the cup. The others moved like rehearsed clods compared to these two. Burns had abandoned all of his fancy steps, those acrobatic twists that made him the ballroom virtuoso, and simply surrendered himself to the caressing waltz music, the rhythmic flow of movement from his possessed partner. Isabella danced as in a trance. Although she could not hear the words of encouragement that Burns whispered to her, she was dramatically aware of his bony fingers tapping weirdly yet compellingly on her spine.

> *"I lost the gladness that turned into sadness*
> *When I lost you."*

The music died out, but into the enchanted silence there poured a burst of applause. This became deafening when the judges with a quick unanimity presented the cup to Isabella. Burns gallantly relinquished any claims to it, and with even courtlier grace returned her to Joey. "Thanks a million," he said coolly. "Thanks." Then he disappeared among his cohorts.

But a new queen of the dance had been enthroned.

The revellers poured out of Stuyvesant Casino and joined the Saturday night throng on Second Avenue. The street was brightly illumined and alive with gay promenaders to whom the lateness of the hour meant nothing, because on Sunday they could sleep late. The gourmets went to Nikolaus' for a steak and French fried potatoes and the crisp onions for which the place was famous, while the others poured into Elfenbein's, where the coffee and cheese cake could not be equalled in all New York.

Joey, proud, despite his fears, led Isabella to a table at Elfenbein's, where she set up the silver loving cup protected by its cloth pouch. At other tables a whispering set up as they pointed her out as the winner of the contest. Isabella had never experienced such triumph and now, relaxing, she flavored it to the full and found it exquisite to the taste, in full accord with all she wanted from life. Her regard for Joey and his love for her, became minor notes. Her life belonged to a shimmering floor, her heartbeats to the beat of a band.

"You ain't touched your cake," said Joey, pointing to the cheese cake and coffee he had ordered for both.

"I guess I can't eat," smiled Isabella. "I'm too excited—too happy." She reached over and touched his hand. "Thanks, Joey, I sure had one swell time."

"I know you did," he said, sipping his coffee. "But you can't be dancin' all the time."

Isabella looked up at him, her eyes suddenly grave. "You don't know me—if you say that, Joey. I can—all the time. I just love to dance."

"But I mean—" He looked at her so sombrely that Isabella had to laugh.

"I know what you mean, Joey."

They walked home, down the illumined length of Second Avenue, left on Houston Street, south again, into the gloomier cavern of Forsyth Street, and into the hallway of their home.

At her door, Joey suddenly seized her and kissed her full on the lips. Her lips clung to his and she felt a great wave of tenderness for him, but even as he muttered fiercely, "You're my goil—Bella," she recalled the bony tapping on her spine and pressed close to her side a little purse in which reposed a slip of paper with the telephone number of Murray Burns.

Joey clutched a stranger to him. Isabella had already been ravished by the gargoyle of the dance.

12

For those readers who still delight in statistics: In 1914, the underground population of New York, not counting the fecund fish in the Aquarium, was one billion rats and mice, thirty-two thousand subway guards and scavengers along the subterranean tracks, who with their long forks pronged the rails like minor devils, ten thousand rag-pickers, junk dealers, shoemakers, pool-room keepers and janitors who spent their lives in basements—and omitting, of course, the uncomputable dead in all the cemeteries who were trying to rise to the surface. The overhead population consisted of the few pioneer dwellers in penthouses, the handful of bird fanciers who still flew pigeons, one million sparrows and other birds in the trees, and the paralyzed and elephantiasic who could only look out of upper story windows on the street life below. But the heavy flow of life, the cream and soot, the blood and the muck was in the vast middle layer that lived on the ground. Nearly eight millions. Whew!

Eugene Murdock re-read the letter from his son.

Dear Father:

> In your last letter you ask me what I intend to do with my future. Believe me, father, I have given it a great deal of thought and am very happy that at last I can tell you. I have decided to become a humanitarian, to serve my fellow man, to do all I can to wipe out the misery of the world. You remember my writing you that my dearest friend in school is a German student, called Ludwig Baum, whose father is an idealist and a doctor. It is to Ludwig that I can be grateful for having shown me the light. Together, we have read Karl Marx and Ferdinand Lassalle and have decided that the greatest evil in the world is the exploitation of the workers by the ruling class. We shall devote our lives to bring about a new order: "The Millennium."

154

Murdock crumpled the letter in his hand. What was this prattle about Karl Marx and the millennium? He remembered them vaguely as phrases he had seen in a Socialist paper left in the subway. What had happened to his son abroad? This foreign education had increased the gulf between them instead of bringing them closer together. And why the devil did he have to worry about uplifting the masses when he was planning to fix up a nice berth for him in the office of Seymour Henderson? He wanted him to be trained for the career of an exploiter. Vehemently he cursed his wife and the son she had borne him. my, the damn fool talked like a crack-brained idealist or a missionary on a spree of conversion. He would cable her in the morning to bring him back. He had a reasonable excuse in that the threat of war in Europe made it unsafe for Americans to remain there. And when he had him alone once more, just father and son, face to face, he would try to beat some common sense into him.

In the meantime, this dilemma called for an antidote, both for his loneliness and for his bitter disappointment. He poured himself four fingers of Scotch and went over to the phone. Polly, round as a Kewpie and soft as pillows, would be waiting.

Elmer Hicks, who was nauseated by liquor fumes and to whom tobacco smoke was abhorrent, had to endure both as he cut a path across the sawdust floor of Donovan's saloon into the rear room which still served as his office. Donovan, who expected him, shook hands and waved him to a chair. "What'll you have?" he asked genially, measuring his man.

"Nothing for me, thanks—I can't stand the smell of liquor, not even beer." Hicks moistened his lips. "Now—to get down to business."

But Donovan forestalled any long recital. "I know what you're after—Goldsmith told me—and I've figured out a way to put it through. Of course, I have to cut in a Bronx district leader."

"What will it cost?"

"I'll know better after I've had a squint at the piece of ground." He smiled at him shrewdly. Then he rose from his chair. "Come—let's hop into my car."

They drove through squalid, shanty-town Tenth Avenue into West End Avenue, which from 60th to 70th Street crawls like an ugly caterpillar, giving no clue to the beautiful butterfly it hatches into above 71st Street. Merely the width of a gutter divides bleak poverty from showy, expansive wealth, separates teamsters, longshoremen and truck drivers, from millionaires. Donovan, who responded to every stone in the town, marvelled at the dramatic, sudden contrasts which characterized the city.

Park Avenue from 34th to 96th Street rears itself proudly as the barricades of the rich; but suddenly, as it crosses 97th Street, it dips into eyesore filth and poverty. Open markets, pushcarts, refuse heaped high, the hot summer cries of children and peddlers exiled to gutters, Negroes, Italians, impoverished Jews—all stepchildren of upper Park Avenue. The same is true of stately Fifth Avenue. Abruptly it ceases to face Central Park, surrenders its aristocracy above 110th Street and permits itself to be befouled by Cubans, Negroes, Porto Ricans, poor Jews and Italians. Fifty-Ninth Street, as Central Park South, from Fifth Avenue to Broadway, is proud and tall and elegant, even boasting its own beautiful skyline to those who travel south through the park or down Fifth Avenue. But across Columbus Circle, Fifty-Ninth Street gives up its caste, shelters Negroes and shanty Irish, grows ragged beyond De Witt Clinton High School and peters out with a down-at-the-heel look into Death Avenue. At Sutton Place, on the East River, a hair's breadth or a million dollars separates the cold-water charity cases from the duplex and pent-house dwellers. The Grand Concourse above 163rd separates the upper bourgeois from the ranks of the struggles. But in Manhattan the contrasts are even more sudden. Seventeenth, Eighteenth and Nineteenth Streets, from the East River, bear on their scarred bosoms the laments and offal of the poor, but suddenly, upon crossing Third Avenue, they take on an exclusive splendor which mounts as they ray into Gramercy Park. And in Brooklyn the pinch-penny, backwoods hunger of Greenpoint, the brutal exile from civilization of those desperately poor who from Kent Avenue can gaze across the narrowest margin of the East River and with yearning hands almost touch the encrusted, gold-splintery skyline of downtown New York, even as they lack the fare to cross the bridge. The stink of the insect havens around Wallabout Market, drawn thin through the decaying, enshrubbed poverty of Vanderbilt Avenue, which, with parallel lanes, spoke into the lush, fragrant, expansive dwellings of the Prospect Park region.

An amazing town that drove its course, letting each man wrest what he could, and dropping its rewards at his feet wherever he stood. A town that laughed at design, mocked at symmetry, concealed neither its running sores nor its tiaras, a town that pummelled its course from river to river, from East New York to Van Cortlandt Park, dropping excrement where it pleased, primping as it ran, but never stopping, never hiding.

Presently Donovan crossed the 155th Street Bridge leading him from the west to the east side of town and approached the vicinity in which was located the parcel of ground that Elmer coveted. He had felt him out on the ride, caught something of his cunning, his anxiety, his lust for land; and he had already determined upon a course of action. As he approached the stink of the hog farm, Donovan couldn't help but admire the aggressive spirit of Hicks. "This is how I size up the situation, Mr. Hicks. I guess I can get that piece of land for you. But," he paused deliberately, "it will take five thousand to grease the proper parties."

Elmer winced. "Five thousand," he repeated, as though he were spitting a tooth out. "It might be cheaper to buy it. They must have a price. Every man has."

Donovan chuckled shrewdly. "If you could have bought it—you would have done so in the first place. Say, I know my business. I'm like a professor. People don't come to me until they've tried all the home remedies and all the neighborhood doctors."

"But five thousand——"

"Take it or leave it."

They were quite close to the parcel of land and the overpowering stench from the garbage at which the pigs fed assailed the nostrils of Donovan. He quickly drove on beyond, although Hicks asked him to stop. When the stink abated, he stopped and turned to Hicks. "If I'd known about this terrible stink I'd of charged you more." Then, regarding him with genuine admiration, "You'll get somewhere in this man's town. Anybody who could smell money under that pile of manure is a genius."

On the way back they stopped at the Hicks Arms to sign a preliminary agreement. And Donovan, who enjoyed having one of his interests nourish another, exacted a little more from Elmer. "And one more favor, Mr. Hicks, considering all that I'll have to do for you, throw in an apartment for six months or so, rent free. I manage a young prize-fighter whose old man is out of work—and they got no place to live. You'll be taking a hump off my back—and I'll make it up to you. Anyway, I want to get the kid off the east side. And say, when Young Samson is champ, won't you be proud to have the lad for a tenant!" Hicks offered no objection. He hated to give anything away, but he was dealing with a sharp trader. Besides, he would need Donovan often. And once the bargain was made, he felt confident that Donovan would fulfill his end.

The plan devised by Hicks and augmented by Donovan was an ingenious one. He had tried without success to interest the lawyers who represented the stubborn New England crone in a sale of the land. Their indifference had its roots in a sound parasitical reason. As long as their fanatical client owned the land, they could charge her an annual fee for managing the property. As soon as she sold it, their revenue was cut off. The thing for Hicks to do was to force a sale.

The first step Hicks took on the advice and with the useful coöperation of Donovan was to enlist the aid of the headmaster of a parochial school, located a few blocks from the land. Father Sweeney, who had been contemplating some action for months, was glad to express his indignation in a written complaint. The pig sty was a distinct menace to his pupils, to say nothing of being a ribald distraction. This letter Donovan brought to the Health Commissioner, with instructions from City Hall to act quickly. And the Health Commissioner, assured that he was acting for the public weal, dictated a letter in his most official style.

"According to Father Sweeney," he wrote to the attorneys for the land, "when the wind blows from the northeast, the odors offend the pupils in the Sacred Rosary Parochial School and seriously endanger their health, in addition to interfering with their studies. There have also been numerous complaints from families in the immediate vicinity.

"In such matters we must take the broader view and discover whether the community has so developed in this region that the existence of such a farm is detrimental to the public welfare and must be declared a nuisance.

"Therefore if my probe shows that this hog farm is not conducive to public welfare, I shall be compelled to order its removal and begin condemnation proceedings."

The next step was to entice the editorial interest of the local newspaper to a condition that jeopardized the health and nostrils of their readers. A reporter was at once despatched to collect the views of those who lived within range of the pigs and this resulted in several columns of verbal indignation, to say nothing of some excellent feature stories written by excellent newspapermen temporarily marooned in the Bronx.

By this time the attorneys for the crusty dame from Boston were ready to sell, and Elmer dallied only to bring the price down so that the seller would bear the item of the five thousand dollars he had been obliged to pay Donovan.

And, armed with the newspaper articles, the threats of condemnation, the official disdain for the befouled land, Elmer sought out the owners of adjoining parcels, convinced them that this campaign would depress prices in the entire neighborhood since it would always be identified with a pig-sty, and secured choice options for large chunks of ground.

Within a month, the deed was signed and the transfer made. On the morning Elmer Hicks became the official, recorded owner, he strode upon the hog farm and notified the swineherd that his pigs' paradise was at an end. The malodorous clod scratched his itchy head and his jaw dropped in stupefied wonderment. "What d'ye know about that?" Then he burst out laughing. "Where will the old woman get her ham now?" Elmer brushed aside his question and gave him an extra two weeks' work in which to get rid of the hogs at market prices (proceeds to go to boss Hicks), instructed him to burn all the shanties and sties on the ground, clean up the debris and deodorize the land.

"What are you aiming to do?" asked the swineherd.

"I'm going to build," shouted Elmer. "This is where the next Bronx boom begins. In Queens they started in a swamp. I'll go them one better. I'll begin on a pig-sty. But watch it boom."

The clod scratched his head.

An Irish subway guard who worked seven days a week and lived with his family on Second Avenue and 93rd Street began to wonder whether he would ever feel the sunshine on his face. All day long he burrowed underground, opening doors, shutting doors, calling out the stations. And at night when he returned it was already dark. On the long summer days he would come home at twilight, but the limbs of the "L" pillars, the railroad ties and tracks outside his windows, and the constantly passing trains obscured the dying sun so that only shadows, memories of sunlight, darkened his cheeks. He used to shovel corned beef and cabbage into his mouth, and wonder whether he would ever feel the warm sunshine upon his face.

13

Detective Scala, tunefully humming "Una Furtiva Lagrima," walked through the streets of New York, looking for what he affectionately termed "my boys." This family of his included weepy-faced grannies who panhandled, breezy confidence men, granite-jawed mugs with heads like totem poles, subway latrine degenerates, angel-faced pickpockets—in fact all the portraits he had been instrumental in sending to the Rogues' Gallery. But to him, and with some degree of stern affection, they were "my boys." He had one of those rare memories that sucked in through one glance the salient lines and colors of a face and froze them in some photographic cell of his brain. There was nothing melodramatic about his pursuits, none of the cops-and-robbers attitude of the lurid melodramas. He hummed as he walked and he mocked as he hunted, greeting a familiar face now squirming a little, "So you're back in circulation? Well—get yourself a job. Keep on the up-and-up and they'll never shave your head. And don't forget—keep your mitts in your own pockets." Scala would laugh and move on. Never an attempt to shake down an ex-convict or to hound him until he was forced to pull a second job. Just a piece of advice, a chuckle—and he moved on. But he never forgot a face.

And so, meandering along West Twenty-ninth Street one afternoon in a neighborhood given over to the fur industry by day and the night life of the Greeks after dark, he caught a glimpse of Googi helping a shipping clerk load several cases of silver foxes from a truck into a freight elevator. "Hard-working dago," Scala mused, "but it must agree with him because he's put on weight. . . . Just for the hell of it, I sticks around," he hummed, trying to make it fit "Una Furtiva Lagrima."

He took note of the number of the street, the surroundings, the flow of traffic, and hung around until after six, when Googi came out clad in dirty work clothes. Then he tailed him back to a rooming house on Tenth Street near Second Avenue, one of a row of brownstone houses with broad steps and spacious windows and conspicuous in the vicinity because they were well-kept. Waiting on the opposite side of the street, Scala computed that the rent, even for a hall-bedroom in a house of this kind, must be at least five dollars a week. "But if I knows my Googi," he hummed to himself, "no hall-bedroom for him."

At that moment a light sprang up in the front corner room and Scala chuckled. "The bridal-suite for the dago. Nothing cheap about him." He waited patiently for nearly an hour, and then Googi emerged, thoroughly bathed and shaved, nattily attired in a blue serge pin-stripe suit, razor edge on the trousers, a silk shirt, Borsalino hat, and the jaunty step of an uptown sport. "He's going to masquerade," hummed Scala and waited until the smart click of Googi's heels faded from the block.

Then, leisurely, he crossed the street and rang the front doorbell. A plump, pink-cheeked blonde in her late thirties opened the door and admitted him into a carpeted vestibule. "Excuse me, madam," she retreated a step and he gave her a winning smile, "I'm thinking of moving and I'm looking around for a nice room. Something cozy in this neighborhood."

"You won't like what I got," she said wearily, "all that's left is only a hall bedroom."

"You can't tell," Scala Italian-smiled at her, "shall we have a look-see?" He felt very playful as he waved her up the steps, humming low to himself. She showed him a dingy cell, and he agreed it was too small, too dark. But on the first floor landing, he ventured, "I bet those front corner rooms are swell."

"Oh yes," she agreed, "I get eleven dollars a week for them—and they're all taken."

"And they must be worth it, too," smiled Scala. "Could you show me one—just in case somebody moves. I'd pay that much for a nice cozy room. Sure I would." He edged her gently towards Googi's room.

"I'll see if the gentleman is in." She knocked twice. "You know how it is—roomers don't like to be disturbed." Receiving no answer, she withdrew her pass key and opened the door. Detective Scala looked inside with those photographic eyes. Googi had left the door of his clothes-closet open, revealing six beautiful suits on hangers, and a dozen pairs of shoes.

"Looks like you got a rich widower living here," he murmured.

"No, he's a young Italian, an electrician, and he must be a wiz at his trade because he makes lots of money."

Scala rubbed his chin and hummed. "You're right. It's a wonderful trade. Sometimes I wish I had taken it up. Well, thanks a lot—madam—and I'll come back soon and try again." But on the way home he abandoned the "Elixir of Love" and switched jubilantly to "Habanera."

Googi, with a springy step, walked down Second Avenue, turned left into Forsyth Street, crossed Broome, and entered Sammy's, a restaurant already noted for the excellence of its food. He had become quite an adept in eating (atoning for the lost, hungry years), and he demanded a juicy inch-and-a-half-thick steak with crisp fried potatoes. While he waited for it he discussed big business deals with Little Rocco, Chick, Lou and other members of his particular fraternity. What added zest to their low-voiced discussions was that at other tables, discreetly distanced of course, judges, assistant district attorneys and fancy mouthpieces also ate thick steaks and discussed big business deals, and all the deals became curiously linked in this particular skein of city life.

Between unhurried mouthfuls of the luscious porterhouse steak Googi expelled little details of information. The men at his table spoke low and tried to listen without intensity. "What I'm saying," he gnawed at a bone, scissoring the meat off, "is that it won't be no cinch." He blotted his lips with a napkin. "The whole sixth floor is wired with burglar alarms—all except the front windows. And if you show me how to get up to them— I'll kiss your tochas." Googi's vocabulary had also expanded.

Little Rocco looked annoyed. "How about the cops?"

"Same old routine—every hour on the hour—but I'm telling you, you can't get in from the street. And the super locks the steel door himself every night. I say forget it."

Little Rocco's candy-drop eyes suddenly flashed anger. "Why don't you put a sponge in your mouth?" He didn't like to have Googi give advice. "Let me do the figuring!" and then, relenting, "—while you do the eating." They all exploded in laughter and that broke the tension. Googi dipped a potato pencil in ketchup and wrote on his palate.

"How about the place next door?" soft-questioned Rocco. Googi hurdled a few words across a mouthful of steak, but abandoned the effort to speak, and chewed vigorously while they all watched him, impatiently, waiting on his words. "There's a small loft for rent—forty bucks a month."

Rocco's eyes lit up again. "Now that's what I wanna hear. You chew the rag and chew the rag and at last you spit somethin' out." Whittling his voice to a sharp whisper, "How much stuff you figure they got there?"

Googi paused. "Fifty thousand—mostly silver foxes and seals." Chick whistled. "But the shipping clerk told me—him and me is friends—there's a truckload coming on Thursday. So that should bring it up to more. Maybe double."

"Oke," said Rocco. "I think Friday. Yes—Friday night looks good." Then brightening over at Googi he grinned, "Is that ketchup on your tie—or a ruby?"

There was nothing dramatic about Detective Scala. He went about the town humming arias from operas, pinning his "boys" up against walls, building fronts, the backs of waiting taxis, anywhere he met them—after conviction—telling them to keep their noses clean, chuckling, walking away. But his pursuit was dogged and thorough, and if he lost sight of his quarry, he never tore his hair, confident that sooner or later the missing cork would bob up again in the New York current.

The following day at a quarter to twelve he meandered down to 29th Street, waited until Googi in his ugly duckling clothes had gone out to lunch, and then crossed over to have a little chat with the superintendent. Could a business man rent a loft, was his question. The super shook his head. Not in this building, knock on wood, hell no, every inch of space was at a premium because the building was so well protected against burglary and fire. Why, one of the largest wholesale fur dealers in New York had the entire sixth floor. So Scala tried to look disappointed and returned to his vigil.

Late that afternoon Little Rocco rented a small loft on the top floor of the adjoining building, and had the sign painter print "Superior Fur Co., Inc., Commission Merchants" on the door. "We handle goods for other dealers," he explained to the renting agent. "The money is quicker and there's no headaches." They moved in some second-hand desks and chairs and in the evening went home like tired business men.

On Friday Rocco, Chick and Lou the Goneff came to work in the morning carrying a couple of handbags, not too heavily laden. They might have been bosses planning to leave on a week-end directly from the office after the week's turmoil. They examined again the contents of the handbags, and then Rocco made a brief excursion up one flight of stairs to test the door to the roof. He tried its lock and hinges and when he was satisfied with it, he returned and all three went down for lunch. They came back separately, between the hours of three and four-thirty, one of them carrying food supplies in a bag, and then they sat down to smoke and wait.

In the adjoining building Googi went about his duties with a military snap, exchanging wise-crack for jibe, but making himself particularly helpful to the shipping clerk for the Hudson's Bay Fur Company, the large firm that occupied the entire sixth floor. A little before six-thirty, when he was through for the day, he said to the superintendent whom he let off on the fourth floor, "Guess I'll knock off for the day. My noodle's dizzy from riding up and down. I'll leave the cage downstairs for you."

"Okay keed," smiled the super, "see you in the morning." Great little worker, the dago. Too bad there was nothing to which you could promote an elevator operator. Well, maybe give him a two-dollar raise on Christmas. Two dollars would be a small fortune to Googi.

Googi rode the lift down to the street level, propped the cage door open with a chair. Then, instead of going out into the street, he went back into the hallway; opening the big steel door, he walked upstairs. He hid himself in the lavatory. Presently he heard the superintendent's footsteps on his way down, then the deafening slam of the steel door and the click in the lock as it was shut for the night. Well, he was locked in all right. Exactly what he wanted. Soon everyone would be out of the building and the power shut off even for the elevator. On tiptoes, he walked up to the sixth floor; in a vestibule from which a short stairway led to the roof he sat down on some steps. He withdrew a dollar Ingersoll from his pocket and kept staring at it. He would have to wait until both hands pointed to twelve. Nearly five hours of ticking, right in his palm.

The hours passed slowly. Standing at a discreet distance from the window in the hallway, Googi could see the life of the street ebb and die. After seven there was the last raucous clamor of the late traffic as trucks and delivery wagons thundered by on long night trips. Following them came the sleek winking of the bosses' cars, glistening conspirators carrying cloak and suit models and pert stenographers off to road-houses with the wives waiting at home. Last in the parade were the tired overtime workers, shuffling figures in grey against a relaxed street.

Googi waited. The watch ticked in his palm and lights glistened in all the first floor Greek restaurants. Googi grew hungry despite his tension and began to gnaw on a sandwich. He munched and responded to the pump of his blood. Minutes might drag their weight across the hypnotic clock, but underneath there was a swift elation. For after this job he would definitely be in the big money. His split alone would run to ten thousand. With a bankroll like that he could follow the horses around the tropical watering places and carry a succulent blonde on the side.

He honeyed himself in sweet dreams, big winnings at the track and crap tables, amorous triumphs, rise in power and prestige. Googi—a sleek, beautifully groomed wise gazabo at the terminus of a long road, the beginning of which was a bootblack on bended knee. Finally the watch ticked both hands to a single dark line pointing to twelve. At midnight, Googi softly climbed up the few steps, softly opened the door to the roof and walked out. The soft light of the sky, the glow of the city, thrilled him. The outlines of chimneys, water-tanks and turrets looked almost human. The low chuckle started in his throat as he stood against the sky, his New York sky, ready for conquest.

Presently the heads of Little Rocco, Chick and Lou appeared as they climbed over the adjoining roof. The roof covering had warped and wrinkled so that even though they walked on tiptoes, their tread created loud reverberations. But they worked with silent speed. Little Rocco unravelled yards of heavy rope, tied a noose securely around Googi's waist and the other end around the chimney.

The plan was to lower Googi from the roof to the sixth floor, where he was to cut deftly a couple of window-panes (make sure the glass falls inside). Then Googi was to fill the dark grey sacks they had given him with all the finished furs in the place. Silver foxes, red foxes, mink, sable, ermine and seal coats. The full bags would be hoisted up to the roof by a second rope to be fastened securely around each bag. When the loft was cleaned out, Googi would be lifted back to the roof. All of them would carry the loot into the office they had rented in the adjoining building. Then all four would wait for morning. At a quarter to eight, Googi would leave and report for work next door as usual. The others would lock up the furs over the weekend and move the stuff out on Monday as regular merchandise. As usual, Googi would go on working every day for at least a week, which would allow ample time to fence the furs; and then, when he got the summons, the pay-off would take place.

As the rope tightened under Googi's arm-pits, he felt a wave of admiration for Little Rocco. You had to hand it to the little leader. Even when a job looked impossible, he found a way to crack it. No wonder Googi had no fears as he lowered himself over the edge of the roof, while his three confederates let the rope out slowly. It was thrilling to be dropped off the edge of a roof—right into a fortune.

Waiting below in the shadow of a hallway on the opposite side of the street stood the patient Scala. Unhurried, undramatic, he hummed an operatic air while his partner Flannagan scowled. "Correspondence school de-tek-ative," growled Flannagan and Scala replied, opera fashion, "Vesti lajuba——"

Behind both stood the superintendent of the building clutching the key to the steel door in his moist palm, and wondering why they had routed him from a warm dinner.

At a quarter after twelve Scala suddenly shed his casualness, clamped his lips on a high note, and stiffened. Craning his neck, peering high up with eyes that penetrated the woolly darkness, he could see a figure being lowered over the edge of the roof. He seized Flannagan's wrist, whose hand instinctively flew to his holster. "Take it easy," whispered Scala, and he led the way, dragging the super back, who was going to cross the street openly. First at right angles for some twenty paces, then across the gutter, then back. The super was for taking them up in the elevator but Scala frowned on that. "Those rusty cables make a hell of a noise at night. Let's walk."

They tiptoed up to the sixth landing, and stopped for breath. Listening with strained ears, they could hear footsteps, soft noises behind the door. Wordlessly, Scala placed the superintendent there, and motioning to Flannagan, whispered, "If you can—cover them. I like my prisoners alive." Then he led the way up to the roof.

But the rusty hinges of the little iron door spoiled their entrance. The roof-door creaked open and Little Rocco heard its eerie note. He dropped the rope, swung around and fired at a shadow. Scala fell flat on his face, and Flannagan tried to slam the door against the bullet, but it stung his fingers. "Sonofabitch," he growled. Rocco fired again at the door and ran for the adjoining roof. Resting on his belly, Scala aimed carefully. He liked his boys alive, but he never took a chance with a desperate gun. He fired and shot through an eye. There was a fiendish scream of pain from Little

Rocco and he fell away from the edge of the roof like a leg wrenched from a table. Chick and Lou raised their arms in surrender.

When Googi heard the first shot on the roof, the sweat suddenly spurted from him and chilled his brow and spine. One minute he had been going about his work, peacefully piling soft furs, wonderful to touch, into a large grey sack, chuckling his low, inside chuckle—and the next minute he knew sickening panic and wanted to vomit. Something had gone wrong. He knew it. Little Rocco was not infallible. His whole system for mulcting New York suddenly collapsed.

He ran to the window and tugged at the rope. No one answered. He had an impulse to fling himself from the window and dangle in the air. But how would that get him to the hard ground? God, to be on firm pavement, running. But he wasn't—and he had to work fast. With agonized fingers he loosened the knot around his waist and stepped free of the rope. Shots rang out above and an inhuman scream filled the air. He ran to the rear window but slapped his own hands down. Even to touch it would ring an alarm and bring a squad of police. He ran to the steel door and jerked at the knob. It was doublebarred. He ran frantically from door to window, searching desperately for a hide-out. But there was no place in the loft. He looked hungrily inside a grey sack, stepped in with one foot, got the other entangled in the rope. Then he heard a scraping at the door-lock. His hand went to his hip pocket and touched the cold gun. He recalled Little Rocco's sly words, "Keep this canister—just in case." Well, he was no punk. He would shoot his way out.

Suddenly, the door opened and a needle of hurtling light stabbed through his wrist and his own gun clattered behind him to the ground. As he sank into a faint, he was aware of a strange relief in being caught. At least they would take him out of this prison.

At headquarters Googi, his composure recovered, at first refused to talk. He called for his mouthpiece and for bail. He acted like the big shot he had dreamed of becoming. Detective Scala talked gently, then persuasively to him and finally lost patience. Scala, who wept unasham-edly at "La Tosca" and got all choked up inside at the sight of a beggar, pummelled Googi on the side of his head with a rubber hose which left no scars but hurt like hell. Scala was unmoved by Googi's screams and continued to swing the hose until the little wop opened his mouth. He spilled a fascinating stoty—"as good as a movie," Scala graded it.

Later, Googi learned of Little Rocco's death and all hope left him, Rocco was the only one who knew anything about that mysterious fund of money to which they had all contributed against the day of just such an emergency as now faced Googi. Where was the money? Where was the mouthpiece? Where was the bail?

Glumly Googi took his rap. As the youngest of the trio and as a first offender he was sentenced to four years in Sing Sing.

The idea is to make a dent in New York—but don't dig your own grave.

14

Drone, drone, drone, through all the evenings of spring, summer, autumn and winter, a constant humming in his mind, little facts propelled by grim teachers, working into his memory as screws driven by pneumatic drills. But in time Peter remembered enough of these little facts to pass a series of Regents Examinations and to acquire the sixty counts which made him eligible for Law School. Well, hurdle number one well taken, and the buzzing head still on the tired shoulders.

And now for a heart-to-heart talk with old Seymour Henderson. Peter, who had the poise and strength of desperation, explained his plan to the capitalist. He was entering law school in order to fit himself for a career in finance. He would grind up all the knowledge there was about corporate structures, financial set-ups, investment trusts, banking dodges, stock and bond manipulations. He would whittle and polish and sharpen himself so that some day he would be of real help to Henderson. But in the interim, however reluctantly, they must part company, for Peter needed a job in a law office. He also needed money for tuition, but it was difficult to talk of that.

The old pirate listened and found himself melting into a human reaction. He liked Peter—not dangerously, for his affection had not as yet made him generous, but he liked the fire and the steel of the lad (nourished by what privations) and he felt an impulse to do something for him. Furthermore the straightforward plan of the young man appealed to him. There was potential value in a young lawyer who could learn to tat with the barbed wires of financial law. Yes, undoubtedly he could use him in his own concern and probably save himself thousands every year in fancy fees to legal specialists. Yes. He felt himself melting and for the first time did not coagulate.

"Peter, I have a great deal of confidence in you," he was talking straight out of the *American Magazine,* "and I've decided to do something for you." He cleared his throat. Peter stood at attention. "I'm going to pay your tuition at school—I know you couldn't have saved very much from your salary here"—Peter wavered on his feet—"that's quite all right— consider it a loan which you can repay when you come back to work for me." He cleared his throat again and steadied the lad with an old wrinkled hand on his shoulder. "And what's more, I'll talk to the firm of attorneys that represents us and see about a clerkship for you."

Peter's knees felt watery. Suddenly the good fairy came along and miraculously swept out the hobgoblins. For so long had the three silent men lived in pinch-penny starvation, for so long had Peter conceived of his career as an incision with fingernails into a world that lay behind a hard rock wall, that this offer felled him like a blow. Tears came to his eyes as it dawned upon him that with no tuition to pay, there would be ample food in the house, perhaps even a doctor for his father's spine.

He was tempted to seize both hands of Henderson and kiss them, but he recovered in time. He knew that any show of emotion would embarrass the old pirate, perhaps make him suspicious of his own generosity. No, better far to thank him with poise and restraint, right out of the *American Magazine*. "I'll do my best to deserve this, Mr. Henderson, my very best."

Peter matriculated in law school, night session, New York University, downtown plant, located at Waverly Place and Washington Square. Here in the gracious shadow of a lovely cluster of trees, here where on clear nights echoes of Bohemian revelry could be heard, was an educational mill vaster than any in the world, a bigger and grimmer continuation of the prep school on East Broadway. Here thousands of students came, morning, noon and night, were exposed to contagion with canned knowledge, and in a few years were discharged as lawyers, accountants and invaders of other desultory professions. What a sight for the rubber-neck tours— morning, noon and night, thousands of law students marching in ranks, each already bearing upon his face an incipient look of stupid importance, each carrying a legal brief case, and each animated by the same wish- dream. That, as he crossed Astor Place, a Standard Oil Company truck would run over a child and he would get the case. And in all the boroughs to which they returned they lay down to sleep like ghouls, envisioning fat bankruptcies and receiverships in which the fees of the lawyers, by some delicate law of balance, just equalled the retrieved assets, leaving the creditors nothing more than a philosophy of life.

Peter, however, had no such small plans. He nourished himself on larger visions, for he had been in Wall Street long enough to understand that the great fortunes, certainly the quick ones, were made through the manipulation of money. And with the aid of the law and the opportunities Henderson would give him he hoped to chart a course for himself across which he could navigate in record time to the charmed islands of the steel vaults.

In the swanky office—four euphonious names in a row, skilled performers on a big-time bill—where Henderson had apprenticed him, Peter was thrice a stranger. First, because he was a Jew. Second, because he was an unfamiliar kind of Jew, his dark Sephardic face, his especial poise and reserve, distinguishing him from the more familiar Russian and Germanic Jews who were burrowing into law; and third, because he was so poor. The other young men in the office who were also serving preliminary clerkships were the favored sons and nephews of the members of the firm or their fattest clients. They wore unostentatious tweeds and good linens bought at the better haberdashers'; they had ample money for their personal needs and spoke of taking girls to dinner and theatre and cabarets. For their actual law studies they planned to go to Yale or Princeton, or at the worst, Columbia.

Because he was the only clerk to whom the small salary actually meant his livelihood, Peter was given all the remote, distasteful errands and the tedious clerical work. But this also had its advantage, for he was permitted to serve the summonses and complaints and the subpoenas, which enabled him to earn extra money since the stipend was one dollar and carfare for every legal paper he served.

His duties as a process server, one of the slimiest occupations in the crevices of New York, had to be performed upon his own time, so that even on Saturday afternoons he was occupied. Yet, for all that it was distasteful to him to startle some unfortunate defendant with a summons to answer a grievance in court "together with the costs and disbursements of this action," or to tag a reluctant witness and make him a tale-bearer in another's suit, this work had its compensations.

It taught him the vast, fascinating stretches of the city. It brought him to all the odd nooks and crannies, opening up little-known veins, the waterfronts from Sheepshead Bay to City Island, the lush jungle growths under the bridges, the fortresses guarded by uniformed doormen ("Who shall I say is calling?"), the correctly fringed green of the nearby suburbs, a map of the metropolis, unrolling, unrolling on castors of debts.

For months at a time he conceived of himself as a sleek, wily fox living on the town, ringing doorbells like a magazine canvasser, posing as a messenger boy when calling up to make sure his victim was home, "I've got a parcel for Mr. Umglick," deceiving wives and daughters and secretaries and doormen whose special duty it was to guard his quarry, yet always ending by placing the despised slip of paper into the right hands because it meant one dollar and carfare.

"Municipal City Supreme } Court of the City of New York: You are hereby summoned to. . . ."

During more depressing months, he conceived of himself as a city ferret, hiding his poverty, hiding the loathsome nature of his errand, the revolting course of his life, tunnelling underground, emerging only to nip with his sharp, bitter teeth, and then to flee. There was nothing to sustain him during those hard, dried months, except the dreams of wealth and success that would one day be his. His home life was silent and depressive, alone with two generations of older men, one nearly paralyzed, the other, the color of parchment and the rare speech of a prophet—two men who lived for him and by him and waited silently for a burgeoning in him that they might also pluck a green leaf. No laughter, no music, no color, not even the voice of a woman to make the rooms less chill and barren. Only the rough embrace of the city and the silence of his own hopes.

His days at the office were lonely because he kept himself busy with all the work he could find. He hungered to learn, to know and to avoid comparison with those who were better dressed, better fed, better sheltered and, what suddenly became important, better connected socially. His evenings he spent at law school, in concert with other lugubrious students, all work-drowsed, bored by the drone of the professors, all coming to life only when they dreamed of escape. What a youth! To pray for the death of each day of your youth, so that manhood might bring a better life. And with manhood on the horizon, middle-age, fringe-around-the-pate, moon-face, lost-navel middle-age, leering from behind the sky.

He had no social life because he could not make new friends and he had outgrown his old ones. His pride was so keen that he would not admit his loneliness. On Sundays, his one day off, he helped tend to his father, listened to his grandfather speak of the illumined life, and visited the Museum of Art, where admission was free. On rare occasions, he walked over to the University Settlement to see what the old boys were doing. Googi, he learned, was up the river, "on vacation"; Joey had become a professional prize-fighter and had moved to the Bronx, Mutt was still a Western Union messenger and other boys were at schools, studying dentistry, or working in offices or shops, or had simply fallen into a void. Once or twice he attended a dance, but contact with the eager girls made him wary. Most of them, physically well ripened, were angling for husbands, making alliances from which the young students would never extricate themselves. But it was not in Peter's program to become emotionally, and certainly not matrimonially involved with a girl from the Settlement. He wanted to live and love out of his class. He had the snobbery of the very office workers who snubbed him. Besides, the pretty girls among them excited him sexually and that upset his equanimity. His formative life was under control, every lust, every hunger must lie dormant until he was a complete and adult lawyer. Then he would begin to live.

Treading air, Bert left the high school, avoided some of his classmates who hailed him, and walked away so rapidly that he broke into a run. He crossed Columbus Circle, heedless of traffic, found an isolated bench in the park and sat down. Then with quivering fingers he opened the issue of the school magazine which he had been clutching so tightly to his side. In the table of contents he read, *"As Plato Sees It:* a dialogue by Bertrand Glass."* Quickly he fluttered the leaves until he reached page eleven, and at the sight of his name in print his eyes became so blurred he could read nothing else. It was the first time he had ever seen it in a magazine, as a full-fledged author, and the thrill of it was sweet and sustaining. He flavored the impression to the full. He looked around and was astonished that passers-by did not pause before him and say in tones of reverence, "Ah there, Bertrand Glass—so you're the author of that brilliant little sketch in the 'Oriole.' Scintillating, absolutely scintillating. Such wit, such biting wit. How did you ever write it?"

He finished the final quip and put the magazine in his lap. He leaned back against the bench, closed his eyes, repeated the printed lines and in a rush it came to him that he had subconsciously remembered some of the epigrams of Oscar Wilde. For months he had been soaking himself in Oscar Wilde. Here were the distillations that lifted him completely out of the life around him. Elegance and refinement in prose, a sparkling venom in dialogue, a concern only with an exquisite upper stratum in life, a life so remote from the lives of the masses, that it might have been lived upon a different planet.

Reading Wilde for the first time on his old Forsyth Street fire-escape, Bert had become painfully aware of the hideous, noisome poverty in which he lived. He wanted to shun it, to live only with the careless elegance of these decadent figures. Here was a life that flowed pure and sparkling above the cesspools, above the slime and stink of the struggling masses. Here were lovely, dissolute ladies who revolved like fatal gems to reflect dangerous color and light to their casually ardent but devastating cavaliers. Sitting on a rusty fire-escape, with the oniony fumes of a "gevetsch" leaking from a window, the rhythm of a straw broom on a dusty and lice-seamed mattress, the lament of a screech-voiced "kooshinerika" who had overpaid by one cent for soupgreens, all this falling on his ears, assailing his nostrils, filled him with a yearning to leave his home, his class, his people, and enter this remote, but for him quite natural society.

Even the move to the Bronx had not lessened his desire for escape. The new apartment at the Hicks Arms had been the last word in comfort and plumbing refinements to his parents and Joey, but Bert felt the depressing weight of the sprawling Bronx upon him. He had been reared on so much harsh and revolting reality that all he sought for the future were the elegant artificialities, the brilliant decadences of English society.

The French and Russian prose masters had nourished his dream-world. But Wilde seemed to shape him for a career, a ladder of escape. The drawing room—the theatre. Ladies and gentlemen, scoundrels with a veneer tilting with the brilliant lines his pen had provided them. He fashioned an epigram. A character is speaking to the perfect back of a divorcée,

"After a grande passion, woman remembers the ecstasies; man remembers the details."

In Mount Morris Park, on the edge of Harlem, twenty acres of trees, benches and tired figures, a heavily garmented old man sat on a bench, munching stale pretzels from a crumpled bag. The crumbs fell into his beard while he licked the granules of salt from around his mouth, and looked up at the observatory on the peak of Snake Hill. A weary Negro plopped into the seat next to him. "Harlem," he intoned, "the black man's paradise. I can sit on the same bench with you. The white man don't hate the black man in New York. That's progress." From his many layers of dark clothes and from his bewhiskered depths, the old man spoke: "There's no use hating anyone in this town, because someone's always hating you. And I know because I got clothes on my back." He shook some crumbs out of his beard. "The history of this town was written in its hatred. The Indians hated the Dutch, and the Dutch despised the British, and the British fought the French and the French loathed the Germans and the Germans battled with the Irish and the Irish beat the Jews and the Jews looked down on the Italians and the Italians booted the Polacks and the Polacks spat at the Negroes. Yet the Negroes feel better than the Chinks." The old man paused a moment and scratched his chin. "No use little people hating one another in this town, because New York hates all of you. And I know because I got clothes on my back." The Negro took a shoe off and cooled his sweating toes. Wistfully, he spoke, "I'd like to have some fried liver and onions."

15

Isabella lived on a hard glass floor. It had long ceased to remind her of a shimmering pond because now there was nothing soft or refreshing about it. It was a glass floor and a gliding life, hard, unresilient, and you kept it up night after night because you too had grown hard and unresponsive to everything in life except dancing and you were too numbed to soften into a change. Every night since their first furtive appointment she would meet Murray Burns in front of Gray's Drug Store on Broadway and 43rd Street. He always looked the same, a lean figure foppishly dressed in the same suit of extreme Broadway cut which clung to him as if it were fashioned of elastic. Above his stiff purple collar which cut tightly around his long neck was his mocking, scooped-out face with the hair plastered back. There were no doubts in him that to be able to dance was the supreme gift of the world, and he looked down with contempt at the couples who were not dancers, spat with his eyes at the fat little men whose movements lacked grace. When his eyes lit on Isabella, dutifully waiting for him, a flicker would light up in his eyes and quickly vanish, and a bored, possessive air would govern his face once more. Like a secret password he would utter between his teeth, "Huntspoint Palace to-night. We'll pick up a cup." She felt his talons clutch her arm and they moved down to the subway.

Isabella had the feeling that the two nickels with which he paid their fares were all the money he owned in the world. And she was right. Familiarity with every special officer at every dance hall gained free admission for Murray Burns and his partner. His presence added interest, because he was something of a drawing card. Girls gaped at him, hoping to ensnare a dance with him, and incipient sharpshooters watched his movements carefully, hoping to learn from him.

Burns entered like royalty, acknowledging greetings, repelling advances, cool and mocking. But with the first bars of jazz his muscles would jerk suddenly and he would lead Isabella out upon the floor. Quickly her fatigue drained from her and the music, the rhythm, the swirl of the dancers pumped artificial life into her veins. The floor was hard and glistening but it must be danced upon. She entered the curves of his arms and body as one sculptured to fit there. His long legs shot back and hers moved forward, her leg with his leg as though they were joined at the thigh, her form with his in a superb harmony. And into all the convolutions he described, the intricate steps, the glides and weavings, she fitted like the key part of a puzzle. But when gentler, sentimental music was played, they danced as two lovers who waltzed to create a memory to warm them when they were old and no longer graceful.

On rare occasions, when she faltered and made a mis-step, he drew in his breath and his lips curled and she felt as though he had spat upon her. He didn't utter a word, but his cruel, mocking silence brought tears to her eyes.

The first cup which he had presented to her at Stuyvesant Casino at their initial meeting was the only instance of his gallantry. After that the process was the same. They would win a contest, the judges would present her with a silver loving-cup, he would take it from her, disappear, and within a few minutes he would return without it. He had a standing arrangement with all the dance halls whereby they bought back the cup from him for from three to five dollars depending upon its size. With the money in his pocket he would issue a curt exit line. "Let's beat it."

Once an unruly claque of west side hoodlums forced the judges to award the cup to their local favorites. This was the first time Isabella saw Murray Burns enraged and it was a terrifying experience. His face, above his tight collar, drained itself of blood and seemed to pump it into a vein that swelled, across his forehead and bulged until she feared it would burst. "The dirty sons of bitches—the stinking rats," he cried, "nobody can touch me for ballroom dancing. It's a steal—that's what it is." And his furious expletives grew fouler. Isabella was frightened by his temper and his language. She thought fleetingly of Joey who not only would never have used such words in her presence, but who would have killed anyone who did. She tried timidly to comfort him, but he shook her off and stormed ahead of her into the street, while she followed like his gypsy woman. At the subway kiosk he paused. "Got a dime?" he snarled. She opened her bag and with his long talons he extracted a dollar bill. "Come on—let's stop off at the automat first."

Once she asked him about his friend, the booking agent, the objective towards which they were working, and he savagely answered, "Wait till you get more experience. That's why I'm taking you around every night."

During these hypnotic months Isabella saw less and less of Joey. They lived miles apart so that there was no opportunity for chance or brief meetings in the hallway or on the street. And then Joey, in whom integrity was a natural trait, adhered closely to the program Donovan had laid out for him. He kept in faithful training, roadwork, shadow boxing, practice bouts at Stillman's, bag punching, a rubdown and in bed every night at ten o'clock. Although he missed Isabella, often acutely, he knew this was his particular road to success. If he kept this up, followed Donovan's advice, some day, perhaps in three or four years, he would be the lightweight champion of the world. For this one could well afford to make sacrifices. And because he himself was so direct and honest, it never occurred to him to doubt Isabella. Why, she had sworn to him that she was his girl, sealed the pledge with a kiss. And hadn't they been childhood sweethearts, even if he did tug her hair when she danced too long or strayed too far from home? He believed what she told him. That every afternoon when she returned from high school she did her homework, took a walk, had dinner, attended a movie or a club meeting at the University Settlement, and then went to bed. The understanding was that as soon as she was graduated and he had won his first major fight, so that his position would be secure, they would be married. Sometimes, Joey reproached himself because he couldn't watch over Isabella personally, not that he didn't trust her, but that the corner loafers flung crude remarks at girls who were unescorted. But then you couldn't complain to a great manager like Donovan who moved you into a swell apartment house in a cleaner neighborhood and told you not to worry about the rent.

On Sunday afternoons, he would come down to the east side and take Isabella to the fashionable Loew's vaudeville house on Delancey and Norfolk Streets. Seeing her week after week in the afternoon light, she looked tired and tense, her face drawn, dark circles under her eyes and a strange fear in them, but Joey attributed that to the strain of study. Since he had never excelled in school, all books had an awe for him and the mastery of strange subjects like geometry, ancient history or chemistry seemed full of barbed hurdles, dark hazards.

Joey took all his problems to Donovan, and he also consulted him about the wisdom of an earlier marriage. "I tink the kid is woiking too hard, studying dem books." But Donovan advised him against such a move. The manager, who perceived the depths of Joey's emotions, always treated his problems with great gravity. He reasoned with him. "What would be the sense in getting hitched so soon? I got big plans for you, Joey. After a few battles, I'm taking you around the country for a little tour. I want you to clean up a flock of second-raters and has-beens so you can build up a rep. Then, when you come back, you're ready to take on top-notchers at the Garden. And if you keep your head and do what I say—some day you'll be the champ." He drove his point home. "But if you get married—you'll put a crimp in the program. Figure it out for yourself."

"But—I can't leave me goil alone—too long." The words thickened out of him. It embarrassed him to admit it, and yet he had never been so earnest.

"Sure, Joey—I understand. Say, wasn't I young myself, once? And I can promise you a fine wedding after your first big fight."

One Sunday evening Joey and Isabella were the guests of Donovan at dinner. Joey proudly introduced his future wife to his manager and Donovan, shrewdly regarding the girl, said, "Seems to me I've met you some place before." The girl twitched her fingers nervously, but Joey laughed. "Not Bella—she ain't hardly been off the east side. She goes to school, comes home, helps her grandma and goes to sleep."

But Donovan remembered. He had once been pressed into service as a judge at a dance contest (he made it a point to attend all the shindigs in his district), and he recalled how this girl had danced. The grace and youth and beauty of her, slender and dark, with a lost look on her delicate face—like a dancer in a trance. And then he also remembered her partner, a tall, cadaverous lizard who handled her as his property. He sobered for a moment in his reflections. Was it always the fate of a boy like Joey to fall in love with a girl who would two-time him? She was not for him, not for a steady lad who, God willing, would go to the top in three or four years and make a fortune for both of them. He deserved something better. But Donovan remained silent. There was no use in puncturing his dream at this stage. The important thing now was to have him win the out-of-town fights.

One night, after a routine at the Audubon Palace which resulted in the usual sale of the cup, Murray said curtly, "We're stopping off at my hotel first. I got a date with the booking agent." Isabella felt a flutter of fear. The clipped, brutal way in which he spoke. Not even bothering to look directly at her.

"You mean—in your—room?" She had never been to his place.

"Say, listen, kid—it's about time you came out of your diapers. Remember one thing—in the show business—everything goes. You could come up to my room in the middle of the night—and nobody thinks bad of you. Besides, this is business." Suddenly he confronted her, eye to eye. "You ain't afraid of me?"

"Why no, Murray—no." Pause. "Why should I be?"

"That's the way I want to hear you talk."

In a small walk-up hotel on Forty-third Street and Sixth Avenue, Murray Burns, prime sharpshooter, lived in a room not much larger than a bath-tub. The "L" thundered by his window, rattling the panes, stirring up grime and fumes, choking him with foul city gases, deafening him with the constant city thunder, running over him with wheels like blades in his feverish sleep. But one block away was Broadway, and for five dollars a week he could live within earshot and view of the glittering highway. He owned nothing but what he wore. Yes, there was one extra shirt, one extra pair of socks, two extra stiff, purple collars and an overcoat with a belt, threadbare at the sleeves and pockets. He was the original hallroom boy without any overtones of jest. He lived on coffee and cake and mockery of the clods who could not dance with the grace that justified his life. Each night he carefully placed his trousers under the mattress and thus his sleeping took on an extra value because it preserved a crease. He hung the coat carefully on a hanger first pulling the wrinkles out of the sleeves, turning the pocket flaps down, examining the worn lining and dreaming of the day when he would own a dozen suits. He hung the shirt on a chair facing the window so that it could dry out under the arm pits, and then he lit a cigarette and wondered when the booking agents would become aware of him.

For brief interludes his dancing partners interested him as women. But not deeply. They were beneath him, certainly not important enough as an ambition.

Murray led the frightened Isabella up a stairway into his tiny room and turned on a bleary overhead light. The downtown trains slowed up near his window with a screech as they pulled in the 42nd Street Station. He drew the window shade down, then carefully hung his coat on a hanger. He loosened his necktie and smoothed out the knot-wrinkles with the palm of his hand. He took his collar off and revealed the red mark around his neck where the tightly drawn collar had been cutting like the bite of a rope.

"Sit down, Isabella." He pushed her gently upon the bed. She sat on the edge, her tired feet hanging. The dancing pumps dropped off and she curled her toes and rubbed them tenderly. Then, as she bent down to retrieve the pumps, he said curtly, "Let them lay." She looked around, frightened by the closeness of the room. She felt choked, she wanted to run out.

"But the agent?" She had to shout to be heard.

"If he comes—he'll be here. That's what."

He snapped the light off and sat beside her on the bed. She felt his arm around her shoulder drawing her down on the pillow. She caught the reek of dried sweat upon his body and her terrified eyes seemed to see the red line around his neck like the mark from which he had been hung. One hand fondled her breast while the other clawed at her thigh. "Let me go," she whimpered, "please let me go." There was a strange strength in his hands and he preserved his usual, almost contemptuous silence against her struggle. Terror froze within her and she believed it was not happening to her. Long fingers rolled her stockings down and pried her from her dress. There was no tenderness, no caress from the man, only a "God damn it—why don't you lay still!" Her mind kept repeating "It's not happening to me." She felt her strength flow from her, flow into the clamor of the street.

The reek of dried sweat made her nauseous, but the pain was unendurable. Suddenly she screamed and her howl of pain and terror were swept along by the thunder of the oncoming train. An hour later, when her sobs had died down, she got into the clothes he had torn off her. His voice, strangely pitched in the throbbing darkness, pelted her. "Everything goes in show business—and you're my partner, ain't you? You stick to me and you'll have your name in bright lights. We'll travel all over together—Burns and Company, Society Spielers." The room pulsed with his ambitions. At the door, he sat up sharply like a roused ghost in bed. The red line was marked around his neck. "Meet me to-morrow night—same place. We'll pick up ten bucks for an exhibition dance at a racket."

Slowly she crept down the stairs and into the street. The lights and clamor had subsided. Like a refrain she said, "It didn't happen to me."

The following evening as she was leaving her stoop Joey ran up excitedly. "I'm glad I met you, Bella—because I won't see you for a month. Donovan signed me for a couple of fights in Cleveland and Detroit, and I'm leavin' in the mornin'." Then, observing her nervousness, the low cut of her dancing frock, the cosmetics on her face and lips, he stepped back, examining her with surprise. "Why, Bella, you look funny—you goin' some place?"

She was suddenly furious with his honesty, his belief in her. She couldn't bear it after the way she had been betraying him. What had happened the night before seemed to raise a wall between them. She wanted to strike out, cause him the pain, the agony and humiliation she had endured, freight him with the burden of the nightmarish months of life she had been leading on a glistening floor. Like a shrew she snapped back at him.

"Yes—I'm going to a dance, your majesty."

"Who wid?"

"Do I have to tell you everything? Are you going to boss me? Well, I'm not used to it."

"But, Bella," his voice was plaintive, "ain't you my goil?"

"No," she shouted, "I'm nobody's girl. I can't worry about little things like love. I've got a career to make."

"But—you promised—you ain't forgettin'?"

"Oh sure—it's all right for you to become a big shot—a champ. But what about me? I'm as good a dancer as you're a fighter. And I'll have my name in bright lights. I can't sit by—and just wait for you."

"But you don't have to wait long, Bella. After my foist bout at the Garden—we get married."

She began to cry hysterically. "I don't want to marry. I want to dance. I have to dance."

He put his arm about her, hoping to quiet her, to lead her away, but she flung it off and tore away, racing down the street. Joey stood there bewildered, hurt. He couldn't figure this out. Here was a situation in life which could not be solved by a sock on the jaw. What had come over his little Bella? For whom was she painting her face, wearing those gaudy clothes? He began to walk, shaking his head, just wondering.

And under the confusion and anxiety that tore at him, he remembered having promised Donovan to be in bed by ten o'clock, because they had to make an early train.

Joey kept walking and wondering.

16

Nearly five years had passed since Eugene Murdock had seen his son. Each contract for a subway extension had been followed by another, but with new hordes of predatory wolves ready to attack the choice carcasses he had staked out for himself, Murdock had been unable to leave his post. He had to be in constant communication with the New York front. Then too, bewildering thoughts about Perry plagued him so that he couldn't quite make up his mind what attitude to take towards his son. Should he censure him for this morass of idealism into which he had sunk? Perhaps laugh him out of it? And while he pondered on the wisest course to take, the years had passed. But now Perry was coming back, and the new life together would begin. Perhaps the boy had outgrown it.

The tension of business had relaxed a little. The major battles had been won. Murdock was entrenched. For one thing, his political connections had been so strengthened that with the aid of Donovan his firm had bought into the official building supply company, Acme Contractors, so that instead of paying tribute on every new city job, they now exacted it from other builders. And the building booms constantly flaring up in all of the five boroughs not only provided ample plunder for everyone, but skyrocketed their own business. Why, in the last year it had expanded to such proportions that they couldn't accurately compute its new dimensions. But Murdock knew that he was a millionaire.

Now, with his family back, he would give up the draughty house in Columbia Heights and buy into one of the exclusive co-operative apartment houses that were being erected on Fifth Avenue in the vicinity of the Museum of Art. He had already looked with favor at a fourteen-room duplex with six baths, and had even consulted an interior decorator about its equipment. He wanted his son to have every luxury that New York and its plunder could supply. Then, of course, he would have to get rid of Polly. He would buy her off with an annuity, and find himself a new mistress. Polly, under the ministrations of good living, had grown so fat and cushiony that he was ashamed to be seen with her in restaurants. It reflected not only upon his taste, but worse, gave the impression that he couldn't afford one of the slender, beautiful chorines that Ziegfeld used to emblazon his chorus.

The future seemed cosy and interesting. All except his anxiety over Perry. That recurred like an old ache which demanded constant massaging. What would the boy look like now? Would there be a warm, father-and-son feeling between them? And again, what was all this nonsense about his being an idealist? He wanted the boy to enter a recognizable groove, to become an extension of himself, in short a real Saturday Evening Post son.

And so upon an autumnal morning Eugene Murdock drove down to the foot of West 43rd Street, to take his family off a luxurious liner. He greeted his wife with an impersonal cordiality (it's been dead between us for so long, he thought). Her first impression was, how gross you look. She offered her cheek and he kissed it dutifully and listened to her comment, with new strength in her accent, "You've gained weight, Gene—a great deal of weight." And then he put his hands on his son's shoulders and regarded him.

From fourteen to nineteen, Perry had grown nearly six inches. He was tall and thin, slightly stooped over with an academic arch; his English tweeds were carelessly worn; his pale eyes and their shy, bewildered expression seemed to emphasize his indifference to the realities of life in America as Eugene understood them. The son greeted the father diffidently. It had been difficult enough to write to him, to tell him exactly how he felt about life, but speaking to him was like addressing a stranger who must be written down as an enemy. The heroes he had worshipped, the friendships that had warmed him, the books he had read, the Marxian philosophy he had absorbed, the vows he had taken with his comrade Baum, all these led him automatically to inscribe a dollar sign upon the ample belly of his father and label him a hated capitalist. Here was the florid face, the predatory eyes, the sleek, glossy front concealing the "I-exploit-labor" look of the robber baron. And this was his father, and it was his money that Perry had lived on.

"Well, well, my boy, it's certainly good to see you. And how you've shot up. Well, after I bring you down to the office—I won't be able to lie about my age." He roared with laughter, trying to create an atmosphere of ease, smooth fellowship and camaraderie. Perry smiled at him shyly, thinking his own thoughts, recording his own impressions.

Murdock had planned to launch a quick if joshing assault upon the ideas which filled the youth's mind, something in the vein of "well, my lad, it's all right to get drunk in Europe, but after all, this is the good old U. S. A. and let's get down to brass tacks." He had hoped to do it in their first talk together so that afterwards the path would clear for a real friendly relationship between them. But there was something about this tall, pallid stranger, his wandering, shy eyes, and his faintly crack-brained appearance that stopped him. It would not be such a simple task after all. And his air of severance from the definite American scene wrung the father's heart. What special irony kept piling distance between these two, making them more and more grotesquely different as the years went on?

So, he decided not to assault the boy, but to arrange luncheon with him for the morrow. He could show him the large new offices, introduce him to his successful associates, obtain for him the obeisance from employes given to a prodigal prince, and then talk to him about the future. Perhaps in the expansive glow of this success atmosphere, the boy would shed these idealistic nightmares as a man throws off fears in the bright light of the morning sun.

But luncheon, the following day, only solidified all of Eugene's fears and made of his son's insanity a high, impregnable wall. Perry, instead of applauding his father's success, deplored it. As he viewed it, each step upward, each new contract, meant more bodies crushed, more workers enslaved and exploited, fresh deposits of tainted money, and more damage to be undone before the millennium could arrive.

Eugene was exasperated. "You're crazy, son, to think that way. Why, this is New York. The slogan of this town is—every man for himself. If I don't do it, the next fellow will. The very worker you say I crush would club my brains out with a baseball bat and climb over me—if I let him. That's human nature. And young squirts like you, with your fanatical socialistic ideas will never change that."

"We can try," said Perry quietly.

"Come on, boy, give up this reform dream—get into harness and do a man's work. Maybe law, or better still, banking. I can get you a nice berth in Seymour Henderson's firm, down on Wall Street. Or, if you like, come in with me. There's plenty of room for you and the way we're growing—in ten years from now you'll be a millionaire."

Perry shook his head and smiled his remote, sad, exasperating smile.

"Then what the hell do you want?"

"I'm going to take special courses in psychology and social service at Columbia."

"Columbia?" Eugene looked disgusted. He had wanted his son to get a degree from Princeton or at least Harvard. "Who will you meet at Columbia? Jews and Japs."

"I'm interested in all people."

Murdock felt that he was addressing a stranger. He toyed with the idea of cutting him loose, letting him shift for himself and then dismissed that. It would bring him more pain than it would to Perry. To bring him back to familiar grounds, he said, "Let's take a look at the new apartment. A fourteen-room duplex facing the Park, better than anything they have in Europe. Come on—and see your new home."

Again, Perry smiled patiently. "I'm not going to live there." He paused. "I've arranged to live at the University Settlement House."

"Where the devil is that?"

"Over on the east side." A dark memory flitted across Perry's face, one that pained him. "I've got to be close to the field in which I'll do my work."

"And what is your work?"

"Change."

"Revolution?"

"Perhaps—but change, anyway."

Eugene Murdock just clenched his fists and bit back his words. He felt both fury and impotence. The boy wanted to do insane, unworldly, unprofitable things. But he wanted them with a maniacal strength and fervor which nothing could budge.

Because of the approaching war fever and war economy of time and emotion (any feeling that distracted from death and profits was considered waste), the dean of the New York University Law School dispensed with the customary graduation exercises; thus cheating the students who had spent three weary, gloomy years of night study, of their one touch of glamor. In three years, a considerable body of young men had developed long, pompously serious faces, grown sparse moustaches, memorized the correct number of correct answers to the recurring examination questions and had dedicated themselves to a life hunt for fees. The sprinkling of older, defeminized women who found in the monotonous stupidities of the legal profession one way of forgetting their lack of charm and beauty, grew beards as well as moustaches, chin tufts or feline whiskers which may adorn the cat, but never the woman. Perhaps the steady bombardment of legal puzzles new to the female brain produced this weird stimulus to hair and pigmentation, and the croaking voice that accompanied it. At any rate, Peter found neither dalliance nor romance among his female classmates to bring a note of color to his weary nights.

Whereas students for generations remember their graduation as a glamorous ceremonial, in which they walk down a hushed path, illumined by doting eyes, and receive a sheepskin from a doddering trustee while friends, parents and classmates applaud, Peter remembered his as an inter-ruption of his sleep. The letter-carrier blew his shrill whistle and shouted, "Men-deez, Men-deez." Peter leaped from his pillow like a fireman into a pair of trousers and clattered down the stairs. He paused at a landing because during the night an Italian girl had died of scarlet fever and the survivors in loud lamentors' voices were already planning a funeral that would cost more money than they had spent on the poor child's upbringing in all of her cramped nine years of befouled living. Peter remembered the smells of the next landing, the vapors from a huge cauldron in which a housewife was cooking mussels. And then the letter-carrier handed him a simple letter in which the Secretary of the Law School of New York University invited him to call for his diploma.

Slowly, a little stunned and proud, Peter went upstairs, and showed the letter to his father and his grandfather. With eager, inquiring eyes they looked at it, and waited dumbly for him to speak. For nothing ever happened to them, and they felt the great world outside only when he opened the sluice of his own gushing world and let it flow in upon them. He explained to them that a diploma was awaiting his call, that he could rescue it after payment of a small fee, and that he would have it framed and hang it up on the barren wall of the kitchen and they could look at it to their heart's content. He also informed them that it was less colorful than a calendar but more useful.

Peter finished dressing, and with the letter in his pocket and no food in his stomach, reached the street. It was a beautiful day in June and the garbage cans overflowed, like small volcanoes which had erupted during the night. It was a lovely day in June, and above death and mal-odor and decay, it tried hard to be lovely even on Roosevelt Street. From the outer reaches of New York Bay, and from the East River, winds arose and went to town, gathering spray and salt-spice odors, winds trying hard to sweep before them the curling stinks of the South Street waterfront that rose like eternal fires at the sacred altars of poverty.

Peter walked into the breeze, turned west along South Street. On this morning, in particular, he enjoyed entering Wall Street through its rear door, as he had in his first adventure. This entry through an unguarded gate had now become symbolic of his whole campaign.

At the law office on Rector Street, he chatted for a moment with the son of the senior member of the firm. He tried to communicate his sense of release, which the letter in his pocket had brought him. But the vested son was too full of his own plans. The young legal forehead, it seems, was planning to expose itself all summer to sunshine at Montauk Point and forget the dreary cares of the office in swimming, dancing, and lovemaking. Work slowed down anyway, because all the important courts were closed in the summer (no justice from June to September—the judges have wearied of dispensing it during the winter months). Then the young forehead drawled, "Really, you should get away, Peter." His concern was one-thousandth of one-inch thick. "Now that you've bagged the old sheepskin—all you've got left is your bar exam—and then you can hang out the well-known shingle," Oh, nothing like tossing off the vernacular.

"Yes—I'll take a rest," said Peter wearily. On my roof, he added to himself. Or, maybe dig a soft spot on the scow that carries garbage off to sea. That's a good way to get sunburnt. But not for long, he clenched, not for long.

BOOK TWO

FRUIT OF THE STONE

17

There are dwellers in the peepholes of New York who love the town with a passion rarely visited upon a woman. Theirs is a devotion as fierce and as pure as that which enthralls the thrice-purged, who with peel-egg eyes glimpse the deity in a religious delirium. It is a passion which, from its first manifestation, gives the lover no peace, thriving on scabrous fevers, constant lice-bites, pin-jabs in the buttocks, drummings along the spine, revolving knives in the heart.

Men toss in their sleep and dream they have become giants who descend on the town and embrace the lower half of the Woolworth building.

Women fall from a great height, navel downward, upon the spire of Trinity Church.

The little lovers move off Manhattan Island on a day's picnic and are seized with distance phobia. Will they ever get back? Others dare not leave the street they know, the very chair in which they sit at their familiar restaurant, dreaming of conquest of the city. Perhaps a blind beggar, sitting on a bench in Central Park, stares buttermilk-eyed at the lake, and considers himself a success because he has loved New York, looked once deep into the sun of New York and had his eyes gouged out.

A millionaire, contemplating his coupons in the cool of a vault, spirals in a heart attack because death will overtake him before he has straddled Metropolis.

Young composers glide stealthily along the town, attempting to trap its peristaltic heavings, its sex gurgle, its pain-blood of birth, its blast of ecstasy. The music of New York beats within their cocky skulls like anvils on a xylophone and, reeling, they write down minute arcs of wooden music. Manhattan Rhapsody—ta-ta-ta-ta-tee-ta-tum-ta-ti-ta-tee-ta. Thin trickle of puny composer's blood along one wall of the many-fortressed town.

Elephant-eared writers spend gaping hours listening to the wise-guy talk at Lindy's, Dinty Moore's, Billy La Hiff's, or record the Bronx and Brooklyn yappings, pack them into blow pipes and bombard New York with confetti. Then they rap on night-club tables and brag of a successful affair with the town. Thin, diarrhetic drool, slimy squiggle on the giant scow of offal that goes out to sea.

Some day the heads of these braggarts will crack like popcorn along the blood-baked city walls and the street cleaner who has made a lifelong study of metropolitan manure will become the anointed, the one designated to write the litany of New York.

Eda Finkel, blonde half-Jewess, bantam, corn-haired daughter of a bland and mildly corrupt labor leader who clung to his accent (vone drink and I'm rollink on the floor like a shikker) and a Viennese mother (remember—you were conceived in Budapesth) was in love with New York. The deeper the love, the greater the mystery of its inception.

Eda's ecstasy for New York, overwhelmed her without warning. It began incongruously with a dentist's evening out. He took her to the Strand on Broadway and Forty-seventh Street to see a moving picture. But as soon as the house was in darkness, he put an explorative arm around her and began to massage her breasts with strong fingers smelling of oil of cloves. The sheer incongruity of his move—rolling the nipple like a pellet of gutta percha while on the screen a chaste heroine received a salute on the forehead—so revolted Eda that she stood up.

"Where are you going?" whispered young Dr. Zemmel, owner of a sign, "Surgeon-Dentist—Zahnarzt" above a giant molar. "Where are you going?"

For answer she spat in his face, and marched out upon the toes of other people. It was not so much moral indignation, as the dentist's clumsy vulgarity, his utter lack of sensing the fine fitness of things, the fine, ultimate order of love and life. Young men had played with her breasts before and, when she wished, she had permitted a caressing hand to glide down below her navel, without feeling outraged.

But tonight the little gestures of men, all men, tender as well as crude, were petty, insufficient, discordant. She swung down Broadway with a growing sense of madness, and when a sidewalk Romeo slid under his toothpick, "Hello kid," she thumbed her nose and laughed out loud.

She crossed Forty-second Street, the bar across the furnace, and entered the cool, dark depths that led away from bedlam. The buildings escorted her, tall, silent escorts, tireless, perfect companions. They clutched her arm, and she found their touch thrilling. Stamping on the pavement brought up coils of satisfying tingles. The dark companion shadows were real, the buildings were alive, constantly stimulating. No small, smelly pressure on her breasts, no clumsy meanderings under her dress, but a tall, broad, crushing lover, a lover that leaned over, dark, fearful and towering. She had an impulse to tear her clothes off and stamp naked through the streets. To roll giddy in the shadows of loft buildings, to rub her back until she bled against the rough walls of skyscrapers, to press her breasts against a revolving door and dance around and around. Waltz me around, New York!

With a rhythmic stride that freed everything in her, she turned east on Canal Street. She sniffed the grated cheese and spaghetti smell of the Italian streets that cross big-girthed Canal and die of fright in front of the Municipal Building and their properly corrupt neighbors of City Hall. She stepped on Manhattan Bridge singing so loudly and so merrily off-key that a policeman warned her not to leap into the East River.

Behind glowed her land-lover, but the river was her rowdy sea-lover. The wind tossed her and she lifted her dress to the hoots of tug-boats. The wind cool-spiralled up her legs and she pounded on the wildly swaying concrete walk.

She sprinted into Brooklyn, and hip-swung along the Navy Yard, telling horny sailors and marines to find a better reason for fighting. Her thighs were singing and every step on the pavement was a smart slap from the man I love. She entered Prospect Park and under the moth-ringed globes she did a Maypole dance and recited obscene ditties to herself. Once she saw lovers heaving in the grass and she lit matches and flung them at their entangled forms. She hallooed to a lone rower on the artificial lake and as he began to row furiously towards her, she pee-d in mockery where she stood.

She stopped Irish cops and asked them in broken Yiddish how to get to East New York and when she finally reached home she collapsed in the hallway, falling on the banister and clutching it in a strangle-hold. A neighbor on his way up pinched her lovely, firm behind and reported to her father that his daughter was drunk.

She was carried to her bed ravaged. New York had raped her.

Perry Murdock became aware of Eda in one of the classes on social service at Columbia. Along a liberal front she was moving educationally towards journalism and she took all the extra courses she could, believing that a crazy-quilt of knowledge was the best equipment for a job on a New York daily.

Her first impact upon him was a fiery one. She had risen to contradict a lecturer who had emphasized the humanitarian impulses of social reformers. Eda pointed out that they extracted as much from the slums as they brought to them, and that in most instances the "work of mercy" supplied a *raison d'être* to people who would have died of boredom.

Perry listened alertly. He had never questioned his own sincerity. What had made him become a reformer? He had never been able to eradicate that first shocking view of the east side, the crowded, dirty streets, the clamorous, weedy life, and that revolting spectacle of the begrimed boys at the water trough. That had been the basis of his resolution to transform the slums. There would be no serenity in him until that memory left him.

"You don't elevate the standard of living of the poor just by giving them a clean room in which to play checkers," said Eda.

"You're forgetting milk stations for babies."

"Contraceptives for mothers might be wiser."

The lecturer accused her of being facetious, and the end of the hour postponed the final round of the battle.

But Perry, overcoming his timidity, joined Eda. For the first time in his life, he felt himself attracted to a girl, an attraction which soon developed into the same fervor that he felt for his career. They were of the same age, except that Eda had been spawned from the salt pillar into which Lot's wife had turned, and her bones remembered bleaching on Asiatic deserts and her flesh mouldering in Indian seas, and when she looked into his young, bewildered eyes she felt older than the Pyramids. Perry, who was experiencing a first generation torment, was drawn to Eda not only by her beauty but by the seasoned quality of her mind, the bitter-flavored profundities of her talk. Here indeed was a strong hand for the bewildered groper. He hoped that it would be stretched out to him.

Falteringly he invited her to dinner. He wanted to empty himself of his dream to change and reform New York, to bring fresh humanitarian currents into it, to beat his dream against the strength of her and have it return resolute, grand, invulnerable. Eda accepted because she wanted to hear his dream, since it sprang from New York, and also because he looked as young and as tender as chicken strips atop a bowl of chow mein. He spoke in rushes, and Eda listened, amused. Bean-shooter against the granite skyline. Row around the Battery with a feather.

"You're not eating," she said.

"It's years since I've eaten." He tried to smile. Eda brought his plate closer to him. She felt like cutting his food into bits and feeding him morsel by morsel.

"It's years since I've slept."

"Bragging, eh?"

"I'm a man possessed."

Eda could not dismiss his torment. She pushed her own plate aside. The word nursery came to her.

Like an abrupt offshoot his voice, now almost in an imploring whisper, flew at her.

"Look, Eda—I must tell you something I have never told a soul. I could never bring myself to talk to my father because he couldn't understand. My mother would try, because she loves me, but there again it would be useless. I have tried once or twice with my friend at school—but I couldn't go on. But I feel that I can tell you—that I must tell you."

Eda smoothed his pale, nervous hand. "Please do. Perhaps I can help by listening." She felt sorry for his torment.

"Even now—it's hard to begin." He licked his parched lips and tried to control his voice. "Something happens to you as a child. Something bitter and strong. It grows within you, feeding on the years—until it becomes stronger than yourself.

"This happened years ago—on my thirteenth birthday. My father drove me down to the east side to show me the tracks he was laying for a new street car line. On the corner of Rivington and Forsyth Streets he went into a saloon to pay off his laborers and left me alone on the corner."

Once again, Perry was a little frightened boy, sitting in the big car, alone. "Outside, there was a trough of water for the tired horses. It was summer. I remember the heat of the day, the dirty faces of the children that played there, their ragged, sweat-soaked shirts, the terrible tenements, the tired laborers. The water in the trough was filthy and foamy."

Revulsion began to rise in his throat but he swallowed his spittle. "And then—I saw some boys of the street drive one of their group right up to the trough. The boy laughed and then he dipped his mouth into the filthy water, shook his head and neighed like a horse, flicked the foam from his lips and ran off. I suddenly became very sick."

"Since then, I have travelled in many places. Always have I been in clean trains, clean ships, clean schools, eaten clean food, slept in clean beds, always have I drunk clear water. But the picture of the boy at the trough torments me. More than anything else, it has drawn me back to New York, made clear my future and my work for me. When I think of changing New York—I think of changing it for that boy."

He lifted a glass, but did not touch it to his lips. "And now I come to the part that I must confess. I am drawn, as by a powerful magnet, by the filth of that trough. I feel that I must dip my mouth into it before I can go ahead with my work. Just as monks drank from the waters of the lepers' feet they bathed, before they were fit to carry on the work and glory of God. It's the only truly religious feeling I have ever known."

"Although I live one block away from it—I haven't dared do it. But I must tonight. I couldn't begin with my plans—until that is out of my life." He paused, sat back. Then, as if gathering himself for another assault, he said: "Eda, will you help me? Will you lead me to it? Come with me tonight—I need your strength."

They left the table and went out into the night. They walked in silence, each absorbed in memories of childhood, the terrible nightmarish sediment that childhood leaves, freighting all life like gall at the bottom of a glass. Presently they reached the corner of Rivington and Forsyth Streets.

Etched in rust against the night were the outlines of the old trough. A yellow-blue flame from the lamp-post bowl above shone upon its filth-laden waters. Upon its surface a watermelon rind sailed calmly, like a candy-tinted yacht.

"That's it," he cried, and began to tremble violently. "All' these years—it has stood there—filthy with the ever-growing filth and poverty of this neighborhood."

Eda tried to steady him, but suddenly he tore himself from her grasp and ran to the edge of the trough. He closed his eyes and with a violent effort dipped his lips into the water. She could see the shudder that ran down his back like a bolt of lightning. He stood up, faint and panting. "I've done it—at last," he whispered, and vomited into the trough.

Eda led him away, as a crowd of kids gave chase with their sing-song plea. "Hey, bum—give us a nickel—throw us a dime."

Sardonically Eda thought: the high priest of New York, the saviour of the slums, is mistaken for a drunkard. He clung to her hand. "Don't leave me, Eda—come with me now."

She led him to his room in the Settlement House. It was a small, square room, as severe in tone as the cell of a monk. From its small window she could look into the tall casements of the public library on Rivington Street, where tired men and women sat bowed over books, reading hungrily, intently, lifting phrases to dried palates, filling empty bellies with words.

Perry, lying on a couch, spoke with an exultant ring in his voice. "At last—I've done it. My real work can begin. Do you realize, Eda—I shall inherit millions from my father. I can use it to leaven the town, to change its hideous face, to heal the running sores of its slums, to wipe it clean of its poverty." His shrill voice charged at her. "Eda—marry me. Together—we can do this great work."

She shook her head. Her own thoughts beat within her. Change the face of my lover? Sacrilege. Aloud, she spoke with a low finality. "No, Perry. I'm sorry. I don't want to change New York. I'd rather destroy it." She paused. "As for changing my own life—with marriage—I think I'd rather destroy that, too."

Perry sank back on the couch, trembling violently. His face and body were wet from perspiration. Eda, like a nurse, removed his clothes, cooled and dried his body, wiped the last flecks of vomit from his unkissed mouth, placed her firm hand on his forehead and left him in bed.

She walked down Eldridge Street. On the comer, it burst into the clamorous brilliance of Delancey Street, the Williamsburg Bridge lights to the east, the "L" tracks and train rumble to the west, the solid front of tenement windows alive with lights and voices, humans fermenting, seething and milling in the streets, each little life bursting its pit, every pit straining at its shell, every shell ripping from its limb, life that hung from its poverty, so ripe, so heavy, ready to explode.

Eda laughed in the street. He change the face of New York? Why, he hasn't got hair under his armpits.

18

Elmer Hicks, having built extensively in the Bronx, sought to expand in another territory. He had been thinking seriously of invading Greenwich Village, and sought out the advice of Michael Donovan who was an authority on that region. Hicks had been hearing and reading about the Village, a territory inhabited by impoverished artists and writers, but which attracted rich Bohemians, the young sons and daughters of wealthy families who liked to live in an aura of creative work, even if they themselves could create nothing, and were willing to pay steep rentals for this privilege.

Donovan approved of the plan. They were examining a row of houses on Christopher Street, cold tenement flats inhabited mainly by Italians with a sprinkling of Greeks and Jews and Irish.

"Now all I would have to do," said Hicks, "is renovate these houses. The timber, the pillars, the flooring and foundations are perfect. They used to build houses in those days."

"I know," agreed Donovan. "I was born in a house like this."

Hicks went on with his computations. "I could cut up a four-room flat into two apartments. Put in tile baths, hot and cold water, parquet floors, and up-to-date lighting fixtures and I can get seventy-five dollars an apartment. Let me see—that makes $900 a year, times twenty."

Donovan chuckled. "Before you count the eggs—remember that the main thing is to get the okay of the fire and building departments on these renovations—and that's where I come in."

Hicks gave him a wry smile. "I always figure you in. You come under the heading of miscellaneous expense."

He went on with his thoughts. He could easily raise the money to lease or buy a block of these buildings. After all land was very scarce in the Village and few new houses could go up except on the sites of old ones. Whereas in the Bronx there were still vast undeveloped areas which, with each new boom, created serious problems for the older builders. Every moving day saw an exodus of tenants into the brand new dwellings which offered new gadgets such as incinerators and built-in showers, to say nothing of a month's concession. Luckily the never-waning tide from the east side continued to fill the senior houses. But suppose that ended some day?

"Let's stop in somewhere for lunch," said Donovan, "and go into this matter. Looks like a chance to clean up for you—with a spoonful of gravy for old Mike."

The increase in Village restaurants had kept pace with the growth in dwellings and population. Where once there had only been three or four bizarre dens like Gypsy Marie's, now there were dozens of real restaurants, retaining only in their names and decorative schemes the Bohemian touch. Quaint nomenclature like "Three Steps Down," "The Open Door," "The Iron Gate," "The Black Cat," and "The Green Hat." Every name and every wall a minor triumph in creation.

They walked through a low door into a warm, cosy interior. Sally, now a waitress, came over to their table. With leisurely movements she set down two paper doilies, two glasses of water, two balls of stippled butter and a plate with thin slices of white and raisin bread. She was clad in an orange smock and there was a strip of orange ribbon around her hair. It was the color that arrested Hicks, and he looked up at her with sudden, keen interest. From her his glance went to the door and he could read the name of the restaurant. "The Orange Peel."

Sally had grown beautiful with the strange, provocative beauty of a woman who goes through life contemptuous of men though desired by them. Her very disdain of men whetted their interest. Waiting on tables in a little Village restaurant was not quite the goal that had propelled her to leave Kansas City. But the years had whittled down the grand ambition until now it echoed only occasionally within her like a loud note she had once sung.

She had begun by modelling for artists, but that, she soon discovered, led to little more than annoyance. The poor artists tried to induce her to sleep with them as a measure of double economy; first, to avoid paying model fees and secondly, to relieve their loneliness. The wealthy dilettantes who fluttered brushes in lavishly furnished studios merely to justify a way of living also considered an hour of posing the prelude to an afternoon in bed. The successful and earnest artists made no advances to her but on the other hand insisted that she pose, which, she soon found out, was very hard work. And after each session of posing, Agatha, furiously jealous of her disrobing in the presence of a male, created scratchy scenes. So that for the sake of the peace and indolence she so needed, Sally soon exiled herself from the world of art.

But other fields beckoned. As Agatha's work with the little theatre group progressed, she grew in power, and soon was able to foist Sally upon a feeble, if arty play in a small role. Perhaps, she reasoned, there was some latent histrionic talent in the girl which could be encouraged.

But Sally was a dolt in the theatre, graceless in entrances and exits and terrified of her own voice when she heard it projected across the footlights. And here too the men crowded about, offering to her special form of lush beauty the free and easy sexual relationships it provoked. So Sally was retired from the theatre. But she had to find some work not only to earn money for extras but to prevent herself from being bored to death.

At this time waiting on tables in Village restaurants was acceptable work for a girl who yearned for the art life but was not yet launched upon a career. It escaped being menial work because in these bizarre and esoteric beaneries waitresses were not expected to be deferential to patrons. In fact the haughtier they behaved towards some of the nibblers, the better they liked it. And what with the gay costumes, the spontaneous singing and the laughter it was more like a masquerade than actual hash-slinging.

And so, to occupy her time, to provide an interest in life and a means of earning money, Sally condescended to wait on whimsical, rickety tables at "The Orange Peel."

Elmer Hicks gaped at Sally. The reddish tints of her hair, the warm, fruity look of her face, the orange of her costume held his eyes. The color itself, orange, imprisoned his private nightmare, but it also had the fascination of a secret link with his one great crime. In all the years that he had been acquiring land and buildings, piling up options, deeds, title policies, leaseholds, he had never, once relaxed. Nights of torment, days of land-lust. Now, staring at Sally, relaxing in the warm rays her colors flung at him, some old desire for human understanding, human tenderness and companionship wriggled faintly under the cement blocks of ambition he had piled upon it. So great had been his hunger for land, so monstrous his ambitions, that they had devoured all of his other appetites. As a man who found no peace in sleep, he was also unable to contemplate a night of love. When a biological need asserted itself strongly, like a hunger apart from himself, he appeased it in a brothel and, disgusted with himself for yielding, he went back quickly to drawing circles around those sections of New York he sought to encompass.

But the orange look of Sally, her soft, fruity contour, stirred a growing hunger in him. Donovan noted his rapt interest in the girl and ordered for both.

"A nice dish," he laughed.

"Where I came from—they'd call her keen."

This was the first human spark Donovan had ever seen struck from Hicks.

"Bet you'd like to go out with her," he followed slyly.

"Could you arrange that? Listen, Michael, I'd appreciate that. I'm much more at home at a title closing than asking a girl to go out."

"Say, there isn't much I can't arrange in the Village. Don't forget—this is my bailiwick."

Donovan called over the woman who owned "The Orange Peel." She was severely tailored and one of the first business women to wear hats while they worked. She was under obligations to him because he had helped lift a fire violation from her kitchen. Michael presented his friend with a ceremonial air.

"I'd like you to meet Mr. Hicks—a big real estate man. He's coming down to the Village to put up some studio apartments—and he'll be eating here often."

"How nice," she murmured.

"And he'd like to have—what's her name—that hot-looking blonde-haired cutie——"

"You mean Sally?"

"That's it—Sally—wait on him. It won't hurt to get them acquainted."

She smiled faintly at Hicks, covering him with an old, mature glance. Business man or artist, they were all after the same thing. Well, all she cared about was a steady flow of patronage. Elmer, under her look, blushed and stabbed at his food.

Hicks returned alone to the restaurant the next day. He was made self-conscious by his amorous enterprise and at the table tried to greet the girl with a hearty jocularity.

"I'm back again, Sally—and you're pretty as ever."

Sally only smiled remotely at him and turned her nose up the moment she left with his order.

But Hicks was an old campaigner. A woman to him differed little from a choice parcel of ground—and his credo was that a man can get anything he wants through the correct campaign. He had his first move ready. He who had hoarded pennies, had deprived himself of food and clothing in order to have big deposits of liquid cash, left a dollar bill under his coffee plate. By his tips would he be known.

Then he sought out Donovan and told him he was ready to acquire a block of cold tenements through a dummy purchaser. It was not only a good investment but would enable him to eat twice a day at "The Orange Peel."

The quarrels that go on in New York, the constant quarrellings. You sit down at a cafeteria table to munch a sandwich. A faded woman reproaches her younger lover for his lack of attention. Her words rise like angry steam from a dish and becloud him. Heads turn towards him, but he goes on eating as though the bitter words were meant for someone else. His indifference shrills her attack and suddenly he swings a hand across her thirsty mouth. She shrieks, a few people rise as if to interfere, and then subside. Many ignore the scene, deep in their own bickerings. In hotel lobbies, from deep, luxuriant seats, under the rhythmic purr of music, little hatreds lash at each other. Possessive women with their devouring looks of hatred. In a business building an elevator door opens and two men enter the car. A hostile word binds them like the unsevered cord of the Siamese twins. Their mouths are close together and fumes of hatred pour out upon each other. You walk up the street. A man's vein-swollen hand suddenly flattens a woman against a wall. "You did so." "I did not." "I say you did." "Honest I didn't." His rage moves him forward, the woman behind him protesting, pleading. Steaming from the keyholes of a thousand apartments, from countless windows upon streets and courts, on Park Avenue, in Hell's Kitchen, in Sutton Place and in the gas-house district, the quarrels go on in New York, the constant quarrellings.

The vaudeville act of "Burns & Co., Society Spielers," broke in at a crumbling, fourth-rate house in lower Williamsburg. Here was an ancient temple of amusement, so sad both in appearance and in the nature of its divertissements that audiences invariably went home in a stupor of melancholy, not knowing whether to blame their own impoverished lives or the unhappy clowns who had attempted to anaesthetize them for the evening.

The program usually consisted of what was known as "family vaudeville" and was as dreary as family life. Six acts and an obsolete moving picture, run off from a negative so worn that the shadowy figures developed a new dimension of thinness and sequences ended unexpectedly while the plagued operator tried to patch the film.

Three of the six vaudeville turns were low-grade standard acts, petrified alumni of the Pantages circuit who, having played the same dopey act for a quarter of a century, repeated it like grinning robots for a pittance. The other three acts were recruited from the try-outs, newcomers to the ranks of "artists," and for these the manager only paid carfare, grumbling always that the novitiates should pay him. Among the small-timers this temple without bells was known as a "coffee-and-cake" house because that was all you could earn from it.

It was in a dank-smelling room of this house that Murray Burns and Isabella were dressing for their vaudeville debut. An agent, in a burst of generosity which he knew he would regret, had advanced Murray the fifteen dollars necessary to rent a shiny swallow-tail for himself and a low-cut spangled evening gown for Isabella. He had seen them dance at a contest in Yorkville and he knew they were good, but as to their future in vaudeville he had his doubts. But he kept them to himself and by dint of strong pleading he had persuaded an assistant from the Keith office to come down and catch the act.

The program opened with an echoing assault of off-key music so fierce and raucous that it roused the audience of laborers, tired housewives, errand boys and five-and-ten-cent salesgirls, to a high pitch of critical intolerance. Instead of lulling them into a gentle mood of anticipation, it filed on their teeth, scraped their ears, jangled their nerves, and caused them to mutter inwardly, "If the ennertainment ain't no better than this, we'll rip the chairs out of this dump."

First of the numbers was a fire-eating act in which a man with a gentle, beaten face, clad in a red flannel costume which he hoped made him resemble Mephisto, but which only suggested the label on a bottle of Pluto water, dipped a long tufted wand into a flame and devoured fire. His wife, an obese squaw with a relish for fire, repeated his stunts. They ate flames for six minutes and then extinguished themselves in a perfunctory spatter of applause. They would never get to the Palace.

The second was a roller-skating act. A woman of thirty-five who grimaced, skated with her husband of forty who also grimaced. Around and around the stage they rolled, hoping they suggested the aristocracy of the Continent engaged in winter sports at St. Moritz, while the band blasted music which was supposed to call up visions of the gentle falling of snowflakes and the jingle of sleigh bells, but which only added to the clatter of wheels on flooring. For the finale the man suddenly lifted the woman off the ground, and, while he clutched her by one hand and ankle, he whirled her around and around. The impulse to toss her into the audience and kill a few blinking dolts was very strong in him, but he had been resisting this for fifteen years and he knew that both his wife and their "public" were safe. This act also received its feeble round of approbation.

Burns and Isabella were waiting tremulously in the wings. "The house is cold," growled the skater, "colder than a whore's heart." His wife agreed, mopping herself under the arms.

It was plain that the try-out act suffered from stage-fright. Murray was worried about the music. In a brief rehearsal he had tried to make the band play a waltz softly, to spin a waltz in dulcet subtleties so as to induce, in this aggregation of lower Brooklyn failures, a nostalgia for the witty, sweetly sad life of Vienna. But the musicians attacked a romantic waltz with intent to rape and produced a clamor that suggested war rather than love. When Murray pleaded with them to subdue the brass and reed, the temperamental leader sulked and furnished an erratic reading of pianissimo music which was so faltering that the rhythm broke through only occasionally, like blisters. Yes, Murray was worried about the music, but he still tried to be disdainful, to feel calm and professional.

Isabella's teeth were chattering and under her make-up she felt bloodless. He seized both her wrists. "Watch yourself—and don't get nervous. Remember—we've got to make good." There was a faint dash of tenderness in his voice, but his heart was too full of bitter memories of the lean, waiting years, too full of his own ambition to think of anything except this chance. The act must go over big.

An usher changed the billing on the rack, "Burns & Co., Society Spielers," the curtain rose and the opening strains of music filled the house. Murray Burns, tall, slender, disdainful, very distingué in his hired evening suit, and Isabella, tinselly, but very pretty in her spangled evening gown, wafted out.

They moved with a grace and beauty that rose above the music, the audience and the crumbling theatre. Here was a fine expression of their burning desire to dance, to become somebody in a city of six millions through ballroom dancing.

In New York there is a place for every sliver of an ambition. Ambition, sandpapered down, particularized until it is one tiny facet of a huge revolving stone. But the whole town watches the slow turning of the stone and men and women devote their lives to be highlighted on one spot. You no longer want to become a great dancer. That embraces too much. You specialize—the best tap dancer, adagio, acrobatic, soft shoe, or the best ballroom dancer.

And this was their ambition. And they were dancing towards its fulfillment. At the end of their first number the audience applauded with a surprising warmth. The cash customers seemed to discern in the flow of harmony on the stage, the one element their own lives lacked. Where they stumbled, faltered, stomped and clodhopped through life, this young, slender, glamorous pair of dancers wafted rhythmically, with a harmony that was beautiful to behold. Lumpy housewives and thick-ankled factory girls dreamed once more of the dance, the romantic prelude to the kiss.

For their second number Burns and Isabella performed a foxtrot, embellished with jerky slides, tricky steps, contortions and twists all designed to exhibit their virtuosity. But the last number was dedicated to the waltz, a sensuous Viennese waltz, back to back, outstretched fingers touching, an amber spotlight on their eager faces; they danced like eternal lovers, working up to a bravura finish in which they spieled, whirling madly around and around and around until the audience broke into wild applause.

They trembled violently as they took their bows; not daring to speak, they rushed down to the dressing-room. The vaudeville agent appeared quickly. His face beamed. "Well, it looks like the rubes fell for you. I think maybe I can pencil something in for you. A couple of months out-of-town and with smart clothes the act should be ready for Broadway. See me tomorrow."

Isabella emerged slowly from her trance. "I wonder," she spoke softly. "Will we ever be as good as tonight? When we spieled for the finish I felt like I was going off in an airship, up, up, among the clouds. And then I nearly fainted."

But Murray was in a practical mood. Once again, he felt sure of himself, and although he realized her importance to the team, he also realized that one mustn't let the female half know how good she was. The thing to do, on the stage as well as in life, was to beat down the ego of women. In the long run they loved it and it made for harmony.

"Snap out of it, kid. You're gonna do better than to-night—or I'll find another dame." He looked at her with sharp, pointed cunning. "Don't forget—the act is Burns and Company—and Company," he repeated, so that his meaning would be clear to her.

Carefully they hung up their rented clothes. There were still two days left of the split-week try-out, and then the real bookings. They marched out into the night, conquering gods.

Again Murray took Isabella to his tiny room. Outside the trembling window, the "L" squealed and snorted and ground its wheels. The city called up from manholes and the hard, blinding illumination of Broadway splintered upon them.

"Don't," she pleaded, "not tonight." But Murray was one with the thundering train, with the grinding wheels. His hungry talons plucked at her dress, and the acrid smell of dried sweat upon him stifled her with nausea.

Before agony overcame her, she had a flash, a clear vision of her life. A moment of triumph impaled upon a crucifix of dried sweat, rape at one tortured terminus, and the bitter doubts of the morrow on the other.

The Cleveland set-up lasted two rounds. Joey tore in and upset him as if he were a cane on a finger. Donovan, watching from the ringside, was jubilant, for he felt certain he had groomed himself a lad with title possibilities. He who understood so thoroughly that there was no progress unless the road was greased had already arranged to sell an interest in "Young Samson" to a syndicate that controlled Madison Square Garden. This would guarantee him choice fights and fat purses in the greatest arena in the world. In any event, better a piece of a money-maker than all of a flop.

After the fight, while Joey was being rubbed down, Donovan exuded good cheer.

"Well, kid, there's no doubt a-tall—you're a comer. With smart handling, you'll be on top in a few years."

Joey stared at him glumly. He couldn't get Bella out of his mind.

"Why the blues, Joey? Don't you feel good about winning? Cheer up."

"I can't help how I feel." He wanted desperately to unburden himself about Bella, but he would have torn his tongue out rather than begin. Donovan looked at the sullen clamp of his mouth, the grooves in his forehead, and surmised. There were some things you didn't have to tell.

"Still thinking about the little girl?"

"She's goin' around wid a dancer—cheez—a dancer!"

Joey exploded and bit his lips tight. It seemed so cruel and incongruous that his Bella, over whose growth he had so tenderly watched, whose hair he had tugged when she danced too far away from home, whom he had kissed and loved and cherished, and who had vowed to be his girl, should now desert him for a sharpshooter and a dancehall lizard, a spieler with a tight suit and a tight collar and no punch.

"So what if she goes out with a dancer?"

"She hadn't ought to."

Donovan spoke hypnotically. "Listen to me, kid—I'm talking to you like I was your old man. You got to think of nothing but fighting. Let her go out with ten dancers. You keep right on fighting and keep right on winning. Get the girl out of your mind until you're on top. But say— when you're the champ and your picture is in all the papers she'll come crawling on her knees to you."

Joey sat up on the table. "You mean—she'd like me better—if I was the champ?"

Donovan examined his eager face shrewdly. Here was a mind that closed around one objective at a time like quicksand.

"Like you better? She'll be crazy about you. And why shouldn't she? Your name will be on everybody's lips. When you walk into a restaurant with a dame—they'll nudge each other and point you out. Say—you won't want to know her then."

"Don't say that, Mr. Donovan. I don't change easy. I'll never change— about Bella."

Joey retreated into thought. Of course he had dreamed about some day becoming the champ. A leisurely growth in the achievement of a remote ambition.

But now he wanted it quickly, in his next fight, with one mighty sock if possible.

There is no repose in New York. The city looks as if it were constantly recovering from an air raid. Scurrying people disappear into kiosks, doorways, holes in the walls. Debris and ruins pile up, wrecked tenements blink through paneless windows, clamor fills the air and the dark sky lowers threateningly. Choice sections of the city strike a truce with the enemy during certain hours of the night. They beg off from terror and dirt and noise. Tall men in evening clothes and bejewelled ladies walk within these barricades and laugh, but not too loud. Fear ripples under the city, from the center to its outermost fringes, far out, where the patient straphangers dwell. As each small home-owner sits on his porch, rocking himself to peace, the mortgage rises over the back yard while a younger man hacks away at his job. There is no repose in New York.

19

On the ferry to Staten Island Peter first saw Eda. He was standing several feet behind her, admiring the contour of her legs which the wind, by whipping her thin skirt between her thighs, outlined with a provocative clarity. And Eda too was enjoying the assault of her sea-lover, the force of the wind against her body and legs, the wind out of New York Bay that pushed her to the rail with the ardent pressure of a lover. Impatient lover, she smiled, with the ferry hardly out of its dock and the glowering lights of the Battery still upon them. As the bow swung, pointing towards St. George, a violent gust of wind lifted the felt hat off her head, and deposited it in the arms of Peter, like a double play. Peter looked at the blonde girl with the wise, suddenly revealed face, bowed with old world elegance as he returned the hat and murmured "You're welcome" to her thanks.

The perfect *Ladies' Home Journal* opening, thought Eda, under the harmless title of Flirtation on a Ferry. Unless, of course, he is the sensitive son of a California oil magnate, alone in New York, a voluntary exile from his materialistic class and yearning for a wistful adventure with a female poet, in which case we'll call it Fantasy on a Ferry. But if he is only a stevedore on a holiday, with pomade on his hair and Saturday night linen, then we'll compromise on Fun on a Ferry. She looked back at him and smiled.

Peter was faintly annoyed. He had been tense and lonely for so many years that he dared not break that encrustation too suddenly. To-night he had fled the heat of the town in an expansive gesture. A five-cent ride on the ferry to Staten Island. It was cooler on the other side and even its smug, small-town depressiveness was a relief from the herded, verminy feel of Roosevelt Street. It was a ten-cent adventure, and in view of the fact that he was soon to be admitted to the bar, and then back to Henderson's office at a real salary, he could permit himself this extravagance.

But he wanted to cling to his fine loneliness a little longer, to abandon it in small ways. Merely to look at Eda from his vantage point, merely to think of a girl, was pleasantly stimulating. God, he thought, how long was it since he had spoken to a girl? He had never taken up with any of the stenographers in the office, because he wished to avoid complications. He had fought too bitterly for his career to jeopardize it with an emotional entanglement with a poor girl.

But Eda, the luscious unknown, the blonde question mark, retreated a few steps as in a dance, and began to induce Fantasy on a Ferry. She had decided because of his lean reserve, his aloofness, his swarthy face, that he was the sunburnt scion of an oil baron.

I'll begin, she campaigned, by pointing out some interesting phenomena in our city of marvels.

"Cold, isn't it?" She smiled at him and Peter flashed his teeth at her. White teeth in a swarthy face. She liked the composition because it formed a night picture.

"Would you believe," continued Eda, chattering in the wind, "that, half a dozen blocks from shore, New Yorkers are sweltering?" There's a tidbit to toss at the handsome visitor from the west.

Peter looked at her with a bitter smile. All gaiety drained from his face. Eda sought in vain for the expression of good-natured, wide-eyed wonderment.

His silence puzzled her. "Would you believe that six blocks from shore———"

"Oh, but I would believe." There was so much acid and bitterness, almost rage in Peter's voice, that she looked at him startled. "I live there."

Fled the oil scion. Fled the gay title. Now it was quite definitely, Fury on a Ferry.

"In that case," said Eda, trying to recover, "may I point out the Statue of Liberty. It rises from the waters———"

"By its own bootstraps."

"Oh, you know about that, too." After a brief intake of breath, "Do you mind if I do a little wondering, out loud, about Staten Island? Why don't more people visit it? It's located on the other side of a long boat ride that only costs a nickel. You can tramp the decks and snap pictures of the shoreline. You can meet the right people and form life-long friendships. With luck, you can get both seasick and the illusion of distance. It easily feels as far away as Philadelphia—and can be just as depressing."

"And far more dangerous. I once served a summons and complaint on an Italian in Tottenville and was nearly lynched. You don't have to sell me Staten Island."

"Say, you talk like a guide. What is your name?"

"Peter."

Her manner was youthful and carefree, like the heroine of a *Ladies' Home Journal* story. But Peter didn't quite fit in the role of hero. Someone had deranged their story.

They leaned over the rail, arms lightly touching, staring at the dark waters in silence. At the landing, they debarked and walked side by side. Across the bay, the shoreline lights of New York crowned the sky. She felt giddy with the power of her lover. How strong and tall and deep, ruthless with conquest, twinkling with a million lights.

"What's yours?" Peter jabbed the question at her.

"Eda. Eda Finkel. You know, Scotch—from the song 'Can an Eda Fink a Finkel, comin' through the rye.'"

Peter laughed, joining her loud, giddy laughter, and as it issued from him he felt surprised. Had he ever before laughed in unison with a girl? A wave of bitterness and misery swept over him, like the return of an old ache. What had happened to him between the time of his first laugh as a child, and this laugh, ages later? Who had boarded up those years like the front of a house whose owner is away on a long journey, years to be spent in darkness, unrelenting work, privation, loneliness. He looked across the dark waters of New York Bay at the monster that showed its grinning, sharp teeth on the other side and he shook his fist.

Eda put her hand up. "Please don't strike—my lover."

But there was no restraining him. "I hate New York. I curse it! My father curses it! And my grandfather curses it!"

His bitterness frightened her.

"Why do you hate it so?"

"You gave me the clue."

"I didn't mean to. Tell me why."

"Because six blocks from where it's cool, people swelter. Six blocks from Wall Street, people haven't got a dime. Six blocks from duplex apartments, people live in hovels. Six blocks from Broadway, people have yet to see a play. Six blocks from the big food markets, people haven't got enough to eat. That's why I hate it."

A slow smile crept across Eda's face. "What is there about me that attracts reformers?" Perry flashed before her. "You make me think of a friend of mine who hates only part of the city. He, too, wants to change New York."

"Oh—make no mistake, I never wanted to change New York. It's myself I had to change."

Peter showed his white teeth. His blue-black hair glistened and his lean, swarthy face, haughty, even spiritual in its hatred, grew taut as he spoke.

"My father dreamed that I would become a wise one among our people. And my grandfather still prays that I shall become a rabbi and dwell in holiness. But I've arranged to become a man of money. The slave, the authority, the lover of money. And I've also arranged to live away from those islands of misery that are so close to the prize centers of New York."

"I shall live very close to its cool forehead, fanned by upper-stratum breezes, close to its hot lips, blood-moist, blood-red, its luscious nipples, its sweet navel—close, very close to the juicy centers of New York." He stopped.

Eda looked at him, startled. The figure he had drawn of his New York had torn her apart, and out had fallen her secret. Why, he regarded New York as a woman, even as she regarded the city as her lover.

"I'm going to mount the town—and make it pay in ecstasy for all it has done to me—and to my father—and to my grandfather."

Gradually his voice lowered and he lapsed into silence. His own vehemence and his eloquence had astonished him. For years all this must have been gathering within him, festering, straining to burst. This was the first time he had uttered it as a challenge. Well, it felt good, exhilarating, to relieve himself even before a stranger. He had flung the glove at the town, a minute, quixotic gesture, but what of it? It was his little challenge, for his little battle was on.

The sad, gentle voice of the girl surprised him. "And you can't be much more than twenty-one." Her hand closed around his arm and the touch of it was good and comforting.

They returned on the ferry and listened to the sea-going musicians who play the same songs four times each trip, stern, starboard, bow and larboard, and keep this up year after year until one day they lose their reason and set sail in their instruments and go to sea.

At South Ferry, Eda asked reluctantly, "Do we say good-night here?"

"No, let me see you home, Eda."

"But I live miles from here. You've probably never heard of the place. East New York."

Peter smiled. "Let me think—I served a subpoena on the branch manager of a bank on Pitkin Avenue. Say, there isn't a part of this whole town, in all of the five boroughs, that I don't know. I have come sneaking through all of its arteries to plaster a curse on some poor devil. If you lived in heaven, I probably would recognize the gate where I stood in the celestial rain with an order in supplementary proceedings to serve on St. Peter."

"Well, that's one way of learning New York."

They took the "L" at Brooklyn Bridge and on the long ride home filled in gaps about their youth, their schooling, their hopes. When Eda mentioned Perry again, she said, "I must have you meet him."

"You want to see the fur fly."

"Oh no. Perry's too gentle to fight. He doesn't shake his fist at New York. He wants to poke into its ashes, stir its conscience."

"The conscience of New York? Poor devil, he doesn't know its anatomy. Well, with or without your reformer friend, I want to see you soon."

They shook hands. Eda walked up the steps slowly. She had the feeling that a human form was standing between her and the Metropolis lover.

20

The fever, hysteria and hypocrisy that swept over America after its entry into the World War developed curious symptoms in New York. The young sons of the socially prominent and wealth-entrenched families, those that dwelt within the fashionably suburban ramifications around the dense tissues of New York, the Long Island and Westchester show places, the smaller estates in Staten Island, the wealthy Brooklyn homes, these gay blades regarded the war as a lark. And indeed for most of them it began as a great holiday. It meant abrupt cessation from the academic burdens of college. You could burn the goddamn books.

It brought unlimited sexual freedom, not with tarts, but with the choice hussies of their own set, because these over-stimulated debutantes, smitten with the fear that they would never see their young men again, gave themselves freely and passionately. Thus fornication without courtship, or the classical ideal, was achieved.

It invested them with the eternally magnetic pull of a gaudy uniform, the definite sense of belonging, power over the lives of men because the well-connected quickly became officers, and the hope of glory upon the battlefield. A few of the more gullible may even have been deluded by the propaganda fantastic agents were then pumping from a gaseous chamber labelled, "War to make the World Safe for Democracy." In any event, since these young men would one day inherit the wealth of New York, it was their privilege to defend it.

The cannier of the young blades, those that tempered patriotism with self-preservation or had a yen for the old carcass, were able, with the help of politicians and influential fathers, to secure for themselves safe berths in barracks and training camps four thousand miles away from the nearest front. Or those that couldn't be spared for the camp life of barracks were given executive jobs in Washington, where they spread well-nourished forms on swivel chairs and lamented their ill luck in not being chosen for active duty. My heart, you know, or my lungs, you know.

But as the war fever swept in towards the poorer centers of town, it met with resistance. There was none of this business of gliding off a fragrant navel at dawn and dashing off to war. On Second Avenue, on East Broadway and Pitkin Avenue, on Southern Boulevard and in Washington Heights, determined bands of Jewish mothers cooked up giant cauldrons of skepticism about the great purposes of war and blew these protective vapors over their sons against the onslaught of patriotic fervors.

But Democracy was relentless in its impartiality. The poor as well as the rich had the right to defend the wealth of the country. And so at the numerous Draft Offices young men were forcibly thrust into uniforms, while little Jewish mothers, wise with the memory of sons and husbands lost in six thousand years of war in all parts of the world, who knew in their bones that death was the most these soldiers could hope for, set up howls and lamentations which converted the olive drab lorries filled with apprentice soldiers into funeral processions for those whom they mourned as already dead.

True, in Hell's Kitchen, along the west and east side waterfronts, in Mott Haven and in the Red Hook section, the fighting Irish went as volunteers and recruits largely for the hell of it. So did the homeless, the disinherited, and the lads in a jam with the police.

But the Italians and Poles and Slavs were bewailed by their mothers, and it was characteristic of the poorest sections of New York that their attitude towards war was the most intelligent. Not that they didn't hear enough speeches, but a two or three-room vermin-infested flat with a layout of Grand Rapids furniture still creaking under its chattel mortgage was nothing to inspire bayonet thrusting.

And they agreed with the most lurid of posters. They did not want their sisters raped, but then most of their sisters had been warding off rape for years or submitting to it as befitted their desires, and there wasn't a gal from the tenements that didn't know how to keep her legs crossed in a pinch.

As American troops poured into France the demand for raw soldiers grew. And soon the reverberations of this demand and the war hysteria reached the prisons around New York. Some of the convicts found in a war, from which they were also shut out, the first gleam of consolation for their dark, mean, beaten lives. They were the lepers of society, not good enough to be at liberty with their fellow humans, and, by that token, not at liberty to be recruited as cannon fodder. They were not even good enough to be killed. Well, upon release they at least would be alive, while hundreds of thousands of law-abiding citizens, their betters, would be bloody dust.

But some of the prisoners who preferred any hazard to incarceration, any danger as a relief from the bleak monotony of prison life, began to complain. What about their patriotism? Suppose they had sinned against society, a little larceny, a snippet of rape, the merest wisp of arson, what about it? They still loved their country, stern as its laws might be, and they sought the right to fight for it, aye, if need be, to give up their damaged lives for their country.

And this subterranean war fever combined with the urgent need for men to fill in the gaps where sardonic military blunders had placed troops within choice range of guns, led to the quiet formation of a legion of the damned. Ironically enough, killers were barred from the army. By some method of cockeyed reasoning, the murderer who had calmly hacked a betrayer to bits or scooped out his treacherous wife's entrails and hence needed no training period in which to lunge a bayonet at a dummy—this accomplished murderer was kept from the ranks. But first offenders, or even young, reasonably hardened criminals who had confined their infractions to larceny or forgery or rape, these were to be permitted an opportunity to retrieve honor on the battlefield, to atone for minor offenses against society by committing heinous ones against a legendary enemy.

It was in this manner that Googi got his chance at daylight. Good behavior, his youth and the fact that he was a first offender influenced a parole for him and made him one of a company that went over as an auxiliary to the Twenty-Seventh Division. His freedom was restricted aboard the transport, but then the boat was so crowded that no one could move anyway. Upon landing at Brest he was hustled to the front at once.

The war transformed timid clerks, slightly effeminate floor walkers, letter-carriers, students, even poets and dreamers into good soldiers. But Googi needed no alchemy to change him. The three years he had spent in jail made him the perfect soldier.

To begin with, he was filled with venom. He suspected the world. He could go for weeks without talking to anyone, spinning his own web of taciturn bitterness. No matter how rancid or decayed the food, he could manage to live on it and still do his work. He was an expert in codes, could communicate a message to a confederate in a roomful of people by taps on the back of his hand, by beats against a wall or table.

He could speak volumes without even opening his lips. His eyes were as sly and as eloquent as those of a forest animal. With one glance he sucked in every important detail of a room, the locations of doors, windows, crevices, computed the strength of each barrier and designed a plan for breaking through it. He could convert a harmless teaspoon into a dangerous weapon and could kill a man as silently as a sigh. He could steal a man's possessions from under his pillow while he slept, and could brazen out an accusation. He could wheedle his way into confidence or threaten so effectively that he gained his ends. He was desperate for life and power, those raptures of intoxication he had experienced on the Bowery fire-escape when he had conceived of himself as a conqueror of New York.

As for death, whether his own or the death of another, he considered it nothing more than a numeral on the dice he rolled.

Yes, Googi was the perfect soldier when he entered the war to make the world safe for Democracy.

In the large, severely upholstered office of Eugene Murdock, Perry told him about Eda. The father grew furious. He had just begun to resign himself to his son's fantastic notions about reforming New York, hoping that a few years of windmill tilting would restore his sanity, when he introduced a new complication. A scheming wench, and, of all abominations, an intellectual Jewess.

"Just what I told you about Columbia," he fumed, "Japs and Jews. And with the nursing milk still wet on your lips, you have to get mixed up with a girl."

"But she doesn't want me," protested Perry, "except as a friend."

"Say, I know that game. Just teasing you along. I warn you, if you get tangled up with this hussy, I'll pack you off to war."

"In that case, I'll disgrace you by declaring myself a C.O."

"Throw her out of your mind."

Perry shook his head and smiled. "You've got her all wrong. But just the same, I want you to help me. Eda respects achievement. Big things done in a big way. She might think more of me—after she's met you."

Murdock relented. His own boy was asking him to help—and he so rarely did that. Besides, he could size up this siren from the standpoint of his own worldliness and maturity.

"All right—let's all have dinner."

"And she's bringing a friend—a young lawyer she thinks I ought to meet. His name is Peter Mendes."

"Arrange it for tomorrow night."

From various ends of the city they converged to meet in the lobby of the Astor Hotel on the west side of Broadway between Forty-fourth and Forty-fifth Streets. Murdock had pictured his son's temptress as a short, dark, plump Jewess, with an intense nose, a radical bob and low-heeled slippers. He dressed her in a middy blouse and short skirt and placed in her hand a placard bearing the legend, "Don't Patronize This Restaurant. The Dishwashers Local 78 Are Out On Strike."

He was totally unprepared for a rather tall, blonde girl, with a fine, pallid skin and as pretty as a chorine, except for the intelligence behind her beauty. She was as blue-eyed as his son, but positive in poise and clear in confidence, where he lacked both those qualities. Perry, with a subdued pride, introduced them in the manner of one who brings together two forces, each stronger than himself.

Peter, immaculate in attire, his dark, bony face, the gleaming eyes and the blue-black lustre of his hair, seemed to be the only serene one. He had learned to control his desires and his emotions. The men shook hands briefly, but Murdock clung for a second to Eda's soft hand. She could tell from the pressure and from the light in his eyes that he did not feel altogether fatherly towards her.

Murdock glowed. "Well—this is an occasion. It isn't often that I get together with friends of my son. I'll give him credit for good taste right now."

"You may regret this compliment," said Eda.

"I'll take my chances. Shall we eat at Moore's?"

They walked up to 46th Street, turned west on Broadway and entered the spacious doors of a solid restaurant. At Dinty Moore's there was a comfortable atmosphere of good food and well-being, of opulence without display. No music here, no gargoylish floorshows, no folderols. Just solid food, well prepared, served in ample portions and at such prices as kept from its interior the poor, the frugal rich and the atmosphere hunters. Gamblers, upper crust show people, lawyers, politicians and big shot racketeers and their women ate and drank here in an atmosphere of complete relaxation and yet maintained all the externals of ladies and gentlemen. For instance, an underworld figure with half a dozen killings to his credit might eat there unmolested, but just let him try to keep his hat on for a moment inside the dining-room!

Peter liked the place. He could see it as the perfect environment for certain kinds of business deals. Soon, he would be able to eat in the best places of New York, and just as he was an authority on its worst, he hoped to catalogue its finest. Seated at a good table against the wall, they looked around. Michael Donovan was present with a party of political parasites, and he came over to greet Murdock, who presented him to his son and guests. Before returning to his friends, Donovan said:

"Say, Murdock, remember that little Jewboy we saw fight at the Forton A.C. prelim? This is years back." Murdock nodded vaguely. "Well, I'm managing the lad and I've got him matched for a semi-final at the Garden next week. I'll send you some tickets." Nothing, thought Donovan, like combining a little business with friendship.

"What's his name again?" asked Murdock.

"Young Samson."

Peter looked up suddenly. Warmed by his drink and by the memory of his friendship with Joey, he spoke up.

"I know him. We were great friends. We used to live on the same block—and how he could sock. Many's the time he socked for me, too. I'd love to see Joey again."

Donovan leaned towards him. "I'm sure he'd be tickled to see you. The kid is feeling kind of low. He's daffy over a girl. Look him up at Stillman's, will you? And don't forget the fight."

Peter returned to his reverie. Joey, grown up, fighting in the Garden, brooding over a girl. He wondered about Bert and the other kids on the block. How the years away from Forsyth Street had melted into a cauldron called time. Eda broke in.

"Will you take me to the fights, Peter? I'd love to go."

"We'll all go," said Murdock. "Don't forget, you're my guests. Dinner first and then the Garden. Perry, you remind me."

"Better leave me out," said Perry grimly. "I won't go to an exhibition of brutality." Murdock had the impulse to slap his son across the face, a perverse impulse to beat him into a primitive masculine reaction. "It isn't civilized," continued Perry. His son harassed Murdock. Just when he thought he was warming into someone normal and human, the boy exhibited this fanatical side.

"There's nothing brutal about fighting." Eda's ears tingled as Peter spoke. His voice had a sharp, almost cruel inflection, the pitch to which it had risen when he had assailed New York from Staten Island. How he and those tones like blades had cut into her.

"Surely it isn't brutal for Joey to fight. Don't forget, we grew up in the same gutter on Forsyth Street. Why, Joey was nourished on fighting. He had battles morning, noon and night—for all of us. Joey with his fists, his father with his eyes, mine with his back." Peter stopped and half closed his eyes. "And all New York trying to strangle and crush us. For Joey to fight in a clean arena, under the protection of the Marquis of Queensbury rules—no bottles, cans, stones or knives, just eight-ounce gloves—no biting, stabbing or eye-gouging—why, that's a holiday for the kid."

Perry, with drawn, blanched face, waited for him to finish. "Did you say—Forsyth Street?"

"Yes, near Rivington." He flavored the memory and the word.

"On the corner—was there—a trough?"

Looking at him intently, sudden recognition flashed across Peter. That pallid face with its greenish tinge of nausea, the frightened face alone in that crude automobile, the pinched, bewildered face on the deck of the ship. The face that had always shone above him with its pale, aristocratic light, now brought down to his level.

Peter couldn't help laughing, as he extended his hand. "Why, Perry—we're really old friends. I remember you now. You don't look much different. Have I changed? I'm one of the water-trough kids."

Murdock felt ill at ease. There was a mocking laugh of hard triumph from this dark, bitter youth, while his son sat there as if bowed by a memory.

Eda tossed a drink down. "Well—it's plain that you two don't need a shodchin."

Murdock began to eat, but there were disturbing vapors about him that had nothing to do with food. Perry pushed his plate away and spoke reminiscently. "I'll never forget the first impression of that neighborhood. God! how young I was." He shuddered.

Then he spoke directly to Peter. "I think you'll be interested in my plans. It all goes back to that one shocking visit. I want to re-make, reform the east side—cleaner streets, better dwellings, more milk stations and settlement houses."

Peter lashed out cruelly. "Why don't you leave the east side alone? What are you trying to do—make poverty palatable for the poor? The hell with the poor! Those that have the strength will claw their way out. The others must suffer until the day they rise up and tear their masters limb from limb."

"You say that?" Perry blinked. The others paused.

"If you must be an idealist, reform the rich. Change Fifth Avenue. Let a little light into Park Avenue, a little humanity into the West End. Yes, reform the rich, and the problem of the poor will take care of itself."

Listening to the bitter force of Peter's talk, Murdock felt himself sympathetic towards his son. Much as he wanted Perry to abandon his crack-brained humanitarianism, he hated to see him bested in an argument. He took up the cudgels for him.

"Don't you feel any sympathy for those poor foreigners?"

Peter laughed with his eyes. "Do you? What did you pay the Italian workers who dug that road-bed for you?"

"The current scale of wages. Besides, that was business."

"Exactly. You have the business. Your son has the sentiment. Did you ever walk through Elizabeth, Mott and Mulberry Streets, through Carmine and Roosevelt Streets and see the havens those Italian workers went to after the day's work? Now your son wants to open a free milk station on Mulberry Street, or open a sanctimonious salon where they can play checkers to make up for what you did."

Murdock found himself stumped and growing angry. Eda tugged at Peter's arm. "You're soap-boxing like a Socialist."

"But I'm not," insisted Peter. "I've paid my tribute to that kind of living. Now I'm on my way out. If I try to help others crawl out, I'll just be a fly on sticky paper—one wing free, the other caught trying to help a fellow insect escape."

Murdock looked at Peter, his dark, sure eyes, his dark skin, observed the rapt expression on Eda's face—it bordered on fright—and the look of defeat that came into Perry's eyes when he saw which way Eda was looking. A great bitterness filled his heart. Why couldn't his son have been as positive of himself, his stand in life, as this other youth?

"I understand you're a lawyer," he said. His voice changed the subject and tempo of their conversation.

"Yes, but I'm leaving law for finance."

"Connected with any house?"

"I was practically brought up in one firm. Seymour Henderson. Ever hear of the old pirate?"

Murdock swallowed his spittle and his mouth suddenly went dry. The girl his son wanted—and the job he had carved for his son, both in the strong, dark hands of Peter. One of the water-trough kids.

"Yes, I've heard of Seymour Henderson." He turned his head away. "Let's have another drink."

Elmer Hicks found himself between two walls of orange. The whirling, tortuous, nightmarish orange that kept sleep from his racked body through the long hours of the night, and the cool, remote orange of Sally that kept him at a distance by day. She was more amused than impressed by his dollar tips, and considered him an eccentric rather than a wooer.

Elmer wanted desperately to deepen the friendship between them, to make her aware of his feelings. But he didn't know how to begin. He cursed himself for his clumsiness and ignorance, lamented his neglect of an art which had now become all-important to him. He knew how to assemble a desirable tract of land, how to extract the largest possible loan upon the smallest security, how to divine a real estate boom, but he didn't know the first thing about courtship. Particularly with a girl who had the knack of chilling him with a glance.

As she set down before him a thin caress of butter, and a few paperweight slices of bread, he asked timidly:

"Don't you ever eat out, Sally?"

"We're not allowed to do that—with customers." A smile whisked on and off her face.

"But couldn't you make an exception for me? We could dine uptown and go to the theatre afterwards."

There was something so pathetic about his plea, that for the first time she really examined him. Here was a slender man, of average height, in his late thirties, with an intense face entirely devoid of humor. His eyes, even behind their glasses, looked very tired and seemed to harbor some deep obsession. His clothes were self-effacing, a medium-priced read-to-wear suit, the collar of his shirt about half a size too large for his neck. He looked far too serious, too pathetic to be a flirt, and Sally couldn't pay him off in the ready coinage she kept for the village troubadours. His fingers tapped the table nervously as he looked up for his answer.

"I'm afraid I couldn't go out. You see, my room-mate doesn't like to be left alone evenings."

"In that case we'll take her, too."

Sally laughed, her shrill, nervous, musical laugh. "Take Agatha? You couldn't get to the door with her."

"But—why?" Elmer looked bewildered.

Her face sobered. "Let's change the subject. I'm here to wait on you. That's all. What will you eat?"

She made a move towards the next table but Elmer seized her hand. She was startled by the heat of his fingers, the moist, burning clasp upon her hand.

"Please, Sally—I really want you to go out with me. And because you've always waited on me so nicely—now please don't think me fresh—couldn't I get you—a little gift?"

"A little gift? I suppose a trifle like a fur coat." That will settle him, she thought.

"If that's what you'd like—all right. When we meet—you can pick one out. A nice one."

His hand still clutched at hers, but she broke away. She couldn't stand the intensity in his eyes. Here was the look against which Agatha had warned her, the look that was charged with the dreadful desire of man. And now, watching his eyes, the twitching of his lips, she suddenly grew indignant, because she felt she ought to.

"Now look here, Mr. Hicks, you can't make such propositions to me. A little fooling is all right—but this is going too far. I'm not the kind of girl you're accustomed to. And you don't have to sit at my table either. Your order, please."

Nevertheless, Sally did not refrain from embroidering the incident to Agatha that night. She hoped to provoke her to buy the fur coat she wanted. But Agatha, who was something of a tactician herself, berated Sally.

"Flirting again? You're no more to be trusted than a cow in heat. Well, give yourself for a fur coat—and see what will happen. Find out what men do." And in that "what men do," she put so much terror, such implications of bestiality, that Sally became frightened.

Elmer, repulsed, kept away from "The Orange Peel" for a few days, and when he could bear the separation no longer, he took his problem to Donovan. Suavely hiding his amusement, Donovan assured him there was no cause to worry, that he would smooth the way for him.

Donovan came down for dinner the following evening and when Sally set his table, he asked casually:

"Seen my millionaire friend lately?"

"Who?"

"You know—Mr. Hicks. He always sits at your table. I think you made quite a hit with the gent."

"Is he a millionaire?"

"Don't tell me you didn't know about Elmer Hicks? Why, he's putting up blocks of houses in the Village alone."

The word millionaire tingled in Sally's ears. She remembered her first ambition, the girl from the west who comes to New York to marry a rich man. And here was an honest-to-God millionaire and she had stupidly rebuffed him.

"No—he hasn't been around in a few days," Sally said, a little slowly. "But I'd like to see him."

"Then leave it to Mike Donovan. I'll bawl him out for neglecting you."

In a few days, Elmer was back at his table in "The Orange Peel." And the fur coat was on Sally's back. She wore it triumphantly even into Agatha's presence, because all she had to do to acquire it was to put her arms through its sleeves.

Elmer Hicks was a tender and timid suitor, whose intentions were most honorable.

Joey, walking north on Lenox Avenue from the Central Park exit, passed Loew's Regent Theatre on 116th Street. He was on his way to an appointment with Donovan at the Harlem gymnasium on 125th Street. His pace was listless, the slow progress of a man brooding.

Pausing before the lobby display of the ornate theatre, he saw, in the show-case, a photograph of a pair of dancers clasping each other in a wingy pose and under it the inscription, "Burns & Co., Society Spielers." Looking closer at the girl in the arms of the dancer, Joey was astonished to recognize Isabella. He stood still, trying to absorb the shock.

She had disappeared from his life; at first an occasional colored card, a line, a greeting, always indefinite; later, nothing, a void of silence. Even her mother, now a mental patient, knew only vaguely that she was on the road with an act. And now she had returned, pinioned before him in a glass case. How beautiful she looked, how willowy and graceful and completely grown-up. Perhaps a little too exposed in that bespangled evening gown, but he felt sure his Isabella was a good girl.

And how that lizard in evening clothes clutched her with a disdainful, proprietary expression. Well, perhaps this intimacy was necessary for the purposes of the dance. Joey examined the man's features more closely and recognized Murray Burns. He clamped his mouth bitterly, remembering how he himself had been indirectly responsible for their meeting. The sharpshooter had not only won the contest at that Stuyvesant Casino dance, but had stolen his girl. A wave of hatred rushed over him. If these were only the days of his youth, when all he had to do to slake his hatred was to sock a guy. But now the code was different. He was a professional fighter, and doubly obligated to behave like a gentleman, for it was the ironclad rule of the ring that no professional engage in fights out of the arena. Pondering the lean, bony face of Murray, goaded by the disdainful smile about his thin lips, Joey computed that one blow from his chunky fist, placed between those mean eyes, would split the face in two and forever change that maddening expression. But he must restrain himself.

He forgot his appointment with Donovan and bought a ticket for the matinee. Far down front he sat, weighted by his own single thought, his hunger for Isabella, while acrobats risked their spines and necks and an Irish monologist extracted gusts of laughter with jokes that everyone remembered.

Then the dancers floated in to the lulling music of a Viennese waltz. Joey watched his Bella dance, gaped at her grace and beauty, marvelled at how tall she had grown, how mature she looked. Why, only yesterday, it seemed, he had watched her circle before an organ grinder in the street, had tugged at her braid to send her home, had seized her arm in anger and wondered why his fingers tingled in secret ecstasy. And now she whirled, smiling fixedly, theatrically, into the contemptuous eyes of a man who had the look of possession, danced with him as one. It was patent to Joey that she moved as a figure in a trance, under the spell of her partner.

Burns and Isabella had added new tricks to their routine and in their second number, an acrobatic fox-trot. He swung her around hazardously, her arms clamped around his neck, his outspread, and as she whirled faster and faster Joey winced, fearing that some accident would befall her. When he could no longer bear the tension, he walked out of the theatre and around to the alley which led to the stage entrance. The crusty doorman stopped him.

"Who do you want to see?"

Joey blinked. He did not know her professional name, nor had any appeared on the billing. "The goil in the dance act—you know Boins and Company."

"Don't you know her name?" The doorman was officiously suspicious.

"Sure—Isabella."

"Does she know you?"

"Sure—she knows me." And a doubt filled his mind. Would Isabella see him?

The doorman was still unconvinced. "Got a calling card? Or, who shall I say wants to see her?"

Joey was beginning to lose his temper. "Tell her Joey wants to see her—and tell her quick. I'm Young Samson, see?"

"Okay, as soon as the turn is over."

Joey fidgeted around until the doorman returned. "Two flights up, dressing room nine."

This was Joey's first visit to the backstage labyrinth, and the back drops, ropes, weights, switches, heavy smells, swift sure movement of performers and stage hands, the sudden appearance of made-up faces like grotesque masks, bewildered him. Quietly he treaded up the steps, and cap in hand, he knocked on the door. "Come in." Even her voice sounded strange, theatrically self-assured.

"Joey—oh Joey!"

She flung her arms about him and kissed him. He tasted the heavy lip rouge and the grease paint. He felt the tears rise to his eyes. She was really glad to see him. And how he had ached to see her. He was afraid to press her to him. She seemed so frail. He merely stood, rooted.

Then, gently, she disengaged herself from his arms, and in a faltering voice said, "You remember my partner Murray Burns." Joey hadn't even noticed he was in the room.

A disdainful face looked up from a mirror brightly illumined by two powerful electric lights. One hand draped in a dirty towel rubbed at the forehead and the voice tossed itself across a shoulder, ironically, "How's the little champ?"

Joey had no talent for wisecracks. Wing a barbed word at him and he could only reply with a snarl or a sock. He tried to ignore the man, although he was shocked to see how few clothes he wore in the girl's presence.

"Cheez, Bella, I ain't seen you in a long time. You just blew out."

"I had to go—sudden-like. Didn't I, Murray?" The intimacy of that "Murray" hurt Joey.

His words were full of sorrow. "But now you're back, Bella, I'm gonna see you, ain't I?" He paused and asked in a lower voice, "You're still my goil, ain't you?" He was uttering a wish like a child. Her little hand went out to him, smoothed his cheek.

"You never change, do you, Joey?"

Burns laughed gleefully. "She's got no time to fool around with second-raters. She's out to make a career. Get wise to yourself."

"Don't say that, Murray! I'll see Joey any time I want."

"Are you forgetting we're booked solid for twenty-four weeks? From here to Denver and back. All right, I'll let you see him—make a date for next year."

Joey's heart grew heavier. She was going away again, far away. "Cheez, Bella—you'll be away a long time."

"A long time is right," Burns cackled. He slapped Isabella familiarly on the buttocks. "Why don't you tell the boy friend what I've done for you?"

Joey felt his anger rising. The way the lizard handled his girl.

"All I know is—you took Bella away."

"Sure, to make something of her. And maybe, when we come back, Bella's name will be in electric lights—and you'll be a third-rate pug." He laughed mockingly.

"Don't insult Joey," cried Isabella. Murray moved towards her, black and threatening. He must show her again that he was the boss. "Close your trap, you punk!"

Joey could stand it no longer. Foul words rushed to his lips but he dared not utter them in the presence of his lady. "You're a no-good guy." He leaned forward, one fist clenched, the arm drawn back. Just one sock, planted between those cruel eyes. He shot the arm out.

Isabella sprang in front of Murray. "No, Joey—please."

Joey tried to pull his punch, but it struck Bella on the breast. She doubled up in pain while Joey bit his lips.

"I'm sorry. Bella—why didn't you let him take it?"

"Because you might have cut his face. And if you had, they'll cancel the act. He mustn't get hurt."

Burns, ambushed behind the girl, shrieked, "Get that gorilla out before I send for the manager!"

Bella pleaded with Joey. "Please go, Joey——"

"I'm awful sorry, Bella. I'd cut my arm off sooner than hoit you."

"That's all right, Joey. The pain is passing now."

"Will I see you, Bella—just once—before you go?"

"Sure Joey, sure." She led him to the door.

Joey walked out. His heart was like stone. All he could think of was that she had thrown herself protectingly in front of Burns. She had taken the blow intended for him. Why, she must love him.

Other thoughts came to him. Donovan had promised him that when he became the champ he could pick up an easy vaudeville engagement. Just rope-skipping, fancy bag-punching and sparring a round with a set-up. Perhaps he would be on the same bill with the dancers and then he could watch over his Bella, even impress her with his own importance so that she would come back to him.

But like a dirge the scene returned. Bella, standing in the way of a blow to shield the lizard. Yes, she must love him.

21

Rain blanketed Yorkville. Sometimes, rain or snow singles out a particular section of New York for its special blessings, or furies. Snow never lingers on Broadway, but it piles high on Avenues C and D, on the mean little streets that slink to the East River. Cold also picks its target. When the thermometer toys with zero, it's brisk walking on Fifth Avenue, but under the Ninth Avenue "L," or where Houston Street crosses Second Avenue, or around the gas-house district, it's blue cold and dirty winter. Looking out of your taxi window, you know it's raining on Park Avenue; but in Bushwick water mains burst; out near Sheepshead swimming pools form in the street and all Queens becomes marshy. The rolling clouds thunder over the city and lift their trap doors where they can bring the most disaster.

Jan Pajalski sat at the window in the Eighty-eighth Street tenement and looked out upon the rain. In Yorkville the sky was the Atlantic Ocean pouring itself through a sieve. The rain fell and Jan was thinking his thoughts. Those new jazz bands which had been springing up all over town were depriving him of engagements. While the earlier immigrants still clung to native customs and loyally supported native music, the younger generation demanded jazz and popular American dance tunes played in those barbaric rhythms which were anathema to him.

Lack of work made him morose. It deprived him not only of his status as head of the house, but curtailed his opportunities to get drunk, to be a glamorous figure, to indulge in back-platform sexual nips. His wife, Maria, forced into work in order to get the little money they needed, cleaned the houses of others by the day, did hem-stitching and needlework on trousseaux, and became the sole support of the family. There was no love between them and the wife allowed Jan food and a place by the fire

230

but no more. There was no money for drink; and with relentless vigor she defended herself from his recurring lusts.

But upon her child, Gina, Maria lavished every care, every tenderness, an unlimited outpouring of all her love.

Jan Pajalski, muttering to himself, revolved these resentments in his mind as he sat at the window and looked out upon the rain. In time he became aware of the ticking of the clock and with that awareness he suddenly started from his chair. Maria had warned him that in the event of rain he must be sure to call at Gina's school with her rubbers, raincoat and an umbrella. No risks must be taken with the health of the child. But it was already five minutes after three. It would take him at least ten minutes to walk over. And the rain was falling in furies.

He re-lit the stump of a cigaret. Well, it was too late now. There was no use in getting himself drenched to the skin on an errand that was futile. Besides, what was the idea of pampering the girl? She was no longer a child. Indeed, with her well-developed body, her rounded legs and her white, budding breasts she gave every lovely evidence of entering maturity.

He lingered in his thoughts of her, and his blue watery eyes blinked. She was very desirable and he couldn't help thinking of her in those terms, even if she was his own daughter. Resentment swept over him. Say, was Gina made of sugar, that a little rain would melt her? He felt pleased, as though he were avenging himself for the cruelty and indifference Maria had been showing him. After all, Gina was of peasant stock, and no rain ever hurt a peasant.

And what made Maria guard this little flower so? Even from him. Here was a situation. She was his own daughter and yet he could never get close to her. Maria had not only blackened his character before the child, but had drawn a curtain across the one bedroom, so that the girl could dress and undress in privacy. At first he had laughed at this, but then he had grown bitter. And curious, too, which was more tantalizing. Although once he had stolen a glance at his daughter, nude. What a figure! The conical whiteness of her young breasts, the little belly. He remembered, with some amusement, his own father, a roistering devil who went about pinching the buttocks of his own daughters and rubbing the breasts of neighbors' daughters and maids, but all in a spirit of fun. That was it, just simple, peasant fun. What was all this American affectation of privacy, of guarding virginity as if it were a gem? It was all right for the rich, because in all probability they had something precious to hide. But the poor had nothing to conceal, and nothing to guard. He re-lit the tiny stump of his cigaret and puffed nervously.

The door banged open and Gina stamped in. She tore off a hat which dripped water on the floor, and her throbby voice and eyes were alive with rage.

"Why didn't you call for me—you old fool? All the girls had someone to take them home with an umbrella. But I have to get wet. Now I'll catch cold, and it will hurt my voice. Wait till mother comes home."

Jan repressed his anger, even enjoyed the way she had lashed out at him. He came up to her like an old man silently pleading for forgiveness and he put his hand on her shoulder to help take off her wet coat. But she shrugged him off as if his touch revolted her.

"Leave me alone. And keep away from me."

"I'm sorry," he said in a sorrowing and peculiarly gentle voice. "I didn't notice the time, and you know how I suffer from rheumatism." Then, more insistent, he helped her out of one sleeve, took the dripping coat from her hands. "Why don't you go in there?" He indicated the bedroom. "Go, my child, and change into some dry clothes."

She searched his cunning peasant face for some reason for this solicitude. He pretended not to feel her eyes upon him. "Yes, I better change," she said.

There was something in the atmosphere that made her wary. She wished her mother were home. Somehow, she never felt quite safe unless the broad-shouldered, buxom Maria guarded her from all the fears, visible and secret, that tormented her. It was Maria who kept telling her that she was a rare child, rare in beauty and in talent, and that she was destined to become a great actress.

Gina walked slowly into the other room. There was no door between the kitchen and bedroom, but even if there had been she would not have dared to close it, despite her feeling of unsafety. After all, he was her own father, even if her mother did treat him like an enemy.

Gina drew the curtain across and sat down on the bed. There was little light in the room. She unlaced her shoes, kicked them off, and peeled off her stockings. The smooth, rounded calves of her legs were wet from the rain which had dripped down from her dress, and, bare-legged, she walked into the kitchen to fetch a towel. Jan stood tense at the window, just sniffing the smell of her flesh. But he did not swing his head until her back was turned. How firm and white her legs were and how well she moved them. Here was grace, balance, all the lovely magic of alive young limbs. He struck a match but did not re-light the butt of his cigaret.

Gina returned to the edge of the bed, dried her feet and calves, wriggled her toes and rubbed them with her hands. They tingled with new life. Then she unsnapped the back of her dress, withdrew her arms and let it fall at her feet. She folded it across the brass support of the bed. Even her underwear was wet. The thing to do was to take everything off, bounce into bed, snuggle under the warm covers until her mother came home. Then she would be served like a princess, hot cocoa in bed, solicitous questions and tender, protective kisses.

She was standing nude, examining with some pride the firm uprising of her breasts, sensing with a flash into the future the power her beauty would one day give her, when she suddenly became aware of her father. Jan had tiptoed in so quietly that she had not heard him. They both stared at each other, one with frank lust, the girl in terror. Perhaps, if she had not screamed, he would have recovered his senses, but her animal cry of terror roused him to sudden action and he seized her, mumbling incoherently, "Don't be afraid—I'm your father—your own father."

Some extra maternal sense of danger, fear for her daughter in the storm, had hurried Maria home. She saw. She did not pause to think. She merely picked up the stove-handle—it seemed the natural gesture, so often had she made this threat—and brought it down upon the head of Jan. His scalp gave a little and he sank to the floor.

Maria kicked him aside and took her daughter into her arms. She quickly examined her, appraised herself of the actual situation and crossed herself in prayerful thanks that no bestial harm had befallen her gem.

Then she put Gina to bed and soothed her with words and caresses. "Don't worry, my child—he'll never touch you again. We'll leave in the morning. Just you and me. I'll take care of you, my beautiful angel. I'll take care of you—until the world is ready for you."

In the rear of the auditorium at the University Settlement Bert stood alone, enjoying intensely his role of solitary and tortured creator, while a troupe of five amateur players performed his one-act play, "The Perfumed

Wall." The words took on new values, even overtones of genius, as they bounced out upon a delighted audience.

He himself had climbed a considerable distance from the ground, and his eager eyes were peering over the edge of the wall, searching for the delights above and beyond it. His driving urge was to escape his early environment, to obliterate the life proverty had thrust upon him. His excursions had led him from French romance to Russian realism, to the mystic pastoral idylls of W. H. Hudson and then to the artificial elegances of Oscar Wilde. And there he remained. This was his goal, the opposite pole.

For years now the theatre had been his sole interest. At first he had combined it with a general interest in literature, science, history, even mathematics, in an effort to encompass a broad tillage so that he could be equipped in all rounded ways for his career as playwright. But so keen did his interest in the theatre grow that he lost all patience with his other studies. He gave up college before he could present his bewildered parents with tangible evidence of his education, a diploma. And after two efforts he gave up trying to explain to them that he could waste no time on extraneous subjects. Then he retired into his little room in the Bronx apartment and began to write dialogue. When he emerged, it was only to visit Broadway, to attend the theatre. In addition to the plays he wrote, he read the trade journals, the theatrical columns and soon had an indexed knowledge of current plays, the relative importance of producers, stars, playwrights, even scenic designers.

It was clear to him that when people sought escape, they wanted to escape upward; and so this youth, who had nourished himself with literature and dreams on a Forsyth Street fire-escape, whose vistas were the backyards of tenements, whose sunsets were composed of colors of wash hanging on lines and food mouldering on window-sills, became an authority on the modes and manners, affectations in speech and artificial elegances of the highest society. The ideal of Mayfair was his special province.

In his own laboratory he had been experimenting with scenes, with dialogue, always remembering that restraint was the better part of expression. True, all about him people gave vent to emotion with an abandon that was vivid and clamorous, an unrestrained outpouring, but he stuffed his ears against such earthy examples.

The playlet they were performing now was his first to achieve production, but he knew that it was only the beginning. And not an insignificant beginning because, with Sebastian Melmoth, he believed that a true artist does not progress, but rotates in a creative orbit, and all of his works are of equal importance.

Bert watched a character make a cross. The girl, equipped with a beak and broad undulating haunches, looked a trifle too plump and too Jewish for the part of the dissolute, satiric actress who had once been the idol of London and Broadway. But he hoped that her lines, epigrams that alternated between brilliance and venom, would overcome her deficiencies in looks and accent. She was advising a young man how to succeed in life. And the sly point of her advice was that his success need have no more auspicious beginning than a little seduction of herself.

Gerald: Success seems so far away.

Cynthia: You give up too readily.

Gerald: What shall I do?

Cynthia: Follow your own impulses.

Gerald: I'd rather have a few rules.

Cynthia: Let me give you the first. Talk to every woman as if you love her.

Gerald *faltering*: That requires considerable practise.

Cynthia *moving towards him:* You may begin—with me.

As the lines pelted him, Bert had to acknowledge that scene resembled the one in "A Woman of No Importance."

Well, even if there was a resemblance, the lines were beautiful. In a few years, he would evolve his own style of writing, a style at once so trenchant and individual that critics would acknowledge him the dictator of wit, the dandy-messiah who brought to the parched public the ultimate word.

The playlet ended and the audience applauded the performers. Bert counted three bows. There were no frantic calls for "author," but such enthusiasm was not yet to be expected. It was sufficient glory that he had been performed on the same program with Richard Harding Davis, Lady Gregory, and A. A. Milne and in all fairness had come off rather well.

But the one who was ready to pay him tribute was his brother, Joey. There was pride, even awe in his face, now battered from the fights he had engaged in. But his eyes glowed. "Cheez, Boit, you made up them lines from your own head. Let me tell you—that's smart. Cheez!"

The contrast between the brothers was vivid. Bert's face had retained, even intensified its pallor. His brow was wider, his nose bonier, the blue tracery of veins etched even more sharply upon his temple and cheek. He dressed in careless tweeds in the English manner, Scotch grain shoes, woolen hose, a flannel turndown shirt and knitted tie. He was nearly a head taller than Joey and thin to the point of a charity case.

Joey's face was tanned and his stocky body moved toward you like an engine. On the occasion of his brother's debut as a playwright of manners he sported a white slit of tape across one eyebrow where a blow had opened it in his last fight. He wore the clothes of Broadway, tight at the waist, broad and padded at the shoulders, his feet shod in small, thin-soled, black-lustre shoes. And his hat seemed part of him, its removal a trial, its replacement a ritual. But he was proud of his kid brother, glad that his chunky fists had been able to send him through college, happy that his share of the purses had been sufficient to keep him at his books and writing, buy him tweeds and flannels, back-stage magazines and theatre tickets. Often he had tiptoed into his room, found him working at his mysterious typewriter with a rapt look of absorption. And Joey would press a bill into his hand, a fin or a sawbuck, something that had nothing to do with his regular pin-money, and say, "Keep on writin', Boit—you'll make it." And now he was beginning to come through, to justify all that hope.

Behind Joey, slowly approaching, were the bewildered and proud parents, little Isidore and his wife, now supported in undreamed-of luxury in the Bronx by their generous prize-fighter son. They were grateful to Joey, but proud of Bert, who had fashioned a language which others spoke gracefully, but which to them was as strange as himself. Every day they thanked God for their two sons, strange, almost fabulous in their separate ways, and also wondered how they had come to them.

On the way home, Bert, thinking back on his play, was surprised to perceive how vividly he recalled one performance. A minor character, the daughter of the dissolute actress. She was a young girl, not more than fourteen or fifteen, entered into the playlet by an elocution teacher. A young girl called Gina Pajal. He repeated her first name. Gina. He must remember her. The girl undoubtedly had rich talent.

22

In Riverside Park an old man sits, regarding the Hudson through his marmoset eyes. His face is matted with hair and his tangled beard is like the inter-rusted brush on the Palisades. Under the warm sun he wears three coats, and all of his sleeves are frayed. He munches peanuts, grovelling slowly, methodically, into a bag filled with them, cracking the shells and spewing the fragments forth upon himself. An evangelist with a large Adam's apple and an ecstatic gleam in his eye sits down beside him. "Brother," he rumbles, "God is everywhere."

"Everywhere," the old man repeats, munching learnedly, "but not in New York."

The evangelist moves away from the halo of the old man's stink. He parts his lips to speak, but is silenced by the deep voice.

"No—not in New York. And I ought to know, because I got clothes on my back. Mister, I know everybody here. I've been living all my life on the town. I meet the best people in the parks. Tramps, whores, down-arid-outers, tired niggers, nurses, millionaires, cops and lovely babies, and dogs that cost one hundred dollars and piss all day long. I eat the best—stale cake from the finest bakeries and T-bones out of West End garbage cans before the flies get at them. And look at the wardrobe on my back. I know everything and everybody in this town—and I tell you, God ain't in New York."

The evangelist, faint, but suffering beautifully, rumbles on. "God is everywhere—in the houses, in the streets, in the subways—in the river. On the banks, under the manholes, in the sky. God is everywhere."

"Maybe," says the old man, scratching his beard, "I ain't been every-where. But—not in New York."

The evangelist moves on.

Something had happened to the plume-like grace, the twinkling sure-footedness of Isabella. Both at the matinee and at the early evening show, she had stumbled, and their whirlwind finish, which consisted of countless spiel turns (they spun like propellers on a plane beyond control until the audience broke into applause), left her so dizzy that she nearly fainted.

"Watch yourself," growled Burns. And then, more cuttingly, "Or are you still in the amateur class?" He smiled to the audience and steadied her with a grip that pained.

For a while he had been jealous of Isabella, sensing that her dancing contributed more to the flash and success of the act than his own skill. But when she blundered, as she had today, he felt his superiority reassured. After all, he had taken her as raw, frightened material and moulded her into the finished dancer she was.

From show-wise girls in dance-units and in tabloid flash acts, and from the jokes comedians did not tell family audiences, Isabella had learned what every girl should know.

And so her own condition, which made her dizzy at the whirlwind finish, did not mystify her. But it did fill her with terror. She couldn't go on dancing much longer, and yet she dared not unburden herself to Murray, for he would drop her instantly. The fact that he was responsible for her condition wouldn't deter him at all. He could easily break in a new girl. He had always dangled that threat over her head, and since the act was called "Burns & Co.," the name of the female partner was of no significance. It was known as a high class Number Three act, and with or without Isabella, it would get booking.

Lacking any intimate friends, Isabella had to confide in one of the show girls who played around the circuit with her. Here was a gutter-wise bleached blonde, sporting one gold bicuspid, a willing navel and the philosophy of the cured. She was the female counterpart of the breezy man of the world who consoles the young sailor in a waterfront dilemma by telling him, "Buddy, it's nothing worse than a cold. You ain't a man until you've had it at least once."

The blonde, wagging her chew of gum, was maternally sympathetic. "Sure, honey, I understand—and don't let it bother you none. If this was Youngstown or Toledo, I'd say walk the floor because you might as well have it. But on home grounds, I say Ishkabibble. Yes, lucky we're playing New York. I know a doctor who'll do it for one hundred bucks.

Say, kid, we all get knocked up—especially the first time. But like I told you—don't let it bother you none."

"One hundred dollars," Isabella echoed faintly.

The blonde popped a gum bubble and daintily smoothed the cud with a pudgy forefinger. "That's all. It hurts a little and you'll have to be off your feet for a week."

"One week—one whole week!"

This, Isabella dreaded more than the fright and pain. How could she explain it to Murray? He would probably assail her for not knowing how to take care of herself and send for a new partner. And then, where would she get the money? Burns only paid her a small share of the money the act earned, explaining that the expenses and cost of costuming the dances devoured most of their earnings.

It was while wrestling with these problems that a solution came from a source least expected. Isabella was removing her make-up before a brightly illumined mirror and Murray was whistling unconcernedly when a loud, authoritative knock on the door was heard.

"Come in," said Burns and resumed his blithe whistling.

Two stocky, pugnacious men, like detectives in a melodrama, entered.

"Murray Burns?" asked one, just parting one side of his mouth.

"Why, yes—that's me, all right."

There was a note of concern in his voice and Isabella caught the growing fright in his eyes.

The inquisitor separated half of his mouth and with a note of mockery said, "Who else could you be? Ain't we seen your act? And you can sure handle those tootsies."

"What do you want?" faltered Murray. The reference to his nimble feet frightened him.

"Well, we're checking up on draft dodgers. Let's have a look at your registration card."

This was the period directly after the costly entry of America into the World War, when New York took on the appearance of a garrison town. The uniform ruled the roost.

Here was an amazingly ironic reversal in public attitude. Directly after the Spanish-American War and during the interlude of peace, soldiers and sailors were barred from every respectable theatre and restaurant in New York and their presence was resented on the main thoroughfares. They were forced to find entertainment at cheap burlesque shows, drink and eat in waterfront barrooms, and obliged to lay up with old hookers and battle-scarred Fourteenth Street buffaloes.

But suddenly, with America's entry into the war, they were elevated to the highest social plane. The bigwigs ordained that for the man in uniform no entertainment was too good, no food sufficiently palatable and no woman fragrant or passionate enough. Convent-bred daughters, directly out of the Social Register, led innocent marines astray for the sake of democracy. Demure schoolteachers and librarians and all the spinsters without whiskers gave themselves gladly to the lads in service.

But all this was done solely for the man in uniform and the young man in mufti was a pariah. And every one of draft age had to carry upon his person a registration card which testified that he had offered himself for service, and was either being readied for the slaughter or was exempted for a good reason.

Murray Burns had failed to register. It was not so much cowardice, not the fear of being killed, but the terror of being maimed that horrified him. If anything should happen to his legs, his long agile legs, anything to prevent him from dancing—he would blow his brains out. He had lived all his life only to dance, had starved, tortured himself for this career, and now that at last he was beginning to taste success, a little bullet or a piece of shrapnel could destroy him. He had nightmares in which in try-outs he performed a grotesque, one-legged dance, a pitiable single begging for time, and whenever he passed a marine in the street on crutches (almost immediately after America's entry, picturesque, one-legged casualties began to beat time on New York pavements) he became ill with fear.

"Well, how about it, lounge lizard—show us the registration card."

Murray's bloodless face grew white. He trembled violently and words came from him in gusts. "I haven't got a card."

"Just a plain case of weak memory. You forgot to register."

"No, but you can't touch me. I won't go—I won't go."

One of the men came over and struck him across the face. "Pipe down, you slacker. You'll go and like it."

Since they were in no danger of serving their country on any of the battle-fronts, they felt keenly outraged at Murray's reluctance to fight. The point was that the young must go.

"How about our—act?" Isabella, who had been petrified with fear, yes, fascinated by this scene, stood up.

"The hell with the act. Dance by yourself." The special agent smoothed her with his eyes. "You'll find another hoofer. Your country needs this guy."

By this time the manager of the theatre had been sent for and when he was informed that a slacker had been appearing on his bill, he looked like a man whose patriotism had been raped. Heatedly the manager recalled that from that very stage which Murray Burns had defiled with his slacker presence tens of thousands of dollars' worth of Liberty Bonds had been forced upon milk-toast patrons, and windy, patriotic frenzies had been pumped into audiences by four-minute men and aged pimps of liberty.

"How could you do this to me, Murray?" he asked, fearing he might be considered a German spy for harboring a draft dodger, or at least a traitor for having allowed a slacker to perform on his stage.

"Get me a lawyer," pleaded Burns. "I won't go."

"Listen, Bud—can the hysterics. A mouthpiece can't do you no good." The detective came over and thumped him good-naturedly. "But don't cringe like that—be a man. Uncle Sam has a heart as big as the Liberty Chest and will give you a chance."

"You mean—I don't have to go?"

The detective, smiling cruelly, shook his head. "I mean—you'll get a chance to make up for lost time. You'll get a chance to go over with the infantry pronto. Say, Uncle Sam gives you guys a square deal."

Shaking with fright, green with panic, Murray was forcibly escorted from the theatre, hiding his face from the jeers of onlookers in the street. He was led into a patrol wagon, into which other slackers had been herded like mangy dogs picked up in alleys and gutters. All of these non-militants without swivel chairs were taken to an armory and there parcelled out to the division first sailing for France. Those that still insisted they were pacifists were given swift trials and sentenced to life imprisonment at Fort Leavenworth. They were known as conscientious objectors, a derisive synonym for excrement.

Isabella was not even allowed to bid Murray good-bye. She felt a curious sadness as he was being led away. All his pride, his scorn, his cruelty had melted into a cringing, whimpering terror. As she tried to instil some courage in him, the detective graciously informed her that her slick dancing partner would be permitted to write to her after he was shoved into uniform.

Although this call to arms temporarily ended her vaudeville career, Isabella felt relief. The act had not been cancelled on her account, and in the interval required by the agent to find her a new partner she could have herself aborted. And when the agent paid over the money due the act to her, she found a new reason to be grateful for America's concern over world democracy.

The following afternoon, the blonde girl friend escorted Isabella to a surgeon whose one regret was that he could never publish papers in the medical magazines on his specialty. The considerate blonde, chewing her wad of gum, was voluble. "I've got everything fixed for you, honey. I've even reserved a room at a hotel near the office so's you can get right to bed."

A woman escorting another to an abortion is the soul of tenderness. There is a shivery feeling of relief in the bosom of the guide, and an unwhispered, "There, but for the grace of luck, go I."

Lying on the operating table, her legs raised on steel supports, the knify pain within her so agonizing that cold sweat exploded in charges from her little body, Isabella thought only of Joey, repeating his name to herself. She hungered for the sight and touch of him as a stifling person cries for a breath of clean air. All her dancing, the years with Murray Burns, seemed part of the nightmare to which this pain belonged. Only Joey was real. Joey was the future. She wanted desperately to be with him, hoped fervently that he would come to her when she sent for him.

The threatening clouds that hover over Manhattan are suspended dreams. The hues that color the city rainbow, the heat that makes the asphalt run, the cold that chills the marrow of the town, the dawns, the noons, the sunsets, all have in them the color and fibre of suspended dreams.

Clarence Dell, dreaming beyond his first conquests, crushing under layers of triumph the young tramp who begged advice on a park bench, the crawling, stinking bum who slept on the Battery grass, the cold-turkey canvasser who wedged his foot inside a hostile door to prevent its being slammed in his face.

Eda, flavoring first love, growing into a full-fledged newspaperwoman, expressing the town that still held her in its thrall, through the people who had chipped off small fragments of it.

Peter, guarding his chink in the wall, fighting off the bitter rivalries of office workers who tried to bind his feet as he strode onward.

Agatha, growing older, still waiting to design that stage setting which would lift her into the front rank of the theatre, nourished by her love for Sally, strengthening her hold on the girl by spider-web threads every day.

And Joey, training, fighting, still cherishing his faraway dream of Bella, fighting towards the welterweight title.

It was in Stillman's gymnasium one afternoon that Joey fell into his first meditative reverie. It was the last place in the world to meditate and dream, for the huge floor was filled with young men engaged in violent muscular activity. In one arena the champ was training, using a big buck Negro for a chopping block. He wore a rubber helmet to protect his ears, long tights, and boxed erect, not using the crouch for which he was famous. After each blow he sucked in his gut to conceal his considerable paunch. He's getting soft, thought Joey. With a nice chunk of dough in the bank and the right to name his own referee in every challenge bout, he looked and felt the cocky champ that he was. Joey, watching him move, felt certain that if they put the gloves on now he would have no trouble in sinking his powerful right into that soft mid-section, and by the time he pulled his glove out he'd be the new champ.

As Joey looked around he was startled to see two other pairs of eyes on the champ, and upon the envious faces that held the rapt eyes he could read the same thoughts that had possessed him. The air was thick with the covetous, hungry ambitions of men. They would claw and tear with their teeth, if necessary, to get to the top. And the thought came to him that even if he were lucky enough to win the title, others would be at his throat trying to rip it from his grasp.

And there were still others, second division men younger than himself, who felt they should supplant him, and in turn become logical contenders for the title bouts. And in one corner there was a Negro welterweight, his powerful black arms glistening and moving like polished steel, who might never get a crack at the title because he was too good.

The huge floor resounded with the rhythmic tattoos on punching bags, the smart flick of the rope as men skipped, the pull of oars on rowing machines; all around, flashing eyes, lean, strong faces, swift, tireless arms and legs growing stronger and surer for the great kill.

Joey felt that he was in a jungle of teeth and muscle, one of a ferocious pack, a pack ordained to hunt until they fell in their tracks and the one to waver would be devoured by its own mates.

For the first time in his life he felt tired, unsure. He thought of all the buoyant fights he had waged as a kid on Forsyth Street. Well, you couldn't regard those as work because at that time he had fought instinctively, enjoying the thrill of every sock. And his first professional fights had brought him great satisfaction. Money for his parents, newspaper clippings, the pleasure of being somebody, standing out from the mob.

In those early days, after eight knockouts in a row, the championship had seemed very close. But he had to admit to himself that since Bella had left him he had slowed up. It hadn't weakened him as a fighter—oh, he was still one of the three most dangerous contenders—but the singing joy and lust had gone out of battle.

He reviewed his career. Thirty-seven knockouts, eleven men outpointed, six draws—and he himself had been outpointed four times. He had never been knocked down. Not a bad record—but where would it lead to?

"Snap out of it, Joey—and warm up."

Joey had been idling, his fingers clasped around the rope handles, just standing and musing.

"He's dreamin' of the belt." A young Italian fighter, a spectacular meteor, grinned at him, flashing sharp white teeth. "Well, stop dreamm'. That belt looks better around my gut."

Joey smiled and mechanically began to skip the rope. First with the left foot, the right held under like a pensive heron. One, two, three, four, five, six, seven, eight, nine, ten. Cheez—a guy would have to have something big in his life, a great incentive, to go on with this life. Just training and fighting. Something very big—like the love of a girl. If only Bella—now with the right foot, one, two, three, four, five, six, seven, eight, nine, ten.

"Hey there, Young Samson, you're wanted on the phone. A dame."

Snickers went up from the cluster of young fighters as Joey, puzzled, went to answer the summons.

The gum-chewing blonde had tracked him down. She knew her way around town. To locate a pug, call Lindy's first and then Stillman's.

"Yes, it's Isabella, all right. She's a little indisposed—" the blonde threw in a tony word; she didn't mind impressing the boy friend, especially since the sweetheart was hors de combat— "and come right over because she needs you."

Joey found Isabella in bed, her blanched, blood-drained face on the white pillow, her dark eyes already hiding the pain, at once showing the joy she felt in his arrival. The breezy gum-chewing blonde who had admitted him sat by the bedside and observed the muted greeting of these two. There was something in Joey's awed worship that routed all her amorous plans. She jerked herself to her feet and swung over to a mirror, where she adjusted both her gum and her hat.

"Well," she giggled, "I guess I can leave you two love-birds alone." Maliciously, she added, "I know it's safe."

"Bella," faltered Joey, "tell me—what happened?"

"She's had her appendix took out," snickered the blonde. "Well, ta-ta, dearie. I'll be seeing you."

Alone with Isabella, Joey stared at the pallid face, at her silent plea for help and understanding and affection, and tears came to his eyes. It was a bewildering sensation, for he had never cried before. A mountainous wave of tenderness swept over him, but all he could do was place his hat on the bed and take her hand. It looked as tiny as a helpless bird in his chunky fist.

"Cheez, Bella, you had ought to let me know you was sick. But I'll look after you now. 'Cause you're still my goil, Bella—ain't you?"

Isabella patted his cheek, his strong, punch-hardened cheek, and through her fingers the strength of him flowed into her.

"Thanks, Joey—for coming here to see me. I was afraid you'd be angry."

"I couldn't git sore at you, Bella."

"I feel better already." Her voice broke in a sob as she pressed her palm against his face. "Joey—don't leave me."

She began to cry softly.

"I'll never leave you," said Joey, "and you'll never leave me. 'Cause you're my goil, Bella."

23

As Peter delved into the private papers of Seymour Henderson and grasped the far-reaching holdings of this financial octopus, he laughed mockingly at those poets and artists who dismissed finance as dull and unromantic. The true epic poem was not the journey of an emotion which finally spent itself in some trivial sexual yelp, but the wanderings of a dollar investment as it went whoring from individual to corporation, from corporation to syndicate, until it achieved its ultimate shrine, the cool vault, in the shape of a gold bond. The peregrinations of Ulysses, Gil Bias, Childe Harolde, became little journeys compared to the crusades of the dollar.

And all these dollars arranged themselves into a mosaic of security behind which Henderson sat, flatulent, piratical, lordly and impregnable. How secure his position was. He was on the Board of Directors of twelve large corporations, mining, railroad, public utilities and shipping, so that he enjoyed an inside track on all new stock issues, was privy to any secret information that could inflate stock prices, and a member of all the private pools that constituted the raiding parties of Wall Street.

When Peter first became aware of Henderson's cushy post, he envied him to the point of hatred. What a warm feeling to be so definitely on the inside! Like never emerging from the protection of the womb. Why, just the twenty-dollar gold pieces that Henderson collected from the various Boards of Directors' meetings could be melted into a little mound of gold. And alongside of this mound of gold could be placed a hill of stock certificates. And on top of it sat Henderson.

Peter, dreaming of the day when he too would control corporations and receive twenty-dollar gold pieces, spent rapt days and nights studying these records of stock holdings, transfers, corporation papers, until he had clearly grasped the vivid panorama of the financial empire which Henderson ruled.

And Henderson, believing that he had enslaved Peter by his single act of generosity, was glad to trust him with new and greater responsibilities. He was not becoming senile, for capitalists rarely grow soft, but he was entering upon a state of gentle ossification in which nothing flowed within him save memories. He felt a little tired of the money game, and had lost his major appetites, so that there was no longer an incentive to gratify anything, not even greed.

Having no son of his own, he fancied himself growing sentimental over Peter. He began to magnify the things he had done for him, forgetting the years of faithful serfdom on Peter's side. He bloated his own image to the proportions of a great benefactor. "Why, the little shaver," he thought. "I raised him in my own office, sent him through college, taught him everything he knows about money."

Here was the one sentimental ray of his old age. It gilded with pure gold the great American legend, the favorite Horatio Alger myth—from office boy to partner. There were many examples on the Street of office boys who had risen to own seats on the Exchange and the surface versions of their success stories were written up in the Sunday supplements and in the *American Magazine* and caused immeasurable unrest on farms and in villages.

Once, all that Peter had built up, the result of all his years of tireless slavery and devotion to Henderson, was threatened by the jealousy of a fellow office worker, one Ralph Plym, who was enraged at the progress Peter had been making, jealous of his reserves of silence and strength, the maddening, still flow of his strength and stride. The man, a born white-collar underling, had been head clerk when Peter entered as an office boy. Resenting him from the beginning as an intrusive outsider, he had ordered Peter around, heaping tasks on him in addition to those that Henderson laid out. And because the boy devoured work without complaint, his dislike of him grew.

As Peter became more adept, he took over some of Plym's duties, at the suggestion of Henderson. In small ways Plym tried his best to impede Peter's progress, but the youth moved on. Plym enjoyed a period of relief when Peter went to law school, but now on his return to a post more important than his own, he was seized with a maddening fury. His jealousy possessed him, crippling him even for the few routine tasks he still performed about the office. It was the fury of an older son who finds himself ousted as the king's favorite and is himself supplanted by a younger son who is brighter, and who possesses an enchanting personality.

On the five-eighteen, going home at night to his suburb on Long Island, Plym would think up schemes to get Peter out of the office. At dinner it was his favorite subject of discussion with his wife. Sometimes, in the office, he could hardly restrain himself from bodily ejecting Peter.

And then, like a gift from the skies, Plym discovered an item in the books which to him was overwhelming proof that Peter had tampered with a client's money. There it was, written in figures, bold and clear. The purchase of a small block of shares with an absent client's money. He could hardly contain himself and at once carried the books into Henderson's office. "I always knew there was something crooked about him. But this is the first time I put my finger on it," said Plym.

The old capitalist sent for Peter. Plym gleefully repeated the accusation. Peter looked at Henderson and it shocked him to see the cold cruelty in those eyes. They were like flint, without a spark of sympathy or understanding, and certainly no forgiveness. All the years of his work meant nothing to the old pirate.

As Plym, with a triumphant smirk, brought the books over, the evidence to confound Peter, Peter waved him away. With his amazing memory for figures, now surer because of the years of training, he disdained help.

"Don't bother, Mr. Plym," he said coolly. "I remember the item very clearly. Five hundred shares of Southern Pacific, bought August seventeenth." With a note of contempt, contempt for the senility that was creeping into the old man's brain and for the stupidity that was destroying Plym, he continued. "You may have forgotten, Mr. Henderson, but I showed you some real estate forecasts about a Florida boom in the fall and winter." He paused. "Then, anticipating a rise in the railroad stock as a result of increased passenger and freight service, I recommended the purchase of the Southern Pacific. You liked it so well that you bought a large block for yourself. We got it at nineteen and one-quarter and sold the small block at twenty-one. You're still holding yours. The profit item was included in the dailies but probably hasn't been entered in the big ledger because it was included with yours."

The flint vanished from Henderson's eyes. He began to chuckle. "I forgot all about it." Then, angrily, he turned to the sagging head clerk. "You should be more careful, Plym, before accusing anybody. That will be all." Henderson waved a dismissal.

"Oh, no," said Peter. "That won't be all. I believe I'd better resign."

"Nonsense," said Henderson.

"I can't work in an atmosphere of suspicion." Peter looked at Plym. He felt a little sorry for the beefy, middle-aged office worker, a servant without imagination, without special drive. He could see Henderson's wrath rising and soon it would vent itself against Plym. The man cringed as before an expectant blow. "Plym—I think you'd better go. You're losing your grip anyway. I'll arrange to transfer you to another office." Plym, stunned by the complete collapse of all his plans to oust Peter, just mumbled, "Yes, Mr. Henderson."

Peter emerged triumphant and was placated with a raise. But he never forgot the cruel glint in Henderson's eyes. He realized now that there was little sentiment in the office. He was kept because he was valuable, very valuable. Why, that piece of foresight alone on the first Florida boom had made a fortune for Henderson, and also a little for himself. But the incident left him hating the old man. There was no kindness, no mercy in Henderson. Well, he would stay on as long as it suited his purpose. But when the time came for him to go, no sentiment would restrain him.

And soon, partly through Henderson's involuntary paternalism and through Peter's own astuteness, money, virtually overnight, ceased to be a problem. While his nominal salary was $5,000 a year, Henderson allowed him a percentage on all deals he originated and consummated, and Peter could see a substantial surplus piling up, piling up.

On some nights, alone in the office, alone in that sepulchral hush that falls on the financial district after the work day, pondering over some clause in articles of incorporation for a new subsidiary designed to circumvent a thorn in the law, Peter would pause in his work. He would think back upon the blue-black days of poverty that stretched like a curtain of black sandpaper across his youth, stretched from Forsyth to Roosevelt Streets, through all the years of his public school and his father's aching spine, through the "Toorkish-a-lemonade two cents a glass" summers, through his years of gathering regents' counts, the nights in law school, and all those bitter thoughts and memories bubbled up in him like vials of venom threatening to burst through his pores, overflow the office, pour into the streets and poison the city. In those moments he hated money and he hated the town. What was the key to this cruel pattern that made a penny, a nickel, a dime important for years and then suddenly, overnight, poured wealth upon him? Why couldn't a little of it have dribbled into the long years of his impoverished youth so that he could have tasted something pleasant when his palate thirsted for it? What ironic gods sitting in what turrets of mockery arranged this diet for him—first, years of gall and then honey?

But even when he hated money most, he did not underestimate it. He must acquire it in vast holdings, if only to atone for the poverty of his youth. He would tap the secret sources where it flowed thick and plentiful to make up for the years when he had gone around beating on stone with a straw.

When his income was reasonably assured, the first thing Peter did was to rent an apartment in the Gramercy Park section for his father and grandfather. The two old men needed pure air and sunshine, and a change in neighborhood.

On the first warm Sunday afternoon, he sat between them on an exclusive bench in this carefully guarded, iron-barred park. The old men sat in silence and basked in the sun, wrinkled patriarchs who had at last found serenity. Peter smiled bitterly to himself, remembering that as a child he had once stormed these very gates, eager to get in; but the park was closed to mongrels, open only to the choice residents of the vicinity. And now the two old men with their withered faces to the sun, his two children, could sit there undisturbed and enjoy peace and fresh air.

New York, the city in which numberless hearts crack from loneliness, is also the haven for thousands of lovers who live together, simply, naturally. They do not flaunt their comradeship as a defiant gesture of adolescent Bohemianism, and yet they turn their healthy backs upon the crochety, verbal pawings of a decayed clergy.

In this simple, natural manner, Peter and Eda went to live together in a small, snug apartment on Barrow Street in the village. There were no pseudo-emotional heavings, no lengthy preludes (preludes wear out ardor) on the moralities and conventions involved. It was the normal behavior of two people who know exactly what they want and are determined not to scratch on back doors and wait for hand-outs from life. They knew what they wanted. They took it.

Almost from their first meeting, Eda had claimed Peter for her own. Here was a mortal symbol of the city-lover that gave her no peace, no hope of anything except mounting desire. With Peter, she could still that fire, a little. The love of a human would save her from the furies, keep her from madness, give her interludes of peace at the feet of the god that glowered above and around her. And if she gave of herself, wildly and generously, she might some day know real oblivion.

But Peter came only part of the way towards her. Much of him remained remote and shadowy, eluding all her cajoleries and embraces. You cannot place the tower of a skyscraper in your lap and stroke its wind-battered forehead. There is no caress for the grinding wheel of a subway train. And when Peter spoke, his inner hatred and bitterness brought a cruel clarity to his desires and ambitions. He uttered his thoughts like a blow-torch, training hot words upon the point to be made, sparing no one. It was grotesque for them to speak of their love in terms of little loves.

"Remember, Eda—I am dry of love. And if ever I marry, it won't be for love. I don't know how long this union will last—but when I have to break it up—I shall." He closed his eyes and thought back. "I've been brought up in a house that never had a woman—raised with two tired, hungry, silent men, and with my own ambitions."

"I'll take as little or as much of you, as you'll give," said Eda. "I love you, Peter—almost in the way—I love New York." Then, half-smiling, "Perhaps I can thaw out some of your hard hatred, melt the distance between us. Perhaps, in time, you'll give more of yourself—than you expect."

And yet Peter and Eda in their hours together were happy—as happy as two people can be who bear within themselves tumult and chaos and fierce ambitions. Only the subnormal ever find that mealy leaven of Christmas-candy happiness. The softening of the pate brings with it a bovine serenity, the kind that permits a cow to lie serenely in the rain, while dogs and humans run like mad.

What helped their love was their complete absorption in their work and careers. Eda had been taken on a morning paper, first at space rates, then as a regular member of the staff. The impact of her vitality, her eagerness to see and do and be, devoid of any wistful lavender, swept her beyond all obstacles. Her work excited her, and every assignment meant a fresh excursion into the city that held her in thrall. She brought life and color to dry interviews. Even the cautious opinions of a public utility menial on light consumption in New York became important because he uttered them from an office on the twenty-fifth floor of a downtown skyscraper. She was always aware that his obedient eyes, if once he wanted to remove them from charts and graphs or the framed photo of a prissy wife, could rest on the East River which separated two boroughs that sprang at each other's throats, while tugs, coal barges, railroad flats and passenger boats calmly disappeared under bridges.

Besides, her work made her financially independent both of her father and of Peter. As she explained quite definitely, in the beginning, "We'll share between us—all of the expenses." Peter, from the peak of his new opulence, protested, but she hushed him.

"In other words, my sweet, I give myself to you. My body shall always belong to me—if only that I may be able to give it—to you."

Work-days and nights they reserved for their masters and their ambitions, but on week-ends they moved into their little apartment together like children who return home after a journey. And on Sunday mornings, lying late in a soft bed, smelling the aroma of percolating coffee, listening to the chimes of a neighborhood church, watching the relaxed movements of Eda in negligée, it seemed to Peter that New York was atoning for the bitter childhood, for the privations in youth that it had thrust upon him.

Thoughts like simple melodies, easily remembered, drifted through his head. "Perhaps I should settle down and marry. Why strive for more than I actually need? I can be happy."

But thundering across the simple song came the roar of his piled-up venom, the clamor of his pent-up ambitions. A derisive roar, a roar of challenge.

The town quits spreading and instead humps itself up in the middle, rising to fantastic heights. A monster, crouching for a leap into history. Skyscrapers are built like steps leading to heaven. The man of the future can climb up in rooflines, up, up, to Mars.

New skylines light up in various sections of the city, and when reporters interview visiting celebrities about the famous New York skyline, they must specify which one they mean. The Battery waterfront skyline which dominates the entrance to the town like a regal diadem. The coruscating and Christmasy Central Park South skyline which is so magical on clear autumn nights that gangsters driving through the park, fresh from Bronx and Harlem killings, clap their hands like children and sing carols. The brooding East River skyline as you cross the Queensborough Bridge. The Brooklyn Heights skyline as you crawl over the Brooklyn Bridge. The Central Park West skyline. The string of pearls along Riverside Drive as you glimpse it from mid-Hudson. New York, scratching the sky in many places, writing its name in flame and terror.

For years now, Elmer Hicks had been watching New York hump itself up in the middle. And taking stock of all his land holdings, his money and property resources, he decided to plunge into the deep center and concentrate on mid-town realty. A handful of enterprising manipulators were putting up towering office buildings across the mid-town belt, and as rapidly as they were completed, their stores and offices were rented. Indeed, some were rented from blueprints months ahead of actual completion. The prosperity boom was always one lap ahead of the builders. It reminded Hicks of his first Bronx apartment houses when tenants would rent rooms by just looking at the excavations.

But what made this amazing concentration of lavish skyscrapers possible was the ease with which it was possible to promote money and arrange financing for a five, eight or even ten-million-dollar structure. If you could assemble a site, any good banking or brokerage house or private banker would underwrite an issue of mortgage bonds which would supply ample funds to construct, and a fat bonus for the promoters, builders and bankers. The bond issues on buildings were absorbed by a gullible public with great avidity. Oil and mining stocks were whimsically called "speculative" issues and passed on to suckers, but your good New York conservative burgher, dipping into his beard for wisdom, or emerging from a consultation with his banker, looked at a bewildering mass of stone and steel and glass and somehow felt that a mortgage bond was a conservative gilt-edged investment.

Elmer, preparing his new campaign for the building coup of his career, began to dispose of his holdings in Greenwich Village and in the Bronx and, through dummy agents, he put out feelers for a site on Broadway between 43rd and 44th Streets. He made a confidant of Donovan, who not only approved of his gigantic plans but pledged himself to help.

And for the financial and legal wizardry behind a deal of this magnitude, Donovan recommended Peter Mendes, whose reputation was growing beyond Wall Street.

"He's young, but he practically runs Henderson, an old pirate who's lousy with millions. And from friends of mine downtown, I've heard the lad's a genius at financial set-ups. I know he's been taking pieces of big real estate issues for a subsidiary of his firm, and cleaning up."

Elmer agreed to check up on Peter Mendes and when he was ready, to meet him.

It was a simple matter to excite men over his vision, but striking a responsive chord in Sally over his dream of conquest was not so easy. They were dining together in a restaurant near the site he coveted and he was telling her about his plan with the ardor of a poet reading a freshly composed sonnet. But it was difficult to impress her, first of all because she was only remotely interested in what he did, and secondly because her skimpy mind could not grasp any of the big strokes of his plans. He tried to picture for her the obstacles in the way of assembling such a precious site, the flotation of perhaps a fifteen-million-dollar mortgage bond issue, the parcelling out of that vast fund, the rentals and revenues which would pay the guaranteed interest on that issue, the tremendous net profits which would accrue to him. But only the word "millions" got a response from her.

"You mean—Elmer—you're liable to become a millionaire?"

"A couple of times—over." He said it with simple pride. He could practically close his fingers around a million now. For the first time, Sally looked at him with warmth, even awe. Elmer caught this new note in her regard and thrilled by it, quickly asked:

"Would you marry me then, Sally?"

Under the table he brought his thigh against hers, but over it his hand could only reach out timidly and caress her fingers. The orange look of her, deepening and ripening with the years, still held him firmly in thrall. But the touch of him made Sally faintly ill. Marriage, she surmised, would be expressed in terms of touching that body, those hands, those thighs, in all the revolting terms that Agatha had been drumming into her head. And yet she could not erase the fact that Elmer would be a millionaire—"a couple of times over." Years before, she had come to New York dreaming of capturing a millionaire. It had seemed so remote, so fantastic, and now it was possible to realize that dream. Yes, even now it would not be too late to return triumphant to her home town, carrying a millionaire in tow, driving up Main Street in a Rolls-Royce with a chauffeur, footman and maid, Cinderella—returning a queen.

"Would you marry me, Sally, when the building is up?" His hand closed around hers a little more boldly. He knew for the first time he was being seriously considered.

"I think I would, Elmer, I really do."

Elmer felt a strange, almost spiritual sensation. Here was the first promise of inner peace he had known since the moment of his crime. He would lose all memory of it in the orange, fragrant beauty of Sally, and live a few years of peace and happiness.

24

The Armistice is signed. Generals turn the war back to politicians. Gold Star mothers clamor for the return of their surviving sons. But it takes time.

Late in 1919, three thousand men and officers jammed the transport that bore Googi back to the United States. The men slept on bunks three high in a cabin, in hammocks swung on all the decks and protected from wind and cold by tarpaulin canopies, endured crowding, poor toilet facilities, bad food, and yet accepted everything with a saintly resignation because they were going home.

These were some of the lucky survivors of the World War, whole men, casuals, heroes, cowards, all bewildered, full of vague but grandiose dreams to be achieved with the help of the everlasting gratitude of a nation they had saved from German rapine. Some regretted not having been in New York on Armistice Day when, as they had been graphically informed, cognac flowed in the streets and juicy blondes and passionate redheads flung themselves at the strategic buttons of any man in uniform. That had been the climactic demonstration of the "open-sesame" power of the uniform. And they had missed it.

But there would be parties at home, and plenty of girls (not all virgins, of course) to seduce with tall tales of no-man's-land. Some, already sobered, even planned to get their old jobs back and settle down.

But for the present, the chief concern was to keep their tempers even and their bowels open so as not to be mowed down by an ironic death, something that came from a little germ like the flu instead of shrapnel or bullets.

In Googi's mind there were no banks of hop-head fog, no vague, seductive dreams about girls under the spell of tales, or employers under the spell of patriotism. He knew quite clearly what he was going to do. He was a grown man now, twenty-five years old, gutter graduate, ex-Bowery ferret, prison alumnus, veteran of the World War and a hero with a decoration. But all this was behind him. Above everything, he was now an ambitious New Yorker. His matured philosophy had firmly convinced him that the only worthwhile ideal was to achieve a velvety life, a life that rolled on noiseless wheels along cushioned tracks in a pillowed car propelled by underdogs. And the great god "bankroll" was the power that performed this miracle.

His life in the gutter and on the streets of New York had so equipped him that no matter where he found himself he knew how to pad his income. And with extra money he knew how to buy protection, extra comforts, safety, even glory. For in Paris he had bought a medal for bravery under fire, a Croix de Guerre, from the first cynical American hero. The medal cost the hero one leg, but Googi got it at bargain rates for one hundred francs and a bottle of cognac.

Aboard the transport, gambling was the chief preoccupation of the returning soldiers. To take some risks every day, if only with money, seemed a natural part of their lives. And gambling, in all of its forms, was a way of living for Googi.

In prison he had majored in courses in shooting craps and "hot" dice-rolling, five- and seven-card stud poker, Black Jack, and other games where percentages and skill in manipulation were fully as important as a lucky streak. On a strip of billiard felt, Googi could shoot craps with the skill of those lads from Georgia who make it a lifelong study. He had supreme faith in his wrist, his palm and his fingers, and also in a kind of gutter god that had watched over him, and when he started out to make six points in a row, he pyramided his winnings, never withdrawing from the pot. He despised that as the cautious gesture of a rube or a frightened player. He let the money lie in a heap, and the dice, too, until he was faded. His little black eyes roved around contemptuously, while from the corner of his mouth he dealt words. "Come on, suckers—cover the bet."

Sometimes, he crapped on his sixth roll after making five points in a row, and greedy hands would plunder the pile of money while Googi coolly said, "What the hell, it's only money." But he already had his plans made for winning it back.

In the main, he was skillful and lucky, and among other bankrolls he raked in was a slender one belonging to a lanky, emaciated doughboy called Murray Burns. The scooped-out face seemed vaguely familiar to Googi, but only because he had formed the habit of searching every face to discover what frailties or strengths lurked behind it. Sucker, wize gazabo, or bull.

Murray Burns, also returning home from the wars, without a buddy, without medals, now without any money, his legs still intact, but the bewildered victim of a grim jest. In the first weeks of his service he had been so terrified at the distant rumble of artillery that he would grow sick with fear. But a tough "top-kick" had slapped and cursed him into some outward semblance of soldiery. Yes, Murray had survived two major engagements and his precious legs were unharmed. But an ironic god still cackled at him.

At night, in a small clearing on deck, Googi recognized this lank soldier, whose money he had taken earlier in the day. Unobserved, he stood still and watched him in amazement.

Burns was dancing all by himself, weaving in and out, forming intricate patterns and steps, his long legs grotesquely clumsy in their badly wound spirals. The dancer held one hand over his heart and the other outstretched as if clutching an imaginary partner, and he dipped and criss-crossed, whirled and spieled in the mad moonlight. Then, suddenly, he stopped, reeled, his nails digging into the cloth over his heart and bent over in a violent spasm of coughing that threatened to break his cadaverous form in two.

"What's the matter, buddy?" Googi ran out of his hiding and supported him while the spasm spent itself.

Burns looked up at him. There was a moony glint in his eye and he broke into a wild laughter.

"God—what a joke on me. You see these shafts—they're my bread and butter—my whole life. I'm a professional dancer—I'm Murray Burns of 'Burns & Co., Society Spielers.' You must have seen my act. I played all the best houses, the Keith circuit. I ducks the war, not because I'm yellow—but because I don't want my legs scratched. Christ—before— they nabbed me—I used to get up in the middle of the night in a cold sweat, dreaming they shot a leg off. So what happens—they shoves me into a uniform—I goes through the war without a mark on my hands or legs. Great, hey?" His laughter grew more shrill. "So what happens? I gets a whiff of chlorine gas in my lungs—and now my bellows is on the blink. So I can't dance anyway!"

Googi, resigned in his own way to the lovely ironies of life, patted him on the back. "That's tough, buddy, but those are the breaks. But don't let it get you down. If you ask me, I think a few weeks at Saranac or Liberty will fix you up." He dug into his pocket. "Here—put this in your kick— it's your own bankroll. And for Christ's sake keep out of the crap games on this tub. There's too many sharpshooters dressed up like doughboys."

Googi led him to a lower deck and helped him undress.

In his hammock, Murray Burns tried to figure it out. In the whole war there wasn't a bullet or a piece of shrapnel with his name on it. But somebody had to carve his initials into that long whiff of chlorine gas, just one deep breath, before he could get that damned gas mask adjusted. It had gagged him then and he had expelled it. But evidently he hadn't expelled all of it. Some of the gas had lurked in his lungs, leisurely cor- roding tissue, devouring the years of his life like a secure enemy who knows he can take his time.

Now he was afraid he was a lunger. You couldn't trust the superficial examination of the army doctor. Yes, he was sure he was a doomed lunger. At best, he had never led a healthy life.

God, those days and nights of his youth, in smoke-filled blast-hot dance- halls, sucking in the sweat of others while you spieled and spieled. Living on cigaret puffs, the cheap perfumes of dance partners, the hot jazz music. Shuddering at the first contact with cold air outside, in your threadbare but pressed suit, the thin collar turned up, rushing to close yourself up in the little cell on Sixth Avenue, to breathe more of the familiar dust and heat while the wheels of the "L" ground over you. No wonder his lungs couldn't stand up.

Well, one thing was certain. Lunger or no, there wasn't a force in the world that could keep him from dancing. He'd round up Isabella as soon as he was mustered out. She had written him once but he had never answered. The hell with writing to women. But she would do what he wanted, just as she always had. With her, they could get booking again. The old act, "Burns & Co., Society Spielers." He'd take new pictures of himself in uniform for the lobby display. Say, you might as well capital- ize on this patriotism stuff even if they did have to carry him off forcibly to war. Perhaps fix up a dance routine that had some military snap about it, he in a smart lieutenant's uniform and Isabella dressed like a nurse. There was an idea. They would do their dreamy love waltz in a clearing in no-man's-land. No, there wasn't a force in the world that could keep him from dancing.

Then Murray doubled up again in a spasm of coughing that not only choked him, but had developed rotary knives which hacked at his lungs and chest while he gasped for breath.

Googi's plans, as the transport landed, were quite definite. He would look up a former prison buddy with whom he had made a pact, and who, in the interval since his release, had become a big-leaguer in the fabulous liquor racket. In Paris and on the boat Googi had secured much desired information from the "blat" guys, for the fraternity of the big-time operators is international. It was easy to weed out the punks and mousy purse snatchers and get the dope straight from the men who were going into the most lucrative industry America had ever known. Bootlegging. Although all of the returning soldiers were full of great dreams of easy wealth, most of them knew they would actually go back into the safe grooves. The killing and looting of war was already a nightmare. But a few planned to make murder and pillage a lifelong profession.

In due time Googi was mustered out from Camp Upton. His debt was paid in full to his country, his state, and to society. The honorable discharge wiped out the disgrace of his prison sentence (an item which he now regarded as a bit of carelessness on his part, something not to be repeated). He laid aside the rough khaki for the silk-lined, shoulder-padded, tailor-made, and began life afresh in his beloved New York. New York of 1919, 1920, the big town rolling in the early period of its most fabulous boom years. The only change he made was in his base of operations. From the squalid, east side streets, he moved to the dazzling, roaring Forties off Broadway.

The military diagnostician allowed Murray Burns partial disability and a narrow white cot in a government hospital for the treatment of asthma at Liberty, New York. Here, high up in the Catskills, where fell the romantic acorns that bloomed into Bronx and Brooklyn weddings, Murray dreamed of conquest. It was only asthma, and he would recover. But a lop-eared orderly, with a shaved head and rolling moronic eyes, insisted he had "galloping consumption."

Half through the night, Murray would toss on his damp sheets, working out nightmarish dance patterns, fantastic steps born of his fever and delirium, until the nurse quieted him with an injection of morphine.

The doctor in attendance told her it would be quite all right to increase the morphine dosage. The cot would be vacant soon, anyway.

In a speakeasy on 45th Street, a few doors east of Eighth Avenue, Googi held the long planned-for reunion with his prison buddy, "Fats" Muldoon, prosperous survivor of a manslaughter charge. They greeted each other like old Yale men, and Fats, embedded in rolls about the girth, congratulated Googi on his splendid physique and the excellent color his life in the open had brought to his cheeks.

"You look like a new man," he said.

"You called your shot, buddy. That's just what I am—a new man," grinned Googi.

Then they sat down to a consideration of the business which had brought them together. Dyed-in-the-wool New Yorkers like Fats and Googi understood that grown men do not come together merely for the sake of wistful reminiscing. Somewhere in the offing, after all the memories have been dusted off, there lurks an honest buck to be made in some legitimate racket.

Googi listened wide-eyed, like Alice in Wonderland, to the tale Fats told him about the money possibilities in bootleg liquor. Years before he had listened with that same rapt attention while Little Rocco opened up a new world for him. But he was better equipped now.

The point was that there was supposed to be no liquor in a land where nearly everyone drank, where fresh converts to alcohol were being made every hour, and where each day the ranks of the drinkers were augmented by new arrivals of soldiers and sailors, packed with resentment against prohibition and boasting of their thirsts. On every transport, in every camp, the lament was, "They put one over on us. While we were fighting for democracy, the bluenoses stole our freedom."

"What a set-up," whispered Googi wistfully.

"Now Googi," concluded Fats softly, "the whole racket is a pipe. The two main things is booze and territory. Now, I can get plenty of hard stuff through Canada. And one bottle of Scotch is as good as two, even three in a pinch. I'll show you the plant upstairs where we cut it with water and flavoring. And then again, I got me a little mob that protects this west side territory. But it's growing, and I need a right hand."

"How about the cops?"

"Oh, cops—they're in on the take. And I shmeer plenty. That not only buys me protection, but they'll even help me unload stuff."

"What a sweet set-up," murmured Googi. "It's perfect."

"Except for one thing."

"What?"

"Other guys muscling in."

Googi looked at him through half-closed eyes. "There's ways of handling strangers." Then he smiled. "But sing on about the dough. That listens like sweet music."

"You I tell it to, Googi. Last week my cut was two G's. That's with splitting with the big shots. And from the way it looks, even that will be chicken feed later on." Fats leaned closer. "The thing for you to do, Googi, is to pull one more job and cop yourself a bankroll. Then I can cut you in legitimate because the buying of all booze is done strictly with cash." Fats peeled off a hundred-dollar bill from a thick bankroll. "Take a yard, and get yourself set. Remember, I got influence." Googi shook his head, and with his out-thrust chin seemed to push the money back.

"Nothing doing, Fats—I ain't taking no chances on a job."

Fats was annoyed. "I'm giving you a good steer, Googi. What do you want to do? Start as a punk here? Tending bar, sweeping out the sawdust, driving a truck, pulling booze off boats? That's for rubes and suckers. I want you in with the big shots."

"That's the only way I go in," said Googi coolly. He inhaled his cigaret and grinned slyly. "I got a little bankroll. I ain't asking any favors. Don't forget, I had eleven days on the tub and two weeks at Upton with a pair of monkey dice and a hot deck. In fact, I got a little bankroll that comes to fifteen grand."

Fats laughed with relief. "I always said you was a smart dago." His little eyes became luminous with greed. "Fifteen G's ain't a fortune—but it's chips in the big game. Come on upstairs and I'll knock you down to the big shots." He put his arm affectionately around his shoulder.

"In no time—you'll be the right hand."

At the door, Googi paused. "Look, Fats—there's nothing stinky about this deal?"

"Ain't I your pal?" Fats pouted and looked mortally wounded.

Googi slowly extracted a medal and decoration from his inner pocket and carefully pinned it to his breast pocket.

"What's that?" asked Fats.

"A medal—that's what I got for bravery in action."

"Yeah! What did you do?"

"I stuck a knife in a Heinie's belly."

Fats snickered. "A lot of doughboys done that. I don't see any medals pinned on them."

Googi looked at him with cool, boring eyes. "Maybe—but with that same twist—I scooped out the Heinie's guts." He spoke with a soft chuckle. "That's what they give me the medal for." His eyes glanced up at the ceiling.

Fats' face dried itself of the snicker. "I get you, Googi. I'll tip the boys off they got to play ball with you."

At the door, Fats paused and whistled.

"Jeez, a guy that carves like you can—sure has a future."

The early part of Peter's comradeship with Eda was the most restful period of his life. For the first time, he knew serenity, surrendered himself to the grateful sensation of having burdens roll off, and leave the mind and body untaxed, fully at ease. And for the first time in his life he was loved by a woman. The silent devotion which his father and grandfather had felt for him had been a tenderness which hovered near, but never quite dared to touch him.

But Eda's love was a rich outpouring, a warmth that strove to reach his darkest, bitterest memories and brush them with love. Even the simple steps of living which he trod with her, relaxed him, lulled him. Dining with Eda, going to the theatre and concerts, filling in the vast wells of loneliness which his bitter youth had bored in him.

Once, in answer to a silent plea on her part, he said, "Eda, we're as good as married."

But she shook her head. "No, Peter. Marriage is a fact. I won't believe this—until it's over."

When he heard her say "until it's over," he experienced a curious sense of relief. However remotely, she was prepared for it to end.

Here was a relationship that had its origin in ecstasy and broadened into a familiar pleasure and serenity. But in time that very quality of peace began to irk him. The city had not fashioned him for peace—not even for those few hours of peace that allowed him to gather his strength for the next day's assault. The mind that echoed to the memory of his father's "Toorkish-a-lemonade two cents a glass," the mind that had been bevelled on Forsyth Street, that had buffeted the waterfront stench of Roosevelt Street, that had been burned in poverty, restraint, endless privations, had been sharpened by too many memories to become blunt and dulled in any kind of contentment.

Besides, he was entering upon the important period of his great ambition. He could envision great financial structures of his own origin, which he would master, and with such dreams in his head it seemed incongruous to return at night to a cosy little apartment where a girl who in many respects was still a stranger to him lavished herself upon him even as she proclaimed her independence. He began to dislike the peace that meant being tethered to a post, the peace that allowed him to roam only so far and then demanded his return.

Even the woman of his life must carry out some part of the dream and drive that gave life to his day.

Like the rustle of the wind in the trees, across the city there blows the sound, pssst, pssst. From the lips of furtive men, the secretive hiss, pssst, pssst. You're standing on a curb waiting for a street car, crosstown to the Christopher Street Ferry, north on Third Avenue, south on Southern Boulevard. A mysterious looking guy dressed in the livery of a large department store drives up in a large car. "Pssst, pssst. Listen, buddy, wanna pick up a dandy fur-piece cheap? A nifty present for the missus, real fox. No harm in looking at it." He springs out, hiding the package under his coat. Already, he has made you feel like a partner in his crime. He maneuvers you into a hallway, and like a magician whisks out the fur. "Feel it, buddy, silver fox—do I have to tell you why I wanna get rid of it? It's worth one hundred and fifty bucks, but—" he looks around and moist-whispers in your ear—"take it for twenty-five." He has shoved it into your hands. You falter—you haven't got twenty-five. He looks grieved—there is heartbreak in his voice. "It's a steal for fifteen." He slinks out with your dough and you clutch the fur. Somehow, you feel part of New York, part of the current of a great metropolis—where miracles happen, where you get something for nothing. You bring the silver fox home and it's cheap rabbit, already half decomposed. You were taken for fifteen bucks.

"Pssst—pssst—how about it, friend—do you need some new tires for the car?" He drives alongside of you, forcing you to the curb. There's a red light on and he talks fast. "Look at this." He lifts up a tire covered in wrapping paper, fresh from the factory. He rips off a piece of the paper for your benefit and you see the perfect tread of a new tire. "It's an Atlas—worth twelve bucks—take it for four." He transplants the tire in your car. Horns are honking, the light is changing—you hand over the money. Your heart beats wildly because you're driving away with stolen goods. At home you examine the tire and only the part the gyp exposed has a new tread. The rest is smooth billiard ball rubber. You were bilked for four seeds.

You stand in front of a store window on Fourteenth Street, Forty-second, Fifty-seventh, Eighty-sixth, One Hundred and Twenty-fifth Street, wherever there are bright store windows. "Pssst, pssst, wanna buy a gold watch? Sixteen-jewel, Swiss movement. Worth seventy-five bucks—take it for a fin." It stops ticking before you get home.

Pssst, psst, you're always going to market in this town, gaudy perfume bottles filled with vinegar, gold-plated fountain pens whose points bend back, pin-seal wallets that are dust in a week, merchandise created by skilled high-pressure men to look and sell right for one minute and then to perish.

Like the rustle of the wind in the trees, across the city, there blows the hiss of the greengoods and confidence men, the fake auction racketeers and phoney merchandise men, pssst, pssst.

25

It took much longer than the "few" days for Isabella to recover from the abortion. For weeks afterwards she felt a knife-like pain in her side when she walked; and dancing, even simple ballroom dancing, proved agonizing. At first panic filled her as she wondered whether she would ever recover her grace, her effortless skill, her endless reserves of energy. But then, as she sank into rest, retreated into a grateful inertia, she put behind her the driving dreams of conquest, let her ambitions slumber while she basked in the warm, whole-hearted love and protection of Joey. For him it was a period of fabulous, serene happiness. The nightmare of Burns was over and at last he was taking care of his Bella.

During this time, because his simple mind was free to concentrate, he climbed higher towards the top rank. Fighting sometimes twice a month in New York and in the large eastern cities, he disposed of half a dozen good second raters and was ready to be matched with one of the three or four fighters that menaced the lightweight titleholder. The dream that had illumined his life, the dream of punching his way from a tenement backyard on Forsyth Street, through walls, beyond fences, way up to the championship and to the heart of little Isabella who sat on a fire-escape as she watched him train, seemed closer to realization than ever.

Joey even mentioned the possibility of a title bout to his manager but the crafty Donovan still wanted him to bide his time.

"We're almost ready," he said. "But let's pick the right one."

Some of the older and tougher contenders were beginning to announce each fight as their last, in the manner of the farewell tours of Sarah Bernhardt.

"Let's pick the right one," counselled Donovan. "Sometimes an old, slug-nutty battle-axe, with only one fight left in him, will upset a newcomer just out of pure cussedness. Better wait, they'll rub each other out, and you sail into a bout with the champ." Donovan was taking no chances, for when the right time came, he would have his first champion in Young Samson.

During these serene, blissful weeks, Joey's chief delight lay in making plans with Bella. There was nothing he withheld from her. He told her to the dollar all the money he had saved, how he had grieved when she was away from him, and all that he wanted to do for her now that she was back. He paid her hotel bills, arranged for special comforts for her mother who was in a sanitarium, bought her clothes, urged her to rest, pressed money upon her, and trusted her implicitly.

And then, because he wanted to flavor every step in his acquisition of Bella, he became formally engaged to her—a simple party at his home, the core of which was his betrothal, the climax, a diamond ring which he placed upon her finger. Joey lived as one transformed by the magic of happiness.

Only Bert, fully emerged from his cocoon of books, free of the glow of the literature of the past, now a little Broadway-lustred, his dreams sharpened, modernized to fit the Times Square pattern, only Bert knew what Joey faced. Only he who followed the theatre so slavishly, who knew about stars, headliners, producers, plays, who knew about dramatic situations and second act curtains, and who now was as deeply engrossed in writing as once he had been in reading and dreaming, only he could properly evaluate the Bella whom Joey placed on a pedestal.

He had never liked Bella. As far as he was concerned, she was a tricky chippie not at all worthy of Joey. He had seen thousands of Bellas on Broadway, blistering their little feet on the pavement, wearing out their smiles in producers' and agents' anterooms, giving themselves to office-boys because it might open a door. Yes, he knew Isabella, the girl born under the unlucky gleam of an electric bulb. And because he understood, he felt sad for Joey, but he loved him too deeply to tell him. Indeed, there was no way to begin to tell him, for whenever Joey discussed his Bella with Bert, it was only in terms of enchantment. Bert simply remained sad and silent, wondering why anyone as honest and good as Joey, must also be blind.

In the beginning, Bella throve and purred under all this attention and devotion. She had been so buffeted and tormented by Burns that it felt warm and human to have someone take complete care of her, blanket her with love and concern. But, in time, particularly as she grew stronger, the attentions of Joey began to irk her. And her conscience troubled her because she felt herself unworthy of the adulation Joey felt for her. He still regarded her as the little flower he had known on Forsyth Street, each petal still sacred to him. Even as Bert, she also tried and failed to leaven this enchantment. Sometimes she hinted that a cruel wisdom had been scratched into her by the vaudeville tours, that her life back stage and her union with Murray Burns had chipped some of the perfection off her, but Joey refused to see or understand. And when he kissed her, there was a worshipful quality in his caress, always of yearning, never of lust.

Thinking, brooding about Joey, the unfairness of their relationship and the new rising tide of her own ambitions, Bella determined, to even the score between them. Perhaps, if she could give herself to Joey, help him consummate the love he felt, her conscience would trouble her less. It seemed like a clever way out. He would have had her, and she would be free to leave him.

One evening she prepared herself for his visit like a character in a moving picture. All the little touches of the scene were familiar to her from having been observed a hundred times. The subdued light, the lacy negligee, the yawning bed, the seductive female reclining upon it, waiting to be touched into life by an ardent lover.

But the efforts were lost upon Joey. He entered, threw his hat and coat upon a chair and simply commented upon what had been prepared to ensnare him.

"Come on, Bella—you ain't even dressed. And I got two tickets for the Winter Garden."

She tried to look wan and to speak in a disturbing voice. "Come here, Joey—sit by me." She patted the edge of the bed.

"Feelin' sick, Bella?" He was full of concern.

"Let's not leave, Joey—let's not go anywhere tonight. I don't feel like dressing—it's so cosy in here. I just want to be with you."

She drew him down to her and kissed him. Her lips lingered upon his, hungering to plant desire into them. She caressed his cheeks with her finger-tips and kissed him again. The heat of the room, the warmth of their bodies, the current of her own dark plans, swirled around them. When he touched her breasts she pressed herself close to him, whispering into his ear, "Joey—I want you—I want you now. Let's not wait any longer. Why—don't you take me? Now! Now!"

Joey moved away. There was shame in his face as he spoke. He could not look at her.

"Come on, Bella—git dressed. We're going to the show."

He cooled his face in the bathroom and when he returned, he spoke curtly and with finality:

"Bella, the way I figure it, certain tings is right—and certain tings is wrong."

That was his simple philosophy.

As far as he was concerned, both the temptation and the incident were over.

Bella dressed in a controlled fury and, completely frustrated, accompanied him to the theatre. The dance acts she witnessed filled her anew with ambition, re-stirring the ferment of her dreams. And at night, alone, she tried to think through to clarity. Well, she had done all she could to pay Joey back. She had offered him her body, offered herself with love as well as desire, but he wanted her only upon his own lofty terms. She would gladly become his mistress, but if he thought he could imprison her in a Bronx apartment and have her become Mrs. Nobody of Mount Eden Avenue, he was wrong. There wasn't a force in the world that could shackle her dancing legs.

The following morning Bella called upon her agent and consulted him about building a new act for her. At first he was dubious, but her fine clothes (Joey always insisted upon the best for her) and her general manner of success and optimism swayed him.

"You know how it is, sugar," he said, "everything changes. That society ballroom stuff is dead. They got adagio teams that do stunts that make the peasants shiver. I'm booking an act myself—s'help me—the guy swings the dame around like she was skip rope and throws her clean across the stage. It's a panic."

"All right," agreed Bella. "I'm willing to learn this new stuff."

"I'll talk to Jimmie Grey, sugar—you know, that Harlem dinge that fixes up all the new routines. What he don't know about acrobatic tap dancing you can print on a postage stamp. But it will cost dough—he charges plenty."

"How much?"

"About two hundred and fifty bucks."

Bella left him elated. A few months of practice, perfection in new routines, rehearsal with a new partner, and she could once again assail Broadway. She was so full of her own new dreams that only dimly was she aware of the item the agent had shown her in "Variety." It was an obit on Murray Burns.

He had died in a government hospital at Liberty, New York. His lungs had been devoured. But he had died with perfect legs.

There now began a new period of deception for Bella. Since she had no money of her own, and dared not ask Joey for funds to finance a course in acrobatic dancing lessons, she resorted to a simple piece of fraud a show-girl had once described to her. She had a duplicate made of the setting of her engagement ring, inserted a "Texas" diamond in it, and pawned the original. On a bull gem market she was able to raise enough money to see her through the course. Joey would never know the difference. With renewed hopes and desperate ambitions, she plunged into the second phase of her career.

She worked hard, torturing her body with cartwheels, splits and distortions, a body which Nature had designed for sheer grace and pure, flowing movement. But if the public now wanted dancers to twist themselves like pretzels, she was prepared to satisfy its taste.

And while she went on with her secret plans (all her lessons were in the morning and afternoon), Joey, blissfully unaware, dreamed of their forthcoming marriage. Every evening when he met her he would bring with him advertisements which he had cut out of the newspapers announcing sales in furniture and linens. He would take her for long walks on Fourteenth Street, on Forty-second Street, even up in Harlem, and he would stare into store windows comparing this bedroom suite with that, weighing the relative virtues of a studio couch or an easy chair, plaguing her with questions as to the type of furniture she preferred.

In his love for her he was still a child getting ready to play house. When he was busy training, he would instruct Bella to look at pillows and rugs and silverware. Once he called her from the gym to rush down to Wanamaker's and take advantage of a sale in doilies and French dolls. There was a great hunger in him for a gentle, cushioned domestic life to which he could go for refuge after the tough battles of his daily work, a blissful serenity in which he could find some compensation for his gutter youth.

And this hunger grew in him as his fights became more important. For he was no longer being fed set-ups, and now was meeting opponents who by savagery, cunning and ring generalship had risen to the top layer.

As the day approached for their wedding—"just the folks, Bella, I ain't got no friends but you—" a hysteria came upon Isabella. She did not know how to tell him. For weeks she had been practicing with her new partner, a skilled dancer, but fortunately a "nance," so that there was no danger of any sexual entanglement. The agent was full of hopes and had arranged a try-out in a Philadelphia theatre.

"If the act clicks, sugar—I got forty weeks' booking for you in picture houses."

It was getting harder all the time for Peter to remain tethered. All the discipline and restraint which had sheltered him so well in his youth, peeled off him like dead skins, and all he felt was an urge to break out. Henderson held him down; Eda held him down. But there was no use breaking away until the springboard presented itself from which he could leap to his millions. Something, perhaps someone, to touch him off.

Donovan had already approached him and there had been one preliminary meeting with Elmer Hicks. That might be the great opportunity. But every day new deals were brought in for his perusal, and on paper, or on the lips of the high pressure promoters, they all looked like bonanzas. Peter's job was to weed them out, and he was becoming an expert in selection.

One afternoon, churning with possibilities of a new mid-town skyscraper, Peter was summoned to Henderson's private office. Seated in a deep chair, outlined against a window, was a smartly dressed woman of about thirty. She had a fair, patrician face, wore sheer hose on fine ankles, and gracefully clasped her gloved hands. The detail of the gloved hands stood apart.

"This is Mrs. Langdon-Chase," wheezed Henderson, "and here is my first lieutenant, Peter Mendes."

They regarded each other with more than casual interest. The woman acknowledged the introduction in a cool, throaty voice which at once placed distance between them. Peter remembered having read of her recent divorce from a playboy scion of a rich munitions family.

Henderson indicated a brief-case bulging with papers. "I'll tell you what the lady wants, Peter," he croaked, a note of regret in his dead loins. "In there you will find a list of Mrs. Langdon-Chase's holdings and, in the divorce settlement agreement, a record of other securities that belong to her. Now make up a schedule that will give her the highest yield in income with—" he coughed—"of course a maximum of safety."

Peter picked up the brief case. Henderson continued to Mrs. Langdon-Chase, touching her arm with a wrinkled hand:

"Peter is a wizard at juggling those things. Don't worry, my dear. I leave you in the best of hands."

Peter smiled and walked to the door. Her throaty voice halted him. "Mr. Mendes, shall I be able to see it—before I leave for Europe?"

"When do you sail?"

"Day after tomorrow—on the Paris."

"Very well. I'll stay in tonight and lay out a rough schedule."

"Good," she laughed. "But it's only fair to warn you that I'm not one of those women who doesn't understand about money. In fact, it's one of the few things I do understand. I intend to know everything about my income."

She held out her hand and Peter clasped it. Her hand brought him two sensations, one of warm, firm flesh and the velvety rub of the glove. The detail of the glove made his palm tingle.

But later, alone, thinking about her irritated him. That cosy, property sense of those damned rich. The way she said, "I intend to know everything about my income." "My income." What had she done to acquire that income except to lower that cool, throaty voice and yield that warm, firm body? Here was a woman who had never felt a shock and intended to insulate herself for life against the danger of any tremors. And that gloved hand, extended!

It was all very annoying, but what the devil did he care. After all, Henderson would charge her a substantial fee for handling her investments and he would get a small bonus from that. Little parasites feasting on her, who had been a major parasite feasting upon her husband, who had nourished upon his father, who in turn had exploited others, ad nauseam.

Peter waited until he was alone in the office. After all the other workers had gone home and the night hush of Wall Street fell on the churchly vaults he opened the brief-case.

His first perusal of those papers widened his eyes in astonishment. Again he felt the poetry, the drama, the romantic biography of finance. Behind the colorless sheets of foolscap, the clear typewritten words and cold numerals, he saw the perfect portrait of Suzanne Langdon-Chase, truer and more revealing than any an artist could paint. What a grasping, acquisitive woman, what a vivid instinct for self-preservation! And how securely she had entrenched herself in a world which still clung to the fiction that men were the marauders and women in need of protection. Graphically he could chart the movements of that small-boned, gloved hand that had reached out and plucked something from all who came in contact with her, practically from infancy, and now defied a world to pry her loose. The cold documents not only painted a portrait; they charted a life.

He could see its origin, long before she was born, with a glint of thrift in her maternal grandmother's eye and that sharp, insistent voice, "Silas, we must husband our resources." A New England housewife who handled the funds of the family so that upon her death there were tidy sums in the savings bank, in the stock of a solid shipping line and in government and insurance company bonds. A modest beginning, but a foundation of solid planks.

These were augmented by what Suzanne's mother had garnered during a lifetime, a note of daring and speculation creeping into the stocks probably from the father's side, so that mining, utility and railroad issues were included. Some of them in their day were undoubtedly wildcat stocks, particularly that early telephone issue.

And then a settlement of a solid million upon Suzanne when she married the pride of a munitions clan. This was in lieu of dowry, and was promptly invested in income-yielding bonds, and General Electric and General Motors. The fool had protected himself against the contingency of death, forgetting the greater hazards of his own amorous carelessness. In a brief marriage period some of these fecund stocks had divided like amoebas, one cell becoming two, and two multiplying into four. And then, most recently, to crown it all, there had been added the divorce settlement, probably a bonus to hasten the scion into another pair of grasping arms.

Peter, studying all those stocks and bonds and debentures and realty holdings and notes and cash deposits, visualized the evolution of a family fortune in a few generations. And he wrote a full biography of Suzanne Langdon-Chase from the financial schedules.

Peter rested his fingers on four million dollars and paused for a moment. He thought of that stifling afternoon on Roosevelt Street when his father in agony had refused to let him call a doctor because the two dollars would buy Peter lunches and carfares for two weeks and still leave a quarter for the gas meter. He thought of all the other privations and skimpings which he had thought were far behind him, but now suddenly rose before him in a living pageant.

But Mrs. Langdon-Chase, with the cool, throaty voice and the warm, gloved hand, was worth four millions. She herself owned enough stocks and bonds to form an investment trust in which other stockholders might buy shares. She certainly did understand money—how to acquire it, how to hold it, how to make it grow.

Well, the thing to do was to rearrange her holdings so as to yield her maximum returns with maximum safety as the bankers promised in their prospectuses. There were a few changes he would recommend. He could convert some doubtful issues into bonds, sell some stocks that were high now and which he knew he could buy back later at a lower figure. He began to make notations, remembering that here was a woman who wanted to know to the penny how much she could lavish upon herself each year.

All through the night, Peter worked. In the cemetery hush of Wall Street after dark he rearranged the masses of her wealth and by six o'clock in the morning he had completed a draft of her new financial picture. Like a skilled craftsman he had touched up the portrait of Suzanne Langdon-Chase, closed a pore here and there against the draught of uncertainty, hardened the glint in the eye, buttoned up a garment, locked a purse against the impulse of generosity, and straightened the seam in the back of the hose so that she could walk with absolute assurance anywhere. And, under all his resentment of her wealth, he felt a little pleased with himself. A parasite, yes, but not just a louse on a frayed garment, but a trained flea who could draw miniature chariots of gold for his daily stipend of twelve drops of upper-crust blood.

He ate an early breakfast, went into a barber shop for a thorough massage and shave and returned to the office a few moments after the arrival of his secretary. Glibly he dictated to her the new financial set-up for Mrs. Langdon-Chase, with his recommendations for changes worded in crisp English, and his reasons for them in logical sequence.

When he returned from lunch, the new Langdon-Chase portrait lay on his desk.

Then he waited for the lady. As the afternoon wore on without a sign of her arrival, he became impatient and annoyed. He had looked forward to the encounter in order to preen himself a bit. The lady of great wealth had challenged him with her avowed knowledge of money and he had wanted to demonstrate that there was at least one field in which he was her superior.

But she failed to come. It was almost time for him to leave when Henderson dropped into his office. "Tell me, Peter," he croaked, "did you get that Langdon-Chase schedule fixed up?"

"I certainly did. I sat up all night wrestling with it. But where the devil is Lady Cheswick?" He handed a copy to Henderson, who examined it superficially and chuckled in approval.

"This ought to impress her."

"It won't—unless she sees it."

"Well, it's like this, Peter. Mrs. Langdon-Chase phoned me a little while ago and said she couldn't come down to the office. She would like for you to bring it down to the boat a little before noon to-morrow. You'll have ten minutes with her—and that ought to be enough. After all, she's a smart woman—and once she develops confidence in your judgment, she'll never bother you." The old pirate glanced at the total underscored on the last page. "Mmmm. More than four millions. Not bad. Handling an account like that will make a neat penny for both of us."

Peter bit back his resentment. So, Milady summons the churl and scrivener to the bateau. And there she will graciously allow him ten minutes in her perfumed presence. Her gloved hand will turn the pages and her small, perfectly shaped head will nod in approval.

The resentment grew in him as he went home. It permeated his evening with Eda. Although he rarely discussed his work with her, preferring to listen to her accounts of the interviews she had experienced, he couldn't refrain from mentioning Suzanne Langdon-Chase. And Eda was a little surprised at the heat of his feeling.

"That's a lot of emotion for you, Peter."

"Well, let's forget about her—the perfumed bitch."

"Yes—let's," agreed Eda, "if you can."

Peter looked up sharply at Eda. There was a clear light in her eye which seemed to encompass more of the truth than he dared acknowledge to himself.

And next day Peter was very much aware of her as he walked up the gangplank. True, there was more assurance in his walk, a note of triumph, too, in that he no longer had to wait below and gaze hungrily at the beautiful ship and the lucky passengers who were able to board it. Why, if he wished, at this moment he could remain on the ship and take a trip. He could even afford a luxurious voyage around the world. And thinking these thoughts which induced excitement in him and a feeling of equality with the most exalted of the first class passengers, he found himself at the door of Mrs. Langdon-Chase's suite.

She greeted him with a cool smile, and the gloved hand outstretched. But there was no hint of apology in her manner, not even the trace of a doubt that, having uttered a command in that sure voice of hers, it would inevitably be obeyed. Instructing her maid to open a trunk, she took the papers from him and ran over them with a look of concentration, astonishing in the midst of all the bustle and clamor of a ship's departure.

"You think we should sell Acme Aluminum?"

"Yes. I happen to know that this quarter's dividend will be passed. After that fact becomes public, we can buy it back at a lower figure. It's still a very safe stock."

She folded the copy and put it in the top drawer of her trunk. "I'll have more time to study this at sea. But it's very clear," she smiled, and there was the first hint of warmth in her smile, "that you know a great deal about money."

"Yes," he said with a faint bitterness, "I learned about money—by not having any for twenty-three years." Then he changed his tone. "Just the same, I'm glad you approve of the schedule." There was no need to tell her that he had given up a night's sleep to have it ready for her perusal. That was like a servant conniving for the approval of his mistress.

"Well, Mr. Mendes, should you get over to the Riviera this winter, do look me up."

She gave him her gloved hand and somehow it felt like more than a hand in his grasp. The touch of it ingrained itself, became stronger as he moved further away from the pier, made him restless, reminded him of all his early dreams of great conquest. It fired anew his lust for achievement, filled him again with his intense hatred and love for money, so that he could not return to the office but instead trudged along the waterfront, pausing on South Street, looking back at his old tenement on Roosevelt and wondering how far away from it he could really spring.

In the parlor of the Glass apartment in the Bronx a little group waited. The wrinkled parents were more bewildered than ever at the forthcoming marriage of their oldest son, not in a hall with a "catered" supper, but quietly, at home. The day before Joey and Isabella had filled out their intention to marry and had received a license in the Municipal Building. On the very steps of the huge building, as they entered, even in the waiting-room of the license clerk, Isabella had started to tell Joey that she could not go through with their marriage. But his ecstatic, other-world look stopped her. It frightened her when she thought of what he might do upon receipt of such a change in plans.

And so, after the license, biting back the cruel words that nearly gushed from her, but her mind fully made up, Isabella had pleaded with Joey to remain alone until the following evening.

"I want to see my mother—it may be the last time." She feigned a twinge of sorrow.

For years, during the entire bitter sweatshop period, Isabella's mother had worked as a forelady in a shirtwaist factory on Canal Street. Her duties were many; she had to be the first to arrive to hand out the piece work to the girls, then to speed up production, and to check on the quality of the finished articles. But her main responsibility was to prevent the girl workers from pilfering shirtwaists. The boss was determined to stop this "stealing" of his wares by machine-slaves who couldn't earn enough in long hours of work to buy the very product they made. And the schemes the girls contrived to outwit the vigilant widow made her life a torment.

The favorite subterfuge was to sneak into the privy, put the blouse on next to the skin, finish the day with it on, and wear it home. And so Isabella's mother had to keep track of when the girls visited the toilet, how long they stayed there, and how frequently they went. She had to apprise herself of their bladder conditions and their periods. Like the villain in a melodrama, she was often hissed for setting traps to catch the new workers.

For this she received an extra few dollars a week which she saved as a special fund for her daughter.

But years of this strain and vigilance and unpopularity broke her health and affected her mind. She became a melancholiac, a mental patient, and had to be removed to a sanitorium.

On rare occasions, when Isabella felt pity for herself, she also wept for her mother. Now, artfully, she began to cry, and Joey, believing the cause was the condition of her mother and the fact that she was practically an orphan, did his best to console her.

"Sure, Bella, anyting you say. But—please—watch out for yourself."

The older Glass had arranged for a rabbi to perform the ceremony and now, in the parlor, they waited. The little father and mother dressed in their best, Bert, sullen, in his tweeds, and Joey lost in rapture.

Joey was thinking of their plans. As soon as the ceremony was completed, he and Bella would leave for a two-week honeymoon in Atlantic City. He would show her a grand time. Then they would return and he would insist upon final decisions on the apartment and furnishings. She had balked at actually paying a rent deposit or making the purchases. Joey smiled. Sweet kid. She was worried about the expense because he insisted upon the best. Well, he would surprise her with the secret cache of money he had saved up for precisely this occasion.

Joey waited.

The note was delivered by a Western Union messenger.

Not daring to face Joey, Isabella had written him. She had tried to compose a letter which would express all she felt, but Isabella was not much more literate than Joey, and upon reading her composition she found that it explained nothing of her real dilemma. So she asked her new dance partner, a youth of real education, to write the farewell letter. He fully enjoyed his part in the drama.

"Dear Joey: (he had snickered at the name)

It is very difficult for me to write this last letter. How difficult, you shall never know. But I cannot go through with our plans. My real ambition is to become a great dancer, and if I consummated our marriage, I would only make you very unhappy. Please try to forget me. I'm sure there are girls more deserving than me, who will make you a devoted wife. Please forget and forgive me, little worthless me.

Love,
Bella."

Joey read it slowly, forming each word with his lips. Then, stunned by the blow, he showed it to Bert.

"What does this here word con-summ-ate mean?" asked Joey.

Bert, aching for his brother, put an arm around his shoulder. As children, Joey had been the one to protect him with his chunky fists, and then it had seemed that nothing could ever hurt the sturdy, fearless fighter. Now Bert hoped to comfort and protect him with what he had learned about life through books, through aspirations, the futility of wooing lost causes, the tragedy of wasting oneself on an undeserving love, the many consolations of life. Bert began to utter words, but there was little comfort in them for the stunned brother who stood like a felled log.

Joey stopped him in a dry, heart-rending voice, "I can't figure it out, Bert. I'm crazy about Bella. And she told me she's my goil."

He shook his head and suddenly ran from the room.

26

Secretly, through several mid-town real-estate brokers, Elmer Hicks began to assemble his giant parcel of land. He had had several conferences with Donovan, Peter Mendes, Murdock and an important politician, and the project looked feasible, with the promise of great profits for all. There was perfect division of labor, each contributing his special gift, and a proportionate share of the initial capital.

The plan was to assemble about one hundred and fifty feet frontage on Broadway, between Forty-third and Forty-fourth Streets, and upon it to construct a spectacular mid-town skyscraper. The public would supply the millions needed with a bond issue and not they, but those of the inner circle, would control it. They knew they were raising a profitable monument on the heart of the city. Once its center had been at Canal Street, then it had moved to Fourteenth, then to Twenty-third, but now it was around Forty-second Street. For as the town grew its heart shifted, and the dream of conquest of all of its plunderers was to spear New York through the heart, a city like a pin cushion, each conqueror snarling over his pin.

The magnificence of Elmer's dream and what it would bring him, not only in the fulfillment of his ambitions but in its effect upon Sally, gave him new reserves of strength, patience and cunning. The obscure insurance salesman who once had dreamed of owning a lot in the Bronx, who had begun by building upon the charred ashes of his father, was soon to construct one of the tallest skyscrapers in the world. And this was something to crown his own life with, and to place at the feet of the peach-down Sally.

It would take all the cash he could muster merely to swing the land. He would have to sell all of his properties in the Bronx and in the Village, but it would be worth it. No man ever entered upon a venture with a greater feeling of security. Land nurtured by the very heart's blood of

279

New York, associates strong in assets and in political and banking connections. Dreamers and plunderers all.

All that night and the following day Joey wandered around in a dazed condition. He still was unable to link Bella, his "goil," with duplicity, with deceit. And if she did have interludes of wickedness, why must he always be the victim of them? Joey brought his problems and the farewell note to Donovan, and his manager quickly applied the familiar poultice.

"Now, Joey, it's plain as the nose on your face that the kid has a flashy eye. She's out to get a big shot. Say, when you're champ, she'll come crawling back on her knees. And it will be up to you to give her a tumble. She just wants the limelight."

"You mean—if I was the champ———"

"I know it."

"Then how's about matching me with Cannonball Wales?"

"You ain't quite ready for him yet, Joey. He's tougher than a side of barnacles."

"Listen, Mike, I can't wait no more. If I put the Cannonball away you can get me a title match. I know I can lick him."

"Sure you can—but not right away. Two more fights———"

"But I tell you I can't wait." Joey was hysterical. "It's him or nobody—I got to be the champ quick."

Donovan wondered whether he had set a trap for himself with this champ talk. He liked a show of ambition in his lad, but Wales, he feared, was too strong, too cunning.

And yet he would have to risk the match or lose Joey.

March of progress in the life of a salesman in New York. You begin as the timid, cold-turkey canvasser who inserts his toe in the crack of a door; you end with the salesman's illusion that there are no doors. From magazine subscriptions with premium sets through Fuller brushes and vacuum cleaners, to the Morocco bound Encyclopedia. House to house to house. From check protectographs to stenographers' hose, to lonely subdivisions, to insurance, to advertising space in benefit programs. Office to office to office. Eventually you land in stocks. Oh, stocks, oh, bonds, oh tempora, oh mores.

A stock certificate, a share in a venture, a fleece-lined bandage across the eyes, fragrant smelling salts to the nostril guarded from stink, the philippic to greed.

In stocks and promotions Clarence Dale found himself completely, grew to his full stature. New York was eager to buy the right to dream. Not great dreams of conquest, of mad love, of vast power—just little dreams of having more money without working for it. It was sated with buying the things it could touch and see and smell and consume. It yearned for the intangibles, stocks and bonds, the marijuana that made their heads swim with illusions of easily-acquired riches.

And nearly all the able-bodied men, all buyers of little dreams, in turn peddled different little dreams to others.

During the boom years of the nineteen twenties, fantasy left the women's pages and magazine sections and flew over to the classified ads. A disturbing challenge was flung to readers in large type at the head of columns of advertising space.

ARE YOU A MAN?

Sometimes it read:

ARE YOU A MAN!!!

Question or exclamation, the advertisements ran on for columns, challenging males to prove their masculinity, not in combat with lions, but by selling stocks to their gullible relatives and friends. And always there was a consolatory note. You could prove your manhood by whole or part-time endeavors.

Clarence was a man! His first job in the field of finance was with a mushroom securities company, selling stock in a huge holding company (incorporated under the laws of Delaware) and based upon a fantastic scheme to acquire a chain of banks in the United States. The logic behind the scheme was irrefutable. America had become the haven of chain industries. Chain cigar-stores, drugstores, groceries, clothing shops, hotels, moving-picture palaces—all links in chains. No matter where you went in the United States you were spared the element of surprise. By building ten stores all exactly alike, and each to be dropped from above upon ten cities, the cost was lowered and a great economy was effected.

Now the plan was to create a chain of banks. And the scheme, for share-holders, included this added advantage. That every time the parent company underwrote an issue of stock, it could allot a pro-rata portion to each of its affiliate banks, which in turn would unload the issue upon its depositors and thus create great profits for the stockholders in the controlling corporation. Here was a simple guarantee of distribution and immediate profits.

Clarence spent the first week in the "boiler room." A huge loft in an old Broad Street building, divided into fifty telephone stalls, a pair of fervent lips implanted in each phone. Sometimes, when the boiler room was operating full blast, fifty impassioned salesmen clamped to phones, hot at their devotionals, singing the canticles of Wall Street, pressing hope and dreams and passion into their rapid speeches, they seemed like figures out of the Inferno, chained forever to telephones, doomed to blast their breath forever into a black hole in expiation for some terrible sin—probably the sin of selling stocks.

More often they were like dervishes rotating around the dream of easy money like flies around garbage. They drew the names of victims from the fat telephone books, hundreds of thousands of gullible prospects. And once a man or woman bought a share of stock, his name went on a special list, which was sold and re-sold to new companies. The sales talk depended not so much upon the force of its argument as upon the speed of its delivery and the ability of the salesman to keep on talking into what seemed a void. Sometimes, a salesman would leave the cubicle panting, wiping the sweat from his forehead, the tension leaving his face, his expression that of a woman who has just been delivered of a cherub, and he would say exultantly, "Well, I hooked a prospect."

"How do you do, Mr. Doakes, this is the Supreme Bankers' Securities Corporation of Wall Street. Mr. Ephraim Zilch was kind enough to refer your name to us and I've taken the liberty of calling you . . . (what about) . . . We're putting out an issue of preferred stock . . . (I'm not interested in stocks) . . . in a chain of banks. No doubt you've heard of J. P. Morgan and John D. Rockefeller and other great financiers . . . (but) . . . well, we're doing the same thing—but on a larger scale. There's no investment as safe as banks. You know that because you're a practical business man . . . (I'm pretty busy now) . . . you read the articles in the financial section of the *New York Times*—you're familiar with statistics—why, last year alone the banks paid dividends of over sixteen percent, to say nothing of the rise on the book value of banking stocks . . . (you'll have to call me some other time) . . . I realize this proposition can't be spread before you advantageously over the phone . . . (I'll have to hang up) . . . so suppose

I drop in tomorrow, say around three, and we'll go into this matter carefully . . . (good) . . . thank you very much . . . (bye)."

Sometimes the prospects were derisive or even abusive, but the salesmen buzzed on, flinging their little pellets against these walls of indifference, knowing that somewhere there was a crack. It was the era of wild speculation in New York, and since everybody except honest manual toilers was engaged in selling some dream, some intangible which came wrapped in a promise to assume shape at a future date, everybody in turn was vulnerable for a salesman. Suckers all.

Clarence was a man! Clarence prospered. Quite smoothly he believed that his success was due entirely to his glibness, his persuasive personality, and he wore his success with a sheen which dazzled prospects like the gleam of armor. He did not attribute it to the gullibility which had seized all of the natives. And this belief in self took on a God-worship which removed all limits from his ambition. His head was light with the gibberish of financial journals, and his body, nourished on the weightless superlatives of the classified ads, made it easy for him to rise. There were no heights in this town to which he could not climb.

With the easy money that flowed in he acquired all the externals of great success. He had a suite in an exclusive apartment hotel on West 72nd Street, near West End Avenue, wore the most expensive clothes, and drove an upper-crust car. He lived in a world bounded on all sides by the "best." He frequented the most expensive night clubs, tossing lavish tips around, so that head-waiters, captains, moved towards him upon his entrance as if he had pressed a button. He associated with the prettiest of show girls, whom he found useful not only for his own entertainment, but as come-ons in his assaults against elderly prospects.

Every person he met was a prospect, and he cultivated a particularly effective campaign against wealthy widows who had just come into insurance money and fat estates. But no matter how high he rose, he never neglected the telephone. It was still the magic instrument that could open any door, a velvety voice entering through all keyholes. So widespread was the money awareness, so intense the interest in stocks, that there were no restrictions, no tradition of reticence, no restraints.

Because of his consistent success, Clarence Dale became the sales manager of the New York division of his securities corporation. His duty was to inspire and instruct new recruits who had responded to the challenge—Are you a man! He would weed out the timid, the honest, the faltering failures and encourage the brassy, the aggressive, the dishonest, and form them into shock troops. He would encourage them to sell their relatives first because of the easy access, and then he would manoeuvre them in descents upon gullible New Yorkers who were willing to exchange money for an embossed certificate with a corporate seal.

And all this proved very profitable to Clarence. He received a percentage of all the commissions earned by his own plunderers, in addition to the profits from his own large deals. His reputation grew as a great sales manager, almost an evangelist among salesmen, the man who could sell "selling" as a creed, as an ideal.

And Peter, whose plans were rapidly nearing the day of execution, arranged to meet Clarence Dale.

A few years before they might have passed each other along the Battery, one freshly risen from his damp bed of grass in the park, shambling along in his tatters, the other escaping the stench of his Roosevelt Street tenement home, hardening his head for the assault upon Wall Street.

Now they sat in the Bankers Club, young, successful New Yorkers, both dream-maddened; Peter, dark, slender, reflecting a blue intensity from the blue-black sheen of his hair to the conservative blue basket-weave suit to the blue-black lustre of his shoes. Clarence, tall, florid, more expansive, his clothes of Broadway rather than Wall Street, but both positive of their power, their mastery of the secret of money.

And Peter, discreetly releasing only little bits of information, sounded Clarence out on the general machinery for putting over a fifteen-million-dollar real estate bond issue.

Peter had not discussed his plan with Henderson, for he knew how hostile he would be to the underwriting of an issue that was new and which he would regard as highly speculative. Besides, he wanted to strike out for himself in this venture. Land anywhere in the city was a sound investment. But real estate located in the choicest midtown section could never fail. And if he assembled this company skillfully and made a success of the campaign, his share would be at least a million and it would be his real springboard into high finance.

Clarence was interested. He believed in banks and bank issues but he knew they were being inflated far beyond their book value. Besides, at the merest hint of a panic, the Government seized the banks first, closing those that were not secure, or at least not favored with political patronage. He knew his banking deal was not a permanent thing.

But real estate bonds were an investment in land. Why, even savings banks could put their money in land, as well as trust funds and pension monies. Besides, he was impressed with Peter. Here was a sure, calculating mind, a man of facts, discretion, knowledge, and secret power. Yes, Peter would be the ideal post to which a flannel-mouthed evangelical salesman could tether himself.

And if the bond issue were large enough, he, too, could make his fortune.

Peter and Clarence agreed to meet again.

27

The fight that Donovan had arranged for Joey with considerable reluctance was held at the Madison Square Garden. It gained importance from the fact that the winner of it would be selected as the next opponent of the lightweight champion. And it drew a huge attendance because in the opinion of several sports writers and the initiate, both men were superior to the champ, who had been sitting on a cushion with his crown between his legs resisting all invitations to risk his title.

At the weighing in both Wales and Young Samson looked in the pink of condition, but each was freighted with an obsession that fortunately did not register on the scales. Each needed desperately to win.

For weeks, Joey had been thinking of victory only as a device to bring him closer to Isabella, as a prisoner dreams of a secret tunnel which will lead him to light and freedom. He had never trained so hard or so faithfully, but his simple mind, designed to carry one objective, winning for its own sake—now ached with an additional burden, the desperate urge to win, in order to impress a girl.

Cannonball Wales, a ring veteran of thirty, knowing clearly that at best he had only a couple of fighting years left in him, and that to get a crack at the title he must win this match by a knockout, decided to take no chances on losing. He had seen Young Samson fight and acknowledged him to be a dangerous opponent. A two-fisted, all-angle hitter, the specialized product of years of street fighting, but inclined to become careless when stung. He had seen a wild punch once stagger Joey, and had watched him rush in, throwing all caution to the winds, pummelling his bewildered opponent. But suppose the opponent had been a ring general?

Wales was strong and cunning and unscrupulous. In twelve years of professional fighting he had built up a solid reputation for hitting low, punching in the breakaway from clinches, and slugging after the gong had sounded on the pretense that he was so engrossed in the battle that he couldn't hear the bell. All these attributes, plus his desperate need for winning, made him particularly dangerous on this night. If Young Samson lost this fight, it would only be a set-back in a younger fighter's career, something to be overcome by a few carefully matched battles. But if he lost—his career was over. He must not lose.

Around the ringside, sat the professionally bored and sated of New York, now gleaming with excitement at the promise of a kill. Here were those that held up the four pillars of New York's sacred canopy, society, theatre, politics and the underworld, the favored few with blood on the tongue.

Had Joey searched carefully among them, he would have noted some of his boyhood friends, the few who had kept pace, and gone up high in the world. Googi with a party of booze barons, an assortment of cosy killers, and an enamelled blonde tootsie. Peter and Eda, the guests of Clarence Dale, and with the promoter, a noisy, bright-toothed widow. Friends of friends also adorned the ringside. Eugene Murdock, with a party of building contractors, and Elmer Hicks with orange-bloom Sally, who had expressed herself as passionately interested in sports. And ranged around the arena, tier on tier, were thousands of others, women to be ravaged by blood, men to realize vicariously the thrill of the sadistic conqueror or the masochistic ecstasy of the bloody beaten—all fight fans.

Within view of the ring, alone, sat Bert, his nails cutting into his palms, his face tight with terror. Although he had seen Joey fight many times and win often, he was not yet hardened to the sickening impact of a blow on Joey's face.

In the preliminaries, the eager novices tore out of their corners like stung wasps, buzzed and winged around each other while small claques yelled encouragement. A dramatic tribute to the lust to kill in man that each could simulate a violent hatred for an opponent he had never seen before.

At about a quarter to ten the principals entered the ring. Young Samson received an ovation, for not only had the sports writers built him up for this battle, but the customers remembered gratefully that he gave them action. He was always good for a crowding, aggressive battle, one that usually ended in a knockout. Cannonball Wales was booed, but he turned his hairy back to the mob like an indifferent animal. What if he was known as a "dirty" fighter? It was a business to him and he must win tonight.

Before the gong sounded, the welterweight champ, an ex-heavyweight champ and a motion picture star were introduced from the ring and the arena was cleared for action.

The dying vibrations of a clamorous bell fell on a hushed mob. Young Samson, heeding Donovan's advice and entreaties, moved cautiously in the first round. It was difficult to hold himself in check, for he wanted to tear out with all the blind rage he felt, as though Wales stood between him and Isabella. But he restrained himself, fighting at long range, keeping his opponent away from any opportunity to dig in with low or "dirty" punches. Wales played in with this manoeuvre for he too wanted to watch and wait. They felt each other out, traded a few blows, led, danced away, but towards the end of the round Joey uncorked a left swing which rocked the Cannonball and drew the first roar of interest from the crowd. Wales clinched quickly and was hissed for hanging on. He knew then that in ten rounds of this kind of fighting the best he could hope for was a draw. He would have to win by a knockout—and soon. The gong clanged and they went to their corners.

One minute between rounds. Wales sprawled low on the canvas seat, his hairy legs outspread. The seconds closed around him like a screen. With rehearsed lightning speed, like a sleight-of-hand trick, he dipped the tip of the right glove into the box of resin. A second cooled his face with a damp towel. His heart beat wildly as he discerned the few crumbs of resin clinging to the glove. Had he been caught he would have been lynched. But fortunately no one had seen him. At the gong he leaped from his seat with magnificent assurance.

One jab in the eye with the resin-coated glove, and victory would be his. It was worth while risking an exchange of wallops. They rushed at each other. Joey caught Wales on the jaw, and the older man thrust the poisoned glove into his eye. Joey felt a sudden sting in his left eye, but any blow would bother the eye until it could be washed out between rounds. But there were still two and a half minutes of fighting until the rest period and the Cannonball concentrated his blows on that left eye. He was rocked twice, he even traded blows, but several times he managed to poke and rub the glove into the swelling left eye.

Seconds washed the inflamed eye—ah, how the lotion soothed, but as soon as the minute interim was up and Joey returned to the ring, it began to smart and itch and tear. He could ignore the pain but the flow of tears was like a film over his eye, obscuring his vision. And while he was shooting at a target that danced behind a screen, Wales kept pounding at that eye. Once, when they were locked in a clinch, Joey could detect a cunning sneer on the older man's face; cruelty and satisfaction were carved there.

Donovan, alarmed at the way Joey had slowed up in the fourth round, questioned him frantically, while the seconds worked over him. Joey lifted his glove to the inflamed eye. There was nothing to indicate that it hadn't been caused by a fair blow. And Donovan, thinking of the money that had been wagered on Young Samson, and the title bout which was at stake, urged him to throw all caution to the winds and try for a knockout. The only chance for victory lay in a fluke punch, because he would never be able to last the full distance.

Joey, now in agonizing pain, hardly able to see, for the watering had spread to both eyes, tore after his man. Like a savage bewildered by an unexpected hindrance and fully enraged by it, Joey swarmed over the Cannonball, hoping desperately to connect once. But Wales was cautious and cruel. He jabbed and hooked at long range, playing on the left eye like a pianist returning to a favorite note. By the end of the round, Joey's face was cut into a gory pattern and his left eye was closed. Donovan was counselled to toss a towel into the ring, and the referee debated the wisdom of stopping the fight, but Joey pleaded, "Gimme one more round. I'll git him."

Gloves like poison darts stabbed Joey, and the ache in his eyes spread through his brain, across his whole being, until each new blow brought quivering echoes of unbearable agony. But he kept on fighting, fighting with the mounting, unreasoning rage of an automaton before running down. He ploughed after his opponent like a blind bear, and every time he missed, there were howls of derisive laughter from those in the gallery who could not see that he had no vision. And inscribed in his pain, in the smears of blood on his face, in the mockery of the mob, was the face of Isabella, now separated from him by the unbridgeable distance of defeat. Every blow that struck him released a yell from the crowd. "Stop it—stop it." Always he had been urged on by, "Knock him out—put him away," but now the pack turned on him. Now they were yelling to heap shame and defeat upon Joey—Joey whose chunky fists had never failed him.

And as he ploughed forward into pain and darkness, the face of Isabella receding, becoming dim and black, a white towel was flung into the ring, and the Cannonball's hairy arm was raised on high, the salute of the victor. Joey was led like a blind man to his corner. Vaguely, he remembered that Wales put an arm around his shoulder and sang, "A great fight, kid, game as they come."

Bert, who had suffered every blow struck at his brother, led Joey to his hotel. Always Donovan engaged a suite for the week of the fight. And after each victory, Donovan would bring some of his friends up, politicians, swells, out-of-town business men, people he wanted to impress, and they would voice their admiration of his Jew-boy champ, while Joey sat around, shy, inarticulate. But now he was alone. Bert was with him but he didn't count. Donovan, who had to square himself with gamblers and sports writers, had been unable to take him home. That's the way Joey wanted to be, silent, alone.

Bert had hardly watched the last two rounds. Once he had glanced up, viewed the grotesque helplessness of his brother, heard the impact of a blow as an axe swung at a tree, and a thwack of pain had seized him in the pit of his stomach. Clattering with cold, his icy hands folded around himself, biting his lips, he had waited as one outside an execution chamber. This was the first time he had ever seen Joey in defeat.

He moved silently around the room. When he tried to help Joey undress, he was pushed away. Timidly, he suggested calling a doctor, but Joey snarled, "For what? For a poke in the eye?"

As he lay on the bed, Joey wondered whether his emotions for Bella had made a milksop out of him. Why, he had taken loads of punishment in his time, a cracked rib, a swollen ear, blows under the heart, taken all in his stride and still he had come tearing out of his corner.

But the pain continued all through a sleepless night. Bert hovered in a chair, wanting, pleading to serve him. Once Joey asked him to wash the eye, and Bert, under the bathroom light, observed a pussy formation. The inflamed, enraged look of the eye alarmed him. He waited until morning and then plucked up courage to rouse Donovan, who came at once with a doctor. There was a quick examination of the eye and a call for a specialist. Bert listened as they made the arrangements to take Joey to the hospital.

"The conjunctivital membrane is badly infected. A granule of dirt, anything hard, embedded in the corner, probably rubbed in every time he was hit in the eye by a glove. I'm afraid there's a rupturing of the blood vessel there. I don't know how the boy was able to stand the pain. A miracle if we save his sight."

The hospital was a place for decisions. Donovan lost a champ. Joey lost an eye.

Bert, sobbing, chattering with cold and nausea, thought once of Isabella. Somewhere in a tank town, in a third rate vaudeville house, at the very moment that his brother Joey was losing his eye, a dancer called Isabella was making an exit on her hands, feet rigid in the air, as the finale of a number two act of acrobatic dancers.

To Elmer Hicks, the fight assumed a curious importance. Once, when Wales drove Joey to the ropes and it seemed that a knockout was imminent, Sally, in an outburst of excitement, flung one arm around his neck. Her white, soft forearm pressed against his cheek; her fragrant hair, close to him, had drawn the blood from his face and made him weak in the knees. He forgot the fight and the roaring mob in his own overpowering emotion. For this and for her, he would build a skyscraper that would pierce the New York heavens.

Although many months had passed, the memory of the gloved hand still proved disturbing to Peter. Sometimes, in his office, or even at the apartment, he found himself examining his palm as though that single contact with Mrs. Langdon-Chase had left a permanent imprint. The rub of a gloved hand, he thought, was like a class ritual, an emphasis of a class gulf. The rich proffered a gloved hand, as though to remove it were to disrobe in the presence of a servant.

But her words lingered in his ears with a different ring. "If you come over this winter, do look me up." That was the invitation one extends to an equal, or certainly to a favored servant.

Peter found himself tempted. All his life he had lived so carefully, by such meticulous reckoning of time and money and emotion, that the possibility of a grand, impulsive, a reckless gesture fascinated him. To pick his hat casually off a hook and say, "I'm going to the Riviera. Back in four weeks."

It thrilled him to think that he was able to do it. But what would he say to her? "How do you do, Mrs. Langdon-Chase. I've brought you some fresh flowers and a new schedule of recommended investments." And even as he allowed the impulse to dribble away, he reasoned not within irony that his greeting to her, which held forth the promise of an increased income, might interest her more than himself.

His lead-weighted thoughts drew him down to earth. Say, Peter, you're still a hireling. You've put away a few coppers in the bank, you own a few securities. You're on the verge of a big deal but compared to the real Wall Streeters, you're a financial pigmy. The office door still reads "Seymour Henderson" in big letters.

Of course, if he could bring a million into the firm, that might buy for him a real share, give him a stronger voice. No, with a million in hand he would strike out for himself. And how he could move, as the husband of Mrs. Langdon-Chase. He ducked imaginary assaults upon him for his impudence. Why not? He could bring an unusual argument in his favor. Where other suitors sought to dissipate her fortune, he wanted only to conserve and expand it. And remembering her interest in money, his knowledge of finance suddenly became an appeal to her emotions.

These dreams and the delay in the Hicks deal made him restless, disturbed the pattern of his life with Eda. She was no longer able to pacify him and to her it was like losing the power of healing.

She too had made progress. She was now a feature writer assigned to interview the one-day celebrities who populated New York. A new face and a new reputation every day. She formed a phrase for her subjects, "Today's man of the hills." But there was no mockery in her writings. Her jaunts carried her around and across the city. And that made each day's work sufficient unto itself. All the rest of her was for Peter, but he was receding. She knew definitely that he had begun to loosen himself from her—slowly, almost imperceptibly, by restless twitchings. At first she dared not face the terror of losing him. But there was nothing definite to point to. They were still together, they still laughed and ate and loved together.

At dinner, Eda was telling Peter of "Today's man of the hills" when she caught a profound expression in his eyes, one of complete remoteness and disinterest in what she was recounting, one of perfect absorption in his own secret thoughts. She felt a pang of jealousy for those thoughts.

"But, Peter—you're not listening—"

"I am, Eda." A startled lie.

"Don't be technical. You are listening—but you're not hearing a word. What did I say about the lecturer's navel?"

With a smile, he tried to swing himself across the great gulf.

"It's round."

"I could think of five men who would listen with rapture to every word I utter."

"You're right, Eda. You're much too good for me." The end of the sentence sobered him, as it frightened her. Perhaps this was the moment when all the little loosenings would come to a sudden end.

"You give me up too quickly. Who is she?"

Peter looked up startled. God damn women. The monotonous accuracy of their suspicions. If it isn't a woman, it's a woman.

"Why, Peter, you're blushing." This was the moment. They had agreed never to hide anything, a childishly cruel vow. "Come, let me in on the secret."

"A client—purely a client. I was thinking of a lady in terms of her investments."

"But I'm a better catch. I own the view from the Woolworth tower. I can cook a meal for you just out of the vapors that steam out of Ninth Avenue windows. In a dark room, I glow like the ferry crossing the Hudson at night. In your arms, I'll smell like Gramercy Park in November. And I'll never betray you except with New York."

Peter listened to her, felt himself inadequate. There were no words he could give her, no assurances he could make. What is a man supposed to feel in the presence of a rare and honest work of art? Reverence, humility—uncomfortable sensations for a male on the upstride. Certainly not compassion.

Eda seated herself in his lap and drew her arms around him in a timid circle. "Peter, I love you. But I know I am going to lose you. Do one thing for me." He was aware of her as a painful duet, the soft pelting of her words on his ear, the thunderous beat of her heart close to him. "When you go, make it sudden. Just go."

"What if you leave me first?"

She kissed his cheek. "There isn't a chance. Please remember, Peter— make it sudden. Just go."

Her arms tightened around him.

<h1 style="text-align:center">28</h1>

On Fourteenth Street near University Place a wizened old man ground out a shrill cacophony from a battered hand-organ. It was a small, upright box, standing on thin stilts, and issuing a cracked, off-key tune.

Upon his shoulders, like epaulettes, the old man wore two white mice. Sleek, pink-eyed, raw, radish-tailed, they crept slowly around his shoulders, whisking their strippy tails against his ears. Sometimes, he could cock his head to one side and press his cheek against the soft, downy body.

The organ-grinder wheeled out his melody and upon a small metal whistle, concealed within his mouth, he kept up a thin, chirping obligato. People stopped before his organ and gaped at the white mice. Men and women shuddered back their horror of rodents, staring, fascinated.

Out of his bailiwick, upon a private errand downtown, Googi stopped before the organ. He glanced at the slowly rotating white mice and a nostalgic smile came over his face. To him this was a poetization of a familiar youthful memory of tough, long rats slinking down cellar steps, or dark, grey mice making free with his Bowery home.

He had never seen the dandified, white relations and they were like symbols of progress. He stepped closer, grinning, brushing one with his finger. The old man perched it upon a box containing tightly folded papers with printed fortunes. The mouse nibbled at one, lifting it up. The old man handed it to Googi, who flipped a half dollar to him.

Googi opened up the blue sheet and read.

"Your Fortune—after Mlle. Lenormand. Deep and dark are the secrets of future, like depths of ocean. Still we have divers who can reveal to us secrets of both."

Googi smiled and read on:

"You have a noble and forgiving character. Your one fault is that you trust too many people, which leads to your being easily deceived, especially by strangers."

Googi laughed, folded the fortune into a paper sword and picked his teeth with it.

In prison Googi had learned the art of silence. In France he had practiced it, and now flourishing in New York, he revered it. It was like the development of a major talent which in maturity grows to perfection. He despised all long-winded speakers unless they were comedians, and then tolerated them only as long as they were funny. He craved dialogue punctuated by laughter, and loathed barren talk. He admitted that mouthpieces had to talk, but if they grew long-winded it was only in line of duty. But he also knew that even a mouthpiece could dispense with talk if he was shrewd and had the proper spots greased.

From his women Googi liked a little baby-talk and gentle crooning. He had narrowed his tastes down to small-boned Kewpie-faced blondes, with tiny mouths, nasal voices, and worshipful stares. Women who were not pretty did not exist for him. They might have been sacks of sawdust sitting at night-club tables. He hated bickering crones, gabby dames, or domineering dolls, and always had an impulse to slap them across the mouth. He despised the men who stood for such women, either as sons, husbands or lovers. And, as he grew in power and wealth, these certainties about women became more fixed in his life.

During his first introduction to his bootleg associates, Fats had done him a great service by whispering to the big shots in an awe-stricken voice that Googi was a killer. Not a bravura or loud-mouthed killer, but one of the grim, silent, methodical life-takers. This was the only reputation Googi wanted, and it had been planted, just as he had intended, where it would do the most good. He was rated a natural killer who did not have to be coked up, who needed neither booze, hop, nor vengeance to take a life, and in this awesome capacity he was a man to be reckoned with. With the mob, this special trait increased Googi's importance.

Then, as a show of good will, he had thrown his bankroll into the common purse—not important money as they reckoned "sugar," but a grand gesture.

And, as final proof of his immediate usefulness, Googi had tapped a fresh source of whiskey supply by contacting an overseas friend, a "blat" guy who operated from the coast of Ireland. Thus he at once became entitled to an even cut, and was admitted to the conferences, where he said little except to advise less talk.

In those first years of the New York speakeasy era, a fellow had to work hard and fast to make a legitimate buck. The world was divided into two classes, the right and wrong people. The right people could be greased and their lips taped and their eyes bandaged. The wrong had to be intimidated or rubbed out.

There were menacing forces, too. Trying to muscle into the choice Times Square sector were ex-doughboys who could eat a sandwich off a propped-up corpse. Ninth Avenue cowboys who had been too young for the war but wanted easy money and excitement, and smart Hebes from the east side, from Brownsville and the Bronx, who were out to duck manual labor. And even as these mushroom gangs fought for choice speakeasy spots, there was the threat of entrenched lords in Brooklyn and in Chicago who looked yearningly at the easy sugar on the Big Stem.

But Googi had been at war all of his life. He had been at war with his father, the truant officer, rival bootblacks, neighboring gangs, policemen, prison guards, and with all of the Germans. He knew military strategy and his sure instinct for what to do against an enemy would have made him a prize member of the West Point faculty even if he was below the regulation height.

And so he prospered far beyond the wildest dreams of the starved and pain-wracked little dago that slunk out of a Bowery tenement in the chill of the morning, eyes pasted together, torn shoe-soles slapping the pavement, shoulder hunched over under the weight of a shoe-shine box. And what was more miraculous, he survived.

Now, for the first time in his life, Googi lived exactly as he wanted to live. He was twenty-eight years old and a complete success. Where Horatio Alger and the *American Magazine* might have shuddered at publishing his biography, the true historian and sociologist of this period would have been grateful for the truthful details of his life and for what they taught as the essential formula for success in any field.

At twenty-eight Googi was not quite five-foot-six, but with the aid of an extra thickness of heel he gave himself a little additional stature, a pardonable bit of petty larceny in a man who sought to plunder millions. He was dark and lithe, his face, body, hands and feet beautifully cared for. His dark hair was beginning to thin but that did not bother him. His eyes were still weak from those youthful sties, stinks and filth that had been applied to them, so that now when he had to see someone clearly he screwed them into little black bullets looking out of dark muzzles. It was a squint that threw terror into the heart of the one scrutinized.

And Googi loved life. He had a suite of rooms atop a Times Square hotel. He owned thirty suits, all silk-lined, all perfectly tailored, broad and padded at the shoulders, tapering at the waist, and the patterns in pin-stripes to lend him added height. He had endless pairs of shoes, all fashioned by an expert English bootmaker, monogrammed underwear, and shirts cut to order from Irish linen or Japanese silk. His vista of ties was a color festival for the eyes. The back of his neck was shaved twice a week and at any hour of the day or night he looked meticulously clean.

He was fanatically careful about what he ate and drank and smoked. He dined regularly at Dinty Moore's, where his lavish tips secured him the choicest of foods and the most attentive of service. He had his own private supply of liquors, and to drink with Googi in the speakeasy era was to sip nectar. And it was a sensual delight to observe him inhale the first fumes of a Belinda fancytail, to sniff the rich smoke and react to its caress with an expression of surrender.

All around town there was a stampede for progress, a lust for expansion. And the mob played along. From little furtive speakeasies they grew to places with a suggestion of decor, with music, and then blossomed into palatial night-clubs. Their most lavish venture was a night-club on West 54th Street called "The Golden Buckle." Here was the last word in underworld swank and upperworld patronage. Food, furnishings, prices, entertainment, habitues—everything was tops. The cabinet that made Metropolis held round-table meetings here, and found diversion and surcease from civic cares.

And from the floor show, Googi picked the tenderest of blondes and made her his own. She was eighteen, satin-skinned, blue-eyed and vacuous. Googi was as generous to her as if he were a millionaire broker, but added the extra quality of being ardent. But he did not talk to her. It was clear that she, as everything else in life, was made to serve him, and that he must taste, enjoy and remain silent.

Sometimes, when they were alone in his apartment, he allowed her to baby-talk to him and to croon for him. He let her babble on like a child in the uncertain voice of a child while he smiled vaguely and lost himself deeper in his own vast plans for conquest.

But when she crooned softly, he listened. A crooning voice awoke a strange hunger and pathos in him. He had never heard his mother sing a lullaby. He enjoyed torch songs, although he had as few illusions about women as he had about men. Still, it was a nice romantic conception that a beautiful young woman would eat her heart out because her man was indifferent to her. To him, love was a manifestation of provincialism. The rubes and the suckers fell in love. He knew that the moment he had no money, his cutie would leave him. That was true of the whole sex in New York. No woman had any use for a man who was broke, if she had any charms left. For that matter, no man had any use for a pal who went broke, because the natural instinct was to shun all those in need.

Well, Googi would never be in need. Each week he went to his vault and into a long envelope inserted a one-thousand dollar bill. This was a personal reserve, upon which he could depend in the event of an emergency. In addition, his mouthpiece had a fat retainer with orders to drop everything and spring any member of the mob that got into a jam, especially any of the leaders.

Two, three years passed. Googi prospered, Googi survived. But the good life in which he wallowed aroused to an increasing pitch the envy of rival mobs.

Towards one midnight in the autumn of 1923 Googi sat at his table, angled into a corner with the big shots. There was a look of irritation on his smoothly shaven face, and his companions looked worried. For weeks now trouble had been brewing on the west side, and several of the speaks to which they catered had been taken over by the Archie Higgins gang. Two of his salesmen and persuaders who had attempted to intimidate the speakeasy owners and bring them back into the fold, had been severely beaten up and given an "or else" warning. Booze trucks had been hijacked right out of city garages and it looked like serious warfare unless some compromise were effected. Chick Schmidt, the big shot of Googi's mob, had arranged a meeting with Higgins, who was on his way over to "The Golden Buckle." He was explaining his stratagem to Googi, whose irritation grew as he listened to the rumble of words, endless words.

"Killings and fights in New York won't do us no good with the cops. They'll have to close down on us just to keep out the federal guys. This is no charity racket and I don't like to give up anything. But I say, let's split the west side with Higgins."

"In a pig's neck," said Googi. "Give up half and you got nothing left. It costs just as much to grease the way for half the booze as for all. And if you let them muscle in—what's to stop Higgins from roping off the whole west side?"

"But he's got a tough mob of cokey killers and they don't stop at nothing." From Fats.

"So what! So hand them everything on a silver platter." Googi's blazing eyes regarded jowl-hanging Fats. He had grown Falstaffian with the good years and wanted nothing to disturb his serenity. There was silence for a moment. The big shot broke in nervously, "We better make up our minds. Higgins is coming over with his right-hand guy to get the new set-up. I think he wants to be friendly."

"Sure—friendly like a dose of salts." Googi looked at him contemptuously. "Why let him come here in the first place? There's no percentage in that. Then he goes back and says to his mob, 'I got them buffaloed.' He says to his mob, 'I'm sitting in "The Golden Buckle" drinking their bubble-wine and they hands over the west side.' In a pig's neck!"

Googi had never spoken so much, or so vehemently in councils, and everyone listened intently. His voice sharpened as he took first command away from the big shot.

"The best thing is, we meet him outside." To Fats: "Get the big Lincoln ready and don't say nothing. We drive up to Chick's apartment in Sutton Place and nobody sees us talk it over. And what nobody sees, you can't gab about."

At one o'clock, Higgins and his bodyguard arrived in a taxi. Googi, Fats and the big shot met them outside.

"Some wolves from Washington are inside," explained Chick.

"And if they see us together, they'll raise the take," added Googi.

"Let's go to my apartment," continued Chick, "we'll spread a feed and talk things over."

Archie Higgins, dapper cocky Irishman, nodded to his bodyguard. "Sure," he grinned. This was no time to show fear. Besides, there was no fear in him. He packed a rod and his lieutenant, Handsome Daly, knew that he had gone for a pow-wow. If anything happened to him, it would be just too bad for Buck's mob.

Googi opened the door of the limousine. Chick entered first, then Fats, then Googi. Higgin's bodyguard sat next to the chauffeur and Higgins planted himself directly in front of Googi. Then he turned around so that he could face all three of the mob in the seats behind him. There was a smile on his young face.

"I think we can straighten this out, Archie," said the big shot in a whining voice.

"That's what I told the boys," said Higgins. "There's plenty for all of us. And anyway, us home-towners should stick together and keep the Chicago mob out."

Fats acquiesced eagerly. He was soft with good-natured fat and life was smooth and cushiony. He hated to have anything disturb it. Privately he thought Googi was wrong to hog it all. The pig was fat and why risk your life over an extra slice? It was the softest dough in the history of easy money.

Googi spoke softly. "You know, Archie, those speaks cost us about ten thousand apiece to fit up. You take over a stack on the west side and that sets us back 100 G's."

Higgins craned his neck around and laughed close to Googi's face. "Take it out of profits. Listen, wop," he continued contemptuously, "my mob is all young Ninth Avenue cowboys. I gotta keep them happy and healthy. Otherwise these micks from Hell's Kitchen will shoot up the town. It's worth a hundred G's to stop the hijacking and to get some dumb bastard rubbed out when he's picking his nose in your soup."

The car smooth-swung around the deserted darkness of First Avenue under the Queensborough Bridge.

Higgins bent down to light a cigarette.

"My very words," echoed Googi. "It's worth all you got to rub out some dumb bastard that's putting his shoes under the wrong bed."

Googi lifted his right hand coat pocket and, shooting through it, fired at the back of Higgins' head. "Keep driving," he ordered as, swinging the coat pocket towards the bodyguard, he fired again.

Higgins slumped forward in his corner, cigarette hanging from his lips. The guard's head remained twisted with astonishment. The big shot turned white with fright and Fats wanted to vomit. Googi pumped another shot close into each of them so that only a muffled report was heard and a little circle of flame where the muzzle met the head.

The big shot opened his mouth but Googi kicked the unspoken words back into his throat. "You yellow bastard," said Googi, "taking all that crap from a hophead kid. I give up nothing. And from now on, I handle the splits in this mob. I'm number one guy."

"But the cops," wailed Fats.

"Nobody knows—that's why I didn't let them go into the club. And the cops will thank you for getting rid of a couple of punks. They ain't like us. We're business men."

At the foot of a dock, near the East River, Googi ordered the car stopped. A few dim lights from Welfare Island winked over. Googi sent the chauffeur out to jack up the car and pretend to be changing a tire. Deftly he went through all the pockets of the two dead men, removed everything, including two guns, cut the initials out of their hats, the labels off their suits, laundry marks off their shirts and socks. Then he commanded Fats and Buck to toss their bodies into the East River.

"Jeez, we took them for a ride," shivered Fats.

"Oh, no," corrected Googi with a chuckle, "a couple of pals went in swimming with their hats on."

They rode back to the club in silence. Only Googi got out. Fats and Chick were to take the car into the garage and bury what they had dumped out of the dead men's pockets. Googi's parting words to Fats:

"Don't forget, Fats—to-morrow you call up Handsome Daly and you say, 'How come Higgins didn't keep his appointment last night?'"

Catechism for a lady forlorn.

When a goddess cuts her finger, does she bleed?

Does a goddess weep tears when her love departs?

Eda had asked Peter to make his leave-taking sudden, and when he left, it was like the swift descent of a curtain.

Is a goddess jealous of a mortal woman?

"Tell me, Peter—what is the special fascination of Mrs. Langdon-Chase?"

"She's above me."

"So am I."

"But she stands at the top of a mountain of dollars—at the pinnacle of a station in society, while you're up in the clouds."

"And you love her?"

"No."

"Does she love you?"

"No, I've only seen her a few times, Eda. She travels constantly. And when she does send for me—it's usually about business."

"Perhaps she can't see you for the dollars."

"That may be."

"And you leave me—for her?"

"No, I'm just leaving you. Eda, let's not quibble. I'm going into the first big project of my career. I must go into it alone—unencumbered."

"Unencumbered? Not even by the financial help of your great social luminary and patroness?" Eda was surprised at the bitterness in her voice. She was beginning to suffer from human traits.

Peter took her hand. "Eda, I was never wholly yours. You were never entirely mine. To each of us—we were one of several interests. My greatest passion has always been success. You knew that."

"And I stand in your way?"

"Yes. I go up from you—if I go away."

"Good luck, Peter. It was nice knowing you."

Eda stayed on in the apartment. In the beginning the void left by Peter's departure was unendurable. It seemed bottomless. She could toss the entire city into its terrible depths and it would swallow it up. It devoured her work, her ambitions, her waking hours and the long nights when she sought sleep alone. There would be flurries of forgetfulness and then the ache for Peter would return, stronger, deeper, almost as powerful as the first emotion Metropolis had aroused in her. She wanted to toss herself at the city, to crush one ache with another.

And as the months passed, her work went on, life by day continued. She began to attract attention as a talented journalist, one of the interviewers who trapped the beat of the city in the daily printed word. She met many men and many women, awed celebrities, resigned nonentities, racketeers, actors, civic leaders, Lesbians, poets and panhandlers.

Above the millions that trod the streets in New York, high up, like special mountain insects that crawl around the very peak of the cone, dwell the leaders. And in her interview with one, she found herself linked with the others. She came to know Googi, Eugene Murdock, Clarence Dale, Elmer Hicks, Michael Donovan, to know about the dream upon which they were all riveted.

And she made it a point to know about Peter.

And of the multitudes she met, many desired her. But when she gave herself with the hope of finding forgetfulness, she became more vividly aware of the tremendous void.

Perhaps the city, Metropolis, was avenging itself for her betrayal.

In a bare Bronx bedroom, whose one window looked out upon a gloomy court forever clamorous with those accents and inflections which were reaping fortunes for Al Jolson, Eddie Cantor, Lou Holtz, George Jessel, Eugene Howard, Smith and Dale and many other Jewish dialectitians, Bert slowly spun a play which concerned itself solely with life in the ultra-smart set of New York society.

For years, he had been nourishing himself upon plays and stories about the fabulous rich. He had steeped himself thoroughly in Spur, Vanity Fair, Tattler, Harper's Bazaar and the society pages of the Metropolitan papers. Like a navigator, skilled only in luxury liners, he could chart the trek of the restless rich from New York to Aiken to Palm Beach to Biarritz to Greenwich to Newport. For him geography was the study of half a dozen cities, three beaches, one ocean and no rivers. He became an expert on the social parasite. He knew what the rich wore that the poor did not wear, and what they ate that the poor did not eat. He could describe the beds they slept in and the period furniture they tripped over when they swayed in the dark. He knew what words they spoke to enrage, placate or seduce one another. His mind was a lexicon of the little phrases they uttered which were indigenous only to the soil of the rich and which if uttered on a Bronx sidewalk would have shrivelled.

From actual experience he knew nothing about debutantes, the horsey set or those daughters of the rich whimsically called "gentlewomen." He had never met a person whose name was in the Blue Book, and he had glimpsed society only as one of a throng outside of a Fifth Avenue church hungrily watching the bridal pair and their guests, or shivering outside the Metropolitan Opera House on opening night as the limousines disgorged the ermine-strangled box-holders.

And yet he was an authority on their lives, not unlike other poor writers who have provided the rich with the correct dialogue.

And so he slowly spun his play and when it was complete, he called it "Landed Gentry: A fable about fabulous women." So completely had he absorbed their routines, the odd, tangent problems that loomed large in their special lives, their nonchalant manner of handling tragedy, that his work had the stamp of authenticity. The fact that most of their emotions were shallow and that their ambitions were small, glibly expressed, simplified his task since it required no more than a veneer to produce the illusion of a solid color.

Further, most of the producers on Broadway were more familiar with life in the Bronx and on the east side than at Cannes and Narragansett, so that no finely attuned ear would listen to detect flaws in the synthetic accents of his play.

Bert, in the tradition of all young playwrights, read his first play to a group of friends at his home. Among them were school teachers, a young lawyer, a medical student and office workers. In the doorway, humbly and timidly, stood his bewildered mother and father, both becoming more wrinkled and shrivelled as a result of an alchemy which baffled them as all life in America had.

In an adjoining room, on a cot, lay Joey, the vision in his one remaining eye still dimmed, shelled by darkness. He was a figure in a black coffin. He would be able to walk and push his hands out, but the dark shell would be forever about him. Softly, he called to his mother to leave the door open. He wanted to hear Bert's play.

Bert read with a glow. From the crisp, freshly typed pages, he drew characters that pranced in a cotillion strange in this Bronx dining-room.

His parents listened with a puzzled expression, pride in their eyes, bewilderment on their faces as he spoke this foreign language. And of the others gathered, only a few grasped all of the upper-crust nuances in his play. But all felt that he had definitely achieved something, and that as a result of his achievement, he would soon be living in the same world that his characters inhabited. They laughed and applauded and joked about the fame and wealth that would be his.

"Soon—you won't recognize your old friends; you'll forget all about us."

And in the tone of one of his characters, Bert replied, "The trouble with old friends is that they won't permit you to forget them."

When all his guests had gone, their praises still in his ears, Bert entered the dark room and sat down alongside of Joey. Here was the one emotional bond that was genuine and lasting in him, from which he sought no escape. He felt guilty because he could see, because he still wanted to laugh.

"Did you really like it, Joey?"

"Cheez, you made that up out of your own head. All them swell woids—cheez."

Joey's voice broke. He was so full of his admiration for his kid brother, the pale-face, the weakling, the mollycoddle who used to grow green with fright at the approach of hostile gangs. He was glad now for his chunky fists. They had sent the kid brother through college, supported him at home while he wrote, taught him all those fine, delicate words, words he would never understand. Perhaps that was the reason he had been a prizefighter. It made everything right, even the loss of his sight.

In the dark, Bert reached over and gripped his brother's hand. But there was nothing he could say, because he knew so few simple words. He had been living so long with his elegant, artificial characters, that this interlude of bitter reality rendered him tongue-tied. This was no time to summon Jenkins for another drink, or to sail on the "Paris" at midnight. He simply gripped his brother's hand and fought back his tears.

On the advice of a friend who was a member of the junior group of the Theatre Guild, Bert submitted the script to a play-broker who had the proper contacts. He reacted to it with even more than professional enthusiasm. "My boy, the play is a natural and Max Graham will lap it up. He wants to spring this new find of his, Gina Page, and in your opera he can surround her with great performers and still give her the fat role."

For ten days Bert lived within a yard of the telephone and then the summons came. The play-broker proudly led his charge into the inner sanctum of Max Graham, who had his office in the Sardi Building on West 44th Street. The building reeked of grease paint and shattered ambitions, but Bert walked on air.

Graham (an evolved name) who still spoke New Yorkese with traces of a Russian-Jewish accent, fell flat upon his meaty face every time an English actor spoke with what he believed was an Oxonian accent. He, too, yearned for Mayfair, and annually he imported two or three English drawing-room comedies, London tripe, which he presented with great fanfare in New York. The English casts came with the plays because they liked the ocean voyage. The plays were slight, charged with small, casual talk, dripped with Mayfairisms which made them difficult to understand and usually flopped in a week.

But Graham remained undiscouraged. For years, he had searched for a counterpart to these English plays of manners, but laid in the American scene, and in Bert's "Landed Gentry" he had found it. The play was patently written by a newcomer and its structure needed tightening and the second act curtain needed a wallop, but in the main, he liked it. He had a play doctor on his staff who could do all this work long before it went into rehearsal. And then, as the play-broker had pointed out, the part of the pretty society crasher was perfect for Gina.

Graham had wondered about its author, for the play had an accent of authenticity which impressed him. While the name Bertrand Glass did not betoken Mayflower or Mayfair ancestry, there was a distinguished Virginia Senator who bore that name. Perhaps the author was of aristocratic American revolutionary stock.

Max Graham regarded Bert with a kindly scrutiny. He took in the careless tweeds, the soft, roll-down collar, the generously knotted tie, the hat with the soft brim crushed in one hand, the Scotch grain shoes and he grunted with satisfaction.

"Young man, I wonder if you realize how lucky you are. Max Graham will do your first play—and your last, if he lives long enough. That's provided success won't make you dizzy in the head. Sit down."

And so the amazed Bert, his fingers trembling and his heart thumping, signed an Authors' League contract for his first play. The clauses and the figures that his eye caught on the run were blurred before him. Something about five percent on the first five thousand—why that was

$250 a week and fifty percent of stock, foreign and motion picture rights. His throat was so dry he was afraid to say "thank you" for fear he would voice a ridiculous squeak. If only he had been able to behave like one of his own characters. To light a cigarette and casually remark, "A bit of extra-ordinary luck, what?"

He came home with a check for $450 (the agent had deducted his ten percent commission from the advance) placed it on the table before his dumbfounded parents and collapsed as he used to after a sixty-yard dash.

Eda was interviewing Perry.

The day before it had been Googi. She remembered his gleaming eyes and the murderous chuckle in his voice. She had written a color story on the killer turned night-club owner. The new hosts and overlords of the city she loved. She did her work well, for now, with Peter gone from her life, work and Metropolis were all she had.

It had been easy to persuade the feature editor that Perry was excellent copy for a long story. Here was a rich reformer, fanatically determined to revolutionize the appearance of the east side. Countless thousands had risen from the slums and gone forward and upward to wealth and fame and security. Few of these concerned themselves with the ratty old tenements that had sheltered them, or with the fate of those wretches who now inhabited them. But here was a reformer from above, one who had no ties with the slums save those that sprang from a rare humanitarianism and who had actually started a movement.

Eda looked at his ascetic face, the blond hair already thinning at the temples, the deep circles under his eyes.

Q.—"Exactly what do you propose to do, Mr. Murdock?" She wrote down her question and poised her pencil for his answer.

A.—"These plans will give you a clear idea. We shall knock down whole blocks of old tenements on the lower east side. Then the entire section will be remapped so that ample grounds shall be set aside for adequate playgrounds. Model tenements will replace the old ones and, because of their added height, the housing facilities will not be diminished. They will rent for a little more than what these poor tenants are now paying. And of course each apartment will have the same modern equipment and plumbing facilities found in the better class apartment houses."

Q.—"How will you go about doing this?"

A.—"A quasi-public corporation will be organized under municipal authority. In most cases the owners will be glad to sell because many of the tenements have already been abandoned. They are unfit for habitation even by those that can barely afford a roof over their heads. There are cold flats near the East River along Mangin Street that are literally crumbling away. The owners don't get enough revenue from these houses to pay taxes and they'll be happy to let them go. Of course, if any should become greedy and hold out, the city can condemn their properties and pay them a fair price."

Q.—"What have you done so far?"

A.—"We've organized a Tenement Commission and we've drawn up a preliminary report for the Governor and the Mayor. Do you know that one-fourth of all the families in Manhattan live in slums? Do you know that three minutes away from Park Avenue's most expensive apartments and penthouse suites, right along Third Avenue, there are 2,000 families without toilets in their tenements? Do you know that more than 60,000 people live in fourth-class structures, hovels that even corrupt politicians have officially characterized as 'unfit for human habitation'? Do you realize that in this ultra-modern metropolis, 30,000 people cook on wood stoves and illuminate with lamps or candles? And sixty percent of the arrests in Manhattan come from the slums. We'll push these figures before the faces of our authorities and prod them into action."

Q.—"Do you expect much opposition?"

A.—"A great deal. There always will be opposition to change, not only from realty owners and politicians, but even from those whom the changes will benefit most. But we're prepared for a long siege."

Q.—"How long?"

A.—"Many years."

Quite suddenly, he stepped out of his role of determined reformer, the man being interviewed. He took Eda's hand and his voice, which had been so confident as he rattled off facts, figures and public betterment convictions, lowered and faltered into a plea. "Why don't you do this with me, Eda? I am terribly lonely. I feel so far away from everything that is warm and alive. My father treats me as if I am a little cracked—and even those who are working with me suspect me because they think I'm meddling. I'm a stranger to every one. But if you worked with me, it would be different. And you do know—I love you."

Eda loosened the hand he had been gripping, set down the pencil he had squeezed between her fingers. She rubbed the little red corrugations the pencil had made and shook her head.

"I'll help all I can, Perry—publicity, advice—even friendship, if you like. But I can't go with you in this—certainly not the whole way. With you, it's love me, love my project." She spoke as one reciting a simple fact. "But I don't love you—and I can't think of New York changing except from its own ferment." She closed her eyes and felt the cruel crush of tall buildings, the hot stench of crowded streets, the cool shadows of the rich, the roaches and rats and lice of the poor, the whole town, criss-crossed, perforated, encrusted, green and dark with a patched canopy of sky, the fearful jungle in which she was a lithe, clawing creature loosed only for an orgy in self-destruction. She shook her head. "Forget love, Perry—and raze the city."

They concluded the interview.

The following day, Eugene Murdock read the interview with Perry, saw a two-column picture of his son in a metropolitan daily, and he beamed with pride. Perhaps in his own eccentric way Perry would achieve the heights. He was willing for his son to succeed, even though this peculiar success would brand him as a lunatic in the father's circle. And while he was engrossed in these thoughts, one of his associates walked into his office, flourishing the same page of the newspaper.

"That boy of yours sure gets a lot of publicity."

"Why not? He's good copy. And that wild scheme of his——"

"That's exactly what I'm coming to." The wily associate lowered his voice. "Maybe you ought to give him a little more encouragement on this plan. Even get on one of the committees. Say, if he puts it over, there'll be a hell of a lot of contracting work let out—and why shouldn't we get in on the gravy?"

Murdock smiled in approval, but when he was alone again, a sadness came over him. Poor Perry, he thought, no matter how high he flew in this town there would be some pitch on his wings. Well, there was no escaping it. If the reforms went through, contracts would have to be let for this vast work and it might as well be Murdock's firm as an outsider. He would bide his time and lead up to it gently.

Then, at the top of the page, under the heading of the interview he read the byline—"By Eda Finkel." He thought of her pleasantly, the clever-tongued blonde Jewess with a swell shape. Several times had he run into her.

Newspaper people were always bobbing up. He had always been friendly to her, but so far she had given him no more encouragement than she gave to Perry. Here was a good excuse for calling her to discuss this big project and she could undoubtedly help handle his son. A cosy dinner would be the best setting for such a discussion.

29

Tucked away in a fold of the brain, on a narrow ledge above the eyes and behind the blank wall of the forehead, a little dream germinates. A man walks the streets of the great city looking very much like his fellow men, but on the narrow ledge, the restless dream has reared itself. It is poised like a bird for flight. And such is the power of this dream that the men who walk peaceably by the side of the dreamer will soon be scattered like peppery granules in a dust storm, fortunes will be shifted and lost, buildings will be razed, a street in a great city as familiar as a finger on a hand will change its contour, emotions will be shattered, love aroused and death accelerated.

The dream of Elmer Hicks, the dream of Peter Mendes, the dream of Clarence Dale, the dream of Bertrand Glass, the dream of Isabella, of Perry, dreams poised on narrow ledges like birds for flight.

On a late Friday afternoon in February of 1925, Peter entered the private office of Seymour Henderson. The old man was seated at a huge carved desk, counting the stamps in a tin box. Peter looked at him afresh, as though seeing him for the first time. Nearly thirteen years he had spent in this office, working for this man. He must be getting on towards seventy, thought Peter. His deacon's whiskers were white except where the tobacco drippings from his cigar had dyed a nicotine-brown rivulet down the center. His eyes, once so sharp, were now a little bleary, and his piratical nose had grown a little bulbous and veined, destroying its cutlass edge and also its ferocity. His hands were rust-speckled, the skin in ridges, like the beach after a heavy rain, and the nails had lost their lustre. But his voice was still firm and his acquisitive greed as keen as it had been at the outset of his career.

Peter smiled. Thirteen years before he had stood, cap in hand, in front of this ogre and had trembled. Now he faced him without fear, even with a little contempt. His own hair still had its blue-black lustre, his face was dark and smooth, and he had supreme confidence in the conservative cut of his expensive blue-black clothes bursting into immaculate white only at the cuffs, the shirt front and the collar, set off by a Sulka cravat. For thirteen years they had lived without love, both touching shoulders only in the march towards money. And now their ways would part.

"What is it, Peter?"

"I want you to know, Mr. Henderson—that I'm leaving."

"Going away on a trip?" The eyes sharpened in their pink-blood rims.

"I mean—I'm leaving the firm. I'm starting a company of my own." The words were applied like a blow-torch.

The old man was silent. He was too old and too tired to bluster, threaten, or fight him. And yet he wanted nothing changed about him. He would have liked everything to remain as it was until his death, which he still hoped and believed was a great many years off.

"You're a fool, Peter, to leave me now. And damned ungrateful. You were a ragged boy when I gave you your first chance——"

"I know all about that. But I also know that I've worked hard for you—managed the office—and your investments too——"

"Is it more money? Perhaps we could arrange——"

Peter smiled and the smile suddenly hardened on his glowing face. "I don't want a raise—I want millions—and this is the time to get them. Not by slow, conservative investments, not by lending money——"

"Some wild scheme, eh? What is it? If it isn't too crazy—perhaps we can handle it from this office."

Peter shook his head. "A fifteen-million-dollar office building. The land is already assembled."

"Where will you get the money to build?"

"From the public."

"Wild-cat speculation," the old man shrieked. "Not for me—and not for you, if you've got any sense. You'll ruin yourself."

Peter stood aloof and firm. "I'm leaving."

Henderson's voice lowered. "Listen, my boy, I'm worth five millions——"

"Closer to eight millions," Peter corrected him. He knew the extent of the old man's wealth almost to the dollar.

"I won't forget you—when I go. Stay on. I'm tired now. Some other day we can discuss it—perhaps we can arrange a larger interest——"

But Peter was not listening. The old fool, trying to be canny and wily, not knowing that Peter had also seen a copy of his will. Remote institutions, colleges, hospitals, churches, orphan asylums would get the bulk of his wealth. And after the inheritance tax and legacies to relatives had been paid, only the good will would be left. And what was that worth in a period of tremendous prosperity, of wild speculation, when firms sprang into being and overnight amassed assets equal to those of aged institutions.

Peter paused. He had wanted to tell him about the years when three men lived on six dollars a week in a Roosevelt Street tenement hell-hole while Henderson had millions. He had wanted to remind him of the time when he was ready to believe that Peter was dishonest and throw him out. But he bit back the memories.

"Nothing can change my mind," said Peter with clipped finality.

"You're a fool," the old man shrieked, "You'll be ruined."

Peter walked out. He would turn over a formal statement in the course of the next week and make the severance formal and final.

Alone, Seymour Henderson fumbled with the stamps in the tin box. He was sorry to see Peter go, but he felt sorrier for himself. Shouldn't have roused himself so. Excitement was not the thing for his heart, especially since he planned to live to eighty. With will-power he tried to drive the turgid blood through his aged arteries. Live to eighty, live to eighty-five, and come down to his office every day. He tried to rise, but a wave of weakness swept over him. His desk swam before him and instinctively he put his hands out to protect his forehead as it fell against the tin stamp box.

Clarence Dale's exit was accomplished without march or emotion. Like the moon, he drew his color and illumination solely from the deal he reflected, and like the moon, constant movement in a large orbit was his way of life.

For several months, he had been on a Long Island subdivision deal where a politician's hazy promise of a four-lane highway had skyrocketed swamp lands into valuable realty. Dale had built up what he considered his most valuable asset, an organization. To him, the men who sold were far more important than the thing they sold. Like a feudal baron, he surrounded himself with an inner circle of first lieutenants. These became his crew managers and moved with him in a body, drawing enthusiasm from him and catch-words which they passed on to lesser salesmen; each lieutenant, in turn the center of the circle that followed him.

Dale, well-nourished, tall, beautifully barbered, his broad shoulders made even broader by the padding on his modish Broadway suit, jauntily walked up to the president of the realty company and extended his hand in farewell.

"I'm off on a new deal—a deal that's got real romance to it. Anyway, you can't unload any more of that swamp land. The suckers are in mud right up to their chins."

"But we're getting another subdivision over in Jersey, along the Palisades—right near the new bridge."

"What have you got to sell? Mosquitoes with a view. No, thanks. Anyway, I'm committed." He pronounced the word "committed" as though, among promoters of honor, the mere giving of a word was a sacred pledge, inscribed in blood.

"Will you leave the men alone? They've all developed prospects and——"

"Count on me. I'll disappear like a magician's rabbit."

All Dale did was inform his lieutenants that he was on a new deal, and the men followed him like sinners in the wake of an evangelist. As he warmed up to the possibilities of the new project, it became "the tallest office building in the world, with the smallest investor assured of the largest return, with the weightiest names in the banking field on the Board of Directors."

Thinking about it in his flashy apartment, while waiting for a beauty contest winner to undress, Clarence Dale felt that at last he had made his dent upon New York, wedged himself in between the golden leaves. Here was the million, the clothes, the apartment, the women, the surfeit he had dreamed of when he lay on his stinking back in the damp grass of Battery Park one dawn.

In a lawyer's office Elmer Hicks placed a certified check upon a desk and accepted title for the last parcel needed to make up the precious building site. He put the document in his pocket and left. In the elevator going down he caught a glimpse of himself in the mirror. He was approaching forty, and his hair had grown grey, a dull, granite, bristly grey. Behind his glasses, his eyes were tragically tired, and his face, never creased by laughter, rarely lined by a smile, was smooth and dead.

Always, after the signing of a deed, all the other parties to the deal had a drink, passed cigars around, arranged for a poker game, a night in the Turkish bath or at a bordello, or a weekend at Atlantic City. To them, it was a punctuation mark in the dull routine of making money, a time to pause and forget business. But with Elmer it was only a link in a chain which he was drawing tighter and tighter around the heart of New York. He could not accept the solace of tobacco, or wine, or women.

As he walked to his little hotel room, the deed rustling in his pocket, he felt tired. Prayerfully, as one wishing for a miracle, he hoped he could sleep. But the orange disks, like fiery grindstones, revolved inside his eyes. He dismissed the hope of sleep. And then, with greater daring and even more wistfully, he hoped he could some day sleep—with Sally.

Tentacles wiggled forth and entwined themselves around the principals in the deal. Peter, who had already arranged for preliminary funding, had carefully drawn the financial structure of the new corporation. One of the main provisions was that all the members of the inner board were to take a special class of stock in exchange for their investments of land, materials and money, and all of these holdings were to be pooled for a period of five years and controlled by a subsidiary company. He guarded against jeopardizing the venture by any sudden withdrawal of capital or the dumping of a block of unlisted shares. A pool would be created for the sole purpose of buying out any member who wanted to default. And, during the initial years, it was practically guaranteed that the small investors would receive their dividends regularly, building up a vast store of confidence, so that in time the venture could be repeated again and again. In the course of five years one could do it half a dozen times, and each venture would be worth millions to those on the inside.

Spacious offices were rented in the Grand Central section and Clarence Dale plunged into the work of inspiring and building up his shock troops. And in preparation for dynamic sales literature and advertisements Murdock's architects had already drafted plans and Michael Donovan had already entertained several of the municipal fathers and their illegitimate offspring so that any obstructive regulations or minor transgressions would be overlooked.

The city itself was ready. The streets resounded like drums to the beat of marching feet—feet marching to brokerage offices. The winds blew across the town, carrying the smell of quick money, spreading a restless murmur. All New Yorkers walked with a fanatical look in their eye, chanting to themselves in fervent voices, "If I put this deal over, I'll be on easy street." Young and old crossed dangerous corners with a dreamy absorption, and as they escaped death from hostile taxis and falling safes, they turned their eyes skyward and intoned, "If Celotex goes up two points, I'll sell out and retire."

Bootblacks, doctors, merchants, chorines, school teachers, errand boys, chiropodists and guerillas, bought three editions a day of newspapers, and turned first to the financial page. Illiterates contrived to read the intricate names of listed securities on the Stock Exchange board more readily than a child's primer. All regular and honest forms of employment were looked down upon with great disdain, as an entire city wooed the new American ideal which was to duck manual labor and live by the sweat of another man's brow.

And Clarence Dale, a victim of this fever, yet able to use it for his own advantage, assured Peter. "We'll put the issue over in six months. This deal has romance—the biggest midtown skyscraper. We'll sell it to the public like insurance—an absolutely safe investment with guaranteed returns."

In the fall of 1925 the project was ready for its actual beginning. In New York, there is no such thing as a fresh start. One begins by destroying what you hope to supplant. The foundation is laid on freshly buried bones. And so several trucks rumbled up to Broadway, between Forty-third and Forty-fourth Streets and the crews of jolly home wreckers rolled out. They attacked with enthusiasm a job that in the main must be very satisfying— the destruction of buildings. And with the speed that characterizes all New York construction—except municipal improvements—a shed was built over the sidewalk to protect the heads of the pedestrians from falling timber and discarded tobacco chews, a wooden fence put up to shut out the curious and a new volley of clamor was added to the noises of Manhattan.

In time Elmer Hicks stood once more upon a vacant lot. Sally was with him. Seventeen years before he had stood breathless upon a Bronx lot, listening to the far-off thunder of the encroaching city, gazing at the glow it cast upon his little sky. He had made his prayers to a steam shovel, silent, implacable, monstrous, like a Balinese God.

Now he had his feet on the heart of the big city. He pawed the mid-town precious earth, to trample on its heart-beats. All the vast fortune that he had accumulated by murder, hoarding, cunning and prophecy lay in this land under his feet. He envisioned the vast skyscraper that would rise here. Eighty stories high. All of his Bronx buildings could fit into this honeycomb. He thought of his earliest years on the farm. Driving cows to pasture. That's what he'd been doing—all those tight, bitter years, herding brick and steel and glass, toward the great watering hole at the heart of Manhattan.

He became aware of Sally, herself awed by the spectacle of a barren acre in Times Square. He went over to her, heavy-footed, digging up his earth, revelling in its feel, and took her hand. "Sally, when my building is up—will you marry me?"

And Sally, dreaming of a triumphant return to Kansas City, a sabled, bejewelled Sally, in an aluminum chariot (don't you remember Sally? Would you believe it—she really married a millionaire), dreamily said, "Yes."

Elmer, for once impetuous (how long he had waited for this) flung his arms about her and kissed her lips. The flavor of orange was in her lip rouge.

In a pit below, a mud- and sweat-encrusted Italian laborer, thinking of his buxom wife waiting at home, muttered, "Dose damn richa people— dey no can wait!"

No dawn, no twilight. Black night. Lying on your back or standing in your shoes, you're in a coffin. Living in a barrel full of blackness. You're got to think with your hands, memorize with your fingers. The chairs kick you in the shins, the table hits below the belt. The street is a jungle alive with wild beasts that shriek for your blood. The gutter was your cradle and you're afraid it may become your grave. You used to live in the street and now you're afraid to walk upon it even when your old father holds your arm. That's the part which is hardest to swallow. It hurts your pride, Strong Joey with the chunky fists, being led about by your old man, like a blind dog on a chain. Carrist! One-punch Joey, tottering around, wanting to cry like a hysterical 'fraid-cat, having to learn all over again how to walk. They even have to lead you to the toilet. Carrist! You used to jump the gutter in three hops, and now you putter across like an old babba.

Remember how you used to duck under the very neck of a truck horse as it clattered down the streets, jump on a street car as it clanged down the tracks at full speed, glide off a truck with a sure-footed leap. You never fell, you rarely stumbled. And on a two-wheeler you would speed down like a racer in and out of traffic, from gutter to sidewalk. Carrist! You almost rode up the side of a tenement.

Remember when you wheeled across the Williamsburg bridge that hot day with the kid brother on your handlebars? And the way you used to skate, sure-footed as a wild goat, forwards, backwards, fancy turns, with all the other kids breaking their behinds through clumsiness and you always on your feet. And in the ring, in all those battles, never a knockdown, standing on your own feet, trading wallops with a slugger or nimbly pursuing the clever boxers.

And now—just a kernel in a hard, dark shell which would never be cracked open to let the light in.

What the hell does a blind pug do? What becomes of him? They run a benefit for you and the first time everybody buys a ticket. "Sure, I'll take a couple of pasteboards. That Young Samson—he was a game little fighter when he had his eyes. Always put up a great battle for the fans, and never turned down a guy for a touch."

But at the second benefit you're forgotten. "You stuck me once before with a couple of ducats."

What becomes of a blind fighter? Most of Joey's earnings had gone for the support of the home, for Bella, for his kid brother, and the manager had always taken a cut. His next two, three years would have been the time of the big purses, the time to sock away the big dough, but he had tried too hard. Fought a little out of his class. The sin of being too eager. Too ambitious—and all to make a hit with Bella.

Well, they won't catch Joey tapping around with a cane, scum in his eye-pits and rags on his back, rattling a tin-cup.

"Cheer up, Joey," Donovan could read some of his thoughts. Sentimental Irishman, his own eyes filled with tears. "You're like my own son, Joey. And if I didn't look after you, every nickel you earned for me would be blood money. You're the gamest Jew-boy I've ever seen—in or out of the ring. And you're closer to me than my own flesh and blood."

"Thanks, Mike—you always been white to me."

"I've got a newsstand for you, Joey. And I had to pull some wires to get it. It's near the subway on Broadway and Forty-second Street. Your old man can help you out while you learn to make change—and then you're all set. A sure living, and healthy too, right out in the open and with people passing all day long you won't be thinking of yourself."

Joey groped for his hand. It was big and warm and friendly, softening to the grateful clasp of his own. And as he thought of a new life opening before him, he remembered the words of Donovan. "People passing all day long." Right in the theatrical district—Broadway and Forty-second Street, people passing all the time, people of the theatre. Surely, among all those thousands, some day, would pass—Bella.

30

Five men in one night, five strangers. Five times to defile the body, five burnt offerings to the great God and betrayed lover, Metropolis.

Eugene Murdock laid his plans craftily, but like all generals he could never have achieved victory without the help and surrender of his quarry. Often you win only because someone wants to lose. He phoned Eda at the paper, and was agreeably surprised to discover how well she remembered him. He dangled before her the bait of a story, some very inside "dope" and she consented at once to see him. Moving his checker one square, he suggested dinner and she said, "swell." Where to meet? Not at the office and not at home. He sewed a lining of discretion into the rendezvous. The good old lobby of the Astor, under whose bland clock lovers go to fornication as by command of the minute hand.

I know a little place. The ultimate baptism of the New Yorker. I know a little place where. In the cab, Murdock looked at Eda and felt himself rejuvenated. In the recent fat years he had bought some of the most beautiful cocottes in New York for an hour or a night. For brief periods he had kept show girls. But he had never deceived himself. He had been buying flesh, fragrant, satiny bellies to rub against and then discard. But here was something that money couldn't buy. A glowing spirit, not heavy-laden and oil-anointed with shibboleth and puritanism, but a pagan spirit, promising delights he had never enjoyed.

I know a little place where the food is marvelous. And he did. He took Eda to the most exclusive swill in New York. It was a small brownstone home in the Murray Hill section, presided over by a French chef who regarded it as his castle. Only a few upper stratum politicians and a handful of judges, corrupt in everything but their palates, knew of its existence. No one came unexpectedly as to a public restaurant. You had to call up in the afternoon and find out if you would be welcome and then order your dinner hours in advance. The dining-room was small and held only four tables. The whiskey, the wines, the brandies were of the finest and came from ambassadors' stock. The atmosphere was one of gravity as befits a place where eating and drinking constituted a sacred ritual and not a springboard into an evening of vacuous levity. And the check, a ditch-digger's wage for a month, was given to you in one sum. The man who asked to have the bill itemized was forever barred from the home.

They were shown to their table in a dimly lit room and Eda flung back her evening wrap. Her shoulders glowed and Murdock felt an excitement he had never known before.

For an aperitif, I would recommend a Dubonnet cocktail. It was like a command, but one pleasant to obey. Half chilled Dubonnet, and half Gilbey's gin, the glass frosted, the mixture dramatic to the tongue as the sweet red beads surrendered to the bitter, white, strong ones. The first dish was a small ice-packed bowl of crab-meat, not whittled into slivers and dripping in sweet ketchup as it is served in barbaric regions, but free of any foreign flavor and cut into sizeable chunks so that their demolition would be the eater's delight and not wasted on a cold pincers. A sauce compounded of tomato extract, garlic, lemon and olive oil was served in a separate dish, so that the eater might dip the crab meat to his own taste. Crisp, heated crackers and fresh sweet butter were served with the course.

"You know what made me think of you," said Murdock, as though it had required an event of force to precipitate her back into his awareness. "That article of yours—about my boy's crazy scheme."

"Let's not talk about Perry," said Eda. She closed her eyes. A wave of sadness swept over her as she thought of Perry. The stark majesty of his dream. Its lovely bitterness in realization. All thoughts drove her back to Peter. And from him to that ecstatic, first awareness of New York, the night the town had ravaged her.

"You can't talk about an old man like me." He knew he didn't feel old. Yes, he had grown heavy and his face was blood-red from good living, but his appetites were young and keen. He wanted her to reassure him that he wasn't old.

"How about the story?" Her question came from a long distance.

He patted her hand. "Later—later." And to himself, "that's if you're able to listen." "Another cocktail—or would you like the wine, now?"

"You could ride to your death on this onion soup," sang Eda.

The second cocktail, the exquisite food, warmed her into a curious gaiety that had nothing to do with the death that lay in her heart. Her eyes danced, her skin glowed, her blond hair held the sheen of aliveness, her breasts felt firm, and her arms moved with grace as she ate and talked.

Murdock was fascinated. To him she was a pagan virgin. "May I pay you this compliment? You're not only beautiful because of how you look, but because of what you say and think. Is there a tribe of blond Jews?"

"I'm only half-Jewish. My mother was a Hungarian servant—peasant class." She sipped the wine, Lacrima Christi. "But when you're half— you're really double. I dance twice as long, love twice as hard and get hurt twice as deep."

"Hurt?" Murdock's face was growing red to bursting, with concern, food and desire. "Listen, Eda, if there's anything in the world I can do for you." He would have loved to be able to give her something that she really needed. O, but to serve my lady love.

"No one does anything for me. I'm the one to do. I'm the one to give."

The press was brought over to their table for the duck. The waiter raised the lid to allow them to savor the fragrance of the roasted ducks, and then, with a deft surgical twist, carved the breast for each and placed the birds in the copper container under the press. Eda watched the process with fascination. As the waiter turned the lever bar, she could hear the bones crunch. From the sauce pan, the distillation of the duck was ladled into her plate. "All that's left of the mortal remains of the duck."

"But delicious," said Murdock, sponging up some of the juice with a soft piece of bread. "And it's just enough."

"Right. Just enough—for the duck, too."

Murdock did not intend to stuff himself. The girl radiated not only provocation, but also hope. He revolved the Napoleon brandy in the large glass, sniffing its vapors. Eda, looking at him gravely performing a ritual to excite his palate, looking at his florid, jowly face and the red, ample flesh of him, thought fleetingly of Perry. Ascetic, cadaverous Perry. Father and son. Holding her glass in a hand that quivered, she laughed.

"Did I say something funny?" Murdock was eager to be amusing.

"No—it's something you did."

I know a little place where the food is marvelous and the service is excellent.

For special guests who liked to loosen their collars and their belts, the host provided a room upstairs. This was a special service extended by a gracious and understanding host to a very limited number of his patrons. They were literally people he invited to his home, for there was no charge for this courtesy. You were led into a room furnished in flawless taste, with library pieces. A Capehart and a selected library of chamber music recordings. In one corner, as an after-thought, stood a bed.

The waiter brought them a bottle of brandy and closed the door softly. Eda thought, I would love to look frightened but there is no terror left in me. I should only laugh and that would ruin everything.

Murdock poured some brandy for her. "Would you like to hear some music?"

"Is that the third step in seduction?"

He stared at her, red-faced and solemn. "I'm crazy about you, Eda, and I have been—since the first time I met you."

"But your son is in love with me?"

"He'll never get you."

"I take it, then, this is part of a campaign to keep me in the family."

For a moment, Murdock forgot his own lust. He seemed to be addressing himself to a great personal frustration.

"He'll never get anything. I used to have high hopes for Perry. I felt he was a piece cut out of me. It was to make things easier for him that I connived and stole and worked. But now he's like a cracked stranger to me. He visits me like a missionary and spouts reform. I'm beginning to think he's not my son. Just a joke somebody played on me."

Murdock comforted himself with a sip of brandy. Eda came around to him and placed her small, white hand against the red expanse of his smooth cheek. She pressed her fingers into the soft flesh and drew them back suddenly to watch the blood flow back into the white runnels. His hand groped for her thigh and he pressed her into position upon his lap. She slapped his cheek, at first lightly and then with greater and greater force as if she were pounding steak. "It's more than love with me. It's worship," he said. "You're like a virgin." He kept jerking his cheek towards the pressure of her hand, clutching her tightly to him.

Then he carried her towards the bed.

Eda cooled her face with water in the bathroom and dressed quietly. He lay with his red, meaty face up, his hands clasped over his protruding stomach, contented as in death. With her lip-stick she inscribed a note and placed it upon his stomach, lifting the coverlet up to keep it in place. The note read, "Thanks for the laugh."

On her way out she smiled at their host and placed a finger on her lips. "Asleep," she murmured, "the gent's asleep."

It was eleven o'clock, not time enough yet for the after-theatre crowds to fill "The Golden Buckle." Eda swept in alone, on a note of gaiety, sobered a little by the presence of waiters hovering over anticipatory tables. The dance orchestra played softly, muting the reeds and winds, accenting the strings. Googi rose swiftly from his table and walked towards her, blocking her entrance into the main hall of the club.

"I ought to sock you in the nose," he said.

"Why? Still sore at me?"

"You done me a lot of harm with that piece you wrote about me in the papers. I don't mind publicity—if it's nice. But making a dummy out of me—a sap that shoots his mouth off—and tells lies." He had a horrified expression on his face as though to tell a lie meant going to hell.

"I'm sorry, I just wrote my impressions. Killers are the new hosts and overlords of New York."

"Well—I'm giving you a chance to make it up. You'll write another story—and this time get it straight."

He took her elbow firmly in his hand and led her out. On the way to his car, he smiled to a few early arrivals.

"Where are you taking me? For a ride?" There was no alarm in her voice. A characteristic big town ending, riddled on a ride.

"You got me all wrong." His voice was an ingratiating whine. "I'm no life-taker—and especially when it comes to ladies. Say, you forgot I learned how to treat dolls over in France. I'm taking you home to show you that croy-dee-guerre so you won't make any more wise-cracks about my service in the war. Killer? Sure—but for democracy. Get me?"

"So that's what burned you up?" Eda chuckled. She knew of the deaths he had caused or perpetrated in New York, and acknowledged them as feats of murder. But because she had doubted his prowess in an organized war, he was grievously offended. A strange streak of vanity.

The car entered the driveway on the side street. An attendant, instantly alert, held the door open, and they took the elevator in the basement and were whizzed up without any stops for other passengers. Two guards at his penthouse apartment sauntered in the narrow hall like guests who have pressed the button and are waiting to go down. A suppressed smile flickered on the face of one as he shot a glance at his comrade. Kind of early for the number one guy to begin his night. This must be a hot dame.

Googi ushered Eda into his living room with a gracious bow. He looked like a head-waiter who has made a fortune through the stock market tips of his important guests. Good living had put weight on him, giving him a friar's chin, a slight paunch, which he did his best to distribute through the aid of a tight, low-cut vest. His hair had thinned and he looked shorter than he actually was. He wore a double-breasted Tuxedo, a center pearl for a stud, platinum wrist-watch that bristled with diamonds which he wore under his shirt cuff for fear his cronies would think him effeminate, and a three-caret sapphire, the dull band on the outside of his finger, the gem resting on a cushion of his palm. His mouth was never entirely closed, lips parted a little and bent to one side like a man eternally on the verge of speaking. And his dark eyes glowed with a murderous gleam.

"A pretty shack," smiled Eda.

"I do all right."

He motioned her to follow him into his bedroom. It was decorated for a queen about to be confined. The bed was wide enough for mother, child and the physician, covered by a rose-satin spread, and weighted with pillows fringed with gold and anchored by gold tassels. The furniture was white, the bulbs rose-tinted even unto the bathroom, upon whose walls she caught a fleeting glimpse of frivolous murals.

"Home sweet home," sang Eda.

"I'm glad you like it," he spoke eagerly. "The style is my own ideas."

"A swell place for a killer to sleep in."

Googi swung around. He suddenly became aware of her as a woman. A blonde. A gorgeous blonde.

"But not alone."

He turned a knob in the radio, but instead of music issuing, a small metal door swung open, and with a key that dangled from his chain he opened a vault. His finger rustled nervously among some papers and then he extracted a medal and ribbon. He kissed it first and tossed it to her.

It was meaningless to Eda but she pretended to examine it. Then she tossed it back to him and he returned it to its hiding place.

"Now—I want you to write another piece about me." He drew closer. "And if you do the right thing by me—I'll do the right thing by you. And more."

"Just—what is—more?"

He turned the lights out in the room and Eda ran towards the window. Suddenly, she was on an island of darkness surrounded by the brilliance of the city. They were high up, and by rotating her eyes she tried to keep pace with the lights that encircled her in dizzy spirals like six-day bicycle riders in a spurt around a velodrome.

She heard him talking into the back of her neck. "I've got a yen for you. I've had all kinds of dames—but you're different. You're smart—a woman of the world. That's what gets me in you. A woman of the world."

She shuddered at the press of his lips, the nibble of his teeth. His hands plated her breasts.

On Rivington near Allen Street, which bore the Second Avenue "L" upon its patient back like a rusty cross, Perry lived. He worked in the very bowels of the region he hoped to transform.

It was two o'clock when Eda's taxi brought her to his house. The street still writhed and gasped like a sturdy reptile which has been hacked at in several places but stubbornly joins itself together in some challenging manifestation of life. As she entered the dark hallway, a couple that had been welded into one by a molten embrace, separated. They were engaged, and so their late love-making was forgiven by parents and overlooked by neighbors. Where else could they steal an hour together? For a second the lady in the evening gown excited their curiosity, and then their moist, bruised lips fused again.

The line of the door was trimmed in light, and it shuddered faintly against the latch, making a noise like chattering teeth. Eda knocked on the door. Behind the wooden barrier she heard the slow shuffling of feet and light slanted upon her. Perry was too startled to speak. She entered and closed the door behind her.

On the kitchen table were spread blueprints, architects' drawings and remnants of food, and to the walls were pinned clippings from newspapers, pictures of model tenements in Berlin, statistical charts, personal notations, and, hanging apart by itself, a photograph of Eda. He seized her hand and kissed it.

"Eda—you came."

"I knew you were lonely."

"How lonely—you'll never know. Blueprints are cold. There's a big part of me that hungers for you."

She clasped his scooped-out face in both her palms. "Poor child—you look so tired."

Tears sprang from his eyes. "I'm not ashamed to cry, Eda. It's like crying to one's own mother."

"Come, Perry—you must rest."

"There's no sleep for me."

"I'll lull you to sleep."

In the adjoining room, the only other in the flat, there was a severe army cot. No pillow at its head and a rough blanket flung across it. They sat down at the edge of the cot. Eda shook off her silver slippers, peeled off a sheer silken stocking. There was a run in it.

"I live like a monk," intoned Perry. The warm flesh-white of her legs, an unfamiliar color, dazzled him.

She wriggled out of her gown, letting it lie at her feet like a cast-off skin. "Like a monk in a cell."

He nuzzled against her soft breasts like a child. She could see his lips form the word mother.

At three-thirty Eda tiptoed down the stairs. From behind a wooden door an alarm-clock rang, rousing some bone-weary worker to open his newsstand or to be on the early milk route. She had made her escape hurriedly. Her hair was dishevelled, there were runs in both her stockings, and along the side of her gown two hooks were unclasped. She lit a cigarette and blew a funnel of smoke into the slit of dark blue that canopied Rivington Street. Her eyes glowed, flames from the flames she had kindled and stilled. Virgin, woman of the world, mother, flames in unfamiliar altars. She walked along, puffing a cigaret, kicking fruit-skins into the gutter.

What was this act of giving the body? Sacrifice or benediction? A social code, a religion, a literature were founded upon the gesture of giving the body. Once she had tossed herself against the city—a gift of violence. To be pierced by a church spire. To rub yourself into a bleeding pulp against its rough stones. To hear your bones crunch under the embrace of its steel. To be blown aloft by its winds of fury, to feel your nostrils torn as its stenches crowded to your head, to be hacked by its wheels, to lie ravaged and dismembered in its sewers.

She had hoped that Peter's love would have hatred and fury and passion in it. But he was gone from her life. He too had saved his violence for his assault on the city. Peter was gone from her life. What was there to pour into a void?

Giving your body to men meant looking the other way. Sad, clumsy gropers, blinded by the sheen of skin, seduced by female aromas, trembling to fuse, hearing passion as a pounding torrent, waking to find it a puny trickle. And forever, running again and again, towards the same mockery.

At Fourteenth Street and Second Avenue two sailors leaned against a lamppost like book-ends. Upon their sunburnt faces desolation was inscribed in a printer's holiday. Sailors, away from sea and ships, in city jungles, look forlorn. Separated from routine duties, from their home on the boat, they are lost. These two looked crumpled and sunk. They had begun the evening jauntily, hoping that the city in its clamorous ferment would toss up a woman for them. Like hungry dogs they had loped along the sidewalks, sniffing eagerly at grease-spots, frisking and prancing to impress, rubbing against dangling arms, passing thighs, hallooing cheerily to phantom females, hoping to appease the lust that raged within them. An elemental, pent-up lust that changed all hungers into one. But of the millions of women in New York, they had been unable to gather one.

As Eda approached, they straightened. Their ears grew to embrace the click of her heels, their nostrils widened to sniff her perfume. A young woman was coming toward them. Alone. From her walk, her dishevelled hair, her rolling walk, she might be drunk. Better luck. Young, alone and drunk. A blonde and good-looking! They hitched their trousers. The older, a gunner, had large eyes, closely set together, a nose squat in the center from a blow in a bout and a Hapsburg jaw, blue with bristles. He ran his tongue across his lips.

"Howzit, sister?"

He gave her an ingratiating smile, his eyes beaming, his teeth flashing in the distortion that was his mouth. Carrist, I'm anxious to please. I'm frisking around your ankles with my tongue out, lapping up the shoe-polish. Mmm-mmm, it's good. I'm turning somersaults in the gutter bouncing my skull on manhole covers. Anything at all to please, please let's get my arms around you, baby.

"Like a little company, sister?"

The younger one stood rigid as a beam. He had a fair face, regular features, undisturbed by intelligence or tragedy, pinched now in a look of desire.

Sex hunger swept out from them and poured over Eda. She knew something of large hungers. She smiled at them.

The gunner jerked forward, rolling his eyes deep into a corner of their sockets. "Can we take you to the subway?" His thick fingers closed about her elbow and he leaned against her soft arm.

Carrist, I'm anxious to please. I'll strut my stuff and jabber like a gabby old dame. I'll sing ditties for you in a funeral parlor, and knock the engineer off his seat so's you can drive the subway. Anything at all to please, please let me dig my nails in that soft rump.

"What's a sweet little girl like you doing alone at night?"

"She must of walked out on her boy friend."

"A bozo is a sap that lets you give him the air. But I'll get you home safe." He slipped a tentative arm around her waist and when she permitted it to rest on her hip, his heart sang.

Carrist don't let my luck change. Sister, tie your legs around me in a scissor-hold. Cut me in half!

"You must be one of them quiet kind. Not a peep out of you since we met up."

"Forgive me—if I seem rude. I've spoken to a great many people tonight."

"And I bet you told them plenty." He was *so* eager to please. "Well it's okay by me, sister, if you're one of them quiet kind—it's okay by me. Just looking at you is an evening's entertainment." He tightened his arm about her waist and with experimental fingers rolled up a fold of her belly.

"Live far?" The younger tried to make conversation.

"She ain't going home," the gunner said. "Stop putting ideas into her head. The night is young and the party is just begun." He pushed him away from her and half into her ear spoke, "Let's go down to my room and pick up a drink." He saw no negative forming on her lips and in his excitement hailed a taxi with a shout. He seized the younger one and growled, "Hand me all the dough you got. Come on, pick it out of the sock. We'll take her down to Whitey's. We can get a room if we buy the drinks. Carrist, what a juicy lay!"

He hustled the young sailor into the cab like a badly tied bundle, planted Eda between them and side-mouthed an address to the cab driver.

"May I smoke, please?"

"I'll cigaret you, baby." He placed it between her lips and lit it tenderly, cupping the light in hands hot as ear muffs.

They pressed against her on both sides, and Eda felt the heat and the hunger of their bodies.

"What's the name of your ship, boys?"

"The Texas." The younger one drove in one line.

"A swell tub, but you can't go to sleep with cotton waste. The grub's all right and the skipper has a heart—but there ain't a seamstress aboard."

"I thought sailors had a sweetheart in every port."

"Sure—in every port you get paid off. But I lost mine in a a black-jack game and Pinky sends his home to the little grey mother in the west."

He caressed the curve of her calf with damp, heavy fingers and rested at her thigh. Carrist, I ain't gonna spoil it now. Baby, I could rip the bloomers off you now and put the blocks to you on this leather seat. I could roll you out of a window and under the wheels of the cab.

"Where are we going?"

"To a saloon off the end of Christopher Street. You look like a dame that goes to town. I bet you hit all them high spots on Broadway. Well, this is La Club Waterfront." He rasp-chuckled at his own joke.

The freshness before dawn blew over the city. The water-front wakes up first, getting ready to feed the big hungry town. Milk trucks rattle, fresh fruit and vegetable wholesalers flit about in long white coats like ghosts.

The saloon smelled of spit, stale beer, old sawdust and chewing tobacco. A bum with his fly open sprawled snoring in his chair, while at another table a Mary Sugarbum crooned eerily to herself in a low voice. The gunner made the arrangements and a bartender who paid no attention to Eda, unlocked a room for them upstairs. The bed had just been used. The gunner tore the single blind down and glowered at Pinky, who stood like a pole.

"Take a walk for yourself. I'm gonna be busy for a few minutes."

Pinky stood there, mute, trying to fashion a protest.

"Get out," roared the gunner shoving him beyond the door and then locking it from the inside.

He slapped the cigaret from Eda's hand and his bloodshot eyes seemed to pop from his head. He fumbled at the clasps of her dress, tugged at it, whimpering with impatience. Carrist, I can't wait. He rammed her on the cot, elbowed down her upswinging knees, zig-zag ripped the next-to-the skin silk and covered her like a coat of armor. A string of beads broke out on his forehead below the dark line of his hair. "Move, you slut."

A sharp tearing, a twitching in violence. I give my body. We'll greet the dawn in a revolving door, waltz me around New York. We'll cool off on a weather-vane, blow me around New York. We'll sing down mail chutes, play hop, skip and jump in the sun-squares under the "L."

There was a timid knocking at the door. The gunner let Pinky in. "Make it snappy. We just got time to get aboard."

Before he left, the gleam of her purse caught his eye. He opened the snap and extracted the bills.

"A slut like you can make plenty of jack."

In a Ninth Avenue coffee pot Eda breakfasted on coffee and doughnuts. Her parched throat welcomed the hot liquid. Not so many hours before she had eaten the tenderest of pressed duck, imbibed the choicest of wines. Old Murdock must be breaking open crisp rolls as she fingered the greasy, rubbery arc of a doughnut. There were a few small delights still left her. Food, a shower, a change of clothes, the blond hair brushed back.

But irrevocably she was nailed to a bed. She would never get off the cross.

Virgin, woman of the world, mother and slut. Five men in one night, five strangers. Five times to defile the body, five burnt offerings to the great God and betrayed lover, Metropolis.

Atonement to New York.

<h1 style="text-align:center">31</h1>

Joey, tell us how the world looks to a blind newsboy. Tell us how the big town climbs off its sky-scrapers, like a herd of black, monstrous elephants, comes tearing and rolling down the streets into a deep pit at your feet, and little black beads rise like licorice spots before the unseeing eyes. The perspective is different. Everything is vast and monstrous far away, and dwindles as it thunders towards you.

But life isn't so bad after all, not when you're a game guy. You're standing on the busiest corner in the world. You're the owner of a newsstand on Forty-second Street and Broadway. Say, that's what you call being a capitalist. Success. You wear a special coat with four leather pockets. Quarters, dimes, nickels and pennies. Those chunky fists that used to sock and spin chins to the canvas, are chapped and red, but you've learned how to make change with lightning speed. Yes, your fingers are as fast as your footwork used to be.

Of course you have to depend on customers to tell you what papers they take. A two-cent tabloid or a three-cent full size sheet. But how you make change. *World-Telegram? The Sun?* (Funny calling a newspaper *The Sun.*) Remember that hot morning in the good old summertime—when the sun rose out of the East River and you ran across the Williamsburg Bridge to develop wind and leg muscles? How young and strong you were, whizzing over the town with Bert on the handle-bars. Oh yes, *The Sun.* Two-bits. Squat thumb on the surface of the quarter for the fine corrugations, into the upper right-hand pocket. At the same time from the left, you extract two dimes and from lower right two pennies. And so it goes all day long while the pockets fill with change.

Everything would be swell except for your little father. He worries you. He gets up at dawn and insists upon riding down in the subway with you. The way he holds your arm, the tender way he guides you. He even combs your hair and dries the corners of your eyes. It breaks your heart. Carrist—you're no cripple and no lady, neither. You can still make your way downtown, and say, there's plenty of steam left in those mitts, if anybody got tough. You've worked out your own system. If a guy gets fresh, talk soft to him to bring him close, then grab him with that left hand and hold him in position and sock with that right. You don't care how many eyes they've got, they'll go down. You laugh as you call that game Blind Man's Biff.

But the old man worries you. Sometimes, you get the feeling that he's staring at you—and crying. Just weeping—right in the middle of New York on the busiest corner. Maybe you're just imagining it, because no grown man would cry on Forty-second Street and Broadway in full daylight, with thousands of people passing all the time. But that's the feeling you have. It gives you a chill down your spine and makes your heart feel so heavy you can't breathe. The old man is looking at you—and weeping. You call out to him and he waits before he answers. You hear him swallow. He's making up a new voice for you. The way his hand touches yours as if it was an accident. The way his hand moves over your face after he's combed your hair. The way his hand passes gently over your face, like a wind, at night, when he thinks you're asleep.

The way he says, "If I could only give you the eyes out of my own head."

But life isn't so bad. You're out in the fresh air and thousands of people pass all day long. Sometime—Bella will pass. And because your lamps are out, you can beg her to come back. Before, when you were a topnotch pug and on your way to a title, you couldn't beg her. But it's different now.

Maybe, she'll feel sorry for you. You'll tell her about the two thousand smacks you put away just for her. You saved that out of your own pocket money, out of the allowance Donovan gave you. You didn't deprive anybody else of a dime. The money came in just the same for the folks and for Bert and for Bella's keep, but you simply didn't spend anything on yourself. You kept away from whorehouses and gambling joints and racetracks and you bought ready-to-wear clothes instead of going to fancy tailors who wanted to hang your autographed picture up on the wall after you became a customer.

And it all added up to a nice two thousand bucks right in the sock. You were going to surprise Bella with it. The eight-hundred-dollar bedroom suite which she liked in a swell store on Fifth Avenue and which she thought was too expensive. Boy, you were going to surprise her with that. Everything in the little apartment would have been better than she expected. And what a kick you would have gotten out of just looking at her face.

Well, you've still got that two thousand and some day when she passes and comes up and says in that little voice of hers, she's only a kid, hello, Joey, and you say to her, Bella, please be my goil, and you beg her to be kind to you and get married, which you can because you're blind and she says all right, you'll surprise her with that two-thousand-dollar nest-egg.

Joey felt someone staring at him. It couldn't be his father because he was away making deliveries of papers to office buildings. This was an intense stare that pelted him in waves even as he bent over to make change.

"Joey," a voice that cut deep into his past, "ritzing an old friend?" He outstretched his hand and Peter gripped it.

"Pete."

Peter usually got off at Grand Central station but on this morning he had shuttled across to talk to a branch manager of a bank which was floating part of his bond issue. First he had stared at Joey from a distance, waiting for him to utter the first cry of recognition. But Joey, it seemed, had looked right through him. Peter, hurt, advanced, and then discovered he was blind.

The knowledge shocked him so that he stood there petrified. Joey, unable to see. The whole mad swirl of bonds, millions and skyscrapers of which he was the center, stood still for a moment while he tried to assimilate the fact that Joey was blind. They hadn't met in years. He had never thought of him except on rare occasions when his eyes glanced over the sporting sections and he saw his name mentioned. But Joey, the leader of the Forsyth Streeters, Joey with the chunky fists, his protector, why—he was one of the deep-rooted realities of his life. He tried to make his voice casual, to ignore the terrible fact of Joey's blindness.

"You son-of-a-gun. You'd never think of looking me up."

"Well—you know how it is, Pete—when I was fighting steady, I was mostly on the jump—and now—I can't do much looking up." He laughed. "I heard about you—who was it that told me—you're a Wall Street broker."

"I'm in finance."

"That's a two-bit woid. Tell a feller what that is." And all the time he was making change.

"I handle money for other people—and make fortunes for them."

"How about making one for me? I got a little saved up———"

"Joey—I'd love to. I've just launched a company that's so safe that all my own money is in it. The tallest skyscraper in mid-town New York. Only a couple of blocks from here. Listen—and you can hear it going up!"

Both paused and cocked their ears. Above the normal thunder of the street, there could be heard a top-layer of clamor.

"Sure—I've got a little sock put away—it ain't much to a big broker———"

"I'll double it for you, Joey." It was never Peter's habit to speak extravagantly, but even if the money came out of his own account, he was determined to make a gift to Joey. But his faith in the venture was so great that he knew this would never be necessary.

As he stood there observing him, the heavy set of his chest, the quick movements of his arms above the noises of the street, there came into his ears the tinkle of bells from a junk cart. He could see the cold winter morning in which he had moved away to Roosevelt Street. The bruised outstretched hand of Joey as he bade him good-bye, the shy, melancholy voice, "Maybe I'll see you sometime, Pete."

Peter shook off the reverie. "In the meantime, Joey—let me give you all my business. Our office needs a lot of papers and magazines. Can you make deliveries?"

"Sure. My old man—you remember him—he takes them around."

"Good. All the papers every day. Put this card in your pocket —that's the name of the firm and address, over in the Grand Central Building."

"Thanks, Pete. All the papers—that comes close to a buck a day. Thanks. And don't forget to say hello to me when you pass."

Peter looked back once and then a volley of people projected from the subway kiosk swarmed before his vision. He sank himself in the crowd.

32

On the day of her funeral, Eda awoke at six o'clock in the morning. I shall give myself the grandest funeral anyone has ever had, a grand funeral to enjoy. Instead of a dozen black coaches with blinds drawn and sniffling relatives, I shall have a cortege of subway trains, trolley cars and buses, the elevated, taxis and ferry boats, loaded with jabbering and laughing New Yorkers, riding behind my corpse. The Italians tread slowly behind the hearse for a few blocks, while a uniformed brass band blows out the funeral march. The Episcopalians get it over with in the chapel of a fashionable mortician and purr out to the family vault. The Catholics go in for a church ceremony and, shrouded in formal mourning black, drive out Queens Boulevard in state and enter a graveyard inhabited by stone angels. The Jews, rich and poor, go to Brooklyn. But I shall have the longest funeral procession of any, from the Battery to the Bronx, from the Hudson to the East River. I shall be the only living corpse, by grace of God, Metropolis, and a special act of the New York Board of Aldermen, permitted to attend her own funeral. A grand funeral to enjoy.

Let's take the body up a steep flight of steps and pay a nickel entrance fee into the other world. Hey, there, mister, furtive pincher of behinds, dervish shuddering against the female thigh—stand away! No pall bearers on this trip! Defile not the dead with the prying touch of human hands. The "L" is high at Forty-second street and Third Avenue. But higher humps the back of town. Down, down, downtown. The body flits from car to car and wedges itself into a cane-covered seat near a window. A funeral with a view.

The "L" is a rusty line drawn across the town. A line with peep-holes. Elegant Hotel, Rooms $5 per week. Lovely Third Avenue chambers, splintery uneven floors, iron cot with a soiled mattress, a roach or two, a little mouse, a crumbling wall, and sparks from the steel tracks. Delightful spot, ideal for draining a bottle of iodine. Fat German lady in a rose-colored slip, dressing before a wide mirror. Glimpse her sideways and as one fat-quivering arm strain-rises up over her piled-high hair, sudden arm-pit smell is released. Bonus to window-riders. Three abashed flower-pots on nearby sill, but the sturdy geranium yields no perfume. The train hisses into a station and in an old-time backyard you see the greenish leafy tops of skinny trees, like the heads of frightened giraffes craning over a fence. Brown-brick, burnt-orange brick, grey brick, whizz-flicker by, open window, barred window, window-shade down, fire-escape iron ladder, clothesline from here to there, roof-cornice, snotty gargoyle water-tank, chimneys asmoke, steaming odors from the pit below, naked fruit smell, Jersey pork, fish off ice, carpet of fruit-skin with a dead cat for a centerpiece, whizz-flicker by, but between blocks the sudden view, like a hand at the throat, of the tall skyscrapers raying out, raying up, Lexing-ton, Park, Madison and Fifth, up-sprouting million-eyed giants, the rusty line cuts across them, hollow-eyed look of vacant apartment, grimy window-panes, abandoned sink, like gentle hills the slopes of a disordered bed, ancient sign of Fat Man's shop swaying in the wind, a pastel of a three-hundred-pounder in skin-tight underwear, King Obese, the Armenian Club, a patriotic note and the train hisses into a station. Below Fourteenth Street, women disappear from windows and become members of an extinct race. The rusty line cuts across Cooper Square, bisecting a citadel of arts and crafts, at whose stone feet crawl the vermin of the town. A building devoted to musical instruments ta-ra-ra-ump-teeay, crockery stores, smell of very old books and magazines like dried tea, pawnbrokers and the arena of the dead. Bowery flop houses, roped in by "L" tracks and hanging on before the kayo. Hunting room of the Dagmar Hotel, porcupine-faced out-of-town guests, holding a conference on the subject of despair around a spittoon, spitting, scratching, spitting. From cubicles upstairs, smell of old underwear peeled off dejected, unwashed bodies, lift a shirt-tail and scratch, and the old distillery stink of "smoke" from the Bowery saloons, nostalgia for the old mission house and the train hisses into Chatham Square. Chinatown, my Chinatown, where the lights are low. Chop suey, chow mein, pickled duck and oolong tea, sugar cane and dried blood of the tong wars, opium and the white loving babies, hot-house, cat-house lotus flowers, Park Row, City Hall. The stony pockets of Metropolis. Lift the corpse on tender hands for South Ferry. The rusty line twists and squirms, strong, fresh-tanned leather smell, olive oil, coffee, spice, chemicals, waterfront, iron shutters rusted shut on warehouse windows, comfort station for seamen and the Atlantic lapping at your feet. Up Ninth Avenue on the big arc through Washington Street, Armenia, Assyria, Turkey and Persia, arak and shiskabob, the vast markets, you could feed the starving New Yorkers on the stuff that rots away, on the food that is thrown overboard, west side Italians, a gash of Bohemia, The Black Cat, The Green Hat, The Orange Peel and into Sixth Avenue. Houses dip away from the rusty line, poor old remains of Siegel-Cooper grandeur, furriers, upstairs Greeks, Gimbel's, Saks and Macy's, Bryant Park scholastic bums, the bookish pouter pigeons and the special pit of despair, the roaring arena of the Sixth Avenue slave market. Employment agencies. On black trunks, white leaves flutter. Wanted, dishwasher, $18 a month, summer hotel. Raw beef hands into steaming cauldrons, soapy, stinky water foaming on plate vomit, dried bean floats, spaghetti flowers blossom, dishes, glasses, knife, spoon and fork, egg-encrusted, coffee-stained, meat-clogged, laughter over the cauldron from the dining-room beyond. Raw red hands, soggy and bloated, cut them off before your loving arms around my baby-mine. Wanted, dishwasher $18 a month, summer hotel. I'll take the job. Wanted, nurse-maid with a nice behind, Selected Help. The rusty line swings around Fifty-third Street, dark gulley for negroes, across the cleft in the bosom of the gay white way, Eighth Avenue, Ninth Avenue. The Columbus Avenue Irish, the Columbus Avenue Negroes, and never the twain shall meet—except as stevedores, janitors, poor man, thief. Under the tracks the Ninth Avenue life goes on and up and out. The corpse stirs, transfers itself to a bus. Death in the open with the winds from the Hudson blowing up the ashes. Beautiful, spacious Riverside Drive, splendor faded so soon, but the River winds its way, and the Palisades crouch on the Jersey banks. Old mansions opened to let in roomers, vacancy, front bay window apartments for vocal teachers, where the rich foregathered, chords are strained, high C, low C, career ahead. East on Seventy-second Street, Clarence Dale, dressing for a date, south to Fifty-seventh, the hippy bus blatting smoke at swank cars behind plate-glass fronts, east on Fifty-seventh, modiste windows full of pert models, more alive than the humans who wear their gowns, and into Fifth Avenue. Noon on the Avenue, twinkle of dainty ankles, click of confident heels, women who belong to the men who belong. Baby Grands, photographers, Black, Starr and Frost, rings for your fingers, bells for your toes, perfume for every crevice, mm-mmm, you smell good to me, baby. The churches that get first helpings at God's table, the side street frontiers of wealth, to swing down Fifth Avenue when your name is in the Social Register and you can fornicate afternoons. The steamer baskets of rare hot-house fruits, Hicks, Park and Tilford, skin a grape as big as a plum, Dunhill tobacco,

Cook's Tours, to go away in season, to eat fruits out of season, open your eyes for the library lions, within, books and humans wither away, department stores, shops, beckon to women, mock at men, how many bodies are bared to buy all these coverings, beyond Madison Square Park, where gentle vagrants, gentle idlers sit, past the statue that guards the entrance to every park, General Leckfertz astride his percheron, down through lower Fifth Avenue indulging the rich intelligentsia, a bow to the Brevoort and into Washington Square Park through the arch. Clang, clang, the crosstown car, Eighth Street yielding inch by inch to its last of Fifth Avenue lofts, book shops, artists' supplies, artists supplied, Child's on your right, Wanamakers on your left, clanging across Cooper Square, diagonal spoke-view of St. Marks on the Bouwerie, into Yiddish St. Marks Place, Polish wedding hall waiters' club, the best pinochle players in town, real Jewish cooking, honest kosher meats in stoop-stores, across Second Avenue into Italian street markets, musical peddlers chingasorde, Hungarians, Poles, vapors from the mixed nationality grill Stuyvesant Square Park, and the free milk station, blue-ivory circles under the eyes waiting for the ivory-blue free milk. Up Avenue A across to Tenth Street, the East River poor who go off on free summer excursion boats, leaking tubs, powered by politicians' spit, the ride is on the city, death is on the house, taxi, taxi, up the waterfront, garbage scows, rotting planks of the wharf, coal-barge with chimney-sweep men, water playing tag with the piles, the lovely morgue, the cool hospitals and in front of them, the pock-marked stones where mothers' tears rained down during infantile paralysis epidemics, packing house, milk loadings, unkosher meat and milk stench, sudden zoom from cold flats to Sutton Place bastille, new fortifications of the chi-chi rich, across the beautiful span of the Queensborough Bridge, steel skirts raised high, mustn't touch Welfare Island, mustn't get contaminated, but in hot, sticky summer, prisoners and degenerates have the best location in town free, look to Harlem, Queens, Brooklyn, a grand funeral to enjoy. The corpse rises for one greedy view, swallow the town, sneak into Greenpoint from freshly barbered Sunnyside, snug coops, cosy tennis, small-limit poker games, across Newtown Creek and with the first sniff of Brooklyn, the corpse chills, Brooklyn, yielding up the odors of its dying and its dead. I've seen enough. I can follow the trickle of sweat from Bushwick to Coney Island, from Williamsburg to Sheepshead Bay, I'll hide in a kiosk, for the subway is my coffin, death has no terrors for New Yorkers, each day they are buried, emerge from a catacomb. Come, return to the swiftly gliding caves, underground, underground. The rooted city sprouts above. I can feel the weight of its fruit of stone, its foul foliage, the bitter poison of its bark of steel, the blood pumped like sap into its glass tube veins, splinter my fingers on the webs in the corners of the catacombs, swiftly gliding caves, in the deep underground, don't push, shove, stand on my feet, rattle your paper in my ear, sneeze in my face, pick your nose in my paper, feel my buttocks, press my breasts, rape me in my very shroud, swiftly gliding by the catacombs, pressure lifts, the Bronx swims up, I smell verdure, spaces, honeymoon-combed apartments, on this very site a farm, a truck garden, greens, refuse and folksy people a generation ago. Crush of New York, stone handclasp of five boroughs, when I am still, my bones shall ache with nostalgia, when my eyes have been picked from their sockets, tunnelling winds will spray my tears over the town, the last grain of me shall sigh in caves swiftly gliding by . . . in the cool, deep underground—swiftly gliding by. . . .

<h1 style="text-align:center">33</h1>

At "The Golden Buckle," Clarence Dale, big buyer of bubble wine, went over to Googi's table. Aside from his breezy assurance which would have taken him anywhere with confidence, he had earned the right to casually drop into a chair beside the number one guy. They were two parallel lines in the palm of Broadway, lavish spenders, easy money boys, wise gazaboes that talked the same language. Googi admired his six-foot build, the way clothes fit him, the ready flow of smart talk from his lips. He knew that Clarence played and lived within the unspoken code, made his money without hard work, tossed it away in wads and let the other guy's girl alone.

Clarence, who had put over some of his juiciest deals over a bottle of champagne or in an unfamiliar bed, had been dropping casual pointers about his new project to Googi. Now, it was time to clinch it, to get back some of the thousands he had spent in this hot spot. Because of the solid structure of the deal, he felt particularly safe in recommending it to Googi.

"Did you have a chance to think over that little proposition I buzzed you about?"

"I never think," grinned Googi. "With me it's yes or no—like that."

"Well, before you slip me a little two-letter word, take the cotton out of your ears. What's twenty-five or even fifty G's for you to sink into something that's safer than a bank and guarantees you about eight percent. I'm putting you in on the ground floor—"

"I get six times eight percent just to stay out of a proposition," Googi chuckled.

"But you need a bullet-proof vest to take that kind of dough."

"Let me worry about what I wear."

"Anyway, there's more than money in this for you." He paused, before turning up the case ace. "Protection. It's an out."

"What do you mean—an out?" No grin on the dago's face now.

"When Uncle Sam starts cracking down on you for income tax returns—you've got something legitimate to show. An honest investment paying honest returns. That's the dough you live on, see? The beer money is all undercover, but this is open and above-board and you cut the White House in for a small piece. But give them nothing, nothing at all, and they'll say let's nail a muzzle on this pig—he wants the whole trough for himself."

Googi listened intently. Shrewd himself, he admired cunning in others. This easy-going promoter had spilled an earful. It gave him another idea.

"Listen, flannel-mouth, and don't let this go no further. If I come in—I come in right. I'm tired of talking business in this place—" he looked around at his night club—"and I don't let strangers into my pent-house. I suppose we could fix up an office in this new building—you know, something special—my own guy in charge of an elevator, special glass on the doors so no punk thinks it's a shooting gallery, and a regular business name."

"That's what I call smart thinking. I'll throw a firm name in as a bonus. Broadway Trading Company—how does that strike you? And to help you out, I'll even stick your name on some of that high class stationery. How would you like to sit on the Board of Directors?"

"Not if you fall off easy." Googi chuckled.

Clerence buttered him plenty. "You'll never fall off, Googi. Anything you sit on—you drive."

Googi, barricaded behind his corner table, watched the first floor show. The after-theatre crowd was in, and under their hubbub and gaiety, under the music to which the line-girls tapped, he pursued his own thoughts, his cosy dreams of greatness. An office in a legitimate building, a swell front since he owned some of the bricks in it, and then to run the beer racket like a real business. He'd get an office high up so that he would be sitting on top of the town.

The head-waiter, with a courtly bow, placed a card before him.

"Come over and join us.
Jane (miss-to-you) Ralston."

Googi followed the glance of his head waiter over to a distant table. A hand fluttered above the heads of people and waved to him. A smile cracked on his face. Miss Ralston—the grand lady of the settlement—the blonde society dame. Once he had been so terrified of her that her presence struck him dumb. He had worshipped her—in a way she had started him on his life-long quest of blondes. And now she sat in his club and was eager to have him acknowledge her. He excused himself and went over to her table. She shook hands with him warmly, presented him to a party of ten, all Social Registerites. And they were all proud to meet a killer, a successful racketeer. He had definitely arrived. Three and four-generation names purred before him.

"Do sit down and have a drink with us." Miss Ralston, once slender and beautiful, had grown fat and gabby and was a little drunk—but she still awed him. Give him ten minutes with her and he'd find her round heels. What a thought. Like settling an old debt with himself.

"In my place you drink on me." Already one of his waiters hovering near, giving him that special attention mixed with fear that even the most prominent guest never received.

"Wine—" he took good care not to say champagne, but the waiter knew that was what he meant— "wine for my friends."

This was success, sitting right on top of New York. He looked over to Clarence and made his decision. Protection—and altitude. Then he turned on the killer's charm for his society friends.

Dinner at the home of Mrs. Langdon-Chase on Seventieth Street, properly east of Fifth Avenue, yet not too close to Madison. An intimate group of eight, the lovely, assured hostess, a middle-aged pair from Detroit (family friends, the male one of the generals of General Electric), a fashionable and conservative portrait painter (she didn't approve of sputtering, fervent extremists), a school chum who had married in Paris, now a widow by grace of the suicide of her husband, a badminton player who had wooed her, a cousin from New England, and the favored suitor, Peter. Intimate dinner at the home of Mrs. Langdon-Chase and then to the opening of the opera season. A familiar opera, "Aida," and one should arrive fashionably late.

Peter enjoys perfection. He finds himself in the midst of it. The appointments, the dress and adornments of the guests, their lineage, the drinks, the food and service, and the perfect poise of Suzanne. Suzy, her school chum called her. Peter watched the ease of her beautiful hands, now ungloved, the first time she had given him her naked hand, the lovely palms in which lay four millions. Those blue eyes, so unblinded by poetic visions, eyes that could discern an unfavorable clause printed in six-point type in a contract. The full mouth, so perfectly shaped, that uttered with such regal finality, "my money is my own."

Suzanne ate little and drank little, but her breasts were ample. Whenever Peter thought of her in terms of a human, a woman to take into his arms he found something in the sweep of that bosom that aroused him. But he had lived all his life by checking his appetites. And he would spoil nothing by haste. He was the favored suitor. Even the society and gossip columns linked his name with hers. But he was not yet the husband. He too ate little, drank little, loved little—a fierce, swarthy ascetic, his nose sharp and straight, his eyes dark and clear, his blue-black hair combed straight back, his strong hands, dark, almost primitively hairy.

After they were married, what could he do to ruffle their cold perfection? Would they make love in perfect taste? Perhaps by appointment on quarter-moon nights upon a mattress crackling with dividend-coupons. Deep within him, a maddening force stirred, like the first boilings over in the earth's center, the harbingers of earthquakes, deep fissures on mountains, the beginning of the crack-up.

A butler, with perfect discretion, spoke close to his ear. "A lady on the telephone, for you, sir. I wouldn't have interrupted you, sir, but she says it's very urgent."

Peter tried to check his surprise and set his glass down. Suzanne with perfect poise, "That awful Hicks building again, New York's latest monstrosity and Peter's Frankenstein." He was grateful to her for easing the way.

In the phone he heard Eda's voice: "I tracked you down, Peter. I'm sorry to take you away, but I must see you now." Her voice was wild and discordant. "It's the only thing I've ever asked of you, Peter. It's the last."

"I'll come, Eda. Tell me where."

"Come down to South Ferry—remember where we met—the first time? I'm in the waiting room."

He was a little annoyed with her. There was the hint of crack-up in her voice. He would pacify her and then caution her never to do it again.

"In twenty minutes."

As Peter hung up and turned around, he found Suzanne smiling at him. "Not the Hicks plan for wrecking homes?" Her voice was velvety, but the whisper of concern in it thrilled him.

"I must go, Suzanne. I'll join you later at the opera. Will you make the proper apologies for me?"

"Of course."

"Our last interruption." He took her hand in his and kissed it. He suddenly wanted to crush it, maul it so that no glove would ever fit it.

"Thanks, Suzanne. You're wise as well as beautiful."

The butler helped him on with his perfectly tailored coat. As he tied a knot in his white silk muffler, he took a glance at himself in the mirror. Perfection was reflected. The tall gent with the topper, the silver-knob stick, the air of assurance, the money in the wallet. He had seen this gent in movies, on the covers of *Vanity Fair* magazines, on the upper decks of liners, sailing away. What had happened to the tenement starveling of Roosevelt Street? Peter pinched himself.

As a matter of fact he had been dining in an exclusive mansion. As a matter of fact he was going to the opera later. As a matter of fact he was keeping a rendezvous with a working girl from his past, the girl who had loved him and given him her all.

In the street he swished a taxi out of the air.

Peter mapped the route for the cab-driver. Down Fifth Avenue to Fourteenth Street, east to Second Avenue, east on Houston, through Forsyth Street, east on Canal, under the Manhattan Bridge to Roosevelt Street, west on the waterfront to South Ferry. Sentimental journey of a successful New Yorker.

Peter leaned back in the cab and wondered about Eda. He had been so absorbed in his plans this past year that he had barely given her a thought. What could she want of him now? Rumors had drifted to him. She was running wild sexually, a brilliant journalist, but loose, unorganized, erratic. Well, as she herself had said so emphatically, "My body is my own." That was her credo. He had known it before any other man, treasured it, used it—and discarded it too, he had to admit. He pressed against the leather back of the seat. On Forsyth Street the same houses were still standing, resisting time and the elements, Lepke's mikvah still a challenge to dirt. The outpourings from the windows and doors, the brick walls threatening to burst under the pressure of the hordes of poor. The very gutters smelled of his boyhood. Phew, how it stank. It terrified him. He cancelled the sentimental journey to Roosevelt Street and ordered the driver to change his course. He had grown out of all this and it was ridiculous to go through it again. Like putting your nose in your own dung. Phew! He would never look at poverty and hideousness again. This was his farewell.

Eda ran towards him as he dismissed the cab. Then she came to an abrupt stop, as if someone had commanded a halt. For a moment they looked at each other. Her hair was dishevelled, her clothes carelessly worn, ill-matched, flamboyant in color. Annoying details to a man nourished on perfection. But her face was so strangely wracked that it went at once to his heart. The blood was completely drained from her cheeks, and yet her eyes held an excited, almost exalted look.

"Eda! You look all in. Have you been—sick?"

"I have, Peter—a strange malady."

"What do the doctors say?"

"They prescribe a long rest."

"You run around too much—and not all of it is in line of duty." He was a reproving uncle, or an elderly guardian. "You're tired now."

"I should be——"

"What have you been doing?"

"Following a hearse. Uptown—downtown—undertown and crosstown. Following a hearse."

"Whose?"

"My own."

He looked at her puzzled, wondering where her sanity had fled. Once she had been tight-encased within herself. But she had given of herself so lavishly, so wildly, abandoned herself to such unbridled love and lusts, wild dreams and garish nightmares, that she had disintegrated. Out of the Battery, a cold wind blew its note of autumnal sadness.

"Peter, you certainly look the swell. Time and Wall Street worketh strange miracles, its wonders to perform."

"Did you call me to mock at me?"

She suddenly fastened her lips to his. They were cold, flavorless, clinging to his as if to draw life from him.

He pushed her gently from him. "Eda—what do you want?"

"A ferry ride with you. My last request."

"Are you going away? A new assignment?" He didn't want to ask too many questions. He didn't want to become involved in her life again. "If I can help, Eda——"

"No thanks, Peter. But spoken like a swell."

Suddenly the ache of exchanging small words with him gripped her. What had happened to the height and grandeur of the love which had been theirs?

They were pushed through the gates that opened and became part of the stream that poured into the ferry to Staten Island.

The clumsy shark-jaw nibbled at the piles, crunched water, plowed into the bay.

"Peter—you've got everything you wanted."

"Everything."

"Including the luxury of still being unhappy."

"I never bargained for happiness."

"No—this is what you bargained for—the silk topper—the white muffler around the throat, the perfectly tailored evening clothes, a box at the opera, a million in bonds—and a lady from the Social Register."

"How did you know about—Mrs. Langdon-Chase?"

"Oh, we newsgals stick together. A society editor told me. Say—I've followed your courtship from the first corsage."

The wind blew trivia from their lips. Eda leaned close against him for warmth, for the warmth of a human. He moved a little away.

"Peter, do you remember how you once hated New York? Do you still hate it?"

"No. I've been too busy marking it up to hate the town." He paused. "And you, Eda—do you remember how passionately you loved New York? You still——"

"Just as passionately. In the same way. Peter," her voice was a cry, "I have it here." He looked around quickly at her, observed the anguish in her face, the wild pain in her eyes. "This is my strange malady. One from which I shall never recover."

"What?"

"I have New York malaise. I am sick with love of the town. I am big with New York."

He avoided her eyes. Their wild glitter drew him to another world, as if she had unhinged her mind and given him a terrifying glimpse into the pit of torment in which she dwelt. He felt uneasy. The ferry docked. People began to cluster about the platform. A guard stationed himself at the swinging gate.

Eda kissed him. "Good-bye, Peter. Don't bother to come off the boat. You stay on—it's going right back."

"But you——"

Half of her face smiled. "Thanks for the ferry ride."

"Good-night, Eda."

"Peter—good-bye."

He felt the touch of her hand and people closed in behind her. All moved in a herd.

He walked to the bow now aimed at the Battery shore-line. He drew a deep breath and felt relieved that he was alone. He had been a tortured person all of his youth and early manhood, thinking one life, living another, twisting, writhing within, curbing, planning, cursing. It was a relief to be ironed out. To move in open, normal channels in big strokes. He had lost his tolerance for an agonized soul. Yes, it was a relief to have Eda out of his life. And a comfort to have Suzanne.

Eda came back on the ferry with a crowd of revellers. She quickly walked down the companionway to the lowest deck where the cars were lined up. Here the boat creaked and quivered as it yanked itself loose from the embrace of piles. It was cold and she was alone below. From above, the doleful music of the ferry musicians reached her.

Midway in the bay, she observed a giant crucifix of light. It was formed by the stars above crossing the phosphorescent gleam in the waters below at the line of the horizon. She saw the brilliance of the big town on one side and the glow of Staten Island on the other.

Swiftly Eda lowered herself into the center of this crucifix, through it, deep into the cold waters. Death poured into her throat, deafened her ears, and she sang back her dirge, "I have New York malaise. I am sick with love of the town. I am big with New York."

34

hroughout the rehearsals of "Landed Gentry," Bert led an enchanted life. This was the world he had dreamed of on his fire-escape. His release was complete. The genteel artificialities of his play, with its raised-eyebrow sophistication, the windy affectations of the players, the special accenting given the play by a homosexual director, all the chichi and counterfeit sentimentalities of the Broadway commercial theatre, the deification of a peep-hole behind golden bars called the box-office, enchanted him. This was where the magic carpet had transported him. And he had been fortunate enough to penetrate it at a comparatively early age.

In its last week of rehearsal the play showed such promise that a premature scramble for credits was launched. The producer bragged about his astuteness in recognizing hit material, the play-broker for bringing it to him, the first reader for passing it, the director for interpreting it in his special sophisticated way, the leading man for enriching the rôle, the stage manager for keeping the cast under control, the scenic designer for his decor, the electrician for the light effects and the press agent for space grabbing. The author had only written the play.

But Bert did not mind. This was the beginning for him. He would write his way into the annals of the theatre with a quill pen and purple ink. And with success, no one could question his right to sport a cane, wear the tweediest tweeds, the woolenest hose, flannel shirts with button-down collars, and while not actually pronounce it dawnce, at least not commit the sharp, nasal, pincer-clipped dae-ence.

And for the first time in his life, he found himself interested in a girl—not as an ear for his epigrammatic twists, but as a human being who aroused a need in him which only she could fill. So absorbed had he always been in his work, so obsessed with the yearning to escape, that he had minimized his need for women. Besides, part of his equipment as a playwright had been a cynicism which grew particularly sharp when visited upon women. And Joey's agonizing experience with Bella had made him doubly wary of falling in love.

But there was no denying that he found himself drawn to Gina Page. He wondered how much of the publicity released about her was actually true. Was she really the daughter of a nobleman? Had she really been reared in a convent? Some day he would ask her to reveal herself to him. Not only was she intrinsically of the theatre, which made her a creature apart from ordinary women, but he sensed that she too had come to Broadway because of a passion for escape. He liked to watch the movements of her hands, the vividly changing expression of her face, the way she cocked her head, flung herself upon a sofa with a graceful violence, the way she stood close to him when she spoke, and yet maintained distance. He liked to think that the words he had written upon paper animated her in this charged, violent manner. To him, they were not exaggerations, but the normal boilings over of a pent-up emotional nature, released at the command of a master of words.

Yet no one actually got close to Gina. During rehearsals of love scenes she flung herself against the leading man, kissing him with a strange ardor, caressing him with her eyes, her voice, her hands. But once the scene was over she retreated into herself. There was no casual or accidental touching of her unless the business of the play called for it. Bert had the flash that here was a woman who could give herself to a man in a play, in any play, but never in life.

And promptly after each rehearsal, out of the shadows of the rear of the theatre, there stood up a matronly figure, a dignified yet worshipful mother to claim her. She made no dates with other members of the cast, did not join in their gossip. Two rumors attached to her. One, that she was the mistress of a millionaire publisher, the backer of the play. The other, that the producer himself kept her. Only to Bert did it occur that she had been given the rôle because she was perfect for it. For all her reserve he had the feeling that she liked him, would unmask for him, be human with him as only two artificial people can be with each other in intimacy.

Once Gina came up and talked to him on a matter that did not concern the interpretation of a line.

"There's something special I should like to ask of you, Bert."

"Of course—Gina."

"When you hear it—you'll probably think I've gone out of my mind——"

"Bring on your little insanities."

"I'm serious about this." There was a fleeting glance of terror in her eyes, a remembered, almost nostalgic fright. "I cannot stand a moustache on a man. Could you get Benton to remove his—it's only the one scene—but it unnerves me."

The scene flashed before Bert. One in which a middle-aged man-about-town attempts a crude bit of seduction. As he recalled it, she did play it rather awkwardly.

"He'll be clean-shaven or I'll cut the scene out."

Gina gave him her hand and in clasping it, Bert again felt himself drawn to her, as in a flash of revelation.

After the rehearsal, Bert took the actor aside. Benton was a foppish hanger-on at the Lambs Club. "You know, Benton—I'd like to compliment you on the way you play that part. It's not the lead—but it can easily stand out."

"Thanks a lot, old man—I'm doing my best with it." He pretended to be shy, but he was delighted, purring and wallowing in praise.

"There's just one thing—a little thing—an odd incongruity."

"I'll be grateful for any hints, old man."

"I never intended the character to be a villain."

"Oh say—am I playing him a bit heavy, old man?"

"No, that's just it—you read him perfectly. I like the nuances, the way you speak those lines."

"I don't quite understand, old man. If I play him, as you put it, perfectly—"

"But you don't look it. I want you to look a little less the conventional suave. You understand, more subtlety in your appearance."

"If there's anything I can do—"

"A simple touch. I've been watching you for days, wondering what it was and I just hit upon it."

"Do tell me, old man."

"Your moustache. If you removed it, you'd be perfect and I wouldn't hesitate to say so to Grahame."

The actor withdrew a pocket mirror and gazed at himself with a perplexed air. The fate of the entire world and its civilization might have trembled on the ends of his moustache. Then with an air of grave finality:

"I'll take it off, old man. I'm always glad for a little hint from the author. Thanks a lot, old man."

As Bert watched him return to the stage, he knew that now he was definitely of the Broadway theatre.

The play enjoyed a swank, black and white opening. Black limousines, black evening clothes for men, white ermine, white gloves, white skin, white diamonds for women. Bert stood in the rear of the orchestra, immaculately clad and pretended that he was nonchalant. He was one of the upper stratum, the gay New Yorker witnessing an opening. Actually he was not yet in this class. In fact one ironic note intruded. He had been obliged to borrow money from poor Joey to purchase this complete trousseau. Actually he was not nonchalant, and his throat was so dry that when a friend came up to speak to him, Bert in answering issued a strange squeal like the creak of a rusty hinge.

In her dressing room Gina was staring fixedly at the program. The name as printed was "Gina Page." From Pajalski to Pajal to Page. Progress consisted not so much in moving forward as in obliterating the past. And yet she had come a long way from a Yorkville tenement, moving always in the protective aura of her broad-shouldered and doting mother. That peasant mother, who had breathed life and ambition into her, who had tended and slaved for her, who had driven her own husband from her life for the sake of the child. Gina shuddered as for an instant the vision of her father intruded. His blue-watery eyes, the face twisted with incestuous lust, the outstretched hands, the fierce moustachios. The call boy's cry of "Curtain," prevented her from screaming. The terrified girl, Pajalski, flowed forward into the determined young actress, Gina Page, dominated by a character out of a play, animated by remembered lines. She walked confidently to her entrance place in the wings.

The audience enjoyed the performance, small claques applauded their favorite players, Gina scored in her first featured part and, with eleven curtains, the general feeling of the Broadway wise guys was that while "Landed Gentry" was not a smash, it would enjoy a respectable run with the aid of cut-rates. And undoubtedly it would sell to the pictures.

Bert was glad that his father and mother and Joey had decided not to come to the opening. They had contented themselves with attending the dress rehearsal. They couldn't stand the strain, they insisted. Their presence would have been an incongruous touch to this channel of escape. And yet when the applause came, he was ashamed of his own severance from them. How they would have thrilled. His little frightened father, his bewildered mother, and awed, blind Joey.

After the performance the producer made up an exclusive party to which Gina and Bert were invited. "I'm taking you down to an exotic restaurant on the east side. I don't know whether you've ever gone slumming—but it's on Broome Street. The food is of the very best." For once Gina shed her mother and relied upon Bert as her escort.

They entered a limousine as dark as a cave and as cushioned as a gangster's coffin. The excitement, the tension, the exuberance of his first opening over, Belt felt suddenly deflated. No success, however great, can produce a continued elation. His heart grew heavy with thoughts of Joey. For all the world that separated them, he had missed his brother. He glanced over at Gina. She looked beautiful, and looked aware of her beauty. Near her sat the backer of the play, a wolfish millionaire with a sunburnt face and drawn-in claws. If he fell in love with her, thought Bert, he would be consigning himself to continuous torture. Men would pursue Gina all the time, heaping gifts at her feet, burning their very flesh in devotionals. He began to feel sad for himself. He was walled out by his own architecture from his family, and afraid to abandon himself to the new green fields of love. There was only his work. Another play about the upper crust, love under a polo pony, seduction on a yacht, romance in a punch bowl, another play in which a professional butler would say, "Begging your pardon, sir, it has been my observation, sir."

On a street familiar to him the car stopped before a bright electric sign. The proprietor of the restaurant, an enormous eater who looked like the sum total of all the meals he had served, greeted them in person. As one gourmet to a kindred group he led them to a reserved table and seated himself so that he could order for them.

"Now what shall we eat," he hummed to himself. "What tickles the palate and yet rests gently upon the navel?"

And he answered himself, "First some calves' brains, and I swear to you that in the days of the heathen these would have been sacrificial calves, so—" intoning now with a curve of music— "calves' brains with delicately chopped onions and chicken fat, and then a big platter of a mixed grill, so, musht steak, carnazei, sweetbreads, and with it some wine and seltzer, and your belchings will go straight to God's ears." Ending his song, "So I order for everybody?"

His dancing eye caught the glum expression on Bert's face. "What torments you, my little bridegroom?"

"When I was a kid," said Bert, half to himself, "I used to sit out on the fire-escape and make a meal out of bread smeared with chicken fat."

The fat proprietor smiled. "Bread and chicken fat? With champagne that's good, too."

"That's all I want."

The savory dishes were brought on while a balalaika orchestra played Roumanian gypsy tunes. Bert listened to the melancholy, nostalgic music, a plucking of tormented strings, watched the others eat, heard their laughter, but he munched his bread garnished with chicken fat, and drank champagne. There was a sadness in his heart which he could not dissipate with neatly turned epigrams, a sadness which lay at the core of him, defying all the counterfeit elegances which he had grafted upon his life.

Seated within the restaurant, in an atmosphere of opulence, bending over a glass of champagne, sheltered, enclosed, he could still smell the street outside, see and feel it more vividly than anything in the room. He knew exactly how that street was littered with rubbish, its turbulent gush where the elevated rumbled above it, its mounting, shrieking, jungle lust for life, and where it subsided to a feather-flow into the East River. He wondered what children were reading what books under dim gas lights, wondered who was practicing scales on violins and pianos bought with tubercular sweat, saw the furtive ones hiding from policemen in cellars, and thought with sadness of those dreaming the delirium of distant lovely pastures that had enchanted him when he was a boy on a fire-escape. The life of all the streets around seemed to flow right into the restaurant and then flow past him to some far-off basin.

The proprietor's moon-face rose in a broad grin. "You think only uptown you have entertainment? Say, I can give you Broadway and good food in the bargain. Look, I'm producing a floor-show."

The lights dimmed, and a spotlight illumined the center of the floor. The balalaika orchestra abandoned the gypsy airs and twanged into popular music.

Into the amber arena slinked two dancers, a rather plumpish girl clad in a cheap green evening gown all a-glitter with spangles, and the man, a sheik-dancer type in worn swallowtails. Their dance resembled a travesty on acrobatic ballroom dancing, and as the girl with heartbreaking eagerness smiled at the uptown party, it suddenly dawned on Bert that here was Bella. She bent back and touched the floor with the tips of her fingers and uncoiled, grinning hopefully at the producer's party. She collapsed in a split and drew herself up, smiling eagerly, always smiling.

Yes, here was Bella, breaking her back, distorting her legs and body in an east side restaurant, smiling hopefully under her pain at a group of people who laughed at her efforts. And this was what is known as a career.

The brutal, tragic horror of it clamped down upon Bert. For this she had broken the line of her life, casting away love and warmth and security. For this poor Joey had become blind. How the dream of those two children, one of her name in electric lights as America's most famous dancer, the other of love and a championship, had splintered over their heads.

Bert munched his bread, sipped his champagne, gave himself over to these tragic reflections. But Bella recognized him. She faltered for one step, and then smiled with special extravagance to him. The producer who observed this and who had the pick of some tasty flesh uptown, wagged a finger at him. "So—you cut up away from home." Gina looked at him with a curious expression. The producer went on ragging him, developing the possibilities of a great secret romance between this faded dancer in a dive and America's most promising playwright. Bert was glad that Joey was not present to hear the opinion of the world, that world which Bella had tried so desperately to make a dent upon. "An old friend," he said, "just an old friend."

"Well, she's trying hard enough," laughed the producer.

Directly after the number Bella, basking in the mock salvos of applause that came from the uptown table, fluttered over to Bert. Avidly she looked at the members of the party, all successful in the theatre, and gravely Bert presented her. She smiled cutely at the backer, hopefully at the producer. But her coquetry was sad.

"Will you excuse us while we talk over old times?" Bert led her away to another table.

At once the trying-hard-to-please grin was wiped from her face. She looked tired, almost defeated. Then gathering her forces, she spoke rapidly:

"Bert, you're just the man I need." There was a look of desperation on her face. "I've been reading about you in *Variety*—and I know you can write smart dialogue. If I only had a smart act—you know, high class patter—I could get real booking. The dancing part is okay, but people out front want new stuff all the time. That's what my agent was telling me—'Girlie, get yourself some snappy talk.'"

"Bella—why don't you give it up?" Bert enjoyed being cruel. It was almost like vengeance. "All the snappy talk and smart dialogue in the world can't help your act."

The lines of her mouth twitched. She was on the verge of bursting into tears.

"Give it up," he hammered on, "you've heard about Joey. Why don't you——"

"You're wrong," she cried, "you and Joey. Trying to keep me out of the theatre. You got your nerve telling me I'm through. Far from it. I'm not through—I'll get someone to write me an act—you wait and see—I'm not through. All I need is a break. I'm not through."

Hysterically she kept repeating it to herself like a wall of protecting words that shut out the horrible nightmare of defeat. She sprang up from the table. The spangles glittered and shook. Her hands flew to her face, hiding it. She walked off in a dancer's stride, a broken dancer's stride. He had never witnessed anything as sad as her glittering, jangling exit.

Bert returned to the table. "I'm sorry—I must get out now."

"Not without me," said Gina, rising in her wrap. She took his arm. There was a finality about their exit that stilled the objections of the backer and the producer and the others in the party.

Outside, he waved away a taxi.

"Gina—you won't like me tonight. I belong to my past. The opening, the play, your success, perhaps mine—all have nothing to do with me now. I feel that I must tramp these streets tonight—the streets I tried to escape—tramp them until I collapse in their gutters. Let me put you in a cab——"

"No—I'll walk with you, Bert."

She looked at him, flashed a strange smile, and hugged his arm to her side.

"I know what you feel, Bert." She sucked in her breath. "You're talking to a gal from Yorkville. There's not much difference in neighborhoods. Let's walk."

35

The Hicks building is up. Fifteen millions' worth of steel, brick, glass, land and water. Tenants flock to it with long-term leases, lawyers, theatrical agents, real estate companies, midtown branches of securities firms, doctors, dentists, business men. Elmer Hicks has realized the dream that pumped him across twenty years of cunning, scheming, hoarding, murder and torment. His lust for land has been stilled, for realty and buildings not scattered but compressed into part of the heart of New York, and raised to one of its highest points.

And now he plans to take a brief respite from land and devote himself to flesh and blood, to become the blushing bridegroom, for Sally has given her word.

And Peter, with the flow of his wealth assured, plans to marry Mrs. Langdon-Chase, a name in the Social Register, a four-million-dollar divorcee, a guarantee of the charmed life.

And lonely Perry is making headway with his plans to entice fresh air and sanitation and civilized habitation to the east side, to make poverty a little more palatable to those condemned not to have.

And Joey, deft with his fingers as he had once been with his fists, is making change with lightning speed, listening hopefully to every voice that calls out the name of a newspaper.

And Googi is finding that the pig is fat, and the world good to carve, with rich rewards for those that live the right way.

Yes—God's in His heaven and Googi's at the trough, and Hicks and Peter are at the trough, and Donovan and Clarence Dale are at the trough, and Murdock is at the trough, and many wolfish mouths are at the trough, sucking away, grunting, gorging at the meat and blood of New York.

360

Within the serene, aristocratic enclosure of Gramercy Park, two old men sat. The skin of one was like ancient parchment, the other's was yellowing into parchment. They were grandfather and father to Peter Mendes. The patriarch was seventy-five, his son twenty years younger. They were dressed in neat, dark clothes, their shoes made of the soft kid leather that old men wear as a comfort to their tired feet. It was spring and the sun warmed through their garments into their bodies. The spine of the younger man still ached when he sat upright, but against this background of leisure and wealth one could bear a little pain.

On other benches, carefully dressed children, attended by uniformed nursemaids and governesses, played discreetly. Within the park everything was well ordered, neatly arranged, as befits a private park, with an iron gate that opens only to residents of this exclusive neighborhood.

Outside the park the city roared, but its rumble fell upon the secluded inmates as from a great distance, like the roar of cannons on some remote battlefront.

The patriarch parted his lips in a prayer to God, an all-seeing, all-wise, all-merciful God who had transported him from many strange lands, who had visited upon him strife and hardship and suffering, but at last had seen fit to lead him to a gentle Garden of Eden to spend his last days. His son joined in the prayer, thanking God for the gift of a son like Peter who had risen to bring glory and pride to God and his aging father.

On the curbstone outside the park, his feet in the gutter, sat an old vagrant. His clothes were ragged, besmeared and plentiful, two coats, three vests, three pairs of pants and an old derby on his head, his matted, unkempt hair a sanctuary for lice. From a greasy bag he withdrew stale cake and munched meditatively, the sugar icing falling in gentle flakes upon his beard.

A street-cleaner passed, rolling a refuse can before him. The old man crumpled the bag and the street-cleaner lifted the lid of the can, and as from Pandora's box, a swarm of city stinks rose up. The street-cleaner, municipal employee, passer of a civil service examination, wearer of a uniform, a man in white, mocked at the old vagrant. Indicating the serene, iron-enclosed garden spot with a broom to whose straw ends manure clung, he cackled:

"That's one park no bum can get into."

The old man slowly turned his massive, alive head and said:

"Brother—this is a two-way town, and I know, because I got clothes on my back. I can't get into the park." His marmoset eyes lingered on the tall iron gate, roved beyond it to the rigid old men like figures in death, and he continued, "But those on the inside—can't get out. Yes, New York's a two-way town."

He rose to his feet slowly, with great dignity, and shuffled away.

36

It is the year of prosperity, 1927.

Spring sun peppers the town, cobblestones, asphalt, warm to bursting. Sap stirs in the skyscrapers, city workers sing along, wearing their clothes like bunting. The flags are fluttering and New York is alive, bursting with life and confidence. The windows are bright and no mourners walk the streets. The boroughs writhe with life.

I place my hand on the feverish brow of New York. Take it easy, big town—take it easy.

One day the "L" trains will run off the tracks and churn through the streets, crushing bones and blood and asphalt. The old street cars will bleat as the crazed tracks rise and spike them. Taxis like giant yellow birds will fly to skyscraper windows and hoot and deafen the city with their screechings. Subway trains will tear beyond their stations, plow through strange holes, perforate the bowels of New York, and the waters from the rivers and the ocean will rush in and flood New York. The town will drown in its own arteries, and the bloated corpse of the greatest metropolis will rise and float across submerged skyscrapers. The first terrible silence will descend upon the city.

Take it easy, New York. Take it easy.